SAINT MONKEY

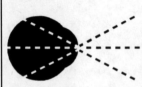

This Large Print Book carries the
Seal of Approval of N.A.V.H.

SAINT MONKEY

JACINDA TOWNSEND

THORNDIKE PRESS
A part of Gale, Cengage Learning

GALE
CENGAGE Learning·

Farmington Hills, Mich • San Francisco • New York • Waterville, Maine
Meriden, Conn • Mason, Ohio • Chicago

GALE
CENGAGE Learning®

LIBRARY OF CONGRESS CATALOGING-IN-PUBLICATION DATA

Townsend, Jacinda.
   Saint monkey / by Jacinda Townsend. — Large print edition.
      pages ; cm. — (Thorndike press large print African-American)
   ISBN 978-1-4104-7302-8 (hardcover) — ISBN 1-4104-7302-3 (hardcover)
   1. African Americans—Fiction. 2. Singers—Fiction. 3. Kentucky—Fiction. 4.
Large type books. 5. Domestic fiction. I. Title.
PS3620.O9596S25 2014b
813'.6—dc23   2014024565

Published in 2014 by arrangement with W.W. Norton & Company, Inc.

Printed in Mexico
1 2 3 4 5 6 7 18 17 16 15 14

To Angela Townsend
and Wendell Townsend,
*who shared their stories
and everything else.*

To David Gides,
*who showed me how
to live life in Technicolor.*

Most of all, to Rhianna Sade
and Fadzai Iman,
*who are the brightest stars
in the darkest night.*

CONTENTS

8

■ ■ ■ ■

PART ONE:
AUDREY

■ ■ ■ ■

THROWN

I see grief every day here on Queen Street. I see it in the hunch of a man who has lost his woman and his job in Cincinnati and come back down to Kentucky after the winter, his head permanently bent by the pelt of hard snow in the absence of a hat. In the dark undereyes of the girl who dusts the ceilings at Huggins Dime Store, the girl who, seven months gone, climbed into the woods of Mt. Sterling to push out her stillborn baby girl, begotten of the frog-eyed, otherwise-married lawyer old enough to be her own father. In the slow gait of a church-hatted woman whose only soft young son has been away to the war and come home to someone else's country with a stump where a leg should be, his military pension only half that of the White officers' and therefore inadequate to buy all the liquor he needs on an empty Saturday night. I see it, but the adults all around me say

13

grief is a thing unknown to children.

Still, my granddaddy built me this porch swing the week after my daddy died, not because he thought I was grieving, but because he meant to keep me amused. "Keep Audrey occupied," he told people. "Keep her around the house with her dress down and her bloomers up." Since my daddy died, Grandpap has begun to see me as a dry leaf in freefall, a wasted petal about to be crunched under a man's foot. He wants me to forget all the boys of Montgomery County and take studies in typing, to let go the idea of marrying a town sweetheart and become, instead, a woman of the city in a store-bought dress and nylons, with my own bedboard and bankbook. I'm supposed to fly and dream about all that, sitting here in this swing. He painted it white, whiter even than the side of this house, whose thin coat is peeling to expose the aged black wood underneath. He painted the wood slats of this swing so white that when you stare at them for a time, they seem blue. Swing high, and the porch ceiling creaks where he riveted the screws: the grown people who walk by warn me. "Hey gal, it ain't a playground swing," they say. For them, for their limitations, I stop pumping my legs, and the creaking

14

stops. But when they've faded down the walk, I fly high again.

Mother never sees me swinging. Mother never sees me. She works days at the county health clinic and nights, without even changing her white nurse's shoes and stockings, she walks up to Seventh Street and gives Miss Ora Ray her bath and bedclothes. When a bad storm comes, or if Miss Ora Ray's kin has come to visit, Mother is home in the evenings. Then, she listens to her stories on the radio, her stockinged feet massaging each other like a cricket's, her mouth and eyes open and aimed at nothing. All her people are down in Tennessee, three hours by the L&N, but she hasn't seen them since my daddy's funeral. She never sees me swinging. She never sees me. She tells my granddaddy that since I talk to her like grown-ass Colored, I can press and curl my own damn hair.

"You keep treating her like she's a baby wolf," Grandpap says, on winter nights when I'm kicking around the bed for the hot water bottle and he thinks his voice is covered by the crackling in the coal stove. "See if she don't bite you when she grows up."

From my swing I'm witness to crooked arm Fridays like this one, when husbands,

15

uncles, sons, and boyfriends pour home from distilleries, tobacco farms, pool halls, or wherever they've gone to stuff their pockets so they can walk down Queen Street with arms bent around bags of groceries, toys, schoolclothes, or coal. Grandpap stopped delivering for Riley's Grocery an age ago; Fridays, he's like an old dog without a bone. But No. 211, the house directly across the street, still gets its tickful, at six o'clock sharp, when Sonnyboy walks through the door with a bushel of oranges for the family, or linen skirts for two girls, or paper dolls for Imagene and a Five Keys record for Pookie. In the first months after Mother got her telegram from the Army, when the sun fell earlier each evening and the wind blew colder each night, when we could still wake up in moonglow and hear Grandpap crying over the bathroom sink, I'd sit in this swing and pretend that Sonnyboy was my daddy. Returned alive from the war after all, and getting paid on a Friday like any other well-behaved Negro. No. 211, in my daydreams, was a detour — a charity — and Sonnyboy'd soon enough be through my door bringing saltwater taffy.

Having delivered, having set off the chain explosion of laughter that bursts out the front window and drifts across the street, Sonnyboy always comes back out to the porch, as if in retreat from his girls' delight. He pulls the maroon shirttail of his uniform over his grease-shined belt and smokes his head into a blue cloud, and I look south for cars and pretend not to watch him. Sonnyboy's the daddy who rescued swollen sidewalk chalk from pails full of rain while my own daddy was inside sketching a car motor, the daddy with such a firm, sure way of moving and speaking that I look down to his feet and blush whenever he asks me and Pookie what we learned that day in school. He upsie-daisies Imagene, sending the frills of her red petticoat floating against a blue sky, and I'm the one who shimmies with giggles. He unbuttons his shirt and chops wood in the backyard, and it's a neighborhood event.

He must've come a little unstacked when Pookie was born — must have — because she's center-of-the-bone ugly. A bit of proof-requiring math, because she's not the sum of two ugly parents or even the average of two mismatched ones — Sonnyboy's wife, Mauris, is pretty enough to hurt old men's hearts. Pookie's younger sister Imagene has dark, smooth skin and eyes as wide as Peace dollars. But Pookie's carrot red hair, freckles, and buckteeth skipped a generation, right from the White man who raped Miss Myrtle straight down to Pookie. "Mauris shouldn't have been out feeding that hound while she was expecting," folks said after Pookie was born, talking about her dog, Sammy. "She marked that baby." And Pookie's head does bob when she runs, and her tongue does hang a little beyond her buckteeth, and owing to her bad posture she has a chest that is not blooming outward but growing more concave, so that even now, as she runs across the street to see me, I think of Sammy despite myself.

"Audrey!" she yells when she gets to my side of the street. "It's Friday, girl. What we going to do?"

"What you think? Nothing."

Pookie runs up Grandpap's three steps and jumps onto the swing with me, cups a ring of her thick, shiny hair in her hand. Her hair naturally curls at the ends like Ava Gardner's, and Mauris never has to run the pressing comb through it or even hair grease, because the White man's texture, too, telegraphed down through the generations. Because Pookie's some uncertain, she hides her vanity from the adults in our town, but any kid in our school who's watched her for even two minutes knows

18

she thinks her hair's going to get her to Hollywood. "In California," she'll say, tossing one thick braid and then the other behind her back. She'll raise her chin to give her hair a few more inches down her back and explain, "up over the hills of Los Angeles." Once, when we were all snapping beans in the kitchen, her grandmama got mad and told her to stop throwing all that hair. "You're lucky, it'll get you far as a big farm out in the next county," Miss Myrtle told her. Other girls with good hair get it ripped out by the roots at school — only because Pookie is so ugly does no one begrudge her her hair.

"Maybe we can dress us up and go down to the Tin Cup," she says now.

"What would we look like trying to set down in the Tin Cup? A couple of fourteen-year-olds."

"We don't look fourteen," she says, removing my thick glasses and folding them gently to put in her pocket. Without them, I can barely see her. "We can draw you in some eyebrows," she says, tracing the bare ridge above my eye socket, "and nobody'll know you got too close to the woodstove."

I slap her finger away, but she isn't looking at me. She's smiling ahead, dreaming, because tall, fine Junebug is coming down

19

the road toward us whistling "Maybelline." Junebug has a jawline like a cornice, eyes that turn up at their corners, and what Pookie calls a meaty butt, and every time I see him walking down the street, I wish he were here in this swing with me.

"Junebutt, Junebutt, fly on over thisaway," Pookie whispers, parting her hair down the middle, twisting the right half of it into a fingercurl. It's her habit, to style her hair when she's lost in thinking. She fingercurls the left half, then shakes her head slightly so the hair falls softly out of its curls and down her chest. She thinks she's gotten somewhere charming, but the halfway points of her hairstyles are always more glamorous than the endpoints. An actress on Broadway would've kept the curls, I want to tell her: it's such bad fortune that, with all her aspirations, she doesn't seem to understand the difference between chorus girl and country mope. "Junebutt Jones," she whispers, and drapes a hand luxuriously over her side of the swing.

Junebug ignores us — why shouldn't he? He's years older and finished with high school and working down at the ice plant with Sonnyboy and probably going to the Tin Cup at night or even riding to Louisville to see the bands that come through the Lincoln Theater, while Pookie and I perch here on this swing like a couple of crows. As he walks closer, I take Pookie's right hand in my left and we both pump our legs, push our backs into the lift of the swing. The eyehooks look ready to pop out of the wood, and the ceiling creaks louder than it ever has, but Junebug is passing right in front of the house and we're giggling so loud to get his attention that we don't even hear the roof groan. Finally, one of the eyehooks breaks free and we're both thrown backwards into the next yard, the air sailing out of our lungs as gravity finds us. Our long skirts and sweaters are covered in Dr. French's freshly cut grass, and as the swing scrapes the porch and comes to land on its one end, we lie there and laugh, watching each other's bodies framed beneath blue sky and clouds, neither of us willing to get up and brush ourselves off in front of Junebug.

Anyone could see it's a miracle our heads cleared the concrete edge, but Junebug doesn't even stop to see if we're alive.

BINGO

Clouds move over spring like a patchwork quilt, throwing us far enough back to winter that the fresh lemonade in the icebox will lose its taste before Mother remembers it. Look up to the sky and ask Pookie what's there, and she'll say the clouds look like nothing. The ornery grain of a burlap sack, she'll say. Failed yarnwork. Miss Myrtle hustles her pots full of tomato sprouts back to her kitchen window to save them from frost, and Percy Greer packs himself and his gin from his porch back into his sitting room to keep his feet warm. Pauline Burke, this Strawberry Winter, skips down the street scratching her dry, dry scalp.

Rays of sun stream through a far corner of sky and Ralph Cundiff balances on the old splintered horse in front of the Colored store. Tyrone Boyd sits under Fifth Street's oldest oak with his legs straight ahead of him, chewing good nickel gum, blowing a bubble big as a frog's head. Working a twig in the back end of a poor stinkbug, but even that must not be enough to soothe his nature, because he gets up, takes a railroad tie from the Flahertys' working pile, and throws it at Ralph's back. For a dodge, Ralph jumps up in the air like a Russian acrobat, but then he comes down on the horse, faltering, and though he leans on his ankle every which way and waves his arms in circles, though none of us can see it coming because he tries so hard in those three seconds to get it not to, he ends up face-down on the ground. Screaming, just as the clouds recover the sun and we all of us, by some instinct, turn and point to where he has fallen. He screams a second time and Tyrone, the only one of us kids not pointing, creeps away, across the sandy lot and toward the alley behind Mr. Barnett's store. He stops mid-escape to wipe sweat from the bridge of his nose, and we can tell by the way he drops his shoulders just before he runs that he'd meant nothing as malicious as what's happened.

Mr. Barnett comes out of his store with his gray apron strings untied and swinging angry counterpoint against his hips. "What happened here?" he yells at us. Cold wind billows the front of his apron but we stand there: dumb, dropping our pointing fingers, unsure. "What happened?" he yells again, this time down to the ground, at Ralph, who curls into a ball and screams a second time, his palm flat against the broken plates of his ruined knee. It takes his starting to cry, pitiful as any baby, before we put our arms down.

"The big dummy," Pookie says to me. "Let's go."

It's 60 degrees, wrong for the end of March and yet when we get to the White people's downtown, where mud meets asphalt and streets become official, the drug store door is open, shooing out the smell of freshly boiled candy and the voice of a radio. Hank Ballard's singing out, "Work with Me, Annie," and we can hear him all the way up High Street, the only Negro voice we'll ever hear coming from Rickles Pharmacy. As we pass, the notes come even to our ears, and at the door, the harmonics reach pitch, but as we walk further on, past the lawyers' offices and the bank and the bakery that's been dead since its roof collapsed in a fire last Christmas, the notes fall flat again. We're just easing down High Street Hill, breathing the scent of candy into the back of our brains, when we run into Miss Wofford.

"Land sakes," she says when she sees me and Pookie, and she puts her box down on the grass fronting the street. Out of her mauve shirt come plump, tanned arms, the freckles dark and so close together as to look like one big cake of freckles, but she lightens at her extremities, and her hands are small, tiny really, with soft white fingers. A wedding band still cuts into her ring finger, because she believed Mr. Thornton last year when he said he'd stop at three wives. Now, everyone in town knows: he sees nothing wrong with courting a fourth.

She pokes Pookie in the chest, just under the V of her cardigan, in the place where any animal is most vulnerable. "We kin," she tells her, and they are, even though Miss Wofford's White, because she's sister to the man who raped Miss Myrtle. "Kinfolk got to help each other," she says. She tilts her head back, sticks her bottom lip out for a funnel, and blows again at her stray hair. "This here box is full of sandwiches I'm carrying down to St. Patrick's for bingo night. I set things up in the afternoon, but then Father Fenton held Business Council downstairs and left the place untidy. Follow me down and help clean, I'll give you gals a dollar. A dollar to share."

The way she says it, it's not an offer so

much as an order, and I would point this out to Pookie, but she's nodding, gone with this already, thinking thirty steps ahead of me and my dignity to what fifty cents might do for her in Hollywood. Never mind that Thurgood Marshall has gone hoarse this winter telling the Supreme Court that Colored children, too, need to look at themselves in clean school mirrors, or that Mauris and Miss Myrtle both would beat Pookie perfectly senseless if they knew she was going downtown to sweep Miss Wofford's church hall. Pookie's following this woman downtown like a baby duckling, and because she's the shiniest pearl I know, because I'm her best friend and not able to think too far apart from her, I'm following too.

In the church basement are fifteen card tables, two of them full of what the Business Committee has left: in one plate, a cigarette extinguished in a mound of un-eaten mashed potatoes; on another, a dol-lop of gravy dried to gel, surrounded by crumbs of still-pink beef; on another, tomato sauce smeared in spirals where someone has sopped it up with bread. Pookie stacks the plates and takes them over to the kitchen and then she's back, wiping down tables, edging sandwich crumbs into the palm of her hand with a wet rag. I'm sitting, watching, in a corner chair whose stuffing is coming out in patches. There's another girl, Sarah, a tall redhead with a mess of freckles on both cheeks — she's taking the sandwiches out of Miss Wofford's box and setting them on green saucers. At the same time, she's smoking, stopping to exhale between plates, and when she drops a bit of ash on one of the sandwiches, she carefully puts her thumb and third finger together and flicks the ash onto the floor. Miss Wofford didn't see fit to introduce us, but we heard her call the girl Sarah when she yelled at her for denting the bread with her fingers. Sarah's thin in most places but heading to plump in her arms, and if we didn't know for a fact that Miss Wofford was a virgin for most of her forty-some years, we'd have mistaken Sarah for her daughter.

"Y'all from around here?" Sarah asks.

"Born and raised," says Pookie. With the rag, she tries to erase a purple stain on a table, first making a tent of her fingers to apply pressure, and then giving it some wholesale elbow grease, leaning into her work, wiping and wiping until she decides the stain is part of the table and moves on.

"How do you stand it?" asks Sarah. "I

27

can't see what there is to do all day."

"Don't know nothing different," says Pookie.

Pookie won't say in front of the White people in town that she's going to Hollywood, because she thinks it'd be disrespecting their own small lives. So to cover for what looks like lack of ambition, I tell Sarah, "We got to finish high school."

"After that, you ought to come to Cincinnati. That's where I'm from — Daddy and me are just down here staying with Mamaw while she gets her gallbladder took out — but if I was home, why, on a nice cool day like today I'd be down to the river with my boyfriend. Watching the boats load up over on the Kentucky side while we eat us a hamburger. We got museums and things in Cincinnati. Fairs, come summer, right when it gets so steamy and disagreeable you'd want to die otherwise. And boys — lots of right-nice-looking boys. Nice-looking Nigra boys, even. You like to never get sad or bored up in Cincinnati."

She twists around to the box to lift another sandwich, and her waist is so tiny that I don't believe she's ever eaten a hamburger in her life. I want to tell her Pookie's thinking way bigger than Cincinnati or wharves or boys.

"How old are you?" I ask.

"Eighteen. Ain't finished high school, though. Quit almost soon as I got there. Drawing isophocles triangles and memorizing caveman books. Boring."

Pookie's on her last table, plunging her dishrag into the white soap bucket, and I'm thinking it's already damn dark outside — probably colder even than it was when the sun was still out — when the first player arrives for bingo. It's Elizabeth Worden, a mess of red blouse unbuttoned in the middle exactly where it shouldn't be, necklace full of fake rubies turned off center, so the biggest jewel sits on the side of her neck like a wound. She lives with her grown son in a decrepit brick house on Harrison, and this is the first I've seen her off her front porch. Generally, she sits there, rocking in her chair with a shotgun in her lap, waiting for the skunks to come out from under the porch. Generally they don't, and curious as skunks are, I wonder if the threat of Mrs. Worden's shotgun has stunted their intellectual growth. One day, I think, they'll figure it all out, or maybe Mrs. Worden will.

"Well, how do, Elizabeth," Miss Wofford says as she bustles out of the kitchen. "Almost finished?" she asks Sarah, and before Sarah can even answer, she's on

29

Pookie. "Looks like you're finished," she says. "Which would be mighty fine, but your friend over there ain't done one drop of work. And I can't give you a dollar for nothing."

Pookie bats her eyelashes, but she knows she'd better not upset some White lady. Instead, she puts her hands in her dress pockets, smiles beatifically at her own great-aunt, and says, "So just give me the fifty cents."

"Girl, you ain't even cleaned the dishes. Just dropped 'em all in the sink."

"I can warsh 'em right quick —"

"You could, and to do right by me you probably should, but you still ain't getting that fifty cents. Deal was, a dollar for both you gals if you both helped clean, and I ain't giving you the dollar to share if you ain't shared the work. Your people got to learn to keep each other in check. As the Good Book saith, 'Wherefore comfort yourselves together, and edify one another.' So next time you got a Nigra friend thinks she's too good to warsh some table, you best leave her behind."

"But Miss Wofford. I worked two hours!"

"Are we done talking?" Miss Wofford asks. "I'm of the mind that we're done talking."

Pookie shoots her dishrag across the room,

but it misses the pail and lands on the table with an angry *thop.* Soapy drops splatter everywhere.

"Have this," Miss Wofford says, and though Pookie's crossed over to me by then and I'm linking her arm, edifying her just like Miss Wofford said, Pookie breaks free of me when she sees Miss Wofford reach into her pocket. She pulls out a broken chain of necklace, dull silver, not real anything. "This was my Aunt Letitia's," she says, as Pookie takes the chain from her and holds it up to the light, inspecting it as though it might have some value that's invisible to the rest of us.

"Thank you," Pookie says.

She crosses back to me, but when she gives me her arm back, I snatch the chain from her and throw it underhand, so it skitters across the floor and wraps itself around a table leg. "She ain't a dog and don't need your collar," I say. Elizabeth Worden clucks her tongue. Sarah giggles, though as we go up the back steps and out the door her giggle goes silent, as though she's plugged it again with a cigarette.

After the church hall's stale breath, the cold air should feel like a gift, but its sharpness turns me nauseous. Pookie and I walk back up High Street behind a hatless man whose face we cannot see. He lists slightly into his shorter left leg, and one thick lush curl has blown, impossibly, over his bald spot. As we pass the bakery, I notice for the first time a tricycle someone's tired of and left. My eyes feel frozen, as marbles might, and I blink warmth back into my tears. It is damn dark, though the moon rises fertile over the horizon. It's the biggest moon I've seen in all my life, a moon glowing with lambent encouragement, a moon bigger than the earth itself. It's so large and so bright you can actually see the eyes and the nose and all the craters around them — it's a moon you could hunt anything under. Deer, or your own destiny. It's pregnant with triplet moons, or stuffed with icing, or perhaps dead and bloated with tiny feeding moon flies.

"C'mon," I tell Pookie, and we turn right at Rickles Pharmacy and head down the narrow alley between it and the hardware store, beating back the dead vines with our legs. On the back face of the pharmacy, iron stairs climb a fire escape, and Pookie and I run up the steps, our feet clanging *thurk thurk thurk* against the hollow metal until we're on the roof, out of breath, rapping our knuckles against the tin heating cone. Out in the county, a trash fire has caught its energy, and a dark plume of smoke pushes into the moon's outer edges before dispersing. Pookie walks to the edge of the roof and looks down to the street, and the danger of it makes the soles of my feet tingle, but I go over and sit next to her anyway. Our legs dangle clear over the edge of the roof, but no one will ever look up and see us; it's not in most people's natures to look beyond what they think they should see.

"Who told you you could talk to some White lady like that?" Pookie asks.

"Who told you you couldn't?"

She laughs. But I mean it. If she's ever going to get to Hollywood, she's going to have to stop believing what's real and start believing what isn't. There are people on far-off continents who must be told the earth isn't flat, and prisoners of war who don't trust that they are free, even when soldiers come to open the gates. They go right back to work, those captives, back to their miserable lives forever. I need Pookie to know: if no one told her, when she was born, that she was going to die, then maybe she wouldn't.

Saint Monkey

Finally, come April, the wind blows down from the mountain and starts to wear warm again on people's bare arms, and Grandpap and I sit out on the porch in the punched iron chairs and play checkers. Grandpap is a master — a wizard, who can beat anyone in the county — and when I come near winning, he upsets the checkerboard. Afterwards, he doesn't apologize or even speak: he steps off the porch, bends over the grass, and picks up three black pieces that have landed there, a constellation spelling his anger. He scrapes the remaining twenty-one off the porch and into his carpeted box while I wiggle myself into my swing and finger a bit of rust already growing on the chain. "Right nice breeze a sailing," is all he says when he comes up and sits next to me. He pushes us back and forth with his feet while we watch the sun sink like a tangerine behind the trees. The forest around Mt.

Sterling is thick in late summer — a forest for trolls, for knights. "Two kinds of people, and some die on their feet," Grandpap says. He says it all the time since my daddy died, and I haven't asked him what it means. I'd rather it stayed a riddle.

Across the street, in 211, two little girls are sitting quietly inside staring at one another: Pookie biting her cuticles, Imagene bringing her wrist to her nose to smell some leftover fragrance; and both of them wondering at, without remarking on, the scratchiness of their father's couch. There they've been sitting while we've skipped past their front window, or not so accidentally hit a baseball onto their front porch. There they will continue to sit, for the unclockable days until Miss Myrtle decides otherwise, because Sonnyboy has killed Mauris and now the girls are expected to stay in the house and calmly mourn their mother. To kill his wife, Sonnyboy chose the most beautiful day we've had yet: April Fool's. The heat had at last tinged the sky the haze yellow of spring, and the day so swelled with the promise of the summer to come that it was heartbreaking for the people of Queen Street, who knew better. He killed her that first honest day of spring but no one heard him do it, and Mauris was such a quiet woman that at first, only the neighborhood men noticed her absence. Treasurer of the Second Baptist Ladies' Missionary, who hid aching shyness under the guise of Christian modesty, Mauris had never greeted the men as she walked home from work. But the men missed, those first couple of days, the *tap tap* of her high heels on the packed dirt of the street, the tight fabric of her skirt giving with her behind, the slight switch in her walk that brought clandestine grins and nods of approval from neighboring porches.

The girls' first motherless weekend, before any of us knew she was dead, Sylvia French and I wandered over to 211 to listen to Honest Harold. Miss Myrtle had come to make her annual inspection of the girls' Easter dresses, because Mauris had never been as good a seamstress as her mother, and her work tended to hang off small shoulders or clench too tightly around waists still domed with baby fat. Mauris had always been happy for the help: she knew her limits. So, in her daughter's house on Good Friday, while Honest Harold wrecked Mrs. O'Day's Warbleware dinner party and all we girls on the sofa laughed, Miss Myrtle bent over her youngest grandbaby and narrowed her eyes at Sonnyboy.

"Where's Mauris gone off to? Ought to be

home now, shain't she?"

Miss Myrtle had straight pins in her mouth, so what she said came out muffled. But I know now that Sonnyboy had probably spent so many hours waiting for the question that he knew instantly what had been asked.

"Been going off like that right often," he said, looking out the parlor's large window. He rubbed the top of his head, stroked the tight place above his belt. "Matter fact, she ain't been home in two days."

Miss Myrtle held her head over and let the pins fall from her mouth down the unhemmed edge of Imagene's dress. "You ain't told me that, Sonnyboy. Why ain't you tell me?"

Sonnyboy shrugged his shoulders. "She just been doing like that come lately," he said, leaving Miss Myrtle running her tongue over her front teeth, wondering at how poorly she knew her only child.

Pookie's cheeks burned red beneath her freckles and she folded her fingers over their opposing knuckles and I knew she didn't want me there. "Excuse me," I told them all, rising from the couch, "but Grandpap's probably wondering where I'm at. I bet your mama is too," I told Sylvia French, and off we ran, out the door and into the spring sun, still so shockingly bright that late in the day.

Sonnyboy held on to his lie for some weeks, until every Negro in Bath and Montgomery counties was certain that he'd been winked at behind his back, that silent, blank-faced Mauris, a child of rape who'd been shielded from men all her life, had run off with some bent rake or another. "Probably in Lexington," people said. "You know how still cricks run deep."

It didn't help that Mauris's one and only friend, Hattie Lee Grainger, had in fact left her husband to go off with a curly-headed insurance salesman from Lexington. Sonnyboy and Mauris had been the first people to know, that opening day of spring, the same April morning the birds set up again in their eaves. Bit by bit the guilt in Sonnyboy kicked its way out, and as he talked, in the by and by, I heard the old people retelling it like a generation of bards, saying Sonnyboy'd gotten an air of something that morning after the girls left for school, a peaty smell of sweat and blood, and he supposed he was going to have to get after Mauris to talk to Pookie about womanly hygiene. But the backroom at Taylor's Department Store was thick with fine holiday clothes in need of alteration, and Mauris was leaving early, so Sonnyboy had to run to the porch if he wanted to catch a word with her. They say he found her bent over the railing, talking in low tones to Hattie Lee, who was so excited she was digging divots out of Sonnyboy's grass with the heel of her shoe.

"Don't tell a soul," Hattie Lee was saying, her bony finger pressed against the big, pouty lips Sonnyboy had been dreaming of since puberty. "Lyman'll be here any minute to get me." At her feet was a lime green American Tourister.

"Clyde been running around?" Mauris asked. "He done laid hands on you?"

"Nothing like that, child. I just heard him put that housekey down on the new sideboy again this morning, and you know I *have* asked him a hundred times." She patted her curly wig, put a hand on her hip. "I just said to myself, 'Hattie Lee, that's it. You ain't never got to hear that housekey again.'"

It came out that during the conversation, little Evelyn Ferguson — one of those gorgeous, obsidian-eyed Fergusons at No. 213 — was standing in the artery between Sonnyboy's house and her own. At ten, Evelyn had already bloomed too beautiful for our memories to hold on to what she looked like if we weren't looking right at her. She was standing there, trying not to pry, trying to sneak a cigarette outside her mama's seeing. Little Evelyn it was who saw, from where she was standing, just behind the porches of both houses, Hattie Lee. She said Hattie Lee patted her wig once more, as though the wig itself could be trusted to hold her secret. She said Sonnyboy leaned back in his doorway, seeming to enjoy the rear view of a wife dressed in polka dot pink and shaped finely as a fiddle. She said he was smiling to himself, rubbing his paunch, probably thinking how fickle Hattie Lee was to leave someone over housekeys scratched against good furniture, probably thinking what a good woman he himself had found, when Mauris giggled.

Just one hushed giggle, according to little Evelyn, who repeated it again and again when her mama cuffed her on her perfect little ear and made her say what Sonnyboy either wouldn't tell or didn't quite remember. A giggle hushed yet throaty enough to make Sonnyboy know that Mauris was laughing not just at Clyde but at the clumsiness of all men. The giggle slipped out of her and stepped on all the ideas he had about women, and according to what he told Reverend Graves through the bars of his jail cell, that giggle kept him from speaking to Mauris about their girls. Instead, he moved quietly off the porch and back into his home that had been his parents' home before his, he retreated to the bathroom, he later confessed, and stood in front of the mirror that had watched him since he was ten. He cut himself four times while shaving and had to press his toes hard against the tile to keep back tears. When he thought back on his life, he remembered not wild craps games behind the Tin Cup or entire Sundays spent swinging on river vines, but a first date in Mauris's parlor within range of Miss Myrtle's keen ears. He remembered Mauris's delicate bare feet drumming the pier while he fished with her at Hikes' Point, and Reverend Owington's proud wedding day smile upon the both of them. Diapers pinned and little girls nursed and bounced on knees. All that he held dear in his life, erased by one giggle. He was in the kitchen slicing ham for his breakfast when Mauris came back in to tell him she was leaving for work.

"Let me kiss you goodbye, baby," he said, with a catch in his voice that said *lost,* because according to what he told Reverend Graves, he'd always been his mama's son first and foremost and now, somehow, that

41

was gone too. Mauris opened a smile and went to him, her lips immaculately rouged, her dress's pink polka dots split in half by the fold of her collar. She stretched her arms up around his neck, and he stuck the knife right through skin and meat, into the place just under her breastbone. Her biscuit-colored skin wasn't as soft as it had looked in the pink cotton, or maybe, he thought, it was the tough, sweet flesh beneath, but he said he'd had to twist the knife a little, and he'd expected screams but was relieved to find that Mauris died as silently as she had lived. Griffin, the black cat under the table, arched his back, yawned, and moved through the doorway into the living room. The grandfather clock rang out eight times. Sonnyboy said Mauris widened her eyes as though he were telling her about the milk bill, as though she weren't surprised but merely prepared.

He told it all to Reverend Graves, how he rocked her a little before he let her to the floor. He scratched a worrisome patch of skin on his chest and took himself back to the living room, where he crushed his boot into the sleeping cat's tail and felt relief to hear the animal screech. The cat escaped, a flash of black fur darting under the French Provincial sofa, and Sonnyboy went to the front porch and called out to Hiram Loving, who was hitching up his bicycle. "Hey, boss!" Sonnyboy said.

It was only Roger Carr who heard him holler the first time, because Hiram's baby girl's nighttime crying was still ringing in his ears. But when Sonnyboy called out louder — "Boss!" — Hiram kicked his leg over his bicycle seat and looked up. "Ride by the ice plant on your way," Sonnyboy yelled, "and tell 'em I'm sick." Hiram nodded across the street and pedaled off into the risen sun.

Nine days passed, and Sonnyboy's children had their beauty shop appointments, their Palm Sunday church play, their night-before-Easter oranges. Come Easter morning, Pookie, after the last joke ever told about her flat chest, punched Melton Boyd square in his moth-shaped mouth. "Damn midget," she said, and he fell to the ground crying, searching on his hands and knees for his front tooth. Grandpap and I were on the porch playing Three Men's Morris, and we saw him get to his feet with his new white suit stained green on the knees and elbows. One side of his bow tie bulged out larger than the other, a sloppy, two-humped camel. Griffin tipped to the edge of Sonnyboy's porch and meowed.

43

"That girl is a monkey," Grandpap said, skipping one of my red pieces.

"She's not a monkey," I told him. "She's a saint."

Melton hiccupped on home without his emancipated tooth, and Pookie went into the house and came back with an early piece of pie for the cat. Miss Myrtle's key lime would go to the dinner table as a fraction, but no matter — Griffin was her mother's baby, more beloved than any girl in the house. The cat's aura was such that he garnered no resentments even: everyone in the family simply loved Griffin most of all, and when Mauris got down on the hardwood floor and put his cloth mouse in her own mouth to play with him the way she never played with her own children, the girls didn't so much as blink. That Miss Myrtle had admitted an animal of any kind into her own home on occasion was testament to the cat's charm.

"I told you, Grandpap. That girl is a saint, no less than Patrick."

"Saint Monkey," Grandpap sniffed. He'd already gotten two of his pieces lined up, and we were both just going through the motions until he won.

Easter left us, church thinned out again, and folks began to notice that Sonnyboy didn't seem mad at his cheating wife or even worried about her disappearance. People talked. His closest friends were chatted up. But what happened first was that the house at No. 211 started to stink. Imagene commented on it first. "I think a squirrel got underneath the house," she told Pookie.

"It's everything under the house. 'Sides, it ain't a squirrel. Smells like a damn polecat." But the smell situated itself, until one evening that week Miss Myrtle came back with Junebug, who disassembled the dead stove and found one of Mauris's small hands, bloated and almost skinless, but recognizable because of the braided gold wedding band that had cut into its flesh. When a piece of the hand's skin slid off, Miss Myrtle fainted and had to be taken to Dr. French's house overnight. Mrs. French put Imagene to bed at her house and Sylvia took Pookie to the show. *Whistle Stop,* I believe they saw, which made the rest of us girls jealous. The law came and got Sonnyboy, who went just as silently as had his wife. Downtown at the jail, he sat across the table from the White men twisting their hands and mouths in disgust as he confessed with all the calm of a choirboy. He told them about putting her hands in the furnace, which she had tended so well; her legs

45

beneath the floorboard of his bedroom, where he had most enjoyed them. Her head (he'd suspected it would stink before any other part) he'd taken to the roof in the night and placed just above the closed chimney flue, so she could look down on her children for always. The rest of her body, heart lungs liver intestine pelvis and wind-pipe, chopped up with the wood ax, sprinkled with lime, and buried before dawn, just below the porch so he could keep her near him.

That was Saturday night. By Sunday afternoon, the news had grown legs that ran through the Black part of town. Children were told to leave backrooms while parents discussed Sonnyboy's strange crime; older women sat on porches and shook their heads, commenting to no one but themselves. "We are surely in the end times," more than one preacher told his congregation that morning.

I sat in my porch swing and watched a steady line of people go in and out of the house at 211 — first ministers and deacons with their Bibles, then church mothers with covered dishes. Then the rest of the Negro community, our fathers and mothers, even the ones who'd looked down on Mauris for hanging her wash on Sundays and going without a camisole under her blouse in the summertime. Mother took potato salad and stayed all night visiting, but Grandpap would not let me go ask to see Pookie: I had to wait until she came outside, just before dusk, with her two sisters trailing out the door behind her. I had to make myself be slow about getting off the swing, since part of me wanted to run over and tell Pookie that my own sweet daddy was dead and I knew how it felt and what to do.

"Pookie," I called out softly, as I got to her yard. The big blue anchor down the front of Imagene's white dress heaved with her shuddering breaths, the aftershocks of her long bout of crying. As I got closer, I saw that the tears had worn lines of salt down her cheeks like nails through candle wax. It had always been her habit to tag along with me and Pookie, gnatlike, but now she ignored me, dipping her head over her knees and biting her lips into her own private coldest midnight. Pookie hadn't been crying. She, alone, saw that she could still breathe air. "Pookie," I said again, hugging her. She felt so soft, but already she smelled like the inside of a grandmother's house — Vicks salve in the morning to fight off sore throats and boiled potatoes for dinner because they aren't dear and the win-

47

dows shut at night to keep the chill out and the house stale. "I'm sorry," I said.

She pushed me away. "What you sorry for? You ain't killed her."

I stepped back for balance and ended up taking some distance. "I'm sorry for your feelings," I said.

"Don't think you know anything about what I'm feeling, just because your daddy died in some war. Your daddy died, but you wasn't living every day in the same house with the person what killed him. The man what kilt your daddy ain't your own flesh and blood who you sprung from and who you'll probably end up just like. Your daddy's fingers wasn't up in no stovepipe. And nobody thought your daddy was a damn polecat." She looked at Imagene, who kneaded her stomach.

"I don't know how you feel, Pookie. But if you want someone to tell it to —"

"I'll never want to talk about this with you nor nobody else. Not ever." She sat down on Miss Myrtle's stoop a fourteen-year-old already defeated. "And my name ain't Pookie. My mama named me Caroline."

CAPEZIOS

Because both murderer and murdered were Negro, the court of Montgomery County never deigned to convene, and Sonnyboy was in the pen before the week was out. Mauris had only what could be called "remains," so Miss Myrtle had nothing to sit in her house until the funeral, no dressed-up body for people to eat and play cards over until it was wheeled out of its house for the last time, no steel casket for the girls to view through the hearse's back window as their mother took her final ride in an automobile.

"No visitation," Grandpap said, when he read about the services in the church bulletin. "No body," he added, shaking his head because he knew what it meant to have a child vanish whole and come back in pieces. No visitation and no body, but still it took Miss Myrtle a couple of weeks to quilt her wits back together and arrange the burial, which turned out to be the biggest — Negro or White — that Bath and Montgomery counties had ever seen. All the Negroes of twelve different towns were there, tottering around headstones and perforating the fresh spring mud with the treads and the heels of their good shoes; even Hattie Lee, returned to Mt. Sterling in black stockings and clumped mascara, without her new man, who maybe had to stay in Lexington selling his assurances, who maybe had quit her already. The old men of the town, dressed in the tar black suits they saved for Easter and their daughters' weddings, my own granddaddy in the Botany that had cost him forty dollars on credit at Taylor's. At my daddy's funeral, it had still given a good fit. Now it puffed like sails where the hanger had built a frame his shoulders couldn't fill.

Since the funeral, kids at school have stopped telling Pookie jokes — no skin pebbly as a pegboard, no legs bowed out like a wishbone. No meanness at all since Mauris was buried and Caroline came to school and cried all day into a burgundy napkin, not even when her pimples jumped out of their hiding places for the summer and turned her face stucco. Clemons Greene imitates my pigeon-toed walk; Wink Loving asks me if I haven't inflated my lips with a bicycle pump. "Fatmouth," they call me. "Boat-nose." "Turnipbutt." And all the while, Caroline keeps an untouchable aura about herself, a certain poise she's found now that the Montgomery County Colored School has forgotten she's not beautiful. She holds her shoulders back as we walk through the high school hall, and makes eye contact with Mr. Pennington, our six-and-a-half-foot principal, and then one night I dream it even, that her fairy godmother has come to her in the night with glass slippers and mice for footmen. It's as though other people are on the edge of seeing her shine, and it makes the shine, for me, all the more precious. When she touches my neck in class so I'll turn around and see Ralph Cundiff sleeping on his math lessons, I push back into her touch, slightly enough so she won't notice me lingering. When we're alone, flipping through the faded, waterlogged issue of *True Confessions* she's taken from her mama's belongings, or painting each other's fingernails crimson in her grandmama's backyard, I study her as one would a frost-covered leaf, looking for the long veins of familiarity under her crust. But I can no longer see my own plainness reflected in hers, and I begin to dread that it might actually be true, that Caroline's leaving me behind.

All the fireworks are exploding this day I've chosen to test her on it, all the bottle rockets and cherry bombs and ground spinners, shooting orange and green sparks from Mr. Nettles's grass. He's cleaning out what he brought down from Ohio last summer, offering his dusty excitement to Melton and Tyrone Boyd so that they might land, for one afternoon, on the right side of boredom. The gunpowder proves itself in a constant attack of sound, from every canister the boys light, and they end up choking the neighborhood with thick smoke that stings my eyes and hurts my throat. When Daddy died, Mr. Nettles sent a flowering plant to the funeral, and now, through the green, mercury-laced haze of a Pharaoh's Serpent, he waves at me as I walk up Miss Myrtle's yard. He sent a plant because he couldn't attend — while Mr. Pinchback was laying my father to rest, Mr. Nettles was over in Lexington, seeing a man about a billiards table. He was back that afternoon: when I went out to Mr. Barnett's store for Mother's aspirin powders I found Mr. Nettles's truck out front, the billiard table leaning against its cab, sinking diagonally into its bed like a wrecked ship. In the store, Mr. Nettles was leaning over the counter at eye level with Mrs. Barnett, so he didn't see me when I walked in the door and tripped the bell: he kept talking. "Young man goes off full of adventure, comes back to his kid in a box," he was telling her, but he didn't have it quite right. My father had never meant to come back, to me or to anyone else in this petty little town, and it's why I still can't decide whether I'm angry with him for dying. "Leave." It's a word you might say two million times in a lifetime. If you're where you're supposed to be, you won't need it as much. I wave back at Mr. Nettles; he smiles and crosses his arms, but seems, behind the smoke, to be already fading to something I won't one day remember.

Miss Myrtle sits on her porch, winding a yard of blue cloth around and around her left hand with her right. "Caroline here?" I ask her. She looks at me for a second, then refocuses on her self-mummification. She points to the door with her free hand, and I let myself in.

A pissy smell of cabbage fills her living room, and from somewhere in the back of the house Dinah Washington sings, swelling the afternoon with romance. Caroline lies asleep on the sofa, with Imagene wrapped around her body like a vine. Their knees touch, and the corner of Imagene's cloud-gray skirt is tucked under Caroline's mint green one. Imagene's thin legs fold alongside her sister's thicker ones, and she's nestled one of her braids under Caroline's chin, and like this, tangled in each other like possums, they remind me so much of the way I used to fall asleep in Daddy's lap that I have to turn my eyes to Miss Myrtle's cabinet. The house's large front window faces north, so sunlight never shines directly enough through for me to catalog all the knickknacks on the cabinet, but every time I come, I do find something different, and this time what I notice is a gray ceramic rabbit on the top shelf. Standing on his hind legs, with his paws bent and his one glazed ear folded over, he looks not at me but past me, as though he's already made up his mind.

"Whatcha know?" Caroline whispers.

"Want to go to Taylor's with me?"

"Sure," she says, and with a ginger lifting of Imagene's arms from her own neck, rolls the little girl off her. *Bamp* goes Imagene's head on the couch, but she doesn't wake: she turns her face away from the cushion and lets out a deep sigh of sleeping. Her eyelids aren't fully shut, and I catch a slice of her deep brown pupils involuntarily rolling back under her eyelids. Caroline leaves her dreaming, and I follow her out Miss Myrtle's door.

We've gone to Taylor's a hundred times before, with and without spending money, looking good and looking bad, with gorgeous lifted hairstyles and with curls flattened by rain, with freshly ironed clothes and with runs in our stockings, but we haven't been anywhere besides school since Pookie's become Caroline, and her coming with me now proves that she still knows we live in the same orbit. As early as fifth grade, other girls had seen our handicaps — mine my intelligence and Pookie's her ugliness — and sensed the tragedy, that we'd forever be unused rungs on the social ladder. They expected the two of us together, and I wanted to disappoint them. When the dodgeball captain picked us for the same team at recess, I sat the game out. When Miss Taylor assigned me to a desk behind Pookie's, I complained that the light from the window hurt my eyes. Eventually, I got excited by the staccato way she struck the words "tectonic plate," and the way she was always the first kid to laugh when something was funny, and now, walking behind her into Taylor's, I know that none of that will ever quite leave me.

We climb the polished stairs to the second floor, because Mother's given me money for school shoes. "Or else," she said this morning, "we'll have to saw your toes off." I was still in my gown, in the hallway, my bare feet leaving condensation on the cold hardwood floor. Mother was already in her nurse's uniform, and the sun ricocheted off the wall mirror and struck the grain of her white nylons, making them look ghastly against her dark legs. She kissed me on the forehead, then licked her thumb and pretended to wipe away the kiss. She smiled while her eyebrows frowned, as if she'd suddenly recalled something profane. The last couple of evenings she'd been in a good mood, breaking her favorite blue teacup only to whistle as she swept up the porcelain, saying, "Oh well," when she forgot a casserole that burned to crisp in the oven. Grandpap joked, outside her hearing, that she must have found a bottle of Early Times in Miss Ora Ray's liquor cabinet. She's given me fifteen dollars, enough for a pair of Weejuns or even Capezios, and Caroline and I circle the table, picking pairs up to look at the price tags on their undersides.

We've gone almost through the whole table before the clerk walks over, tucks the blond hair of her bob angrily behind her ear, and says, "You done picked up ever single one of them shoes. What *are* you looking for?"

"Shoes," Caroline deadpans, and the blood comes to my face as I laugh silently into my own throat.

"Shoes," the clerk repeats, making herself miss the joke. She has a stub nose that reminds me of pork, and a cut in her right eyebrow that reminds me of butchering. Her name tag reads WENDY, and though I've never known her name I've known *her:* she was one of the six filthy children of the coal washer who used to live right across Fifth Street, in the part of Shake Rag that's White but just barely so. There was one summer when we were all seven years old, she'd run across the street to play jacks. Now she pretends she doesn't recognize us, doesn't remember having touched our hands, looked into our eyes, and wanted what small piece of metal we held.

Caroline hands her a pair of pumps, smart brown ones with straps. "I'll try these on."

"No you won't," Wendy tells her, mashing the three words down to one syllable. She points to Caroline's sandals. "You ain't got no socks. The Health Department got regulations."

"You got footies, don't you?"

"I only give 'em out to paying customers."

"Who says we ain't paying?" Caroline asks.

Caroline's voice has taken on sad water; it sinks me with everything that's wrong in her world. "Take my socks," I tell her, and we both lower ourselves into the shoe department's soft leather chairs. I slip off my loafers, peel off my socks. I feel my bladder getting full, and I think about how Gloria Fugate said she snuck into the Whites-only bathroom here. Clean as a whistle, she told us, with a towel machine so you could wipe your hands after washing. "What size will you need?" I ask Pookie.

"Seven and a half," she says, looking to Wendy, who still stares at us, still angrily. Eight years have elevated her Whiteness, and she wants us to notice. Caroline must read her mind too: halfway through pulling one of my socks up her calf, she straightens up and says, "Please, ma'am," creating a gulf where before there was none.

"Well, all right, then," Wendy says. She saunters to the cash register like a queen through a garden. "But I got to count these bills before I wait on y'all." She punches the register open and the bell echoes through the empty second floor, punching the downbeat of the waltz being piped in through the

58

ceiling. Off the tiles of the furniture department the bell echoes, and against the metal
racks in girls' clothing, over the curvature
of the fine china in housewares.

"We got all day," Caroline says. "We really
do."

Wendy counts bills, licking her finger for
help when the corners stick together, glanc-
ing at us out of the corner of her eye before
she recounts the same stack. We're sitting
there, Caroline tapping her heel against the
chair leg, me fighting the urge to go home
and pee, both of us watching Wendy count,
when a White woman comes up the stairs
with her little girl trailing behind her. "Can
I help you?" Wendy asks, dropping her stack
of bills back into the drawer.

"Just looking," the woman sings back.
She's large, shuffling, perfectly waistless in
her housedress. Her daughter grabs her
behind in a hug, making her amble.

"Well, we got cute little girl shoes," Wendy
tells her. "We got 'em with bows right across
the toe." And suddenly, it seems, the number of pairs on the table grows. When she
describes them, there become so many that,
were I offered a pair for free, I'd have to
say, "No thank you," because I would have
lost myself in the choosing. She picks up a
black patent leather pair, turning them so

that the overhead light drifts across the shine of the toe. "Perfect for church," she says, covering her speech with a veneer designed to distinguish herself from Shake Rag. While she talks on — *we got leather we got heels we got buckles* — Caroline pats me on the arm and we rise from our chairs. We pass behind the clerk, so pointedly close to her that I can smell the cheap toilet water she's dabbed on the back of her neck, and then we run down the stairs and out into the summer heat.

On the way home, I crunch acorn caps under my shoes with each step and wonder where, now, I'll get my Capezios. We pass Mrs. Dickerson's meditating scarecrow; Mr. Eblen's scorched rosebush — trying to die, trying to bloom. Melton and Tyrone have left Mr. Nettles's yard, and the smoke has risen to hang over his slanted roof. A plane passes overhead and I think how Grandpap says it's an abomination, metal wings that far above the earth, higher than any bird, mocking God. Caroline hasn't said one word. On her long legs she's walked too fast for me, and my blouse, under my sweater, sticks to my back. Beneath all that I'm wearing a bone-colored bra, a new B-cup Mother bought me for Easter. It's satin, and the cups are glossy under a certain light, and I wonder how Mother found the meekness to go to Taylor's and buy it.

CINDERELLA

Now finally, now that the trees have filled green and the last day of school has come round, and we pupils are stacking chairs and dusting erasers, the boys have to break their recess from cruelty, because Caroline is, despite my worries, irresistibly ugly. I hear them laughing from across the room and feel it, familiar and dreadful as the hotcomb come too close to my neck: they're laughing at us. Mr. Pennington has turned his radio's full power down the hall to propel our cleaning, and as the Clovers sing "Fool, Fool, Fool," the little boys from the lower grades pile atop each other like puppies sliding around the hardwood floor. A new boy slams his full weight down on the others with each new verse of song, and Evelyn Ferguson coughs, under attack from the dirt she's kicked up shelving spellers in the coat closet. Ralph comes to us like a war veteran, favoring his good leg, limping to spare the kneecap that will never heal to wholeness. "Ah-buh-buh-buh-buh beanpole Betty," he says into the silent space of the disc jockey's switch, when everyone can hear him. "What's this for?" he asks, snapping Caroline's bra strap. "To remind your chest that you're a girl?"

Everyone laughs. Even Mrs. Dickerson smiles — I catch her before she catches herself — and it's a relief when the tears come to Caroline's eyes, when we take leave of Ralph, his laughing friends, the entire school. Clouds hang low and dark but it's not yet raining, so she leads me out to the schoolyard, to the edge where it meets the forest in a stand of honeysuckle. As she leans down and picks a bloom, I can see that the palms of her hands are peeling, as they always do when her nerves get the best of her.

"Forget him," I say.

"It ain't him. It ain't none of them." She pulls the stigma and breaks the stem, sucks the wee bit of nectar and closes her eyes until the tears come. She rocks herself into crying, and I spread my hand across her shoulder. Not to rub it, because she's not a baby, and not to pat it, because I'm sincere. Just to touch her. To absorb, through her clothes, some small ounce of her pain. To feel, in the tightness there, everything she needs to say.

Some of what she tells me I already know, because after Pinchback & Sons Mortuary buried the baby-sized casket with her mother's head and hands, she momentarily came back to happiness. She dug two yards of squares for hopscotch and hid from the boy who was It. On Hiram Loving's handlebars she hitched rides into town, smiling all the way, as if she were realizing that the world itself wasn't broken but just her murderous father. On that first 90-degree day, when she got home from school and slammed the storm door back against the wall, she unwrapped herself from her sweater, set her pink parasol abloom, and wandered into the alley behind the Tin Cup, whose owner summoned her with a whistle. Oval Murden, who'd been walking down the alley on his way to collect Laura, one of his mama's chickens who'd stopped laying, told us that the owner of the Tin Cup coughed before he spoke.

"Hey there!" he yelled.

"Sir?"

"How'd you like fifty cents?"

Of course Pookie was fourteen years old, on the edge of something big — the Rest of Life. She stood in the alley, Oval said, appraising the owner's polished shoes and his pearline false teeth, turning up her little bean nose to sniff the air for the Duke the owner used to slick his conk. You couldn't get Duke in Mt. Sterling — Pookie knew that much.

"I'd like fifty cents, sir. I'd like it a bunch."

Oval Murden, too, had been appraising. He told us he'd watched Pookie's face as she'd spoken and seen how it was set in smooth skin that hadn't yet erupted in hormones and worry. He'd looked at her plumb little legs and her child's way of standing with them spread far enough to make her woman's dress look wrong, and decided she was still so young that if she fell, it wouldn't hurt. When the owner said, "Get in here, then," Oval Murden didn't give one thought toward warning her not to. He just kept walking for his mama's house, with the smell of a frying hen already up his nose.

Pookie tells me now about the particulars, how the owner told her she'd make her daily fifty cents off of exactly one person — Percy Greer. When he sank down to the bar and into unconsciousness, the owner dragged him by his feet back behind the blue store-room door and Pookie left her place behind the counter. There, in the box-strangled closet, where moth wings floated down like confetti around the lone fluorescent bulb, the owner showed her how to soak a rag in water and wring small drops onto Percy Greer's chapped lips until he woke up in a paroxysm of startled blinks, and could be sent home to his wife, his woman, or his devoted auntie. Despite Percy's jaundiced liver, his eyes, and only his eyes, were beautiful, for he'd managed to carry through the fifty years of his life the long, thick lashes he'd had at birth, and when the owner went back to tending the bar, Pookie sat in the storeroom and watched Percy's beautiful lashes as he attempted to blink off his liquor. She listened to Percy lick his lips as she noted how the owner had stacked the boxes of cherry syrup so neatly, in the staggered pattern of bricks in a wall. She cupped Percy's forehead in the palm of her hand and picked dust from the floor out of his hair, until, in the confusion that remained within him, Percy called her by his wife's name. "You, sweet Lucy, are the most precious thing in my world," he said. He frowned in embarrassment, but still he put a hand on the little bump of her left breast. "Thank you, my Lucy," he said, pinching the rosebud of her nipple.

Pookie screamed. She ran back through

the door and into the bar. "Mr. Percy's touching on me!" she said.

Oval Murden had beheaded Laura by then and returned to the bar while her feathers boiled off, and he told us that when Pookie accused Percy, the men laughed until they cried. "What you think some drunk old man going to do?" asked one. "Sail you a paper airplane?"

She looked to the owner of the Tin Cup for justice, but his mouth stayed flat and even over his false teeth. Between mixing drinks he was keeping his accounts, and now he lifted his pen to his mouth and tapped his lip. "He touch you?" he asked her.

"Yes, sir."

"And you don't want him to touch you?"

"No, sir!"

The owner sighed. Dropped his pen on the lined paper and its many figures. "Listen here, gal. What you going to do with that fifty cents?"

"Buy white bread for my sister. And some cornmeal and fish from Burtis."

"You're going to like that fifty cents, huh?"

"Yes, sir."

"You're going to like that fifty cents, and I'm going to like Mr. Percy not trying to touch on *me*." The men around the bar issued another movement of laughter. "You think on that, little bit. Ain't nothing I can do about Percy Greer touching you." He reached under the counter and brought out two quarters. "Here's for today. Mr. Percy probably in there right now tying his shoes together." He rang the money down on the table. "Now get. This ain't no place for children."

Pookie took the quarters, gathered her parasol from the other end of the bar, and skipped out into the bright sunlight. From her mind vanished thoughts of buying chalk for hopscotch in the school's drive: the whole world might not be broken, but the right way in it was. She'd always had a hard time putting words in paper dolls' mouths and could never make out a shape you suggested in a cloud, but now, the dog recited poetry if she got too close, and the lamp on Miss Myrtle's dresser did a ballerina's pirouette each morning when she awakened. The day Percy Greer touched her, she ran home from the Tin Cup and fixed herself a saltine and cracker dinner, stripped off her pants, and went to the lemon yellow room the girls shared.

While she sat before the mirrored table, brushing her hair, Imagene sat in the corner playing with the cat. Pookie didn't wish her good night. She simply went to bed, turned her face into the wrinkled sheet, and lost herself in sweaty, frantic dreams. Soon an itch in the crook of her knee woke her. Through the worrying of skin it spoke, commanding her outside, where she discovered that the moon was broken exactly in two. It wasn't passing through clouds or behind a tree — it was simply broken, floating in the sky in its two pieces. The itch worried her until the tactile became the auditory: she had to repair the moon somehow, the itch told her. She had to reach the moon and fix it.

She didn't know how she would fix it, but she did know that Imagene needed five minutes' worth of help tying her shoes in the morning, and Griffin jumped to the bed and crawled over her heart in the night. She knew that Imagene had smashed Miss Myrtle's papier-mâché angel that morning without explanation, and that Miss Myrtle'd had to buy the groceries on credit that week. She wasn't sure whether the woman on *Your Show of Shows* had spent the spring of her fourteenth year washing piss out of bedsheets, but there were dogs who'd live better lives than hers, she knew that. There were just so many orphaned problems in that house now. So much need.

Earlier in the day, while Caroline and I dragged down the school lawn, laughing and trying to decide what *was* that running down the leg of James Whitfield's pants, Imagene had walked straight past us and all the way home from school for the lunch recess. She'd tell Caroline the whole story later, out on the back stoop, where she wiped the girl's swollen red eyes with a washcloth, how she'd been at Miss Myrtle's house alone when Mrs. Caldwell came across the street knocking, and how the door, in need of Sonnyboy's oil can, screamed as Imagene pulled it back on its hinges.

"Why hello," Mrs. Caldwell said, but Imagene didn't smile and didn't speak. Mrs. Caldwell told it over at the Ladies' Missionary Meeting, said Imagene just stood in the door staring at her with those little owl's eyes, boring a hole so deep into the old woman's soul that discomfort forced her to ask, "Ain't your grandmama taught you no manners? Ain't you going to say how do?"

Imagene nodded.

"Well, then, say it."

"Yes ma'am. Hello."

Mrs. Caldwell wrapped her bony hand around Imagene's and pulled the child out the door and off the porch. They walked the length of the house next door until they reached the back of an asphalt-sided bungalow, one of many that faced the alley behind Queen Street. Mrs. Caldwell pointed to an open window seven feet from the ground. "I'ma lift you up in that itsy-bitty window. Then you crawl in and unlock Mr. Anderson's front door. You hear?"

Imagene nodded. She'd tell Caroline later that she did feel something wrong with Mrs. Caldwell's directions, but she hadn't believed, after all, that the woman would be able to lift her — Mrs. Caldwell was wrinkled and thin and looked as if at any moment she might fold over into pieces. Well, she must have been built on some core of strength — must have — because she grabbed Imagene by the waist and swung her right over her head. She grunted only once, then said, "Now get yourself on over in there."

Imagene used her little arms to swing the fifty pounds of herself into the windowsill, and ducked her head in to see how far she'd have to jump. A braided oval rug covered the floor of Mr. Anderson's bedroom, and a small green dresser sat in the corner with coins arranged atop in stacks according to their denominations. Just beneath the window, as if waiting for her, was a bed: some-

71

one had taken enough care in making it to turn the sheet under the pillows. She swung her other leg in the window and dropped onto her back. Bounced halfway to the ceiling, making it to her feet on the way down so she could bounce again. She jumped creases into the bedspread. This was fun. Like being in a circus. Pookie would be sorry to have missed it. The house breathed a quiet perfection, a still so solid that the only noise she heard was that of a small child crying somewhere in the alley. She walked to Mr. Anderson's dresser and took the stack of pennies in her hand and as she was counting 1-2-6-4-8 it struck her — this house smelled of something magnificently frightening. A smell familiar and not at all familiar. A smell big as the inside of a whale. The odor made her tiptoe, though she couldn't have said why.

She crept through the kitchen and down the shotgun hallway and then she saw him, Mr. Anderson, his hand on his chest, eyes lifted to heaven, the rest of him dead as forever. A fly landed on the corner of his mouth, and his glasses lay in a gym of twisted wire, their left lens smashed beneath the paws of his Doberman. The dog lay with its chin on the ground, and its belly didn't fill or empty with breath, but when Imagene looked into the dog's amber eye, she saw it move, saw the dog actually *blink,* and then it was the discovery of life rather than the discovery of death that finally made her move: cursed with knowledge, she threw down the pennies and ran to the front door. Turned the deadbolt and threw it open. She didn't even see Mrs. Caldwell standing on the porch, and so she ran right into her, butting her shoulder into the hardness of the woman's thin thighs. "Must have been dead three days," Mrs. Caldwell was saying to a woman standing in the yard. "We ain't seen him since prayer meeting. Strange, the dog ain't barked."

Gertie Loving had to run halfway to school to find us to come save Imagene, who wouldn't stop crying no matter how many Mary Janes they gave her.

"You sent her in there knowing he was dead?" Caroline screamed at Mrs. Caldwell, when she got there. I'd run all the way to Queen Street with her, fear just as sharp on the back of my tongue as it was on hers, but when we got there, I knew she was the rightful owner of the outrage. I hung back with the growing crowd, and flinched with everyone else when Caroline yelled, "Not a one a y'all had sense enough to stop this bitch?"

After she said it, no one could keep eye contact, and Mrs. Caldwell's ladyfriends looked down to their shoes. "Low-down dirty old bitches," she kept on. "That dog could of killed her. Come on here," she said, grabbing Imagene by the wrist, which made her wail even louder. As the two of them disappeared across Mr. Anderson's backyard together, I did hear some of the ladies chiding Mrs. Caldwell for sending a little girl to discover a thing so gruesome, while others wondered aloud who else but a child could have gotten through Mr. Anderson's window. Here in the schoolyard, Caroline tells me, breathing into her honeysuckle. She's beginning to understand the very final way her mother is gone, and she knows now that she'll never again hear Mauris singing Helen Forrest's part in "Comes Love," garbling the words loud and high over the running water before she spits toothpaste. She'll never peek around her mother's bedroom door and catch her knotting her stockings at the top. She's already forgotten the shape of her mother's hands, she says, and I know because it's already happening to me that many years later, whenever anyone says the word "mother," she won't think first of her own. Screaming at those stupid old women, none of whom cried at her mother's funeral, did make her feel better, she says. But that afternoon had suddenly seemed like an opening, through which more outrageous things would come.

GRIFFIN

The woman sitting in front of me, the one with her hat ribbon turned three full quarters past its right place on her head? That's Delia Alice Loving Wilson, with cheeks smooth as an olive's and a voice hoarse with cigarettes and snuff and yelling her two boys into submission. Delia, who got up in church three Sundays ago and testified that the Lord and not any fool doctor saved her from dying of the walking pneumonia? That Delia has four children, and each of these four has two feet and two hands: sixteen. Count the two arms and two legs apiece and you get sixteen again. But think down to the five fingers on each child's hand and the five toes on each little foot, the uneven sinews of muscle and the ragged bunches of veins and the tiny capillaries you couldn't see to count even if you skinned the brats alive, and there's no way you can honestly get to 256, which is the only perfect number.

I've been calling Caroline by her right name for two years now. She's moved every single teaspoon and every last houseshoe from her house to Miss Myrtle's, six homes and one weedy lot east of No. 211, almost at the corner where Queen meets Fifth and social graces disappear. That block of Fifth sees naked children running in yards and plaid couches rotting on front porches; that intersection marks the line our mothers forbade us to cross when we were little, lest we stumble into the drunken path of leathery old Mr. Fleenor, who liked to grab small children and squeeze their shoulders until they cried. Now Caroline can stand right in her bedroom and watch Mr. Fleenor spitting on his own porch. Small changes seem to have happened in her, shifts like the panels of a three-dimension comic, reconstructions of unhappiness that leave her face stern and her mouth closed over her rabbit teeth. Life has sanded her down and left her with sharper corners, oppressed her with its omissions. I can never get to 256 thinking about Caroline now, so I stop remembering her so much.

Up on the mourner's bench with Miss Myrtle for Mauris's birthday, Caroline jerks in waking as Miss Aileen pounds out the opening of "Great is Thy Faithfulness" and the three gray-headed reverends push from the arms of their chairs to standing. The rest of the church rises to sing; jackets are pulled over healthy stomachs and long skirts fall into place, but Caroline sits with her hymnal open and her eyes closed, and Miss Myrtle won't dare touch her disrespect, since Caroline, last hog-killing season, brought more money into the house than she did. Only one pew back from them, I watch Caroline's hair drape over the set of her shoulders, and I can see her take a breath of grief and tilt her head to an angle I've seen at school a thousand times in the last two years. *What are you thinking of?* I've passed her in notes, but I always get the same answer written back. She's imagining herself in Louisville. Chicago. Anywhere that isn't Mt. Sterling, Kentucky. Hollywood. Broadway. The moon.

William Travis, who comes down the mountain from his stone-pocked, bountiless farm to be our school janitor on Tuesdays, looks out from the choir stand and throws Caroline a frown so hard it's meant to compel her to stand, but she ignores him, so he goes back to singing, in a voice so loud and a hill accent so thick that no one need see him to know it. Grandpap calls William Travis "the Indian," because he has not one or two but six feathers sprouting out of his favorite Homburg, but most adults call him Buddy, because that's the sort of man he is. He cleans our school on Tuesdays, and because he's an adult, no matter what his job, no matter how much moonshine he's spilled down the bib of his overalls, no matter how brown and thick and cracked are his fingernails, we children greet him as Mr. Travis. Caroline's the only one of us with gall enough to call him Buddy. "Thanks, Buddy," she's forever saying, because he's a distant cousin on Sonnyboy's side and forever dishing her quarters. She never looks at him when she thanks him; I think he embarrasses her.

By the second verse, everyone else in the congregation is busy pretending not to watch Miss Beulah Pike up in the choir stand fan herself and cry, and even if they weren't, I'm the only one close enough to see Caroline drop her chin and smile. I would wonder, except that Reverend Wyatt, half-deaf Reverend Wyatt who moved up from Alabama five years ago and has been living in Miss Lila's row house ever since, is shifting in his seat, smiling just a little, too.

"She's in a better place," he'd told Caroline at Mauris's funeral, though he hadn't sounded that sure about it. He'd put his hand on Caroline's back and lingered there, regurgitating scripture in a consistency that a teenaged girl was supposed to chew on and redigest. I'd been standing right next to them but he hadn't once looked at me. Occasionally he'd lifted his hand from her back, letting it hover an inch away from her sweater while he emphasized one of God's truths. He'd replaced the hand, like a broken gate fastener, further down each time, until he put it in the small of her back and I coughed. He didn't notice me at all, and it salted up the difference between us. Tortoise-shell glasses, shit-colored wool stockings, a head full of high-flown literature, and hair that never grows longer than two marcels on a bumper, is what I've got. Two different bloods don't meet up in my face and explode there: I'm not capable of riling up some minister enough that he starts quoting scripture at me.

"Bad breath," Caroline had said of him when he finally walked away. "Too bad they ain't passing out mints with the communion crackers."

One thing I've learned in the distance between me and Caroline: she's nobody's mother. Imagene spent the whole of May to August last year scratching bug bites on her face, and came to school wearing dirty fingernails and no slip. Asleep in Dr. French's hammock one day, Pookie menstruated right through the back of a white dress, bleeding a stain in the shape of Argentina. From Grandpap's porch I watched her limp home unembarrassed, and though she did wash it, she mustn't have used cold water, because here she is in church with that same skirt on and it's still there — light beige and even brown in places: Argentina. A mother would bleach it; a mother would *burn* it. Caroline's too distracted by youth to even notice.

She spent the last half of our fourteenth year watching television at Sylvia French's house. Most days they didn't even invite me, but when Dr. and Mrs. weren't home, and Sylvia turned the show up to full volume, I'd hear them both through the open window, laughing. Evenings, I'd see the flicker of the television through the lace curtains of the Frenches' living room, whose side window faced mine. They'd watch television until Imagene came telling Caroline she was hungry, for emphasis putting a long "o" where the "u" should have been. The Frenches' front door would slam shut and Caroline would yell something unintelligible at Imagene and then the television volume would go low, way low, and in the relative quiet, I could more easily hear Sylvia's laugh. Alone, she didn't laugh quite as much.

At Thanksgiving, Mrs. French hauled Sylvia down South for what Sylvia called her annual gentility lessons, so it was just an accident of unavailability that put me there when Caroline burned her arm. Mr. O'Neill up on the mountain had let her have a bucket of hog fat after she scraped more rind in a working day than anybody else, and Imagene had walked up and down Queen Street, knocking on front doors, telling everyone how her sister was going to have soap to sell. I'd never seen it made, so curiosity sent me over to her house, where she was already waving her arm in the air, crying and retching over the edge of the porch where the bucket sat, full of bloody fat, next to the lye can. "Tell me what to do," I yelled at her, but she couldn't speak for the pain.

Mr. Nettles came over with a bottle of vinegar and poured it over her arm, which he held aloft while she doubled over in a fit of moaning. "Damn fools," he called us, and he hustled Caroline away from me and over to Dr. French's house. The scab on her arm puckered up like something alive. It dried up and fell away after a couple of weeks, but the lye had already eaten a nasty scar into her left arm, right on the forearm's most defining part of loveliness, the part visible when she was walking or even sitting, the part she herself would look at while she sewed or washed dishes. The scar has changed color over the last year, from an angry pink to a soft brown, and sometimes it seems it's shrunken from the size of a palm print to the size of an ink spill, and then I get anxious, but it turns out she's just handing me a note and has her arm turned out the wrong way; she goes to flip a page of her speller and the scar is terrible once again. My disappointment is that it doesn't make her uglier. Rather, she wears it like an extra mark of grace.

Caroline turned fifteen in February, on the sixth day of a persistent snow, a snow so light that the wind wouldn't let it settle, and it blew impossibly upward, and then straight across the horizon, and finally in semicircles that mocked Caroline through her window and drove her crazy. It was moist enough that it didn't stick; it simply turned dirty on everyone's front steps and puddled in the mud of the street. The mailman tramped through Miss Myrtle's soggy front yard the morning of her birthday, turning black bootprints up out of whitened grass. He was bringing a letter from Sonnyboy, who by then had already written Caroline exactly three times from Eddyville. The first time, she'd come and got me and we sat out on my stoop crouched over the letter, which relayed his daily schedule. We hadn't exactly been wondering, but there it was: 6 am MORNING COUNT; 6:30 am CHOW; 7 am LAUNDRY DUTY; 11 am CHOW. On it went, in script so small and cramped it hurt to look at, until it ended with 10 pm COUNT; 10:30 pm LOCKDOWN.

"He killed my mama and left us scrambling around for money and that's all he got to say," Caroline told me, as she crumpled the page, and the letter had ended there, with LOCKDOWN, not even offering a complimentary closing of the type we were taught in school. But he'd been a good father, I wanted to tell her, and you could see it in the way he'd included punctuation. Whatever he really had to say was there, between those semicolons, trapped under all the cowardice in that cubic space of air stretching from the paper up to the universe. Caroline tossed his second letter into the fire without reading it. She read the third as soon as she got it, but she hadn't shared it with me. She told me only one thing Sonnyboy'd written — that he had a seventy-year-old cellmate who'd been in prison for thirty years, getting regular meals and regular hours. Because of this, Sonny-boy had written, the man still looked to be forty. That fourth installment, the birthday letter, Caroline claimed to have tossed immediately. But I'd been outside upending Mother's flowerpots to keep the snow out, and I'd seen Caroline run in the house and slam the door when the mailman handed it to her. She said she burned it, but I didn't believe her.

She spent that whole fifteenth year at the Colored store, staring at the nail on the wall behind the soda jerk, listening to the gossip of senior class girls who wouldn't, in a million years, have actually spoken to her. She said they spoke of how three of Michelle Turk's girdle hooks had come unsnapped during the Pledge of Allegiance and they spoke of boys who'd asked to touch their breasts, and, listening from three feet away, noting who interrupted whom and which voice's desirous tone most betrayed its owner, Caroline said she felt like the girls were telling her more about themselves than they were telling one another. When Caroline's Great-Aunt Patty walked by Miss Myrtle's house one day and found Imagene standing ankle-deep in mud, bawling her eyes out over a lost cicada shell, she asked Miss Myrtle if she might take the girls for a spell. She told Miss Myrtle it looked like they needed more taking care of, but it turned out she needed considerable help around her own house, and when I visited, I had to talk to Caroline over the scrape of the Brillo pad she was using to clean eleven years' worth of grease off the dimmed black face of the stove.

Then too, Mrs. Patty's neighbor kept thinking Caroline was White, kept waving to her when he rounded the corner in his truck and came upon her walking the road. He'd always drop his hand and turn his eyes straight ahead under his engineer's cap when he saw her swollen lips and realized she was just some nigger girl from down the way, but he couldn't stand the gaps of reason the mistake would leave in his mind. He made sure to mention the new tenants to Dr. Mayer, who owned the house and was letting it to Mrs. Patty on a discount. Caroline and Imagene were back at Miss Myrtle's before the week was out, Caroline sitting on the front porch, knitting potholders to sell in the White downtown, and Imagene rebicycling the deep ruts into Miss Myrtle's lawn so Jesus could find her when he came back in disguise.

Yesterday, when Caroline popped out onto Miss Myrtle's front porch in her black boots and mackintosh, there was only a slight drizzle, and you might have forgiven her not shooing Griffin back in the door when he strutted out after her with his long tail thrown out like a question mark. But she couldn't have been five minutes gone when thunder opened the clouds, and everybody on Queen Street knows that Mauris never let Griffin know weather. He rolled on his back for some time, his four feet crossing each other in the air, the lone white paw bent with the effort of trying to find a dry patch. A little sister who'd play with her always; hair that made her an angel; and a cat who saw her hard days, climbed in her lap, and purred — Caroline didn't deserve all she had, and if she couldn't show kindness to the least of His creatures, I'd have to. When I rose from my swing and yelled for Griffin, he shot down the street like a spark. Stood on our top step and purred, his rain-slicked tail ticking back and forth. Mother was out getting a side of beef from the Maynards, and Grandpap lay in his easy chair snoring chains. "Come on in, cat," I whispered. "Let's have a bite."

The milkman had come Friday, so I tipped the bottle and let Griffin lick the bit of cream left at the top; since Grandpap had eaten the cold cuts down to nothing, I gave Griffin the tip of casing that the icebox had dried to crisp. Griffin moved his entire head with the effort of mashing it between his teeth, and every time it crunched, he raised his pointed ears in surprise. Finished, he sniffed the greasy spot on the floor and meowed. Mother'd left a green tomato pie in some tinfoil atop the icebox, and I cut a slice onto a plate and set it on the floor, but Griffin just ran his whiskers round the edge of the plate.

"Choosy beggar," I called him. He sniffed the toe of my sock, then stretched, letting his little black feet skid across the floor to rejoin the rest of him. I wrestled his front paws and let him play at putting his teeth around my finger until he drew a bead of blood, though when I kicked him across the floor, he cocked his head in innocent confusion. He trotted into my room to look out my window, meowing as he curled his tail into his body: what he'd brought into our house was a small portion of the sadness that had been filling up the girls who'd used to live at 211. Mother complained of smelling onions in my room when she got home, but Griffin wasn't going back. Caroline didn't deserve him.

When the rain cleared to an icy sunset, Imagene started calling. "Griffin!" she yelled, walking the street, her head turning so hard in the search that the crocheted lilac ribbons in her hair shook. She got keys and entered 211 looking for him. A few boys from Seventh Street had climbed in the back window of the house that first winter looking for Mauris's ghost, coming back out only to tell us that the pipes had burst, leaving the floor flooded and buckling in places. A family of opossums had taken over 211's front porch — I saw them at night, curling around the wrought iron columns — and none of us could even begin to imagine what had decided to live *inside* the house, with all that mold: when she'd decided she wouldn't find Griffin inside, Imagene couldn't get out and bolt the door back fast enough. As she walked back to Miss Myrtle's house, I saw her absently tap the side of her head, as though trying to shake what she'd seen from her memory. Miss Myrtle had never been one to leave the house on leisure — never had, even when Mauris was alive — but in the evening, when I went out on the porch to swing, I saw her walking the lengths of houses, peering under porches, pulling back vines and looking into rosebushes as if divining the future. Griffin stayed in my closet all night, not once purring or scratching to get out, and at daybreak, when I went to take out my good satin dress for church, there he lay, on his side, blinking, blinking. *Sick,* I thought, and then I thought again, *maybe just homesick.* He'd have to adjust to a life within the four walls of my room. "You stay put," I told him. He'd eaten all the tomato pie save one last sliver of onion, and I took the plate for bleaching. "You'll have more cream after church," I said. Now, as I look down at my oxfords and notice that despite the four perfect eyeholes, the laces cross only once, I wonder where I'll find cream on a Sunday.

The arched ceiling of this church was designed to evoke eternity, as were the three concentric circles that make up each chrome light fixture. A wood balustrade separates the pulpit from the pews so that the ministers look, to the congregation below, as though they are floating on divine air. Jesus is pressed flat to the wall by oil paint, his reed-colored hand held out to a background of green pasture that stretches beyond the corners of the ceiling into infinity. The walls are so plain of ornamentation that in summer, when beetles fly in church and light, you can look over and count whether they've kept all six of their legs. But whoever bricked Queen Street Second Baptist into being built it all wrong. Jesus is painted a little off, his forehead unnaturally bloated. The balustrade walls off the ministers like they're a museum exhibit. And even if it means I might reune with my daddy, the thought of eternity scares me. Eternity isn't 256. It doesn't finish in fours.

The reddest of cardinals is visiting the yew tree outside the open window. Thunder scrapes heaven. A chill spring wind plows the grass and darkens the earth. Mother stands next to me, squeezing my hand. She exhales whiskey and a single tear winds down the curve of her high cheekbones to settle at the corner of her mouth. In her haste to get us here early, to get a seat up front near Miss Aileen and her Howard upright, she forgot the pearl earrings that go with her two-strand necklace, and Mother could just as well be crying over that as anything, since she always says a woman with holes in her earlobes is not, by a long shot, a lady. You'd think she's an emotional drunk, but she's not — we're just singing benediction. She didn't cry at Mauris's funeral just like she didn't cry at my daddy's, which is a shame, because my mother, with her flawless skin and keen nose, is a beautiful crier.

"Amen," she says, tapping her foot in time to Miss Aileen's playing. Praying down into her purse while people stand and leave with the Holy Ghost gathered into purses and pockets, until we're the only people left sitting. Caroline's already out on the church lawn trading lemon drops, or maybe even on the road back to Queen Street, and I hate Mother for making us stay after, listening to Miss Aileen's tedious chords, watching the folds in the velvet curtains that hide the baptismal pool and missing Grandpap's pork chops with black-eyed peas and all the other beautiful things of this world. Mother smiles her lopsided lipstick and bobs her head, because we're sitting close enough for Miss Aileen to feel the waves of admiration.

"Amen," Mother says for the last time, after Miss Aileen tinkles the high register and closes her hymnal into the case of her piano bench. She links my arm to drag me out of the pew and toward the piano. "Aileen," she says. "How do."

Two deacons in short summer sleeves chat in a corner, one with his arm resting on a windowsill and the other caressing his tie. Mrs. June Webb bumps clumsily down the aisle with her son, Lester, who has wrapped the top half of her ninety-year-old body in his arms. Wind has cooled the earth, but in the after-service quiet, the church feels warm and close, as if the Holy Ghost is enfolding us in one of His sun-dried bed-sheets. I've never been in church this late. The Spirit has finished His performance. It's a feeling like watching your father's train pull out of the station without you, or going to bed with your mother having forgotten it was your birthday.

" 'Naitha," Miss Aileen says with her hymn-warmed voice, though the stare she gives Mother is frozen. Anybody with half a nose can smell the Sambuca cloud.

"I want to talk to you about my girl," Mother says, unlinking her arm to push me forward as she wobbles from the sudden lack of support. The youngest reverend's wife walks the front of the church with her white patent leather purse draped over the crook of one arm. She fingers the dirt in the pots to see whether the lilies flanking the pulpit need watering, shakes her head to herself when she finds that they don't. "How much you charge for lessons?" Mother asks Miss Aileen.

Miss Aileen gives me a doubtful look that involves her eyelids almost closing, and I'm reminded of Griffin, and my stomach burns with the thought of him escaping if Grand-pap opens the door to my room. "Audrey's old for lessons," Miss Aileen says.

"But she's played for years." Mother's voice rises and strains over a hard place in her throat. "Her daddy taught her." Though Mother doesn't care about my carrying on where Daddy left off. She doesn't think of me as special, or talented; she doesn't even know whether I can *really* play. But she knows that Grandpap started asking me to sit down and look at songs last year, and she knows that he kept asking me, even when I rolled my eyes at him. He stopped asking me when he didn't have to anymore, when hours outside Mr. Barnett's store turned into hours sitting at my daddy's old piano, when the music became a math problem that I'd solve by playing in a different key and with different permutations of my fingers on the black keys so that every song sounded like the bebop that Guy Jones pipes in our radio from Lexington on Saturday nights. Mother has always been a person of spring planting and fall preserving, and though she understands that circle, she knows nothing of the satisfaction of grace notes. But she knows that if Miss Aileen will pass her torch to me one Sunday a month, she'll pass along a portion of respectability that I might use as I grow. And in twenty years, when Miss Aileen gets too old and feeble to learn the new songs, I can take her place on Sundays and Wednesdays and there'll be thirty dollars a month I don't have to scrape up from the White part of town.

"Here, then." Miss Aileen pats her bench. "Sit down and play for me."

I shake my head no. Silently, I've passed gas, and all three of us can smell it. I can feel the glacier of unlove my mother blows onto the back of my neck.

"I always did teach her modesty," Mother lies. At home, she calls me an alley cat.

"Play for me," Miss Aileen asks again, her voice warmer now, and something does come to my ear and ask to be let out, the one song my daddy never taught me, a three-quarter mountain tune he played sometimes to get me to sleep when Mother wouldn't let me into their bed. He'd tack it to the end of a boogie-woogie, after he'd buttoned my gown and braided my hair.

"Play for her," Mother says, closing her hand around my wrist, and the three quarters for twenty-four bars leaves me and I'm thinking instead about four quarters for eighteen bars and Griffin trying to claw his way out of my closet, and the way Daddy brushed my back teeth last thing at night until I was eleven years old and Mother

95

screamed that he was turning me into an invalid, the way he used to clip the very ends of my braids the night of a full moon to make sure the hair grew. I lower my head and raise my eyes and pass Miss Aileen the look that will let her know — I will never, ever do anything Mother asks. And I will never let Mother hear my father's songs again.

"I'm too old," I say.

"Well." Miss Aileen frowns at my belligerence, or maybe at my flatulence. She speaks to my mother in a confidential tone, as if I'm either deaf or an idiot. "She is a league older than the girls I teach. But she can come over to the house. Thursday after school, and I'll see if there's anything I can still do with her."

"You won't be disappointed," says Mother. She's left nail marks on my forearm.

"I'm not promising, mind you, that I'll take her as a student."

"It's all right. When you hear her, you'll want to," Mother lies, as if she has any idea.

Finally we strike an exit, but we've taken so long fooling with Miss Aileen that Caroline and the other girls are already long ahead of us on the road, too far ahead for me to catch up without running, which

Mother would no doubt cuss me for doing in good shoes. As we navigate the upward slope of a rocky hill, this sun passes over the trees a perfect ball, and I can see how the Indians thought the sun itself was God.

"I don't know what —" Mother begins, the anger cutting sap from her voice. "Who you think you are to sass me in front of people like that."

"I didn't sass."

"Oh, you just stood there and made me into a liar without you even saying nothing. Made yourself into an idiot."

"I'm not your trained seal; there's one thing I'll never make myself into."

"Shut up," Mother says. Her strides grow longer and faster, even as she wobbles on the gravel, until she's a few yards ahead of me. "Your old daddy died trying to give you some kind of a life, and here you just want to sit on the porch and play checkers with yourself. Terrible little bitch."

I run then, good shoes be damned, all the way home, past Mother — *Set that dinner table when you get there,* past Caroline and Sylvia — *Hey! Come back here, Flash!,* past a knot of five- and six-year-old girls, stopped in the middle of the road to see how far their skirts float when they twirl. I run all the way home, where Grandpap sits on the front porch fanning himself with the Sunday paper from Owingsville. "Whoa!" he says, when he sees me cross through the yard. He smiles and waves his sheaf, full of the world's whispers, but I charge past him, into the house and down the hall. In my room it's quiet, too quiet, and I'm afraid for a second that Grandpap has heard Griffin's yowling and tossed him outdoors. But there, in the closet, is Griffin, on his side with his paws stretched ahead of him, his one eye open to the ceiling in a way that can only be Death's. His front leg, when I stroke it, is already stiff, and just in front of his hind leg, just where he should be the softest, is a hard, diseased knot. Caroline was better to him in her neglect than I've been in my caring, and now he's been sacrificed, this small gift of grief from across the street. I'm incapable, perfectly incapable.

The old Panama rice bag from under the sink is just the thing, then: holds his body shapeless without letting fur show through the holes, and who's to say I'm not carrying rice to the Deimers and their eight pissy-smelling children? Who would Mother be to question Grandpap over such a trifle as an empty rice bag gone missing? It's perfect, except that Griffin is heavier over my shoulder than he was when he was alive, so the twine drawstring cuts my palms as I run across Second Street and then Third and then down to the Fourth Street bridge. It's an empty Sunday, with no people or even cars, and the only sound is the churning Hinkston, still narrow enough at Fourth Street to swim across, still rocky and deep enough to kill a man if he jumped. The black patent leather of my shoe is gone dusty; my good satin dress is pasted to my back. Death has been there, pressing against my clothes. A tree, uprooted by winter, groans in the distance, and instead of watching what I'm tossing over, I shield my eyes from the sun to watch it sway. When I hear Griffin crack the river's surface and sink into the current, I dip into my pocket for the butterscotch I stole from Grandpap's coat. Mauris is in heaven and knows it all, down to how many hairs I had on my head when I locked Griffin in the closet with the tomato pie.

JUPITER

In May comes a blizzard. A freak snow, a covering of inches such that the strongest tulips find themselves peeking out of ice. Excitement in town, and trouble up on the mountain — seeds frozen as they are planted, a power line that collapses under the weight of ice, a stove fire that kills three. We girls have to wear our ugly snow boots for the school picture. Caroline and I walk the cold in ours, tramping past the riverbank that has grown itself over the years into a muddy bog. The surprise of cold has frozen the Hinkston into a second sheet of trees and sun, a reflection so crisp that we can see the thin needles of minor branches and the hawks' nests they hold.

Imagene trails a few feet behind us, kicking a squared stone. When it doesn't roll where she wants, she follows it out into the road and kicks it back, or she wanders into the high grass and stops to search through frost. Pookie almost didn't come. She's begun imagining things that aren't happening. She hears castle doors closing and summer frogs growling, hallucinations she knows will become bigger as time passes, until she's seeing purple stars and Negro presidents. Some days she sleeps during the daytime, while Miss Myrtle is in the White part of town cleaning houses and Imagene is up the road at school and she can be certain, perfectly certain, that none of the sounds she hears are true.

"Ain't you cold?" Caroline asks me.

"Warm and cold's all in your head — t'ain't real." I wore a summer dress just to spite my mother, who says I'll be the only girl wearing one in all this snow. It's blue cotton with white flowers, and my menstruation will stop for months because of it, she says. All the better, I say. "I got a coat on, Caroline, and a sweater you can't see under that. It ain't the material, anyway — it's how many layers."

"Yeah, and your mama probably hit you with a shot of devil water so you'd stay warm."

She herself is wearing a shawl soaked in all the colors of the dinner table. There's a green stripe like asparagus knitted across, and a purple one like a rutabaga, and a piss-colored one like a bell pepper rotting. There's even a little pumpkin orange, knitted into a border around the collar. Against the bloodless snow all that color, all the life it implies, actually hurts my eyes, and I can see why she never wore it when her mother was alive, even though Mauris spent the better part of a summer knitting it. Miss Myrtle has marcelled the ends of Caroline's hair so that each curl finishes in a straight edge, and in the winter cold her skin has gone clear, and I don't think I've ever seen her so pretty. We pass Henry Robert Sells, checking the ice in bottles at the edge of his yard, and Caroline gives him that particular look of mistrust she saves for the elderly.

"Your Cousin Harrel coming home this summer?" I ask. Her Cousin Harrel is short and skillet-headed, not so good-looking, but he always drives home from Chicago in a long black Cadillac and throws quarters around and takes us girls to the drug store in Lexington, where he orders in a cool steady voice that makes the White people hurry to get our sodas. Last summer, he showed me and Caroline which gears go with which sound of the motor, and for two whole weeks we drove around and honked at boys and didn't have to worry about what to do for fun.

"He ain't coming this year. Grandmama told him to save his money and send it down instead. She say we hurting."

"So what're we supposed to do all summer?"

"What we always do. Nothing."

"But it's summer. We got to do something."

"You go on, Huckleberry. My summer'll never be over."

"What you mean?"

"No more school for me, sister. Miss Wofford going to get me on over to that slip factory in Camargo. Grandmama say we need the money."

"How she going to get you on at any slip factory?"

Caroline shrugs. "I saw her coming out the dime store. She poked me in the jaw with a finger and said light as I am, Mr. Robideau might think I'm a White girl anyway. She said kinfolk got to stick together. She crazy as a pineapple sandwich."

Miss Wofford's genes are, in fact, tangled with madness, descended as they are from the touchy Scotch Irish sheep farmers up the mountain. Sam Wofford, Caroline's granddaddy, is one of the meanest men in the county, an auctioneer who swindles illiterate farmers and shot his daughter's

103

puppy on a Sunday before church, not because the puppy was sick or worrisome, but just for the hell of it. With Sonnyboy on one side of Caroline's blood and Sam Wofford on the other, she doesn't stand a chance.

"I make enough money," she says, "I'ma hop my ass on a northbound bus." She sings it into the air but it doesn't ring like it should: the odd weather has frozen even waves of sound.

"You can't just skip out of school," I tell her. Without her, I'll be alone with my thick glasses and my chewed-off hair and the countdown in my head. "Why can't you just work in Camargo for the summer?" I ask her now.

"Need money to eat on all year."

Imagene kicks her stone from the salted road into the shoveled school drive, and Caroline picks it up and puts it into the front pocket of her mother's dress. "I'll save it for you all day," she says to Imagene, "promise," and Imagene runs away in her own thick white shawl, off through the snow to the iced-over tire swing hanging from the school's shortest tree.

"See you later," Caroline says, as she heads for the base of the front steps, where the boys in our grade sit smoking Kents and shooting dice and trading playing cards with naked White ladies on their backs. We girls bind our breasts under adjustable elastic and cover our scent with deodorant while the boys celebrate their puberty, stroking the beginnings of mustaches and checking their own widening shoulders in mirrors. A high yellow boy named Ralph Cundiff takes it upon himself to practice the roll of snuff in Caroline's mouth: he turns out the pink rim of her bottom lip, packs the leaves into her gum with the same grimy finger he's used in his own mouth. They both work their jaws as Ralph taps his foot to count to ten: he spits, she spits, he spits, she spits, his juice arched gracefully by a magic of tongue and palate, hers at her feet, in little brown inkblots on the freshly salted walk.

"Aim for that piece a ice," he says, and though she misses when she spits again, they both laugh. Ralph's mother is president of the Second Baptist Ladies' Missionary and would have a fit if she heard it, but Ralph laughs a gurgle like water down a drain. Caroline's laughing so hard she can barely get her shawl off, but she does — she wads it up in a little woolen ball with all the colors of the planet Jupiter, and she throws it toward the steps, where it unfurls itself into one big sheet of color and floats to the ground. Her dress is wool too, brown and black houndsteeth that belonged to her mother. Caroline's thinner than the dress, and her neck pokes out of the Peter Pan collar like a dish soap doll's, and the hem should fall below the knee but instead splits her long legs in half. Still, she laughs. She's still laughing when William Travis comes and takes her by the arm with such force that the Peter Pan collar slides over to one side and shows her collarbone. "Stay away from those silly boys," Mr. Travis tells her, "whose very names spell trouble."

I'm sitting on the top step pretending to read *Giovanni's Room* and after hearing what Mr. Travis says, I start to go down the list of them — one is named Tyrone, there's Ralph, and another named Otis, but just as I'm realizing no boy's name starts with "U," I see Mr. Travis dragging Caroline up the steps by her elbow. I raise my book even farther toward my nose and count the lines on page 92 to make my face look purposeful, but they're soon up the steps and on me. Even with his heavy winter coat and gloves, Mr. Travis looks desperate: the effort of shoveling all morning has broken a sweat on his neck and forehead. "Lookit Audrey here," he says. "Smart. Ladylike. You should be 'ssociating with her."

"Smart?" Caroline raises her head to a queenly angle and smiles disdain with the chapped apples of her cheeks. "Smart?" she repeats, sizing me through the slits of her eyes as she works snuff between her front teeth. "Before I even get here in the morning, I done combed Imagene's nappy head and massaged my grandmama's corns. I can add up how much money I'ma make down to Camargo while Audrey sets here in school figuring up how much she'd weigh on the moon. Audrey ain't got no more sense'n I do, maybe not even as much. She just lucky."

Mr. Travis frowns at me, doubting himself. He's confused into giving Caroline and me both quarters.

"Thank you, Mr. Travis."

"Yeah. Thanks, Buddy."

Rocking forward on the balls of his feet, he pushes his gloves to tightness in the crevices between his fingers. "Candy money," he says. "Money for hair ribbon. It ain't for snuff." He strides away on the juggernaut of his salt-bejeweled work boots, and Caroline and I both put our hands in our pockets and hunch our shoulders against all kinds of cold.

We both finger the stray threads in our dress pockets and we both close our eyes in seconds-long blinks of hurt, parallel movements we can feel through the quiet cold even if we're unable to look at each other. The silence hurts Caroline more, I suppose, because she's the first to speak. "Picture man's here," she says, though I too have seen the photographer wander into the yard of playing children. He's the same man who came over from Hope last year and the year before that. Each spring his temples are grayer under his derby, his cinnamon skin always slightly more paled by the preceding winter. He tips awkwardly through a second-grade snowball fight, holding his tripod aloft so the frost won't cling to its metal legs and make rust. He dodges a little girl running with her hat in her hands and makes for the steps, where he'll set up his equipment.

"Good morning, Audrey. Morning, Imagene," he calls, because like everyone else, Mr. Rollins has confused the celebrities from Mauris's funeral. Pookie, who barely cried, was given an iced cake by Mr. Pennington the Monday after, while little Imagene, who went through an usher's entire box of Kleenex, was ignored at recess by the girls in her grade. The upper school boys talked about how ba-a-ad Reverend Graves's new Ford Fairlane looked parked in front of the church, but no one mentioned Miss Myrtle's performance of shouting and fainting and low blood sugar. Caroline, whose stony funeral face lives in my mind like a gorgon's, got wolf-whistled at that Monday on her way into school. The only person who tried to comfort her was Mrs. Dickerson, who turns doorknobs with her handkerchief and has a page turner near her desk because she refuses to handle our schoolbooks. The Monday after Mauris's burial, she hugged Caroline from a miracle of distance, an enclosure of limbs held slightly aloft that let only her hair touch Caroline's face. "Caroline Wallace," she says now. "You'll be in the back row of girls because you're tallest. And Audrey! Didn't you carry a change of shoes?"

"No, ma'am." The other girls — even Caroline — have gotten themselves into high heels when I wasn't looking.

"You'll be in back as well, then," she says with a disapproving tick of her tongue. "Short as you are, you won't even show up on the picture."

Everyone shuffles, everyone pushes. Everyone wants to be seen, to be acknowledged by a future they don't even know. Girls are sent back inside to wipe rouge from their lips. Boys are told to turn down coat collars and straighten gators. The world is suddenly frozen, the Rome Treaty signed amidst deepening recession and Mrs. Dickerson shaking her head at my winter boots. I run, then, away from her judgment, away from the senior girls' indifference. Away from the little kids, from poor Imagene and her mossy, unbrushed teeth. Past the steps, where I take Caroline's shawl by its edge and unfurl it like a flag in front of me. Behind the school, where I unlatch the door to the crawlspace and throw it in, making of it a carpet for huddling mice. I turn on my heels and feel the stiff backs of my new boots dig into my Achilles tendons, and I run just to run. Toward the backs of my posing schoolmates, their sweaters and coats dark as pilgrims'. After a spring snow comes warmth, always. Caroline might miss her shawl on the walk home, but she won't be cold. I'd never leave her cold.

We're all in line then, being hushed by Sylvia French, whose thin finger makes a cross with her lips. "Children," Mrs. Dickerson says, as she passes Mr. Rollins to take her place at the end of the front row. She picks up the chalkboard, on which she's written in careful script: *Montgomery County Colored School, 1957.*

Caroline and the senior grade girls in my

row are all half a head taller than me, and even the junior and sophomore girls one step below are taller: when the photograph comes back to hang on the school wall, no one will ever be able to see my face. But if they look just under the top of the school's tallest window, they'll find a half-White girl with as serene a smile as Mona Lisa's. One of her last, a smile Caroline sent away when she found her shawl gone missing, a smile turned to fallen hardness as she sat on the school steps after the last bell, shaking her head and refusing to walk home with the rest of us girls, refusing to tell why.

And if someone were to step close to our class photograph and focus, if they were to look at the end of the row of girls, they'd see the grains of portrait that make up Mrs. Dickerson, the sallowness of her cheeks and the malevolent thoughts behind her eyes. Even closer, just past Hannah Cosby's left arm, they'd see that I'm the only girl who, just before Mr. Rollins ducked his head under the drape and released his shutter, slid her coat to her feet. And if they looked two rows up, if they blocked out all the other cloying faces and concentrated on the black-and-white-and-gray boy with the soft charcoal cap and one jaw bulging with snuff, they'd see that his eyes are trained

not on the photographer's lens but on the V
of my dress back, and all of my future that
the camera cannot see.

Coal

By the time Russia launches Sputnik, Caroline has stopped telling me anything. Grandpap turns up the bombs in Saigon from Tuesday's *Lexington Herald*. *VIETNAMESE COMMUNISTS BETRAY THEIR COUNTRY,* he reads; *13 Americans wounded.* The skin of the newspaper shakes with his hands; he reaches up and folds the page in a clumsy half. He reports in a voice dry of sorrow — "Guerrillas have assassinated over two hundred Vietnamese officials, says here" — and moves on to the racing page without further reflection. When his hands begin to shake again, he steadies them against the kitchen table. If not for the war just passed, my father would have been here with us, but I wasn't enough to keep him. I was eleven then, when he left, and much smaller — a presence demanding hugs and glasses of milk. Not enough to keep him here, safe and alive. He felt he had to leave, even if that meant he might have to die.

A cold misery warms the roots of my teeth, and I go outside to lie on the porch under the ghost of my swing, which Grandpap has already chopped up for next winter's stove. Battered into slats, its white paint sanded off and the chains broken out of its arms, the swing now seems, in the backyard woodpile, as though it never could have cradled me or Caroline or anyone else. The porch L's around the front of the house like a blank stone tablet, a fair and just plane that cools my back while it flattens my hairstyle. Grandpap whistles some sad Cole Porter and I know he's thinking about another Asian country, another chain of death, a morning three years ago, when he read the last day of the war that killed my daddy. NORTH AND SOUTH KOREA SIGN TRUCE, he'd read then. *South Korea to gain 1,500 square miles.* At 52,000 of our men lost and 1,500 of their miles won, our United States gave 36 men per mile. One Nebraskan for fifteen palm trees, one Mainer for a den of panda bears. My father for one copse of trees and a cave, I figure, and I hear a door slam and know that Caroline has run out of her house again and down the street without speaking to me. North and South Korea are living as neighbors, and downtown at the

114

bank, the branch president has raised the American flag back to peak every day since the Army stopped telegramming death from overseas, but my daddy isn't coming back from there. I hear hard-soled shoes running back up front steps, Dr. French's beagle laughing at the morning, a thin wood door slamming, Caroline shouting Imagene's name down Miss Myrtle's cellar stairs. Last July, Althea Gibson won Wimbledon. This morning, at dawn, it rained through sunshine, the devil beating his wife, the dew above Mt. Sterling painting two intersecting rainbows. Daddy won't come back, but still, the world keeps spinning wonders.

The last Caroline spoke to me was the day school let out for the summer. Nothing at all significant, just one girl commenting to another on the stench of chicken liver coming from someone's kitchen.

"Gah," she said. "Smells like my grandmama's underpants." We were walking home for the lunch recess — me to Grandpap's neckbones, swirling in a pot on the stove, and Caroline to whatever she'd left for herself in Miss Myrtle's pantry — and when she said it, she turned for approval to Ralph, who walked one pace behind her. Humidity being what it was, Caroline had taken to twisting her hair into one tree of a braid to hide its greasiness, and though her neck seemed less a giraffe's than a swan's that last day of school, and her chest had finally puffed out enough to hold up the two circles of lace on her shirt, her face had rededicated itself to growing pimples. Ralph's skin, as if in correction to Caroline's, was so perfectly smooth that it seemed, under its light sheen of sweat, to glow.

"Your grandmama's underpants probably got green cheese in 'em," he said, and pinched her behind, which made her slap the air where his fingers had been. But then she put her fist on her hip and threw a switch in her walk. He looked at her behind and matched her smile without even seeing it, and she belonged to him in a way I hoped I'd know someday. "Audrey —" he began, because he'd caught me staring. "What you doing all summer?"

Tyrone saw a nickel in the street and cut in front of Ralph, blocking my answer, planting a nebula of body odor I wouldn't talk through. I turned, then, back to the road ahead of me, back to whatever we were all walking toward.

I've seen them together since, Caroline and Ralph, stepping into each other's shadows on the paved sidewalk of the White downtown, taking the shade of a tree at the Baptist district meeting, changing themselves so cleanly and secretly into the habits of one person that the grown-ups don't even notice they should be separated. I've seen Caroline take on composure as though she's an unplugged jar being filled at a well, as though Ralph has opened up a fatal hole to pour in his attentions. She's told me nothing of their relations — we haven't talked since before the beginning of Ralph — but I imagine if she were still speaking to me, she'd tell me, between giggles, that she thinks, in his absence, of the depth of his voice and how it lifts his heavy Adam's apple. She'd tell me that she's tried her name with his (Caroline Cundiff), and that when they walk to the edge of Mattie Gibson's corn and hold hands, she feels the wind blow through the eyelets of her dress and knows what it is, after all, to be a modern girl of 1957. She'd tell me that she's equally in love with each of his three brothers simply by virtue of their being blood related, that she's picked out children's names (Ralph Jr. and Raylene) for the days to come with him, and that anyway we were wrong, love is none of that, love is nothing we've imagined at all. It isn't just holding the envy of the lower-grade girls or

117

feeling a boy's stubble against your forehead but just. Just wheeling around town knowing that someone in the world thinks you're A-all right. I rescued her woolen Jupiter from the crawlspace, washed the spider eggs out of it, and laid it to dry. I twisted and retwisted its fringes so they hang just right when I sleep in it at night, pull its neck around mine. But Caroline's found Ralph. She's found love. She's found it.

To fill another day without her, to till love of my own and make Grandpap happy by conjuring his son, I play the old upright in the living room. It starts as me dusting the pearline surface of the keys, then mixing baking soda and salt to scour away whatever's gotten in the grooves of the ivory since Daddy left. But it's deep under the keys, a fungus that refuses to be conquered, and the more I try, the less I can stand the wrong notes of my cleaning, the hammers misstriking. I pick up a rhythm to soothe the old board, to apologize to the undusted half notes; first an easy boogie-woogie like Daddy never played in front of his father, then the church songs Grandpap taught us both. "We'll Understand It Better By and By," and "The Last Mile of the Way," and without knowing, I start humming deep in my throat to fight with the bass, until

Grandpap says, "People want to hear you play, girl, not hum." And in fact Miss Aileen, after hearing me play just one time, said she had nothing else to teach me save to keep the humming in my head, told Mother I should be teaching *her*.

"Well," Mother said when we got out Miss Aileen's door, "guess you're ready for Carnegie Hall, then." But it wasn't kindly said, and when we got home, she handed me a basket full of laundry for folding and went off to listen to her afternoon story. The memory of her lying flat on the sofa, eyes to the ceiling, makes me stop humming, and the fight of this song squares my shoulders until I'm actually standing, hovering inches above the bench. To this physical error, Grandpap pays no nevermind. He sings, he taps, he stomps, he cries, and I know he'll never tell Mother: it's our secret, until the doorbell rings and I brake on a G major.

"Coal," comes a voice. Even through three inches of door, the pitch is so familiar I hear it more with my skin than my ears. I open the door to let Caroline into our lives and find her with Ralph, the two of them standing like twins in brown caps and knickers, with blackened palms and circles of wetness under their arms. Swaths of ash across their foreheads where they've forgotten and used their dirty hands to wipe sweat. The prickliest part of the picture they make is Caroline's hair, which is gone missing. A tiny tail of auburn comes out the back of her cap where someone has severed the braid. Behind them, a wheelbarrow full of coal tilts down to Grandpap's yard.

"Pookie Wallace?" Grandpap asks, shielding his forehead from the sun's attack. His eyes have gone buggy with wonder. "That you, little bit? Out selling coal?"

"We're selling it cheap," Ralph answers. He parts his legs to swagger.

Grandpap asks Caroline, "Miss Myrtle know you out doing boys' work?"

"Her grandmama know," Ralph says. "We're selling it cheap."

"She still got a tongue to talk for herself?" I ask. Caroline's a study in evasion, lips drawn over her horsey teeth, eyes focused so hard on the grass I think she might set it ablaze. She's defeathered, lost in something I cannot touch.

"Y'all need any or not?" she finally asks, as though we're wasting her afternoon.

Grandpap limps out to the edge of the porch and bends over to inspect the wheelbarrow. "If you're selling cheap coal cheap, it ain't no bargain. But you ones is too young to have sense enough to figure on that. Ought to be home reading books or some. Figuring out the world you just got born into." He turns around to Caroline's back, the slow bullet of her hair just hitting him. "Little girl, what happened to your hair?"

"Cut it off," she says, staring at Grandpap. "Don't need it." The summer has grown her so tall that she doesn't even need to look up to see Grandpap, who's been watching the crown of her head since she was a baby. Now, at his eye level, she chews her gum and blows a bubble whose root thickens between her two front teeth until it pops.

Grandpap throws both his hands in the air as if to say he's giving up on all humanity, but he's just a buzzing white-haired midge, one more set of judgments this pair of doves won't hear, more of that code so old it is written into the stones of this earth.

Ralph backs off the porch and tips his cap. "Come on, Caroline," he says as he descends our three steps, and he seizes and rights their wheelbarrow. Having stared at Grandpap just long enough to make her eyes involuntarily roll when she turns away, Caroline lands her gaze momentarily on the emptiness where the porch swing used to hang. She tugs at the phantom braid still hanging over her shoulder and walks away into the sun.

From the porch, Grandpap and I stare down the street after the two of them. "Lord hammercy," Grandpap says, shaking his head. "That boy's got her nose blown wide open." He grunts to second himself, and my morning becomes even more miserable: eventually, everyone leaves. One day, it will even be Grandpap.

In the westbound lane of Queen Street the seafood truck splashes by, a new black Ford with a custom metal tray in its bed and LIVE FISH painted in candy apple red down its side. Water leaks out the truck's back end, and a larger catfish leaps out of the bed to writhe in a circle on the hot dirt. "Hey hey," Grandpap says, running his hand down the front of his yellow plaid shirt. "Burtis in town with the fish."

The street's children break from jump roping and footballing and run to tease the fish where he lies flapping his giant arteried gill; the boys squat, hold out their hands, and try to catch him, but each time the fish surprises them with a lift of its barbelled head and a violent twist of its body. They fall bad, girls and boys both, in giggles and squeaks, until a mother yells out the front door that that fish will surely cut one of their arms wide open. She slams her door shut over a pillow of dust and the children deflate of purpose, so that one by one they return to their chanting and leaping. There remains, finally, only one pigtailed girl who bends over and studies the gill that flaps more and more slowly in its death of oxygen.

"Fish for dinner?" Grandpap asks.

"But the truck's gone. Burtis didn't even stop at Mr. Barnett's."

"Must not a had enough this time, but he'll surely be gone to sell it to the White people." Grandpap gives me two quarters, and when I stall, gives me a quarter more for myself. A third quarter will buy me plenty — fifteen Mary Janes or three packets of Necco wafers or even a tin of lip rouge — but a fourth quarter, a squaring off of the silver rounds, will keep me safe. One. Two. Three. Are difficult. I close my palm over the triplets so I won't have to see them. I daren't ask Grandpap for the fourth, because he'd never understand about the protection of even numbers. He'd only believe me greedy.

"Be back in an hour," he says. "I got to have time to clean it."

Along the route to the White grocery, I pass everyone and everything in this town. I walk up the hump where mud meets side-walk and the ground under my feet doesn't give. Past the abandoned brick newspaper building with the cleanness of S.Q.U.A.R.E D.E.A.L. left behind the missing steel letters where the brick had dirtied all around them. Past the young couple, their arms full of seed, who raise peacocks up on the mountain and speak to no one in town, the girlfriend in a pair of jeans as dirty as any man's and the boyfriend with hair longer and darker and shinier than hers. Through one thick spiderweb that survived the rain but not my body, past drops of moisture still left on a town park bench. Past Lucille Grady and Pauline Burke, girls from the grade ahead of me, Lucille switching in her sandals with the newfound elegance of the formerly fat and Pauline piebald with psoriasis save for where makeup forms a brown carapace on her face. Into a sharp right, down the 700 block of Chestnut Street, and suddenly behind the crisscrossed suspenders of Ralph, who has mounted his hand atop Caroline's on the wheelbarrow handle. The houses have gotten bigger, the yards greener, the playing children whiter, and she and Ralph leave the wheelbarrow to thud against the sidewalk while he chases her in the street far ahead of me, and then

I'm just following ghosts.

To move out of the way of a passing Packard, they clip back to the sidewalk and almost run into a White woman who, when she walks past me, says, under her breath, *niggers.* Ralph catches Caroline around the waist and swings her in the street, and she grins my way when she finds me watching, but her teeth seem like weapons. Whatever friendship we had has slipped away in dark waters.

Burtis's truck is parked in front of the White grocery but I can't see Burtis himself; the store window offers rows of canned goods, bags of flour and sugar, a bushel box of tomatoes, and no Negro fish seller. Even Burtis — rangy, fish-perfumed Burtis — has been called away to some glorious point beyond this town. The sun elbows its way more strongly through the clouds and the window more cleanly reflects what's behind me: White children paying dimes to Ernie Hodges's three-horse wooden carousel. The children turn and scream, and it takes four of their revolutions for me to realize I'm not going in the White grocery. I'll lie to Grandpap, stanch his disappointment with a can of sardines from Mr. Barnett's. I'll play his son some more, clean the house to make Mother feel guilty. She'll come home then

125

in the afternoon and press my hair, thinking the cleaning was for her, when I've simply enjoyed the rhythm of a house being able to dirty itself one day and come clean the next. Mother will light the flame for the stove and watch the match burn down to its quick, remembering all her four thousand days with my father in those seconds the match burns. When the stove catches, she'll blow the match but it won't die; it will flare up again in orange-blue glory, reminding her for that panicked second of the joy she has in the stout-bellied man she thinks she's keeping a secret from me and Grandpap: she'll run the match under the sink and sigh. Mt. Sterling is a palsy, a consumption, a slug drying from the salt in the soil beneath. It's a hunchbacked woman who cannot walk straight, a torpescent blight on God's map, a crooked spoke in His well-oiled wheel. This morning was the last morning I didn't know: if I stay here, I'll begin to rot from the inside out.

■ ■ ■ ■

PART TWO:
CAROLINE

■ ■ ■ ■

RHOMBUS

Back when Audrey's daddy passed, she cried like a whitegirl, with that look on her like she'd just left all of us and warn't coming back. Her mama ain't cried one drop, and she give Audrey tissue to fresh up her face but Audrey pushed it away — just let them tears roll down her face and then down her chin to salt up the neck of her sweater. What really did it was when she bit her lip, just *like* a whitegirl, in a way that said *This will hurt me forever and I'm just going to let it.* Like her mind warn't ground down by balcony-setting and back-door entering and settlement-cheating and other general whitefolk treatment, like she ain't got the White kids' used schoolbooks just like the rest of us, handed down to the Montgomery Colored with *Nigger, can you read this?* written across all the pages in red ink pen. Like her mind was free enough with time enough that it could skip around in whitegirl spaces and just grieve. Like she ain't have to have the same stone-cold heart as everbody else out here under God's gaze trying to scrape up two nickels, and that's when I first knew Audrey thought she was better'n the rest of us. 'Cause she couldn't stay cool at a funeral.

Come a couple years later, when Emmett Till got kilt, she come running over to the house all upset, with her fifteen-cent *Jet* magazine what done come in the mail to Grandpap Wallace for the dime subscription, telling me to look at them pictures of Emmett in his casket. "Look like he ought've had sense enough not to look at some White lady," I told her, but she ain't heard a word. I was soaping down the base of Grandmama's door where the dirt daubers done stuck nests on it, and Audrey got down on her knees and opened the *Jet* out where both of us could see it.

"Here's what his mama told them," she said. " 'I looked at his teeth, because I took so much pride in his teeth. His teeth were the prettiest things I'd ever seen. And I only saw two. Where were the rest of them? They'd just been knocked out.' "

She read on to me, like I wasn't setting right across the doorway from her reading it for myself, and it sounded like she was fixing to cry just reading about them teeth. But to me, look like them teeth'd been the least of old Emmett's problems — looked like his face'd been shaved clean off'n his head. I was thinking on telling Audrey, but she whipped that magazine right out of my face and held the page with the pictures up to her chest. "I cannot believe someone could do this to another human being," she said. "In America." She shook her head so hard her glasses slid down to her nose. *"America."*

She ran her mouth about it for long about a week, and it got to where I could see her across the street and hear the name "Emmett Till" running through my mind. She talked more stuff than the radio, about how sick it was, and how those poor Colored people down South done suffered long enough, and how we was all suffering — all us Negroes, everwhere around the world — and how enough was enough and we all had to pick our nappy heads up and do something about it. I ain't said a word. Just nodded and said mm-hmmm, thinking maybe she'd shut up and give me a swig of her soda. But wouldn't you know when we went downtown to the Varsity to see *Love Me or Leave Me,* she went right through the main doors and sat downstairs. Tried to get me to set down there with her — pulled on my arm and asked me what sense did it make to sit in a balcony. "It ain't logical," she said. "We got eyes to watch the movie just like they do. We paid the same price to get in the door."

'Course, I wanted to ask her why she was whispering if it made all that much sense, and why she kept sneaking an eye back to the girl selling the tickets, like maybe she wanted to make sure the girl didn't see her walking through that downstairs door. And maybe it didn't make no logical sense for all the Coloreds to set up there in that pissy balcony, but for me, it didn't have to. I wasn't like Audrey, always needing ever little blessed thing to end up in a square. I was paying for a different experience than the White people was, and warn't no reason to buck it, far as I could tell, so I broke away from Audrey and went on up to that balcony like I had some sense.

By the time I got up there and looked back down, she done already sat down middleways to the front of the theater, but the funny thing is, none of the White people noticed. She looked this way and that and hardly watched the movie a tall — she threw herself into a phony coughing fit, even, but all them White people was so hung up on

Doris Day kissing James Cagney, ain't nobody seent her. Nobody but us children up in the balcony, and we was all just a-laughing at her, aiming popcorn at her head and such. Emmett Till hollering at her from the grave, his mama putting them awful pictures out to throw the whole country off their appetite, but didn't nobody notice Audrey setting there trying to make everthing right. Come the fifth or sixth dance number, she just got mad and stood up out of her seat, and knowing how special them Martins think they are, I was afraid she might start screaming or somesuch, but turnt out she just walked out the theater and missed the rest of the movie. Like the regular miracle of a good show just wasn't good enough for her.

And then there was her whole to-do about that house out in the county, which anybody else would of give their eyetooth to live in. Out there on that meadow, she didn't last one week. "Caroline, you got to come see this mess," she told me. Me, tossing out dead mice in the morning and raising myself up ladders to patch shingles on my grandmama's roof, and her, complaining about an upstairs-downstairs dream. Her mama'd moved them out there with big-bellied Mr. Barbour, who'd been watching Danaitha's ass for years. Miss Ora Ray down Seventh Street had finally passed on (though Danaitha celebrated so much in the three days after, she was too drunk to make it to the lady's funeral), and since she didn't have a night job no more and no excuses neither, Mr. Barbour say why don't she just move on in with him. Mr. Barbour's people in Indiana in the house-renting business, and he has more money'n he know what to do with nohow, so he started hisself a tobacco farm and built a house what ever corner is seven degrees off.

"Seven degrees," he explained to us, when I finally got the time to go out there and see for myself. "Seven is a powerful number." It may and it may not be, but I was studying those wood floors, sanded clean as limestone without a knot anywhere. Them windows in the front room, big enough to let the whole day through. The three climbing stones of the walkway, carried in from the Camargo quarry by Mr. Barbour hisself and laid into the hill up to the yard, at an 83-degree angle from the road. Danaitha moved them in there and out of Grandpap Martin's house thinking *peculiar* meant *fine* — Audrey's mama, too, believes deeply in fineness — but them corners upset Audrey something fierce.

"Looka this," she said to me, in a parlor that was a trapezoid. Mr. Barbour'd been baling all morning and was asleep on the couch, looking forty ways to gruesome, with his eyes half open and drool running all out his mouth. "This shit is as crazy as the day is long," she said. Asleep, Mr. Barbour couldn't fight her on what she was saying, even with his mouth wide open. And anyway, the house *was* awful unsettling. "Clearly, he don't want me in his house," she said, taking me from room to slanted room. Felt like standing sideways in a milk carton.

Her mama loved it, she loved them wood columns staggered by seven degrees on that big old front porch, and them stairsteps that rose to an angle so they landed seven degrees left of where they took off. But Audrey couldn't see the point. The point seemed to be to set her off. "Mr. Barbour built this house 'fore he even knew you," I told her, but she shook her head.

"I'm out soon as I get me some bread. Me and you can go to Lexington and find us a couple a cityboys."

I just been swallowing Tyrone Boyd's tongue out behind the Colored store, and some folk didn't have to go all the way to no city to find them a good man, I wanted to tell her, but looking like she did with them glasses, like Poindexter, it didn't seem right to say. "I'll come visit you," I told her.

'Course it warn't just the crooked rooms, or Mr. Barbour looking like a ghoul when he slept (which was just about always), or even the smell of cow shit from his tobacco field. Mr. Barbour done changed Danaitha too, to something fake and phony-dripping that jangled its bracelets when shaking hands with strangers and used a voice like sherbet when it said how do, and Audrey warn't never going to be happy about that.

Long about the time they moved, Miss Tallulah Gorton over to the African Methodist Episcopal stroked up and knocked out the whole left side of her body. Audrey started to play for her on Sundays, and so when they left her granddaddy's house, they strapped that big old piano on the truck with them. Took four little hungry men from Shake Rag to scoot and push that big piano out the house, and when it landed down on the porch steps you could hear the sound of all eighty-eight of them coils banging at once. The noise set Grandmama running to the window: she looked down the street and said a piano nice as that weigh about six times what one a them little men do. She made me go out to the front porch to watch:

Mr. Barbour standing next to the truck with his chest puffed up like the king of Kentucky; Audrey's granddaddy standing on the porch with his lip poked out like they sawing off his arm. But then onced the piano got to the new house, with Audrey hollering to put it on a inside wall to keep the dew out its guts, Mr. Barbour went sour. "Can't stand to hear it," he told the men down to the Tin Cup. "Works my nerves. She plays a little nub of a song without finishing, or she goes down the same piece a road over and over."

Was a family by the name of Simmons what lived out by Mr. Barbour, renting a little shack on his property what used to be a curing house. Didn't even have no plumbing, even, but them Simmonses seemed so low-down and trampy we figured they didn't mind, even if the mama did have three childrens to wash and cook for. They'd lived all over everwhere, it was said, and Oval Murden told us he'd beat the father once in a card game all the way over in West Virginia. It was said the father (we weren't sure he could rightly be called the husband) shaved his head ever time they moved, and by the time it grew out again, he done ruined his reputation in the new town. The oldest girl, Ruth, was in our class at school, and she bragged about all the places they done lived and all the things they done seent, said they used to live in a big mansion in Lexington and once at dinner with Sammy Davis, Jr. She told us all the details of it, down to how the color of Sammy's fake eye was a little lighter than the color in his real one, and she built the lie up so pretty you didn't want to break it down yourself, but then we saw her mama down to the Colored store, dressed in Mrs. Gertie Woodrow's skirt she done stole out the trash, with its old elastic hanging off her belly so she'd had to knot it on the side of her waist. She slumped her shoulders when she walked, and spoke so low Mr. Barnett had to keep yelling at her to tell him again what she needed. "Sack of flour," she'd say, and you could hear the tears in her voice. We knew such a person as that ain't never shared candied bacon with no movie star.

Well, after I started going with Ralph, old Poindexter ended up hanging tight for a spell with Ruth Simmons. Ruth couldn't hardly read her speller at school, and she was just as confounded as anybody else when Audrey opened her mouth and started talking about all them books she ordered through the mail, but they was the only two Colored girls out on that particular county road, so Ruth would come set on Mr. Barbour's porch and play checkers with Audrey in the afternoon. Ruth told Audrey all her lies and Audrey told Ruth all her truths, not knowing that Ruth came to school and retold ever single bit of it. It was Ruth who told us that Audrey's own mama eventually turnt sour on her piano playing. Asked her not to play lessun Mr. Barbour was out the house, but then he started complaining he could hear it when he was in the field picking his tobacco. His hired hands hummed the pieces of songs while Audrey played, Ruth told us, and finished them a capella when she stopped, and generally made things worse in Mr. Barbour's head.

Danaitha had them four skinny men come back out to the meadow and scoot and pull the piano back onto the truck. Ever single one of Audrey's other valuables fit in a big paper sack from the Colored store, and Ruth said Audrey threw that in the bed of the truck and then climbed up there herself and started playing her piano, all loud and happy, just to get under Mr. Barbour's teeth. He pushed his hands in his pockets and started whistling and shuffling and jangling change and generally trying to ignore her, but she stood straight up in the back of the truck and played louder. Put her foot up on the high register and beat on the black keys with the toe of her shoe. They started the truck, but even with all that jumping and bumping over that dirt road, she didn't miss a beat. She played all the way into town: "Leaning on the Everlasting Arms." The four skinny men sang with her. Then they scooted and pulled that piano back into her granddaddy's house, and her granddaddy stood there flashing his false teeth, handing out five-dollar bills. "Two kinds of people, and some of them stand on their feet," he was saying. I was walking home from the fruit market when I saw all that commotion. She told me howdy. Said she was moving back to Queen Street. Told me she couldn't decide whether it was a battle she done won or lost.

According to Ruth, she did go back to spend the night with her mama on weekends, but onced the piano was gone, Mr. Barbour wanted it still quieter in the house, told Danaitha to tell Audrey she was not to leave her room while he was napping. She had a might pretty little room, with the wood floors bleached to pink, a strong cane chair, and even a writing desk for Audrey to get her lessons, but seem like setting round looking at the nails in the wall made her feel like Rapunzel. Ruth told us one Saturday, Audrey walked down to get a glass of milk and Danaitha met her at the icebox. Danaitha had a glass of whiskey in one hand and a wet dishrag in the other, Audrey'd told Ruth; Danaitha'd had water fighting to stay in her eyes and a layer of flush under her cheeks.

"What you trying to do to us?" she said, and she slapped Audrey so hard with the dishrag that Mr. Barbour woke hisself up and ran in the kitchen. Audrey and Danaitha stared each other down, altogether ignoring Mr. Barbour. Audrey blinked first, though, and when she felt that one tear dripping down the side of her face, she ran out the front door, clear back to her granddaddy's house. Four miles and she ain't even stopped to catch her breath. She played at church that Sunday with a welt on her face, but the next weekend she went back to stay with her mama again anyway.

'Course she didn't have no bed when she got there, and no dresser neither, on account of her mama done moved all her furniture out to the barn. Where Audrey's bed should of been, it was a little crib, painted pink and set over a pedestal. In front of the window where Audrey'd looked out and dreamed that the meadow was an ocean rolling her straight to Paris, Danaitha done put a rocker chair with the outlines of baby ducks carved into its back. Audrey stood in the middle of the floor and watched the room, and her mama stood in the door and watched her watch it. "We can make you a pallet downstairs in the parlor," Danaitha said. "You're going to be a big sister."

"A what?"

Danaitha blinked, blinked and then smiled. Her little nose went up and down one time like a rabbit's. "Mr. Barbour and I are expecting," she said.

"Ain't you kind of old to have a baby?"

And then it was Danaitha's turn to blink first. She smoothed her dress down over her flat belly. "I ain't had my ministration for three months now."

"Ever think you might just be going through the change of life?"

You'd think Audrey would of been happy, since it meant Mr. Barbour'd marry her mama and they'd be living out there in that big old house for perpetuity, but Audrey'd always been her mama's one and only baby, even if being Danaitha's baby ain't meant much, and now her mama had one on the way and a grown man what done already replaced her sleeping downstairs on the couch. Ruth said Audrey sat herself down in the rocker, hugged her own neck, and got to going back and forth real fast. Said Audrey got to thinking about the last time she seent her daddy, how he hugged her and her mama too, too tight; how he jumped on that green Army bus and told them out the window that everthing would work out, they'd see. Audrey'd heard him tell it so many times — he'd come back to Kentucky and make a doctor, just like Sam French, and then they'd have all that money and a big house somewhere. I remember how happy Audrey'd been when her daddy told her all that over his dinner plate, and how good it'd made me feel just to know that somebody in this town was aiming to kick up his feet and dance a little harder. It'd been enough to make Audrey eat her liver without Danaitha asking her, and it'd been enough to start me dreaming about getting out of this town myself. Now, 'course, her daddy's dead and gone forever, and everything's different. I got two dead parents, a mind what feels like it's cracking like an egg, and no decent way to get myself fed for the winter let alone get to Hollywood. All Audrey has is Grandpap Martin, who's going deaf and more and more can't hear what she's saying noways. She had me, but now I got Ralph. She's got her piano, but you know music just travels.

"Well, listen," Audrey said then to Danaitha, up in that pretty room what used to be hers. The rocker chair'd made so much noise against the floorboards that it'd woke Mr. Barbour, who was stamping around the kitchen slamming the lid to the breadbox. He'd turnt up the radio real loud, so Lowell Fulson was shouting "Reconsider Baby" up the stairs at them. They could smell the cinnamon what was boiling round the sweet potatoes and the vinegar bubbling up through the greens. "Y'all have fun with that baby. If you need somebody to mind it, don't call me. You won't be able to. I'm leaving town."

"Don't know where she thinks she's going," Ruth told me, sucking her teeth like the business she'd just finished putting out in the street done let off some bad smell. It's why I can never be Ruth's friend — she don't know a thing about dreaming something up on her own, and she don't know, neither, how to just stand back and enjoy it when somebody else does. I want to tell her: don't doubt Audrey. Look at her old daddy. Both of them wanting out of this town, and ain't neither one of them caring about the fallout. Them Martins is a little bit like wild birds — you can't never know where one of them's going to fly off next.

Peanut

The Friday after Thanksgiving, Ruth Simmons's daddy fell down dead. Me and Ralph was kind of surprised, on account of we just seent him two days previous, the day a cold rain blew in and knocked the seven big cursive letters off the top of Taylor's Department Store. That happened in the White part of town but Pauline Burke saw the whole thing on account of she done went to Nessum's to buy kerosene, and she ran in the Colored store yelling that the Taylor's sign done fell to the street and broke in two, right between the "Y" and the "L." I know when she said it that Ralph was fixing to walk me down there to see it, rain or no — Ralph thinks ever day of life ought to be an adventure, and lucky me, he sees fit to pull his girl along with him. Well, we ain't even fully rounded the corner of Sixth Street when here come Zill Heller busting out the front door of the Tin Cup with Ruth

Simmons's daddy hot on his back, Simmons with the hat on his head what was so old, the inside rim was an oil slick. Two green duck feathers stuck out of the hatband so filthy they was gummed together in places, and the back of his corduroy jacket was so eat up with moth holes you could see the green of his shirt peeking through, and yet still he had the gall to be shooting his mouth off at Zill Heller.

"You want that money back, you gonna have to pick me up and shake it out of me," he was saying. "I ain't a bit more giving it back to you than the man in the moon." Even pulled out his knife, he did, and waved it at Zill, but then Zill threw up his hands and yelled something about G. L. Horst over in Judy and "wouldn't he be interested in the matter," and well I guess Simmons must've owed G. L. Horst an even bigger scratch of money, because when Zill mentioned him, Simmons closed his knife up with a bothered little *click* and put it back in his pocket. He pulled the sides of his jacket straight, like he was the one in the right and it was Zill Heller's face he was saving, and then he walked on down Sixth Street and disappeared in Ophelia Loving's house. Hiram was at the ice plant until four, and everbody knew it. I just wondered what her and Simmons was going to do in there if that baby woke up from her nap.

It was some of us thought somebody might've poisoned Simmons, all the trouble he done rustled up in town, but Ruth's mama told the coroner the way it happened, all quick like, couldn't have been nothing but his heart. Said he gave a little yell and fell over — looked like he was dead before he even hit the ground. I wondered why nobody suspected Ruth's mama in the whole business, but the church collected some money and give it to her to bury him. It was a well-attended funeral, because even though they'd only been in town two weeks, Simmons'd made quite a magnificent impression. It wasn't that people wanted to pay respects, and not even that they wanted to make sure he was in the ground. More like we all just wanted to get a good look at lightning that hot while it was setting still.

I figured, much as they moved around, the mama would've been out of town — *bam* — just like that, but she stayed on. Matter fact, she got herself a job at the post office, and now she's the first Negro — man or woman — to deliver mail in Mt. Sterling, Kentucky. Twice a day now she comes walking down Queen Street handing over letters and parcels, shuffling and hunched over and looking at people's feet while she speaks, like she's still embarrassed by a dead man. That big leather bag they give her is right smart, and she's got a United States Postal badge slapped right on top of her heart, but the way she tips up to people's porches and dashes off into the snow soon as she drops the letter in the box, she looks like somebody's runaway child. She crunches across Grandmama's sidewalk salt to bring me another letter from Daddy, hands it right into my hand without even looking at my eyes to see whether surprise grabs hold of me, and I think it's a relief it's just Ruth Simmons's mama bringing the mail. Second off, I ain't sure she's smart enough to know what "State Penitentiary" means. And first off, she's new to this town and her opinion just don't even count.

Cold as the devil's eyeteeth, but I stand there on the porch for a while, noticing how Daddy — or somebody — licked the flap and sealed it just a little bit off'n its glue, and I have half a mind to run after Ruth's mama, ask her whether any other house in town gets letters marked "Stanton Wallace, c/o State Penitentiary, Eddyville, Kentucky," but then I ain't expecting my daddy has any friends here on the outside: after they heard tell about Mama, seem like everbody in

148

town turned on him overnight. Already, the other men down to the ice plant done cooled it with him; they thought he sounded a little too happy gobbling down those sandwiches he made hisself, and they didn't trust the look of good sleep on the face of a man who didn't know where his wife was. Daddy was on his way home from the plant while we was digging around for the rest of Mama's body, and he made the front porch just as Junebug was walking out the house with Mama's hand wrapped up in a handkerchief. Junebug was headed straight to the police, so when Daddy spoke, he just walked on past. It was all a mystery to poor little Imagene, and when Daddy walked in the house she turned her big pretty eyes on him and ran to hug his legs. I just sat there with my mouth wide open and nothing coming out.

Grandmama done cried herself to sleep on our couch with her feet propped up on the armrest, and I'd been rubbing her shoulder trying to get her to wake up. But when Daddy just stood there tickling the snail of Imagene's ear, laughing along with her like he ain't done nothing, I stood up and dropped Grandmama right to the floor. *Bamp,* went her head, and that did get her awake, and she sat up from the floor and rubbed the back of her scalp. "You ain't heard?" I screamed at him. "Get out!" I took the poker from the fireplace and threw it at him, and lucky thing Daddy ducked to his knees, elseways I might've been the one going off to the pen.

Daddy ran out the house and off to the Colored store for cigarettes, but Mr. Barnett threw his nickel right back over the counter at him. Daddy went in the Tin Cup to have a drink, but they say when he walked in, the place got quieter than a barn — the laughter on them bar stools just went dead. "We got no call for whatever just came through that door," said Percy Greer, with his back to Daddy. The owner wouldn't have him served. "I hope they throw you *under* the jail," he said.

Ain't nobody warned him about the police wagon waiting out front. The whole of Sixth Street watched the White policeman cuff Daddy's wrist, but the way they was all standing there with their arms crossed, looked like nobody was even afraid for him. The police forgot to duck Daddy's head down getting him in the wagon, and Daddy hit his face against the door and hollered, but didn't nobody from Queen Street so much as bat an eye. Didn't nobody shift their weight to even their legs, nor turn their face to shoo off a fly, nor uncross the gate of their arms to let in answers that shouldn't be asked for. Didn't nobody stop looking, not even when the police wagon disappeared three miles down that flat road and then over the curve of the earth. And ain't not a one of us seent him since. Nobody gone down to Eddyville to visit, not even his people what live down in Princeton.

I imagine when he gets out, there'll be people what wants something to do with him now and again. He might get his job back on account of he worked so hard busting fifteen year worth of ice, and he might be able to take whiskey at the Tin Cup again, because really the owner would take money from a Martian, long as it spent. Women. There'll always be women — even right smart-looking ones — who'll have anybody. There'll be women who'll love Daddy all the more because he's in need of their fixing. But he'll never have friends again, not real ones. He's marked as one of the devil's for life. Can't nobody understand why he killed Mama, who never so much as raised her voice to him, and that mess he told those White men down to the courthouse is just plain ignorant. About the onliest person in the world who maybe could've made headtails out of any of it was Audrey's

151

daddy. Too bad for Sonnyboy, Lindell Martin's dead and gone, blown to bits over in Korea.

The day Danaitha come telling him about the Army's telegram, Daddy just sat there in his chair and stared at her. Even after she walked back across the street to Grandpap Martin's, with the belt of her dress dragging the ground behind her, Daddy just sat there — he slid down in his chair and put his head back into the cushion and stared at the ceiling. He looked awfully uncomfortable slouched up like that, but ever time we'd look in on him we could see he ain't moved not one inch. He ain't even eat dinner when Mama brought the plate and set it in his lap. Imagene was still a little-bitty thing not really talking, and she waddled over and tried to climb up in Daddy's lap, but he patted her on the back a couple times and told her to go find me. Me and Imagene started running back and forth across the living room, tagging each other in the porch door and then again in the kitchen, tripping each other and falling down just so Daddy might show some concern, but he ain't told us to be quiet or even really looked at us. He just sat there, with his hands folded in his lap, staring at the ceiling until it got so dark in the afternoon he couldn't even see that, and then he got up, cleared his throat, and went about the business of sweeping the kitchen, which is what he'd been about to do when Danaitha knocked. Considering what a shock it was to his nerves when Lindell died, I guess it ain't so strange that Daddy keeps mailing me all them stories about him. He still ain't apologized for killing Mama, and he ain't explained it, neither, and half the letters I just throw in the fire. But sure enough, when I rip open the flap on this one and read past the three paragraphs he done wrote on how the sun was shining just right through the basement window when the warden come down to compliment him for his work in the laundry, here Daddy comes again telling me about Lindell Martin.

"Friends since we played ball together in school," he wrote. "I had a big pumpkin head and Lindell had a bitty nut perched on his neck, and the joke was we had to be walking side by side just to think straight." "Bighead" and "Peanut," he says the girls called them, but their freshman year of high school, they beat out every White basketball team in eastern Kentucky, because the White coaches was so curious to see them play that they suspended segregation for all the winter of '19 and '36. Mongtomery

County Colored was the first Negro team to go all the way to State, and the coach and the principal and the A.M.E. bishop and damn near every Negro in the county begged them to keep playing, but Lindell'd already got Danaitha pregnant, Daddy wrote, and my granddaddy (who had five young'uns standing shorter than my daddy) had stroked up while he was out shoveling snow and lost all the words he'd ever meant to have. With Danaitha all poked out like a watermelon and old Mr. Martin's mouth hanging down off its corners like a handlebar, Lindell and Daddy both dropped out of school right when ball season was getting hot. The White people was relieved; look like they donated more coal to the Negro community that Christmas.

The more I read all this in my daddy's letters the more I'm some surprised, on account of it sounds like the story of a flop. Sounds like life kicked Lindell around, and he just curled up in a ball and covered his head. But you know, at some point Lindell must've uncurled hisself and hollered — if he hadn't, he wouldn't of never got out of Mt. Sterling in the first place. And so I keep reading, because life done kicked me too, and I want to hear how to kick it back. Well, Daddy said he got hisself on at the ice plant, and Lindell started cutting tobacco. But to hear Daddy tell it, Lindell hated the juice getting in his clothes and the chiggers biting his ankles. 'Course, Grandpap Martin and them always did talk so proper that it would hurt them even to say "how do" in some heat, and Lindell didn't much like the baling twine cutting up his pretty piano hands, so when the first frost hit the fields, Lindell took his darlin' little fingers off to Lexington and started fixing cars at a filling station, figuring that the grease would at least keep his hands soft. Come the mornings you'd see him with his heavy coat on, hitching the half hour to Nicholasville Road.

Long about five year, he was able to afford a little piece of car for hisself, and generally he'd chug back to Mt. Sterling after his workday and him and Daddy'd spend the afternoon fixing whatever'd gone wrong with its engine that week. It kept Lindell out his daddy's house, and my daddy away from the damnation of one little noisy girl and another on the way, and if Daddy's remembering right in his letters, seems like it was pure accident about the Lyric, because really Lindell was supposed to be home nights keeping up his routine of fixing the car and helping Danaitha drink her bourbon. But one afternoon when the wind was blowing snow into Lindell's eyes and Mr. Combs was about ready to let him go on home, Lindell happened to pump some Esso Extra for a conk-headed half-breed on his way back to New Jersey. The man rolled down his window and put a bug in Lindell's ear that Cab Calloway was playing in town.

"The Lyric Theater," said the mulatto. His eyes were gray like rainclouds. He blew into his closed fist to warm his hand.

"And where might that be?"

"Corner of Third and Elm."

"No kidding," said Lindell, and after that, Daddy wrote me, if'n you wanted to see what Lindell and Danaitha looked like in the dark, you'd of had to hike yourself up to Lexington. Audrey was coming up on eleven year, and Grandpap Martin was happy to keep her home Lyric nights to teach her checker games. Danaitha hid her whiskey in her coat pocket so she could take it in the Lyric with her: it was known that the Lyric only let in Negroes aiming to be proper.

Lucky thing they took Daddy with them, too, because Lindell couldn't much dance and didn't want to noways. Daddy wrote it all down in the seventh letter he sent me, said he was grinning all over hisself, bouncing around, trying to keep a proper distance from the places on Danaitha's body he couldn't help but study. Meantime, Lindell was standing out front of the velvet curtain, looking round the ballroom and laughing to hisself with joy over the big ocean of Negroes, more Negroes in one place than he'd ever seent or even imagined, all of them clapping and moving and spinning each other and having a swank time after a week's worth of mule work. The big grand piano onstage, eight foot long and shiny enough to give off a reflection of the pianist's gold rings, got Lindell's nose wide open. "Hey," he yelled at Danaitha and Daddy over the noise of the band. "When the show's over, I want to see what that grandpa grand's like." Daddy was on the dance floor with another girl, so close to the stage that the bell of the trombone blew spit over his head: Danaitha was pouring more whiskey into a cup. Danaitha nodded at Lindell when she twisted the cap back on her flask, but Lindell still ain't asked her to dance.

They did stay quite a time after the band packed up and left. Lindell sat a spell picking out tunes, but then he got all excited about the piano's guts. He slid his fingers down the strings, then stood up and watched what the action did when he stomped the damper pedal. Without the music, Daddy had to hum while he pretended to swing a skinny girl in his arms, but there was so much happy left over in him, he didn't complain. It was a lady janitor at the Lyric that year — she kept her hair short and nappy, but Daddy said if you looked at her from behind you could tell from the fit of her pants — and when she came cross the stage with her wide-headed broom, she smiled with her head cocked to the side like only a woman would've.

"You sound right nice there, boy. Shoot, I thought the show was still playing. You belong to one of these here traveling bands?"

"No'm. I just play at church."

"Well, don't waste the talent the good Lord gave you at church, boy — you oughta be up there playing with the Duke hisself!" She laughed at her own joke, and they all heard how hoarse and pitchless her voice was, and even my daddy knew that neither it, nor any other part of her body, had ever truly touched music.

"Yes, but," Lindell said, hanging his head, watching the hammers jump as he struck the chords to "Ko-Ko," "I'm just some hillbilly two-cent piano player. Some black peckerwood from up the mountain. I ain't going nowhere."

The sweeper laughed again. "Don't you know, boy? All these people what got theyselves orchestras now wasn't nothing but black peckerwoods theyselves at your age. Duke Ellington, matter fact, come up from some little holler down in North Carolina. Hear tell his daddy was a slave. Everbody got to come from somewhere, boy."

"But you know, ma'am, he must have gone to New York City to make it big like he did. How am I even to get to Cincinnati when I have a woman and a child to feed?"

Daddy said that sweeper looked up to the corner of the ballroom like it was giving her the answer. Said, "Join the Army, boy. The Army got a band. Good as you can play, they'll put you to work entertaining them soldiers sure enough."

Daddy said he could tell she was just talking. It was nary a bone in her body what could've felt talent, he wrote, and she ain't really seent in Lindell what Lindell done seent in hisself, but Lindell was a country boy didn't know nothing about nothing and, so, wanted to believe everthing. The sad part about it, Daddy said, was that Lindell would die thinking what that sweeper said was true. "Matter fact," he wrote, and there was a space where his pen had picked up between the "c" and the "t" and I could almost see him setting there, scratching a place between his thumb and forefinger where the laundry starch done dried his skin, "that sweeper's what made him go strutting off to Korea in the first place."

Well, Daddy's letter pretty much ended there, but I got the rest of the story from Ida Mae Harris, when I went across the street to get a hula hoop Imagene'd left on the edge of her yard. Ida Mae was a tall, big-boned, red-skinned lady who dressed all her days in blue jeans, and she had a dog named Shep what was part German shepherd and part chow, and even though he ran with a limp, and Ida Mae tended to set there on her porch with his leash pulled up short and wrapped around her wrist, I could see how Imagene'd probably dropped her hula hoop and ran off scared when he barked — even Ruth Simmons's mama didn't want to get too close to him, so she pitched Ida Mae her mail from the road.

"It was a starless night when Lindell told us all," she said, "a night the whole county'd remember come a long time afterwards." Shep was setting between her legs, and he shifted hisself around so his shoulders was poking up behind his head. His chain clicked against the edge of Ida Mae's porch, and she petted him behind the ears and kept on talking. "Weird thing was, warn't no moon outshining the stars, and warn't no clouds hiding them neither — it just warn't any stars." Ida Mae told me Lindell's big sister Juanita was in town for church revival, though Grandpap Martin nor nobody else knew she'd really packed herself up on the bus from Knoxville College in order she'd get to see Ida Mae.

"Lindell, you think they'd let me on up at the filling station?" Ida Mae'd asked him across the dinner table. Her and Juanita'd made sweet potatoes with marshmallows on top, just like Juanita's mama taught her before she died. Grandpap Martin kept leaving the kitchen to go move the knobs on the radio, and ever time he did Juanita kissed Ida Mae, each time swallowing more of the girl's lips with her own, Juanita's lip-sticked heart mashed against Ida Mae's plain one.

"A gal at the filling station?" Lindell asked. He never seent Ida Mae knife a cow's neck while it mooed, nor slide lard up a mare's private parts to get it to foal, nor shovel shit onto an entire three acres worth of soy. But he told them all then at the dinner table that he had seent Mr. Combs reslide the creases down his shirtsleeves when he thought no one else was looking, and he done seent him carry money to the bank folded over in a money clip inside a leather pocket inside a steel case. He said he done seent Mr. Combs eat his fried potatoes with a fork and knife, and otherwise announce the limits of his mind to the world. "Mr. Combs would never let a girl do that work, not even a Negro girl in blue jeans. For one thing, it wouldn't sit right with the customers. Lexington people are city folk."

"What about another Negro man, then?" asked Grandpap Martin. "They say Preacher Fletcher's son Priddy back from Chicago looking for a job."

"Well, he can have mine."

"Lindell," Danaitha said. She said it surprised-like, Ida Mae told me, but then she chewed her roast slow and let the rest of the table wait for her to say any more. Ida Mae said she figured Danaitha's mind was an exclamation point looking for more whiskey to calm itself down, but she always did try to hold it together in front of Lindell's daddy. "Lindell," she said again. She smiled like she done ate him. "You going to get a job here in town?"

"No. I'm going into the service," he said, and two pairs of silver rang against two tin plates. Danaitha'd gotten the plates from

162

the dime store over by Rickles Pharmacy, so even though the tin was painted over bright yellow, the forks made the sound of cheapness, and in Ida Mae's ear they sounded like everthing that was wrong in all their lives.

"Lindell," Grandpap Martin said, meaning to set him straight. "You ain't going in no White man's service." He folded his napkin and smacked it on his plate for the last word.

"What this country ever do for you," said Juanita, "you got to go off and get kilt for it?"

"G.I. Bill, my dear. This country is going to give me a college education."

"Gonna get you kilt, nigger, that's what," said Danaitha. She didn't seem to know she done got up from the table, and she shook some on her feet.

"Uncle Sam is going to give me a loan from the bank to buy a dairy farm when I get back. Send me to a Negro medical school with five hundred dollars a year to spare."

Ida Mae laughed then in her telling, told me that when Lindell said that about the five hundred dollars, everbody else round the table calmed down and put their eyes back to normal size. But Danaitha laughed.

"You come back to America with one arm and a pinned-up shirtsleeve, how you going to milk cows?"

" 'Naitha, it ain't been a war in five years. And whether I come back with one arm or two, you're going to sit around this house turning your liver into soup, so it seems to me it's none of your concern."

Right about then, Ida Mae said, Danaitha coughed like something done caught in her throat and she run on into the living room. Grandpap Martin looked on after her, but Ida Mae said her and Juanita kept on eating like ain't nothing been said.

"What's your opinion, Ida Mae?" Lindell asked. "I know you to be a wise person. Would you be willing to stay here in Mt. Sterling, Kentucky, when the Army wanted you to play piano all over the world?"

"Piano!" Juanita said.

"They going to let you play piano?" asked his daddy. "You ain't got to twirl no rifles nor nothing?"

"The Army has a band. I can audition."

"Audition," said his daddy. "Audition don't mean play."

Lindell sighed. "Being in Mt. Sterling is like being on a ship sailing to nowhere."

"Well, it was a good enough place to raise you up in," said his daddy. "Good enough

164

for my daddy to raise me up in, and for his daddy to raise him up in, and good enough for all us Martins for as long as I can carry it back. You tell me one thing wrong with this town. Or one thing wrong with this house. One thing wrong with your wife and child, who you want to leave."

"What's wrong with my daughter," Lindell said, tapping his glass of water so rings jiggled out on top of it, "is that she has to watch her daddy go off and pour grease fourteen hours a day and have nothing but a messed-up piece of car to show for it. What's wrong with this house is that I could be going away from it to make something of myself." He lowered his voice some. "And I know you didn't raise me up just to go pump whitefolks' gas. To be grinning at Mr. Combs when I'm a fifty-year-old man going bald. I know, Father, you didn't raise me for that."

Ida Mae said it all sounded right nice to her, and she done moved on anyway to eating her chess pie. She was thinking about Audrey, she said, thinking that the child's very own daddy could go all round the world playing his piano and then come home to wear suits every day, like Dr. French, 'stead of just on Sundays like all the other Negroes in town. She thought

165

about Audrey with a powder blue sweater and a satin bow for a belt, and all them furry soft flamingoes on the bottom of her long skirt, and she felt warm to the bone, like Juanita was sharing hot apple cider with her during a kiss. 'Course Danaitha was still setting in the living room crying puddles, but when she overheard Lindell talking about making a doctor, seem like she stopped some, and Ida Mae said the way Danaitha was, she bet she was feeling a mink stole creeping round her neck, and the bomber seats of a brand-new Merc fitting to her bottom. Said she bet Danaitha was setting there already looking out over her new French headlights while she drove up to the first house they didn't have to share with Lindell's daddy.

Ida Mae thought about how Juanita was down in Knoxville on scholarship, and how that meant she had to wash dishes at the girls' dormitory while her girlfriends got their lessons. She thought about how, for want of money to go to Kentucky State, Juanita was living on scholarship in the worn-out dirt of Tennessee, going on dates with boys for the sake of appearances. She thought on a day when they were all three just kids, when Lindell tackled her to the floor and tickled her with one hand while he played Hot Biscuits with the other, and she knew he didn't deserve to be cooped up like a dog in Mt. Sterling. Ida Mae said Grandpap Martin, who'd been planning on bullying Lindell into the bushels of grandbabies he wanted, had cheeks red with heat. Somehow along the way, his son done become a man.

But then again, when she excused herself to the bathroom, it come to Ida Mae that maybe the stars'd hidden away that night so they wouldn't have to hear what Lindell done gone and decided. Ida Mae didn't love men, but on her way to the bathroom, when the uncooked air in the hallway shifted to coolness and a screech owl rattled his call through the open back door, she felt a peculiar sadness in her heart for Lindell. *But he ain't my brother, and not my son, not my husband or my daddy,* she said in her head. When she was finished with the toilet she washed her hands and then said it out loud, answering the question Lindell done asked, way long after he done forgot it. "Ain't none of my concern," she said. She walked back to the dining room, and started to clear plates.

SAVED

Boys, you know, they don't notice my teeth so much when I got lipstick on. I make sure to keep them brushed clean so the lipstick don't stick, and I don't take coffee nor tea nor soda. I blot my lips with Kleenex ever so often to make sure I ain't smeared, and I say to my mind over and over again to keep that mouth closed. *Shut your trap, shut it, just shut it,* I tell myself, and sometimes I tell it until I'm almost humming it, and my lips are sore from being pressed so tight against each other, but it works. When I smile at boys now, they look at my eyes.

'Course, in private it's a different matter altogether, but that ain't about my teeth. The surprise of it all, when I finally let Ralph, is that he doesn't even kiss my mouth while we're doing it. It's the end of lunch recess, and Imagene done already hopped herself back to school, and it's cold against the wall on account of it being the dead of February, but Ralph pushes me up next to Grandmama's front window and squeezes my bosom, and then he pulls my skirt up and I let him. He turns me around and backs me up against him. He says, "Put your hands against the wall," and I lean over and do that too, on account of he quit me last October and this is the first time he's been in Grandmama's house since, and I'll do anything he says long as he never leaves, and then he's got both hands around my waist with my long skirt piled up on my back, and last year at the soda counter I overheard Colette Smith telling Pauline Burke that the first time hurt her something terrible but Ralph's inside me and making a sound like it's over before I'm even able to decide whether it does. My panties are draped over my shoes but I still turn around and move up close to kiss Ralph, and the thing is, even though I'm holding my mouth closed, he looks right at my lips and then drops his eyes like he's just now remembering who he's with. His eyes land on the scar on my arm, that damn thing, and then he catches himself right quick and winks at me like he's just trying to be fresh, but we still end up not kissing, and I pull my panties up and move away from him.

We set there on Grandmama's couch

after, and he holds my hand but he holds it loose, like he's holding a piece of his scarf or a cartoon ticket or something else he don't care too much about, and I keep squeezing his hand to get warm but it's just from my end, all that squeezing, and he don't squeeze back not once, and just about the time he's starting to look sleepy, and I've decided we probably ain't going back to school this afternoon, somebody knocks on the door.

I put a finger to my lips to tell Ralph to be quiet, and I go answer it and it turns out it's Ruth Simmons's mama with a letter from Daddy. "I thought you might want it soon as you could have it, 'stead of out the box," she says, and she moves her thumb from where she's put it on purpose over the return address, and now I know the bitch can read.

"Thank you," I say, just because it's what Mama always used to tell us to do whenever somebody handed us a piece of paper. But I snatch it from her, just quick enough to let her know.

"What's that?" Ralph asks, when I close the door on her.

"A letter."

"I can see that."

And then I'm stuck, frozen right to the

floor in Grandmama's front hall. I want Ralph to stay and then I don't, and I want him to know the letter but I don't know how to say it, and I sure as Sam don't know how to say that the letter's from the very last person it ought to be from, and that I'm embarrassed to even be reading it. I could tell him how I'ma throw it in the fire right after I do, but that ain't any kind of redemption. Even when Ralph buttons his coat, which he never even pulled off in the first place, I can't say it. Even as ever little part of my tongue wants to move and ask him to stay put just a spell, even as he makes for the door, I'm frozen.

"All right. Bye," he says, and I guess that's the end again. To get out the door, he has to push me aside with his shoulder.

Well, once I open that letter and start reading I'm too mad to cry, because here come Daddy again asking for Lindell's old story reel, on account of they got a new reel player at the penitentiary for the inmates to play things. He's been writing and asking and asking and writing for that reel, and I just keep throwing them letters right in the fire. He ain't asked for nothing normal — not the one photograph of all us girls together, standing on the porch at Christmas, smiling in our gowns at Mama's little

Kodak Brownie even though we was just about froze to death. Not even any of the pictures he had of Mama — not the one from before she ever kissed him, when she was seventeen and grinning secret wishes into the Woolworth's Photomatic, and not the one she took the day she got married, when she was nineteen and had to take both her fists to bunch up the sweep of her wedding dress. He ain't asked for a bit of that. Just that old story reel, the one Lindell sent up from Mississippi right before he got shipped off, with him speaking all them big words like they done made him the general. This time, when he asked, Daddy done at least got polite about it. "Please," he wrote. "If you got any remembrance of your father at all."

I guess he thinks maybe I done forgot him on account of I ain't answered a single one of his letters, and I ain't intending to, and I damn skippy ain't fixing on walking down to no White people's post office to mail any package full of a reel-to-reel to State Penitentiary, Eddyville. But it's something about the way Daddy wants just that one thing so bad what makes me want the thing too, so since I ain't going back to school I carry myself down the street to our old house.

When I turn the key in the lock I hear

something scramble across the living-room floor, and whatever it is must have sense enough to run off into the kitchen, because I hear the old cast iron pot fall to the floor. I open the door and it's two dead birds in the corner of the living room and one more in the hallway, and the roof over the furnace is hanging right into the room. I don't really want to see more but I keep walking, to the middle of the house where I can look in on four different rooms: the floor in the kitchen is bucked and cracked so bad I can see clear down to the foundation, and the outside wall in Mama and Daddy's bedroom is covered in black mold. I know that reel-to-reel is down in the drawer where Daddy kept his special things, and I don't fool around getting it. It ain't all the little rats rustling around behind the walls, and it ain't the mold neither — it's that all of a sudden, it feels like my mama's standing right there looking at me, and I want to get away from her. 'Course, it feels a little funny, being afraid of my own mama like that, but well. No matter how much you love somebody, once they're dead you want them to stay put. I run out the house without even locking the door back, and Ida Mae's dog is barking at me like he knows I ain't supposed to be there. I want to bite his tail and pull the hair out of the little mole on his snout. I want to send that big happy dog running crazy.

I still remember the day Daddy got Lindell's story in the mail — he took it out the box and stacked the two reels on top of each other so he could turn them round and round on his finger. 'Course we all knew what a reel-to-reel was, even though ain't too many people what had them when we was little, but it seem like right then Daddy ain't understood how he was supposed to listen to something that small and get something as big as his best friend's heart. He took it down to WCFL to see if they might let him play it on their reel, and suggested to the manager that he might be interested in running a regular program of reels from men in the service. According to Daddy, the station manager was all excited until he took a hearing of it with Daddy, and then all of a sudden he went sour. Said that tape wasn't even fit to listen to.

Well, Daddy told Mama it was on account of what Lindell said wasn't at all complimentary to White people, and when I bring it back to Grandmama's and put it on her player, there's Lindell, proper as usual, telling his story, something about a man named Sims:

" 'You will take the test again,' the man told me, 'in my presence.' Asked him why, he said, 'Because I'm saying so, son, and this is the armed service of the United States, and if you want to join up, you'd do well to become accustomed to taking orders.' "

Lindell went on, on the tape, said it warn't like him to question much noways, and I figured that was on account of he was so used to taking orders from his daddy. But Lindell did say he was powerful mad, in the moment, at this Sims feller. Said he'd made the trip all the way cross Lexington to take the Army test the first time, and now this second time was going to take up all the half hour in pretty weather that he'd wanted to spend getting his shoes shined up for Lyric night. It was two sets at the theater: Freddie Ferguson and His Hot Peppercorns, who played like they done paid the devil for music, and Valerie Wilson the singer, who had a twenty-inch waist and legs like Coke-Cola bottles. Look like them shoes'd have to stay muddy, though, 'cause Sims flipped a sheet of paper out at Lindell, and Lindell sat hisself down in the same chair he'd sat in the month previous. Sims rolled a pencil cross the table. "You got two hours, son. Never met a Negro 'fore you," he told Lindell, "but I figured I done listened enough on the radio to know plenty about them. So when your test came back and the service said you got only one out of a hundred questions wrong, I reckoned there was something awful strange."

Sims sat in the room and watched him grind in the circles with his pencil and finish the test just as fast as he had back in June, and he tapped his forehead, Lindell said, like he was making sure the day was real.

"Stay put a minute, boy," he said. Lindell tapped his foot and twirled his hat brim while Sims compared the answers from Lindell's first and second tests. "You changed one," Sims said. "You changed the one you got wrong the first time."

"Yes, sir," Lindell said, trying to be right nice so maybe the man would let him leave. "Between now and then, I've added the word 'phaeton' to my vocabulary, courtesy of Webster's Dictionary. It's a type of ancient carriage — did you know?"

Before Sims touched Lindell, he tapped his own forehead all over again. "Son," he said, testing Lindell's shoulder like he was seeing if it was flesh, "do you know you are the only recruit in the history of this office to score in the ninety-ninth percentile of the AFQT? You qualify for Coast Guard. Air Force. Hell," Sims said, and with his excitement, his hill accent started to show up, "you could probably go to pilot school. You could do radar repair. Hell, son, smart as you are, you could make a general." Sims nodded fast. "How about it, son? Air Force or Coast Guard? I got to re-send this test, but that's just a formality."

"Sir, as I said before, what I really want is to play in the band, so —"

"Right, right. They don't put tubas on boats. We'll sign you up for the Air Force."

Sims fixed him right up the minute the test come back, and I do remember when Lindell got called down to Lackland, since it was about that time me and Audrey got baptized. We weren't that good of friends, then, I reckon because we were the girls what got picked on most in school, and we knew that running round together'd be kind of like water rising only so far as its own level. That spring when Lindell left we were both fourteen, which at Second Baptist is kind of like being seventy, if you ain't been saved — the preacher will mind you that much over your lost soul. Matter fact, me and Audrey was the oldest girls in church who still ain't accepted the Lord. Mama was still living then, and she kept saying it was because we reckoned we was smarter than anybody else. I think we was both just angrier down in our hearts.

I still wouldn't of been saved, neither, weren't for Audrey Martin, for warn't no holy feeling sent me to the front of the church to that empty folding chair, no voice of God nor no dream of Moses neither. It was jealousy, p.o.d. jealousy, what sent me up there to that deacon and his empty chair.

Lindell was down in Texas mailing home half his pay, which meant Audrey was getting picked on a lot less, because ever time her mama opened that envelope full of money, she stopped drinking long enough to hit the stores. Audrey still talked more proper than any of us thought necessary — she couldn't help herself on account of that book-eating daddy of her'n — but her mama went down to Taylor's and bought a pair of saddle shoes with the middles so black, people couldn't hear how long her words were for staring at theirselves in the shine. Her mama bought fancy little writing pens with caps to match the color of ink inside, and lace bobby socks enough for ever day of the week. Which left me kind of the odd girl out at school. So, that last Sunday of revival, when Audrey ran up there and flopped her sadicty ass down in one of them three folding chairs, I got mad as hell.

Reverend Owington been talking that day about Pharisees or Saducees, or maybe plain old Jews — I don't remember myself which, because naturally all us children sat in the back pews and did everthing but listen. We whispered, and we drew notes and flowers on the church bulletins, and we linked our feet and swung them in a chain all the way down the pew, and we always had a right good time until someone got too loud or slapped somebody else upside the head, and then Reverend Owington would stop his sermon to make us all go set on the front row. Even then — matter fact, *specially* then — we didn't listen, because setting up front, we was all struck deaf with fear. All three of them preachers could watch our arms and legs then, and all our mamas and daddies and grandmamas and schoolteachers could watch the backs of our heads to see if we moved. We rocked on our haunches to toughen them up for when we got home. One Sunday, when we got called to the front of church, Imagene peed her dress.

Anyway, back pew or front pew, we children never heard the sermon, lessun the preacher got to talking about lust or sins of the flesh, but that ain't necessarily speaking for Audrey, because she always been just the type to actually listen to grown-up talk and make sense of it. Whatever it was Pastor said or didn't say that Sunday about them Pharisees, it got Audrey up out of the back pew and sent her straight down to that folding chair. It was so close after the end of the sermon that Owington was still wiping sweat off'n his forehead, and a couple of old ladies was still passed out on the floor from getting happy. Harry Greaves, the biggest fattest deacon in church, was standing to the side of those three rusty chairs he always got out for Invitation, and the church was on their feet singing and looking right at nobody but him, which always made him fiddle with his jacket buttons. You'd think he'd of got used to people looking at him after all them years of Invitation, but ever Sunday faithful, he got up and we got up and us getting up made him fiddle with his jacket buttons, and generally nobody joined church anyway, so the chair stayed empty, which made him fiddle with his buttons even more.

That Sunday Audrey went down there, Greaves got hisself all spun into action, nodding and asking, "Let the church say amen." Audrey's Great-Aunt Hesterline started stamping her feet and screaming, "Thank you, Jesus!" Danaitha didn't cry nor shout. She just bent a lazy crook in her mouth, smiled so small she might just as well have been watching a dead leaf sail down the river. She didn't have to get herself happy about Jesus no more on account of she was getting that good Army money through the mail and that was better'n anybody's revival. It like to make me spit nails.

So just when Harry Greaves got out his pencil and pad and Miss Aileen started playing the last verse of "I Do, Don't You?" and Deacon Britton got up and started folding one of them rusty chairs, just when it looked like Audrey might be the star of the show that day, I went on down there myself. When I stood up off the back pew, Britton unfolded that chair right quick, and Miss Aileen started her song over at verse one. It was the longest walk, down that church aisle. Felt like ten mile. A walk full of knowing I warn't doing right, and wondering if God might cause the roof to fall in on my head. While I was walking, the church got about two thousand times louder. Them ladies down front had came to, but two girls getting right with Jesus 'stead of one like to make them pass out all over again. All the old people got to stamping their feet and carrying on, and the air got thicker and hot-

181

ter, and my mama started crying into her dress sleeve, and Imagene and the other little girls got to laughing and making faces at me from the back pew, because by then, the sanctuary was so whipped up, wasn't nobody watching them.

When Harry Greaves came over to my chair and pushed his glasses back up his nose, his face didn't seem real at all — seem like he was made out of bean wax. "These young ladies come to be baptized in the name of the Holy Ghost," he said, but I stopped remembering my own physical body, my heart and my lungs and my hands, and then I stopped remembering there was even such a thing as the earth we was spinning on, and then I fell out.

"The Spirit just took you for a spell," my grandmama said later, but Imagene funned on me all week, falling out on the floor and then making her voice waggle up and down like the Holy Ghost. She got more and more fancy with the voice part, until Grandmama heard and came out to the kitchen to whip her with a little green switch she made Imagene go break off the hydrangea bush herself. That just made her do it silently, falling out on the couch so she wouldn't make any noise, and then holding her hands straight out for waggling her ghost fingers. I was a grown girl, going on fourteen, but something about it like to make me cry.

The next Sunday like to make me cry even harder, because Pastor made us stand right in the pool — with our feet soaking in all that cold, dirty water — for all the singing and scripture what went on before it was our turn. Mama give me a good breakfast — eggs and smoked ham and coffee — but when a little piece of scum bubbled up from somewhere and started floating across the pool like it was alive, my breakfast started roiling round in my stomach. My ministration done come early that month, and I kept wondering whether there was any blood on the back of my white dress, on account of the cold making it come faster. My hands and feet was already getting waterlogged, and it was a little bit of hell right there in that church. Audrey's mama had got her a swim cap from in town so her hair wouldn't draw up and lose its press, and Audrey was standing there looking like a spaceman, and that made me like to cry too, because it reminded me I wouldn't be sinning no more on this earth. And then, if I got through my whole lifetime without sinning, I'd end up in heaven with nothing to do but watch a bunch of sheep playing harps for the rest of eternity, with not even a game of spades to keep my mind busy. I couldn't think round how long eternity might be — forever would just never finish. It scared me just about to death. To stop the tears from running out, I made myself think about how my hair was going to curl up and be even prettier when it got wet: there's one thing I had on old Audrey.

The cold water made my cramps pound like little men was beating hammers in my stomach, and long about ten minutes I couldn't even feel my feet (that's how cold the water was), but Reverend Owington just kept on talking. "Therefore we are buried with Him by baptism into death, that like as Christ was raised up from the dead by the glory of the Father, even so we also should walk in the newness of life."

Was only the second time I seent Audrey without her big old Poindexter glasses, and I was watching the side of her head, studying on how her nose curled under and looked just like a button, when she turned to me and smiled, for a long time, like we weren't standing in all that freezing water. She was that happy to be getting saved. She believed in the whole Bible thing, I reckon, and when she reached out and held my hand, I reckon I did, too.

"For if we have been planted together in

the likeness of His death," Pastor said, "we shall also be in the likeness of His resurrection." He took Audrey by the forehead and dunked her, and while she was under, I squeezed her hand to keep her safe and felt her heartbeat jumping around her palm. She came back up looking like an egg, with the white plastic all dropped down over her eyes, which she'd popped wide open like she'd seen some miracle down there in that dirty water, and it scared me, because I started to figure that since I ain't come to be baptized out of holiness, I might see the red devil down there instead. "Knowing this," Pastor said, and he took and turnt me to such an angle that I had to let go of Audrey's hand, "that henceforth we should not serve sin."

He dunked me 'fore I could even ask him to please not, and when Audrey went under it'd felt like a long time, but when I went under I was out the water 'fore I could even see if there was more scum at the bottom of the pool. We was both shivering, and seem like the louder the singing got, the colder I felt. Mean old Miss Hesterline came with two towels, and Audrey took her swim cap off and her hair stood up in all kinds of places. It'd lost ever last bit of its style, but Audrey didn't even bother to try and pat it down some. Both our mamas was setting on the front pew just a-crying. Imagene was setting there too, but she wasn't making any faces and she wasn't even trying hard not to. She just looked sad, probably because she figured I wouldn't be serving sin with her no more.

Next day at school, 'fore the first bell, I tried to set down with Audrey on the building steps. She was so deep in her book I could only see her glasses, and her eyes behind them were some wet, like she was taking a fever. When I got down next to her she even turnt a page before she noticed I was breathing in her ear, but I didn't care what was eating her mind. I couldn't of told you then, but I believe I was trying to get some more of that good feeling she give me when she squeezed my hand.

"How does it feel, being a Christian?" she asked me.

"Well, you're one too now, aren't you?"

"I guess so," she said, all disappointed that I wouldn't have much to say on the matter.

I could of told the truth, and it weren't that I was afraid she'd tell anybody else, but more like I didn't want to upset her. *I like cookies and juice at Sunday School, and the way Miss Aileen puts a little twist on "Just a Closer Walk with Thee," and how good Dea-*

con Hines looks all dressed up in a suit, and I believe in church more'n I believe in God, I could of said, but it would of been overdoing things, like swatting a dead fly just to watch its wings fly off. She smiled at me again, just like she had the day we got baptized, and now that I knew what her eyes looked like without them glasses, it seemed like a shame she'd got herself to wearing them by reading all them books.

"I feel . . ." she started, and her eyes swam around all big behind her glasses. "I feel different inside. Like I got all this still and quiet in my head."

Well, I reckon she did feel special, on account of she'd probably had a big day of it that Sunday. I suppose her granddaddy had fixed her a big fish dinner after church, and her mama maybe give her another new dress, and she maybe gone down to the Colored store to take a long-distance call all the way from Texas. But there was two of us girls in my family, and things was never that proper in our house, and an hour after I got baptized, I was scraping grease out the pork chop pan while I boiled the water for washing. "Maybe you heard the Lord's voice a little louder'n I did," I told her.

"Jesus has no favorites," she said back, and she closed the book she was reading,

187

which had *Cane* written on the front in fancy gold letters.

She was trying to make me put some work into getting that special feeling back. "Bye, Sister Christian," I told her. I stood up and brushed the dirt off my dress. "Tell your nose to have a good time in that book."

LACKLAND

Meantime, down in Lackland, Lindell was telling that story reel how it seemed like he was calling on the Lord ever five minutes. It was his first time not sleeping under his daddy's roof, and those first few nights in the Army's hard bed, he actually cried. Seem like all the kitchen knew how to do was bread and gravy, and Lindell watched the rest of the soldiers gobble it on down, but the gravy looked too mysterious for him to even sniff it. So he just ate bread, which stopped up his bowels. The Army issue socks bothered his feet something terrible, and he'd be practicing how to wrestle the enemy to the ground when he'd have to duck away from the man he was fighting to itch his foot. He wrote home in all them letters how he was about ready to audition for the Army band; how he done learnt how to set out in the desert with no water, just like Jesus; how the sky over Texas was bigger and oranger and more mindful of the good Lord than the sky in Mt. Sterling. He wrote Danaitha that he was a better man and he wrote Audrey that his belly was hard as two tree trunks, wrote them that he might be stationed in Omaha or even in France, that they might could come live with him overseas and eat little paper-thin pancakes with sugar sprinkled on top. But he didn't believe one smear of it, he told that reel. Was a piano down in the mess hall, but Lindell was too scared of his training instructor to go over and play it.

'Stead of taking a bath in the water Danaitha boiled on Saturday nights, he had to take showers under cold Lackland water, straddling his poor itchy feet over a rusty drain in the middle of the concrete floor. He always felt the other forty-nine soldiers in the showers with him was laughing at his shrinking balls, even when they wasn't, and the soap the army handed out never really rinsed off, so his feet itched even more powerful. By the time he finally got called up to Mississippi, he done figured out a way to wash his entire body in ninety seconds so he'd have another ninety just to rinse his feet. Lindell'd left Mt. Sterling trying to move hisself to higher ground, but he said that by the time he finished the rounds ever day, he reckoned he warn't the magical Negro he'd thought he was. At night, when he laid in the pitch-black barracks and listened to the boy in the top bunk worm his hips around and spoon out loud through his soup of dreams, Lindell thought he might oughta cut his own feet clean off.

After all he been through in Lackland, he felt like a king when he got on the bus to Biloxi. They'd just built a new barracks and mess hall, and put fancy toys in their electric labs that he couldn't wait to get his hands on. He spent one long night on the bus not asleep but looking out the window at the flattest land he ever seen. No tall trees to speak of — just lone bushes standing like simpletons under the power of the moon. Round midnight, the bus ran longside a train, and on the sides of the boxcars, his mind put movies of all that marching he'd done. It'd started ever morning at four thirty, when the T.I. blew his whistle, and it hadn't ended till ten o'clock at night, when all them soldiers marched theyselves off to the barracks and over the cliffs of hard sleep. They marched to the undersides of jet planes and they marched to the hot gymnasium for push-ups, and then they marched to a clearing where they got down on their bellies and crawled through the mud like gators. It'd got so even when they was supposed to be walking normally, Lindell felt an urge down in his spine to march. Said it made him appreciate Mt. Sterling and the feeling of going nowhere, on account of he ain't never been so tired in his life as he was trying to get somewhere. He was like Jonah, he reckoned — he done got out the whale's belly, but he was all covered in spit. The force promised less marching in Biloxi, and more time off base at night. They promised shorter mess lines, too, though they ain't promised better food. And they ain't promised not one thing about the White peoples of Biloxi, Mississippi.

Lindell got hisself a right smart interduction to them his first day on Keesler, after he woke hisself up with the birds to go see the ocean. He'd read about the sea in books, so naturally he wanted to see if it was like they said. The sky over Texas had grown his heart right up, with ever cloud what floated by telling him he needed to go pretty places and do front-page things. And there were the words *Son, you could be President* bumping around in his head, even if he warn't paying them much never-mind. Sims'd told him he was right smart to think of making a doctor, but he also promised to send a note up the chain about Lindell trying for Army band. Either way, Lindell would put hisself in a bigger life than any other Colored man in Mt. Sterling'd ever let hisself imagine. Seeing the ocean would be just the first of it.

He stretched on his airman's first class uniform and saluted as he walked out the gates of the base and down Irish Hill Drive, and when I heard him saying it into the microphone, I could just see him smiling into the air around him, remembering. It was so early in the morning, warn't even no cars about, he said, and all he could hear was the ocean. He said the breeze blew right through the gathered legs of his new pants, but it warn't the kind of cold that would upset a body — it was a soft, warm wind like you'd never catch in Mt. Sterling. He'd seen drawings of the sea in his books but he'd never seen it in photographs, and now he still couldn't see the water for all the houses up and down the boulevard, but he could smell how clean it was in the air, how the ocean done took all the dirt of Mississippi far out to sea and left it. Said he smelt a nothing in the air like he never smelt in Mt. Sterling: everthing the ocean'd washed up to shore, it done already cleaned the night before in its fearsome bowels. When the sun started to make light and Lindell looked at his reflection in the window of a closed thrift shop, he stood up a little straighter and threw his arms out in front of him and imagined hisself leading an orchestra. He could of made his right several times, but the streets was narrow, and anyway he could hear the ocean getting closer, which meant when he finally did make his turn, he'd be right up on it.

He got hisself to St. Francis Street, which was so wide he knew he couldn't walk all the way cross 'thout seeing the ocean, so he closed his eyes.

"Might oughta watch where you going, boy."

Lindell said he looked, and found hisself standing not two feet in front of a couple of farmers. He knew they was farmers on account of the sun done burnt their necks so red. Their pants was brown, but you could see how they'd been white in some season previous, and sweat had got their collars stiffer'n any woman's starch.

"Where you think you going?" asked the short one. He chewed his tobacco like a cud.

"I'm on my way to the beach, if you'll excuse me."

They both laughed, and Lindell said he figured by the lack of scratch in their voices that the wrinkles around their eyes wasn't speaking to their true ages — they was young, maybe even young as he was. The tall one wasn't chewing, but he spit tobacco juice anyway, in the sand right next to Lindell's shoe. "Naw you ain't. You ain't a bit more going down to that there beach'n the man in the moon."

"Must be one of them air monkeys from up North," said the short one. He wasn't smiling anymore, and now he was chewing so hard his nose moved with the force of it. "He don't know we don't *let* niggers on our beach."

"You best get your black ass to base," said the tall one.

The short one winked without smiling and spat again, this time right on Lindell's shoe. They walked on, but Lindell done forgot right then how to move. He stood in the middle of the street so long that a city bus had to slow down, honk, and drive around him — so still that a man in a cotton truck drove a little bit on the sidewalk so as not to hit him. For long about an hour, Lindell said, he just plain couldn't remember how to move. He stood in the middle of St. Francis Street with the waves crashing not a hundred feet from where he was standing, and he heard men shouting at each other while they was searching through the waves

195

for oysters. But Lindell wouldn't look. Matter fact he'd never see the ocean, long as he lived. Turnt out he walked down that street ever weekend on his way to Joe's Oyster House, and he could of just turnt his head a little to the right and seen all that great deep water, but he knew it would of made him just as mad to look as it made him not to. He'd lie in all his letters home, tell Danaitha the ocean was even bigger'n the sky he'd seen over Texas, but the picture he'd have in his head was from a program he saw on the television.

The Air Force didn't apologize none for the situation, but they did warn him, after the fact, because he got back to base that first day just in time for a special briefing for Negro airmen. It was seven of them, standing out in the hot sun in a straight line, with the sergeant yelling at them through a megaphone like they was a hunderd. They wasn't 'llowed to set foot on the beach, Sarge said, and they wasn't supposed to set down in Whites-only establishments. Sarge yelled out through that megaphone like he was being cut with an ice pick: they was not to be seen riding in a car with a White airman. His voice sounded specially angry right then, and Lindell said he knew it wasn't your regular Army angriness, but he couldn't decide whether Sarge hated the Negroes standing in front of him or the rules the White peoples of Biloxi had made to keep them in their place. Lindell looked out the corner of his eye at the six other brothers to see if they was understanding the situation like he was, and sure enough he saw mouths set in "I'll be damned," eyebrows crooked in "What've I gotten myself into?" Seven hundred fifty miles south of Kentucky, and Lindell was already in enemy territory. There was rules of engagement the Army didn't even know about. Sarge yelled out that the Negro airmen was to ride on the back of the Biloxi buses, and that's when Lindell fixed it in his head he warn't going to be riding on any city buses.

And his voice was different while he told the rest of it. He said he stepped out for fried okra on Saturdays because he could walk right down Columbus Street to Joe's Restaurant, but outside of that, he didn't leave base. He stayed in the rec room and played the two pinball games — KnockOut and Skyway — and he read ever crazy story he could get his hands on through the by-mail book club. He started out with all four books by Claude McKay, and then he found hisself getting more and more peculiar in his appetites, ordering books about monks and priests and even nuns. The light in the rec room was none bright, and he missed the Lexington Public Library with its lamp at every desk, but he figured Negroes warn't 'llowed nowhere near the Biloxi one.

He made hisself quite a few friends, and they never stopped asking him to go see a football game at Our Mother of Sorrows. They just about begged him to get on the bus and go out dancing. "You some kinda queer?" they teased him to his face. "Weird, anyway," they said when they thought he warn't hearing them. But he didn't never go into town with 'em, not even on the Fourth of July. It got to where he done read all the books about Irish priests and moved on to the American ones. Nobody could beat him at pinball anymore, and the other soldiers liked to just stand by and watch him spin those little wood flippers, his hands rolling from the side of the machine to the front about as fast as they churned over each other on his piano back home. It was other times, after their long nights of carousing the Colored part of town, they'd find him setting in the room's maroon reclining chair rereading *The Cardinal,* and they'd sit around on the couch and whisper about the thighs of girls they'd met while they watched him speed-read. He was special and un-reachable and plenty of fun to watch, Lindell figured — like a dog they could pet when they got back to base.

It was prostitutes what walked theirselves right outside the base at night there on Irish Hill Drive, but apart from Joe's Restaurant, Lindell said he didn't even fancy going that far. For love, he took to playing the Lyric's black baby grand in his dreams, so much so that the wood floor next to his bed began to sink under the dream piano's weight. At inspection, when he stood next to Lindell's bed, Sarge kept saying he felt shorter than usual. Said he never did understand why.

DETAIL

Grandmama ain't give away if she found out about Ralph coming over to the house when she wasn't in it. But she been looking at me right dirty ever since, like she knows everthing swimming around in my head from the beginning to the end, how I want to screw with Ralph over and over and over again until he falls in love with me; how I see other boys, and grown men even, and wonder if they'd feel any different inside me than Ralph did. Maybe they'd move different while they're doing it, or make more noise when they're done. Maybe after, they'd love me. Grandmama never has told if she knows, but she's been dropping Alka Seltzers ever morning, like something's bothering her so bad she has to fizz it away.

School's out for the summer and the kitchen's all mine this morning on account of Imagene still sleeping, and I'm going to set here and think while the dew melts off the new flowers and the world gets hot. I done collected my mind in the months since Daddy killed Mama. Ain't like some big thing happened — God did not appear to me in the bottom of my soda pop and tell me to cut it out. It's just that when I heard Lindell on them tapes, following his dreams off to nowhere, and then I subtracted the difference between what me and Grandmama had for Imagene's school shoes and what they was actually going to cost, well, when I thought on all that, being crazy just did not seem profitable. I pour orange juice, and an ant floats up with the juice to meet me, but then here Grandmama comes looking for her Alka Seltzer and I know she'd cuss me for pouring good juice down the drain, so I just sip around that ant and watch her. She never has been a big talker in the morning, so it seems natural not to say nothing, but when I don't, she gives me one of them foul looks. "Well, good morning to you too," she says.

"Morning, Grandmama."

"You going to fix that thing today?"

She means the blender she got on layaway from Taylor's. She ain't known a thing about blending — she just bought it on account of Siddie Sims got one, and she sure ain't going to let low-down Siddie Sims with four children by four different men have anything over on her. It's a manual what goes with the blender but Grandmama don't read long words, so the blender been setting there with its innards on the counter all week since it came home. We moved the radio to the window to make room while we put it together, but that just means we ain't reached up there to turn the radio on for all this time, and yet we still ain't got no chopped-up food out the deal.

"Yes'm. I'll read the manual and assemble it."

She drops her tablets in the water, and they sink to the bottom even as their little bubbles float to the top, and when she leaves out the kitchen I bring her glass to my ear to hear the fizz up close. It's little bubbles hitting the side of my face, and that phony lemon smell is coming so powerful I can just imagine little Speedy singing at me. *Plop, plop, fizz, fizz:* I hope I never turn into my grandmama. "Here, Grandmama," I tell her, when she comes back in the kitchen with her thin spring jacket on. "I shook it up a little so the tablets'd break faster."

"You ain't supposed to shake that," she says, taking the glass, and her eyes flash blacker behind her glasses. "They break up when they want to. It's medicine, girl. Medicine."

She drinks it down faster'n you'd believe is good for her, and then she packs some Kleenex into her handbag and leaves for Dr. Stone's house, and when I'm sure she's a good piece down the street, I reach back into that window and turn on the radio. Jimmy Giuffre's tooting out "Iowa Stubborn," and I turn it so loud that it powers out the sound of the screen door slamming against the doorframe, so loud that the hearing it powers out anything else I might feel of the world, and I'm floating down Grandmama's steps 'stead of walking. I lay out in the grass with that manual and I ain't been there three minutes when here come Audrey running out Grandpap Martin's door to lay in the grass with me. "You going to Lexington with Sylvia, too?" she asks me.

"No."

"Oh." Back when we was both flat-chested, we used to lay on our bellies and close our eyes into the cool ground under our faces, but now we both have to lay on our sides with our trussed-up bosoms aimed sideways and our arms cocked under our heads, so she's facing me when she asks why I ain't going. "Sounds like it'll be right fun, anyway," she says.

"I don't even know what you're talking about. Sylvia ain't asked me nowhere."

"Oh," she says again, and we listen to the radio a little bit longer, a song what sounds like Paul Evans singing it but I ain't never heard the music before, and then Audrey gets up and brushes off her dress. "Bye," she says, and runs back across the street.

I wait and wait for Sylvia to ask me, but she don't say a thing about it. I even treat her to a milk shake at the drug store in the afternoon, and then on Thursday she asks me over to her house to watch *The Danny Thomas Show,* but I don't get one word out of her about fun, or Audrey, or Lexington.

I don't get one word of it until the next week, when I hear it from Hannah Cosby, that Sylvia took Audrey to one of her Alpha Kappa Alpha Cotillion dances. "Said you wouldn't even believe how splendid it was," Hannah tells me, when I see her at the Colored store, and she tells me how Audrey said the AKA ladies decorated the Lyric with fancy streamers and shimmery strings up in the rafters, and how the Colored girls in Lexington know how to pick up the right fork for their beef, and how to set with their ankles crossed for a group photograph, and how to curtsy so low their dresses sweep the floor. I'm thinking a hilltop blackberry like

Audrey couldn't of made out too well up there, but then I hear it from Ruth Simmons, how Audrey's mama bought her a new pair of Capezios and a purple dress with gossamer over the skirt, and how it all must've worked, because old Poindexter took off her glasses like she was some sort of swan and danced with four different boys that night.

Well, I ain't asking her nor Sylvia not one thing about the whole business. Won't give them the pleasure. And anyway Tyrone Boyd done invited me to go see *Porgy and Bess,* and before I know it I'ma be over in his mama and daddy's bedroom, testing out how he sounds and how he feels when he's doing it, and won't neither one of them know a thing about *that.* And I got something over Audrey, something she won't even know, because I ain't never going to let her hear her daddy on them story reels. I been thinking on calling her over to give a listen, get her all excited about the sound of a ghost, but now I figure she can just set over there and dream fancy with Sylvia French. Too bad, 'cause she won't never know how her daddy's story really ended.

Lindell told it all to that recorder, the part we all knew already, and I do remember it very clearly, how Grandpap Martin was walking so tall around town at the time on account of his son done stood up to some muckety-muck down in Mississippi and lived to tell about it. Well, the way Lindell told it, it was a senator by the name of John Stennis who came to base, telling them servicemen about how "the United States will put a man on the moon before the God-abiding state of Mississippi integrates Nigras and Whites outside the walls of this base."

When he wrote home to his daddy, Lindell wouldn't be able to tell him what made him get up by hisself in the middle of that senator's speech and march back to the barracks in 115-degree heat, but he told that reel recorder. Said his sergeant trailed his heels the whole ways, wiping his bald head with his cap and hollering for "a damn good explanation," and Lindell could've told him he was tired of watching all them cityboy airmen fall out like fleas in the heat, or that the lack of sex in his life done finally made him crazy, or even something a little like the truth — that his daddy'd always told him it was better to die on your feet than live on your knees. But Lindell told that tape the true nitty-gritty — Senator John C. Stennis'd just plain made him mad.

"My father taught me to play by ear

because the notes were no count," Lindell said, "and without a piano to play, I'd begun to think perhaps my father was wrong, because at night the notes were all that came back to me. I'd dream up an entire six-part quadrille and see every accidental. Well, just then in that grandstand listening to the senator, the notes left me, and I reckoned my daddy must have been right — the important things in life get played by ear." He said he ain't even had to think about marching back to barracks.

It was June 28, and a war'd been going on in Korea for three days, and Lindell'd tell that tape he figured getting sent off to it all had to do with Senator John C. Stennis, and I do remember Grandpap Martin, in the short time between Lindell's letter and the Army's sad telegram, walking round a little bigger, a little stronger in his knock-knees, even telling the White druggist downtown to please get his heart pill order right. I remember Audrey telling me later that her daddy never loved her, that he went over there and died on account of he was so in love with his pride that he forgot he had a little girl. And listening to that tape, I get right sad myself, on account of I done spent eight years thinking Lindell was some Negro what flew away from here, and it turns out once he got where he was going, he got his wings clipped just like anybody else. Lindell got them papers to transfer to a deploying unit, and he told the tape that after feeling some afraid he reminded hisself how he walked out on that speech, and he got to feeling like the biggest man at Keesler. And that was the end of Lindell's voice, but here it turns out that ain't even half the story.

Audrey told me, just like Sims'd told her mama — back in Lexington, when he got the Army's telegram, Sims had actually fainted. He'd done a little work on Lindell's case, he had, and it turnt out the Army radio service was putting *Jubilee!* back on the air and they needed a piano player, and it was a letter saying so chasing Lindell all around the country. The letter'd get to Korea, but too late, and Lindell'd never know why he went off to war without even the regular week off to go see his family.

Now it was a man by the name of Paul Sacks, what came down to Mt. Sterling from Cleveland one day not long after Danaitha got her telegram. Said he reckoned he was the last person who seent Lindell alive, said he wanted to share Lindell's last thoughts. He'd been in the unit all the way from Keesler, and he said Lindell told him it was a minute or two, when they was all

208

about to get on that transport plane to Kadena, he thought he might jump off and run. Desert, he kept saying. Go AWOL. Even when they stopped to refuel at Pearl Harbor, Paul Sacks could see Lindell looking round at doors, maybe thinking he might hide in the men's room until the plane gassed up and left, make his way through the Hawaiian jungle and get hisself a little hut with a hula dancer inside peeling pineapples. He ain't seen his babygirl 'fore he left, he done told them over and over, and he wanted to just stop everthing and get on a boat back to the mainland. He wondered if God was trying to tell him something by him not having seen his baby girl: either he'd make it for sure, or he for sure wouldn't. Either way, he said he wouldn't let God beat him with signs — he needed to get off that big jet plane and go home to his Audrey, spoonfeed her oatmeal and tuck her into bed just one last time. But when he smelled the gas burning off the engine, and he looked down the tarmac at the new friends he'd made, boys as young and silly and scared as he was, he told Paul Sacks he knew he wouldn't let the rest of the company down. "He was a man like any other man," Paul Sacks told Danaitha and Audrey, "and I guess he loved being a man more'n he loved anything else."

And so he found hisself not even one day later, dying in Kunsan, his head in Paul Sacks's hot lap, his burned skin flaking up and peeling off his meat like he was an onion. He still ain't seen the ocean, he told Paul Sacks, on account of he'd kept his eyes closed getting on the transport, and while he was laying there dying, another bomb blew up, right across the airfield from him and Paul, and he should've screamed but he didn't. Fire was everwhere, eating up the high grass, crawling up the trees, rolling across the sky, but when Paul asked him Lindell said he wasn't even hurting. And not afraid of what might happen next, either. More'n anything, he said, he was surprised. Surprised his life wasn't flashing backwards before his eyes, but going around in circles in his ears. Maybe it was because his ears was so big that they was how he'd lived all of his life, but Lindell said he was hearing everthing, from the coughing fit his mama had right before she died to Audrey's first words ("dog dog") to the very last chord he'd played on his daddy's piano. He heard the *clack clack clack* of a little monkey on a string he got for his sixth Christmas, and he heard the water dripping in his mama's bedroom ceiling while he held her

210

hands and cried. He heard the terrible empty crash of the bomb that threw him eight feet in the air, and he heard Danaitha's low laugh when he slid off her stockings. He heard the taps on the new shoes he got when he started high school and he heard his mama's heart beating while he sat in her belly and sucked his toe.

It all went round and round, he was telling Paul, in no order a tall, until finally something did come to his eyes, and the fire all round him seemed to be dying out in a driving rain but nothing got dimmer. 'Stead, things got brighter, he said, and he was seeing minutes and hours he'd never see, Negro men and women wading in the beach at Biloxi while White men swung tire chains. The Negroes singing, their children flinching, photographers from up North snapping pictures, all them Negroes looking pleased to be beat. And living — *living, living* — on their feet. Said he saw Danaitha drinking whiskey over his remains and he saw his babygirl running into the sunflowers, and then he said everthing did get brighter and brighter, until the light was so bright it hurt to look at his babygirl's face.

"He was whispering by then," Paul Sacks told them, "and I could barely decide what he was saying, but he said he did look. He said he looked right into the middle of Audrey's pretty brown eyes until the light didn't hurt him no more, and then he said he felt his nose against her smooth little gumdrop nose and saw the corners of her eyes turn up in smiling."

" 'Mother's going to be so angry with us,' " she was saying. Lindell took a shallow breath and said his babygirl had fallen down in the field of blackberries, and her white dress was stained blue at the knees.

"Don't matter, babygirl," Lindell said, and Paul Sacks said he eased his head off'n his lap so he could run hisself into the retreat. "Don't matter one bit," Lindell kept whispering. "Turns out almost nothing does."

Paul leaned over for one last listen before running.

"I love you too, babygirl," Lindell was whispering. "More'n anything. Forever and ever."

■ ■ ■ ■

PART THREE:
AUDREY

■ ■ ■ ■

Mr. Barbour

Mother received the telegram on the fifth of July, but on the third, I woke up tasting blackberries. Fat, knobby, indigo blackberries, leaking juice so tart they made me get out of bed and check in the mirror that my tongue wasn't blue. I dressed and ran up the mountain to our secret hill, the one where Daddy had found the blackberry patch. I picked enough to fill both skirt pockets: Mother and Grandpap and I ate blackberries with cream all day on the Fourth, and I was baking a cobbler when Mr. Sims knocked on the door. Mother screamed. She ripped the buttons off her blouse.

"My father," I told Sergeant Sims, as I stepped in front of her to the door, "isn't dead. He's coming back to pick blackberries."

Grandpap came crying with his eyes closed, a wet cloth for Mother's face draped over his arm, but I returned to the kitchen and finished sugaring my crust. Mother stayed between her bedsheets for the two weeks of waiting for his body, but I kept riding my bicycle to the Colored store for Coca-Cola and reading my Langston Hughes at the kitchen table through lunchtime, and I didn't believe Daddy was dead until the Army shipped his teeth. Some kind of ignorant, childish grief, folks thought, but I just knew there would be another day on the hill — that's all. When Mr. Pinchback let me hold the box full of Daddy's teeth, when that box weighed nothing and rattled hollow, then all the pain of a lifetime came crushing down upon me like a mountain. It's pinned me down ever since.

Before my father died, Mother hadn't believed in dressing to blend into the shadows. She'd never owned a simple black dress, and since she was abed with misery all those weeks after she got the telegram, it fell to me to go to Taylor's and buy a mourning dress in a ladies' size four. The first one on the rack had a butterfly collar. Too modern, all wrong for someone with Mother's constitution, but the White saleslady with no other customers smiled too lazily at me, and the girl working the register frowned with too much energy, and I got nervous and paid for it. Mother didn't even open the bag until the day of the funeral, and even then she dressed without protesting the collar. But it was the last time she dressed easily, because after Daddy's funeral, she stopped being able to decide on a simple thing like which clothes to wear. She accidentally set the mantel clock for two minutes late and then decided she liked it that way. If those two minutes hadn't yet happened, she told me, then perhaps the month preceding it hadn't, either. She was exactly two minutes late everywhere she went, and she often smelled of bourbon when she arrived, and if you watched closely as she walked down the street, you'd see how much slower was her gait. Sometimes, she cried as she walked. But the doctors at the city clinic kept her on out of sympathy, and Miss Ora Ray's daughter gave her night ironing to make up for our household's lost income, and Mother started drinking Early Times as if it had been prescribed. She'd always been a beautiful woman, my mother, but she swept the porch and canned the tomatoes and kept her business so well, she didn't appear to need a new man to take care of it for her. Folks around here thought she was too strong to make room for a man, so she didn't find one until Mr. Barbour

217

decided he was even stronger than she was.

He's not stronger than me. He can't even pronounce the word "piano" properly. "Stop banging on that *pinetta*," he'd say when I was still under his roof. "People are trying to think." He makes Mother open every piece of mail that comes to the house, and I wonder if he can even read. He thinks Mother is standing in the garden enjoying his conversation, when really, she's standing there waiting for my daddy to come back from Korea and take her dancing. Her mouth is moving, launching words she thinks Mr. Barbour will like, stringing phrases along so that they sound like some kind of future for them both, but all the while she's talking, her hands are getting ever stronger with bringing my father back. She's cross-breeding and cultivating and tending her blooms to grow a fragrance that will reach him wherever he is. Mr. Barbour thinks my mother is sitting on the sofa enjoying the feel of his hand on her thigh as they listen to *Backstage Wife* on the radio, but all the time they're listening, Mother is watching out the window for Daddy. She's listening to the radio for the sound of crackling as she remembers it coming out of my father's little 1937 Magnavox, listening for my father to laugh even outside of the right places. Where my daddy was an ocean, Mr. Barbour is a raindrop. Still, I thank God for him, because he's the one who pushed me out of town.

Mt. Sterling was growing tinier and tinier, even if nobody else could see it shrinking, and I'd made up my mind to leave before it winnowed away to nothing. But lightning has to strike ground before it can burn up the sky, and that little town loaded me down with a lot more misery before it would let me go. First, my soul began to hollow, until it emptied so fully that you could knock on my back and hear an echo. Missing Daddy was only half of it: the other half was that God left me, eventually, with nobody. Grandpap had always thought his son was the very axis on which the world spun, and Daddy's death only made him believe it that much more. After we got the telegram, Grandpap searched in vain for a watch identical to one he'd lost when Daddy first left for the Air Force, a silver Hamilton with a tessellated weave engraved on the back where Grandpap might look and find his happy memories. Grandpap took out a duster each morning and cleaned the three gilded frames that held Daddy frozen in time — one around a painting of Daddy as a little boy in knickers, one around a *Herald*

Leader photo from the 1936 basketball season, and one around a shot of my parents in front of the house that Dr. French had taken to christen his new camera. To keep the moths out, Grandpap folded and refolded Daddy's shirts, as if Daddy were going to come back to life and need to wear them. Of course dusting and folding wasn't living: Grandpap just wasn't there anymore. He waded through his days patting indigestion back down into his gullet and misting his dry eyes with a spray bottle. Watching the checkers in my hand without noticing the girl moving them down the board.

My mother had cleaved tight to my father since the day she met him, and for some time after he died, she did nothing and said nothing, and I wondered if she might discover me. She didn't. She found Early Times down at the Tin Cup, and then she found Mr. Barbour at a dance over in Hope. God galled me. I stopped praying. Stopped reading my grandmama's leather-bound Bible, and left the ribbon marking my place in the book of Ruth. I still attended services, because the A.M.E. paid me fifty cents a Sunday for playing, but I didn't believe a word that dropped out of Reverend Graves's mouth. When the old ladies down front got happy, I felt sorry for them. The usher would hand me my communion wafer, and I'd slide it between the sixth C and D on the piano.

Then, as if to show me how much power He actually had, God took away Pookie, who had been as close to me as my own brown skin. She was falling in love with Ralph, and I had nothing, not anyone or anything. Just a bunch of books I'd already read. I had music, but it felt formless. I didn't know enough yet to love it the most.

The Saturday before the Sunday our church went visiting in Versailles, Mr. Barbour drove up to the house and interrupted my porch reading. He was slouched on the wheel in arrogance, and his cap rode low over his eyes. "Your mama misses you," he said. He had a fresh cut to his hair and mustache, but he looked every bit as foul as I remembered. "Come on out to the house and have dinner, what say? I'll ride you back to town in the morning."

Grandpap asked, "Let's say she wants to come back this very night. You going to carry her back?"

Surprise sat Mr. Barbour straight up behind the steering wheel, because he hadn't seen Grandpap sitting behind the screen door.

"Let's say Audrey wants to come back

home after dinner, even. You going to carry her on back?"

"Yes sir. I will."

"All right, then. Audrey, do you want to go with the gentleman?"

I didn't. But I hadn't received a new book in the mail for two weeks, and I'd been sitting on the porch rereading the first six chapters of *Quicksand,* letting Grandpap win at checkers, listening to the same Dinah Washington song on the radio four times a day. "Sure," I said. "I'll go."

Mother was surprised to see me walk through her front door, even if she did hand me a bowl of cornmeal and put me straight to work. After dinner, she insisted on washing my hair, and then she pressed it and marcelled curls for the first time all year. "Got a long head, girl," she said, as she clicked the bumpers from one clip of hair to the other. "Such a long head." She hooted laughter over the kicking furnace. It was August, and starting to get cold in the night. "I'd forgotten how long your head is. Just like your daddy's. Long as a peanut."

She was seven months gone, and her body had grown soft and enormous, as if it were holding a large, gassy planet instead of a small, thin-limbed baby. She sliced parts down my scalp to the nape of my neck, and when she bent me over to do the crown of my head, her belly was so close that its warmth pressed against my face. "Hear tell Ralph gave Pookie a promise ring," she said.

"Where'd you hear something like that?"

"Mr. Barnett. Said Miss Myrtle told him."

"Well, there's a piece a news. I wouldn't know nothing about it."

Mother dipped the bumpers into the lard, then brought them out and cooled them in the hair-stained towel. "Something happen 'tween you and Pookie?" she asked. "Ain't like y'all not to be speaking." She rubbed grease onto my scalp, more gently than she had before.

"I'm just busy, Mother. I'm more serious about life than she is."

"You think?" she asked, but it wasn't a question. She took the back of my neck in her hands and pressed my whole face to her belly, and my throat started to ache with wanting to cry. "You and Pookie are too much alike to ever, ever lose each other. You both just got to do some growing up for a minute." She rubbed my neck with the tips of her fingers. From the living room, Nina Simone sang "I Loves You Porgy." Mother asked, "What you so busy with you can't keep friends?"

"Me and Mr. Baldwin Upright," I said,

getting myself out from under her fingers. "Practicing. For when I get out of this no-horse town."

"Just like your old daddy," she said, in a manner that suggested she'd found a way to let him become a simple nodule of her memory. She thumped the comb against the side she needed to part, then marcelled my hair all the way down to the roots, like I was never able to do by myself. I still needed her, but I didn't want to. "Why don't you stay the night with us? Jonas'll get you back in time to leave with the church, if that's what you're worried about."

"Nope. Got nowhere to sleep. You put my bed in the barn. Or don't you remember?"

"Got a nice new sofa down there, softer than that bed ever was. Your daddy got that bed on credit at Taylor's. It was springs poking through the mattress 'fore he'd even paid it off."

"Yet and still, it was my bed."

She thumped me again with the comb and finished my hair so we could go sit down in the living room with Mr. Barbour and listen to the news from out of Lexington. Senator McCarthy's voice echoed off the walls: *Point of Order!* He talked through his nose at cool old Joseph Welch, and I knew that every Communist in our country could feel his heart clenching. Barry Bingham, the Louisville millionaire, had been visited by Lee Remick the actress. *Miss Remick and I had a fine time at the Downs,* he told the radio announcer, *and the lady certainly does know how to pick a horse! All of Louisville was honored by her presence.*

"Whyn't you come on and stay the night?" Mother asked again, but already, she was sitting on the sofa holding Mr. Barbour's hand.

Mr. Barbour was sunk in the boxing scores. He picked his nose with his free hand and frowned.

"I'm ready for you to carry me back," I said to him, but his mind stayed wherever it was: he might just as well have been flying across the sea. "I'm ready for you to carry me back," I said louder and he made a big show of rising to his height and drawing his pant legs up at the knees before he stood. I caught a look on Mother's face, a quick scrunching of the bridge of her nose that I'd seen two thousand times when she was about to take a swig of whiskey, and I had to look away because I didn't want to read her face further.

Mr. Barbour made all kinds of noise putting on his coat, groaning as though his sleeves were biting his arms. "Alrighty

225

then," he said, and I got up and left my mother sitting on her brand-new cherry-legged sofa. On the way to town, Mr. Barbour made certain to swing his 210 through every rut in the county. He turned his radio to the worst station, and we drove through the four paved blocks of town listening to "Buttons and Bows." WLEX. Soulless treble. Simple manna. Mr. Barbour even had the nerve to sing along. "Don't be a stranger," he said when he drove up in front of Grandpap's house. "When you think you might be out our way next?"

"When my mama's a widow again," I said, and I got out and slammed his car door hard enough for him to yell *Hey!* I ran up Grandpap's porch steps and tried to put my key in the lock but it kept missing. The moon was new, and it was so dark out that I could see the sparks fly off the metal.

"Your daddy's dead," Mr. Barbour yelled out his car window. "Better get used to it." He backed up and turned his headlights onto the porch so I could fit my key. If he'd crashed himself into a tree on the way home, I wouldn't have been happier.

The radio had lulled Grandpap to sleep, and when I finally got in the door and out of the dark, I found him stretched across the couch, his feet hanging over the armrest, the extra space in his socks pinched up past the toe. Frank Sinatra singing love into his dreams. I threw a quilt over him and tipped across the blue braided rug, down the hall, and into my bed. The night was cool with coming autumn — a perfect night for rest — but when at last I lay down, I found that a ball of Mother's corn bread had lodged itself at the gate to my stomach. I didn't want her, but she was with me.

PUFFER

I'd been afraid that night, wondering if I'd live the rest of my life and die in the hills of Mt. Sterling. Watching Grandpap's complex sorrows ferment into simple bitterness, watching Pookie and Ralph chase each other into the confines of everlasting love, watching Mr. Barbour speed by me in his 210. Not even a month later, I wonder that each New York day isn't my entire life. I hadn't known how much I hadn't known; I hadn't fathomed not even a quarter of the depth of my ignorance. I'd never realized that Queen Street isn't a street at all but a cowpath of baked mud, a corridor past the waving pickaninnies, through the west part of town to the shops in Lexington. One turn of the calendar page, and I'm living in a basement apartment in a strong brick building on a street of solid asphalt. A world lives beneath my feet, even — water rushes by just under manhole covers, and passing subway trains throw skirt-lifting breezes from metal grates in the sidewalk. Rats peep out of the corner rain traps, unafraid, the bones of their inner ears absorbing the thrumming march of the city's pedestrian army.

Every day I've lived here, the same man has stood on the corner in his blue bowler collecting the numbers. He's as regular a part of my days as Hiram Loving once was, ringing his bicycle bell as I waved, but here in Harlem, I'd just as soon wave to a stranger as saw off my own hand. People rush by the numbers man, for the most part, in such great hurries they threaten to topple him, and if a beautiful woman brushes his coat, he'll sweep himself up in her wake and follow, silently, as though he means to have her. When she steps on a motor bus he'll stop at the apple seller, realizing, and watch her as she takes her seat and the bus lurches forward. His jolly eyes will follow her bus down its route, but his sad fish lips will draw his mustache down to their corners, because Lenox and 123rd is, after all, his post, and he cannot follow her. I hadn't known that desire can have such practical limitations, that love can so willingly accept defeat at the hands of money.

I hadn't known that our stores in Mt.

Sterling were general mercantile, that there exist markets solely for the sale of fruit, or seafood, or lamb. On the ground floor of my building, women pay the Lenox Avenue Fish Shop for their lobsters, string them up by their tails, and carry them onto a city bus. During this year's three days of Indian summer, brine-filled flies gave chase and mated in my window. I hadn't known they actually mount each other, like cattle. On the third, topmost floor of my building, a Negro woman lives with a White man and their child, a beautiful little cinnamon-colored girl with big brown eyes and dark curls that brush her shoulders. Their mailbox is marked "Mr. and Mrs. Donald Green," so it seems they are married, and yet when they walk down the street together — their arms linked, their shoulders touching, their little girl tottering in front of them — no one jeers or even stares. Mr. Green's father, a tall man with stately, metallic gray hair, comes to visit, and twirls his beautiful, smiling, cinnamon granddaughter in the street before they stop in the drug store for soda. Sometimes I hear Mr. and Mrs. Green in the stairwell as they argue; her soprano smacks up against his basso profundo, but he never calls her nigger. After they argue, he'll bring home the groceries in two big sacks like nothing has happened, and they are still together, this White man with his sandy red hair and this Negro woman dark as molasses. I hadn't known such a thing was possible.

I know things I cannot stand to know, like how dirtied the floor of a subway platform becomes after a rain, and how that filthy, spit-splattered floor can come back to me in the night and make me count 512 over and over again until sleep comes. A roach on my wall, fiddling its one leg like a bow against another, can seem to stare into my morning tea. Men can wander the streets crazy and drugged with no family to keep them, and even low as they are there are men much lower, men with employment and wives and children, men in full possession of their faculties, who nonetheless abuse themselves on the roofs of neighboring buildings while dewy young girls fresh from the country extinguish their lamps and watch. Waking in New York City, you'll find the morning rich with possibility; you'll open your window for fresh air and find, instead, a bustling crowd, and in that crowd all the millions of possibilities that might collide that day with your own. By the time you retire in the evening, you may find that the possibilities weren't all opportunities, and the collisions weren't without their damage. Negroes can eat in restaurants with Whites and have nothing come of it, I've learned, but I've also seen that a fish can be made to eat its own dying body. After sixteen years of innocence, my mind is growing fat.

The morning after I insulted Mr. Barbour's car, our church went visiting in Versailles. The choir was to sing St. Paul A.M.E.'s Sunday afternoon service, with me playing "Precious Lord" behind Althea Marks, who was such a beautiful singer that Mother said any accompaniment at all was charity to the pianist. Versailles was fourteen miles beyond Lexington proper, and passing through the city's downtown, all we ladies leaned our satin head scarves against the bus windows and watched the locked doors of the shops. The older ladies closed their eyes, righteous in the knowledge that no good Christian would think of spending money on a Sunday in the first place, but the younger of us sat hotly disappointed, and my second cousin Maylene, up on the fourth seat of the bus, actually folded her legs under herself to get a better look at the mannequins in the window of Snyder's.

From his place on the first seat, Reverend Graves saw Maylene in the bus driver's mirror. "Think," he said, turning just enough that all of us could see his brown ear graze his white starched collar, "how great the fellowship we're taking to our brothers and sisters in Christ. It is a much greater thing than any yard of fancy cloth." In profile, silhouetted against the bus windshield and its vista of city streets, he truly did look like Providence, and the whole bus said amen. But when we got to Versailles, we found a funeral. Cars stuck end to end on the street fronting St. Paul's; cars wedged into the yard at the side of the church; cars covering every square of grass in the empty lot across the street. Three horses, tied to a porch post, drank water from a trough, whinnying and swishing their tails when the flies stung their backsides.

St. Paul's face wore high stained-glass windows and a spire running up its front, and we'd never seen the Crucifixion baked into glass, and even though we all knew those cars couldn't possibly be waiting for a visiting church choir, we felt grander getting off the bus than we should have. We pushed through St. Paul's door and squeezed, single-file, down the side aisle, to the choir stand. Arranged ourselves into two rows and looked over the pulpit into the casket, which was made of gray reflective steel and held a spray of red roses across its closed top. Four of the most beautiful ladies in all of Kentucky's history sat on the mourner's bench, leaking tears through their four handkerchiefs and down the necklines of their four identical black dresses. They didn't look like sisters, exactly, but all four of them were tall and smooth-skinned and had the same style of long, thick hair — narrow over the ears and full at the shoulders. Nested in misery, they crossed their legs in the same direction — right over left — and even the Mongoloid child sitting between them, with her eyes slanted upward in their lack of full under-standing, sat with her thick little legs crossed. The congregation, lost in an old spiritual, tapped their feet. In the corner panel of stained glass, Jesus met His mother.

I sat down at the piano and Althea stood up in the choir stand, and St. Paul's minister nodded to me, absurdly pronouncing his overbite. He wiped his sweaty forehead and drummed his finger on his knee as I took the congregation to the key of D flat. I'd get seventy-five cents for playing a funeral.

"Precious Lord," Althea sang, "Take my Hand." We'd only made the first bar, but already one of the four ladies on the mourner's bench had popped out of her seat to

234

commence the most terrible kind of moaning, throwing herself down into an unfixable misery. Althea sang, and the woman bent over double, and a nurse in a white uniform came and stood next to her. The retarded child shook with a strange kind of anger, and a tear dripped off the end of her nose. When the bent woman began to thrash and scream and cast wild shadows against the small bit of sun coming through the stained glass, the minister finally spoke. "Give God back what's His," he said. "We'll understand it better by and by."

I started to wonder what had happened to the man in the casket, whether he'd spent his entire life in Kentucky, and what he'd done to the bent woman to make her love him so. Having caused such love, he now slept. He'd rot to teeth and bone deep beneath the mud of Versailles, his fingernails curling long against his hands, his hair coiling out to super lengths atop the mossening of his velvet casket, his flesh wasting until it lost all human form, and she'd still be loving him. Whatever had killed him would no longer be — a gunshot wound would no longer pucker out of a hole; a tumor would no longer lodge itself as a lump — he would lose all the scars and scratches of his man-life, and become nothing more than a skeleton, even more unfettered by flesh than he'd been on the day he was born, and still, he would cross the woman's thoughts every morning as long as she lived. Thinking about it, the repetition of her want, my own ribs began to ache in my chest, and the white keys on the piano began to feel as narrow as the black ones, and I saw again how my own life up to then had been a death. Althea was deep in the theater of her own voice, squeezing tears from some place that had nothing to do with the man in the casket or the beautiful screamer now sprawled on the floor, but when she heard me play the final chords a full two verses early, Althea opened her eyes just a slit and frowned. I tinkled out the ending anyway: that screeching widow, the casket, the dead man himself — if I let them, they'd pull me into the grave.

Althea had brought up such a commotion that no one noticed when I stopped playing and ran to the back of the church. I pushed open the front door, letting myself into the country sun. I stared so long at it that I thought I might go blind.

"You all right?"

He was sitting on the steps, right at my feet. The sun had burned itself into my eyes, and when I looked at him, he blazed red.

"What's a matter?" he asked. "Can't talk?"

"Just tired, that's all. Didn't sleep much last night."

"And played like that?" He whistled. "Hate to hear you play when you're wide awake."

He'd solidified into his normal color, which was still light as any phantom's. He chewed something not snuff, something that didn't make him spit.

"You from around here?" I asked.

"No, ma'am. Visiting. I'm an associate of the deceased."

"Then you know how he died?"

"Poisoned. James Parks could play a fat hand of poker. Should've known better. Never lick your fingers in a house where you're winning every round. When you're a winner, you ain't popular."

"Yeah. Well, he's got *some* folks in there all broken up."

"Widows."

"Plural?"

"All four of 'em. Concurrently. Never divorced a one — real-life, modern-day harem — your menfolk down here in Kentucky got it made." The man chewed some more and looked away from me, off into his own daydream. "Tell you something else," he said, after a time. "Wonder why the funeral had to be on a Sunday?"

"They ain't got no Black undertaker?"

"Negroes 'round here are doctors and lawyers and such. Sure, they got themselves a Black undertaker. But your specimen James Parks in there, he messed over this woman and he fooled around with that one, and then he messed around with the undertaker's wife."

"And when you're a winner, you ain't popular."

The man laughed. His voice was expansive yet brittle, as if something had been sautéed on his throat. "Come time for James to be embalmed, the undertaker wouldn't even look at him. Body started to rot. Pretty James Parks, ain't looked shabby a day in his life, started to stink so bad you couldn't even be in the same room with him. His wives figure they better get him on in that ground."

The shouting and moaning in the church seeped through the walls, a fever spreading to the outside. The preacher's noise occasionally cleared the crowd's. "This nasty life ain't where it's at, beloved," he was saying. "Death! Huh! Death is the party."

"Better get back in there," the man said. "Ain't no party like one with a gal talented as you at the piano."

"I still got a minute." I was trying, still, to catch air, trying to make my lungs keep up with my galloping heart. "So what else do you know? That James Parks's kid up there?"

"According to that tall fine woman of his, a mermaid brought that child. James couldn't handle it — you know — the girl's condition. She was his only child." Whatever sat in the corner of the man's mouth peeked out at the edge, green like a sprig of jungle. His gold incisor flashed in the sun. "You're smart," he said. "You ask all the right questions. You married?"

"You White?"

The man had a nice, even row of teeth, but he was almost as old as Grandpap, and lighter-skinned even than Pookie, with freckles in all the same places — under his eyes, on the tops of his ears. "I'm what some people call White, yes," he said.

"Some people. Well, since we're being honest here, I'm not married. Not looking to be, neither."

"Good, good. Keep yourself out of trouble, not like our friend dead-ass-James in there. How about your kinfolk? You think they'd let you go off to New York City with me?"

My kinfolk almost didn't.

A White man, Grandpap said, after Mr.

Glaser came out to our house, begging. *New York hustler,* said Mother. But then Mr. Glaser took us all to a ten-dollar-a-plate restaurant in Lexington, a whitefolks' establishment where the owner let us sit at a back table and order whatever we wanted in peace. Mother asked for soup with a spoon, then went back to rearranging the three different forks that gated her plate. Mr. Barbour ordered prime rib. Grandpap, thinking we weren't watching, ate three pieces of the soft, white bread the water brought in a basket. He had a hard time managing with his false teeth, and though we all pretended not to notice, Mother did suggest more butter. Mr. Glaser ordered raw fish that he said came from Japan.

"You really gone eat that?" Mother asked when it came. The poor fish was alive still, turning its head and gasping for water, its backside sliced open to expose its bloody spine.

"Blackspotted puffer. You should try some yourself," Mr. Glaser said. He slid the plate over so that the fish, its gills flapping, was an inch away from her arm.

"I think I just got throwed off my appetite," she said.

Grandpap, on the other side of Mother, averted his eyes from Mr. Glaser's plate, and Mr. Barbour frowned at the fish as if it had just cursed him out. While he looked, he sliced his beef, steadying his knife between the tines of his fork. "Audrey's too young to go running off to New York by herself," he said. "I believe it's out of the question."

"You ain't none of my daddy," I reminded him. He flared his nostrils at me and looked at the door like he wanted to leave, but then he looked at all those White people at the other tables and went back to slicing his beef.

"Your Audrey is an incredible talent," Mr. Glaser said to the table. "Pianists of her caliber make seventy-five dollars a week in New York."

"Seventy-five dollars," said Mother. "Takes me two months to make seventy-five dollars." She dabbed her napkin at her mouth in a halfhearted way that made me feel sorry for her. She spun a snow pea in the air with her fork. "But she's only seventeen."

"I'll be eighteen come January."

"Madam," said Mr. Glaser. "New York is full of eighteen-year-olds."

"Where will she be eduated?" Grandpap asked.

Mr. Glaser leaned across the table as if he

241

and Grandpap were plotting war strategies. He quieted his voice. "Sir, this child is too talented for school," he said.

Grandpap's eyes grew shiny with moisture. His daughter had shipped herself across two states to go to a college he'd never heard of. He'd sent a son away to the Air Force and never gotten him back. The man who had stolen and impregnated his dead son's wife had also taken the last piece of bread.

"She's finishing high school, at least," Mother said. She dabbed her mouth again, with more force than before. "You'll see to it, Mr. Glaser, or we'll see to it that she comes on back home. And what about a chaperone?"

"I'll be her chaperone." Mr. Glaser's lips smiled without the help of his eyes, and a piece of flesh fell from his chopsticks right onto the tender gray edge of the fish's mouth. We all watched as the puffer involuntarily jerked, sucking down its own body. "Goodness," Mr. Glaser said, but he laughed as he said it. Grandpap, Mother, and Mr. Barbour all stopped chewing and watched the fish eat itself, and to stop what I was feeling, I had to giggle. Such a man as Mr. Glaser no doubt kept the company of murderers.

"With all due respect," said Mr. Barbour, "you might be the reason Audrey needs a chaperone. We'd appreciate some letters of reference before she travels."

I didn't sass Mr. Barbour that time.

Three letters came, all on the same day. The thickest wore a return address of 253 West 125th Street, Harlem. Twenty-five fives, so I opened it first. "Joseph Glaser is a prince among men," it read, in typeface whose serifs supported its honor. The words *The Apollo Theater* looped across the top of the creamy paper, and six inches below them, a Mr. Jack Schiffman, Owner, had signed. The second letter came from a Miss L. Jones on 116th Street. A dancer, she wrote, her career managed by Mr. Glaser, and in beautiful, accomplished handwriting, she hoped to meet me when I arrived in Harlem. She'd chosen my favorite shade of lavender for her stationery. "Joe Glaser wouldn't so much as hurt a fly," she wrote, though Grandpap pointed out that we already knew that not to be true. She'd signed her name bigger than she'd written the word "sincerely." The *L* in *Letty* wore a small, practiced bead to the left of its head.

The third letter was the only one that stopped Grandpap from fidgeting, as it was folded around three ten-dollar bills for my travels. "I regret that I cannot accompany Audrey on her journey," Mr. Glaser wrote, "but I will meet her at Penn Station." The L&N came through Mt. Sterling four days a week, and we knew every single body who descended its steps. It never occurred to us that the scene at Penn Station would be any different.

HARLEM

I'd pulled apart and eaten all of Mother's fried chicken while waiting to switch to the integrated train car in Cincinnati, and as the chain of twelve cars clacked down the middle of the long, lonely rectangle of Pennsylvania, I'd strained my eyes to make what I could out of darkness, felt up through the grease-depleted bottom of my paper bag, and found the red flour tin with Mother's biscuits. Under the glass domes of Penn Station's skylit ceiling I was hungry, dirty between my legs from two days of squatting over toilets and sour in the mouth from drinking PET Milk. Fifty cents of my thirty dollars had gone to advise Mr. Glaser of my arrival via telegram, and yet even after I'd been sitting on the schooner-length bench for three hours, watching the giant face of Penn Station's all-seeing clock until I could close my eyes and still find its long and short arm burned onto my retina, I didn't see Mr. Glaser. On either side of me, a steady procession of men sat down, bit into sandwiches, checked their watches, and hurried back to offices; women sauntered through the station with glossy department store bags draped over their arms; a fourth and then a fifth hour passed, and still I hadn't seen him. At the ticket booth, I asked a clerk whether he'd seen a tall, dark-haired White man with fine Italian shoes. "Seen about a thousand of 'em today," he told me. "And gal, I dunno where you're from, but around here, you'd better keep an eye on your suitcase."

Late afternoon lay itself atop the station's glass domes and glanced off the black steel beams; the sun disappeared from the highest ceiling glass and streaked through ventilation shafts along the wall. A poor, trapped bird flew the length of the station to light on a beam, and I wondered whether fourteen dollars and forty-three cents would buy me a week's worth of lodging, and what kind of employment I'd have to secure when that money was gone. A plump grandmother in the station's balcony turned the violet grosgrain ribbon around her hat as she looked over the railing, and I wondered how many streetlamps and how much danger lay between me and the genteel parlor of

Miss L. Jones of 116th Street. I imagined Caroline telling me what a damn fool I was, and wondered how, if she were there, she would go about finding the address. In the exact middle of the station, a young girl about my age paused just long enough to spit her gum on the floor, then stood there, swaying at the waist, looking this way and that at the giant clock, oblivious to the disapproving glances of the few people who'd witnessed her transgression; I wondered how long New York would take to make me so bold. I never once wondered whether I should catch a train back to Kentucky.

Over the next hour the hall grew crowded with commuters in various stages of catching their trips. Some stood and waited, holding their purses and briefcases and suit jackets, watching the schedule board turn its letters, rearrange hours, subtract suburbs. Others were runners, dodging these waiters so that they might board nearly departing trains. In the middle of all these people, a hunched, balding man swept the glass brick floor. He was as old as Grandpap, with the same bushy eyebrows, but he moved with an effort of spryness I'd never noticed in any of the old men at home. He had more fight about him. In New York, he had to.

The girl's gum had dried and hardened, and the old janitor squatted to scrape it from the glass with his dustpan. Scraping and chipping, he squinted, and I could tell that the trick of afternoon light made it impossible for him to work easily. Mother had always been fond of saying that nothing good happened after dark, and at that time — just fallen off the train, watching the women's tight silk blouses stretch over their chests, listening to the men at the shoeshine stand whistle at them, watching them offer up rouged smiles in return — I imagined that Mother's warning applied especially to New York City. A red marble plaque over the big arched door at the end of the hall read WEST, so I set out of the train station toward the setting sun, my coat in the crook of my elbow and my suitcase heavy in the opposite hand.

For a young woman alone, the suitcase was poorly sized, and its bulk forced me to amble out of the building as a three-legged stool: halfway across the street, the weight became more than I'd realized. While a red light held cars at the intersection I set it down in the middle of the street, right atop a line of tar that bled through a crack in the asphalt, and breathed. In, out, and the city's steam filled my lungs to let me know I was staying here. In, out, and the buzz of five million people filled my ears so I'd have faith. I felt watched, though the sheer number of hurrying people told me otherwise: I felt watched by someone who was not there. Not my father, who knew already that I was here, living what he hadn't dared. Not my mother nor Grandpap, though I should have been thinking of them, wondering how they'd know I was safe; what they would think of this mammoth city if they ever got to see it. I wasn't thinking of any of them, I realized — I was thinking of Caroline, wondering how she'd rejected someone who could find their way to something as magnificent as this. The light changed and I picked up my suitcase to run, and I thought this — I thought that I must push her from my mind once and for all. I would make new friends and a new life, and memories of her simply wouldn't be profitable. Tar had stuck on the suitcase's bottom, and then it stuck to my nylons, and though I was hurrying, a couple of drivers honked as I made the far lane, and I knew that this was something I'd always remember — my clumsy entrance into Manhattan. I stepped up to the sidewalk and found, in the corner trash can, a perfectly uneaten birthday cake, and an uncapped lipstick that someone had tired of. To my left, beyond the tall buildings overhanging the street, the avenue dropped off into the Hudson.

I walked on, and my right arm blanched and then reddened, and began to hate me for all the useless dresses packed, the extra can of Bergamot hair grease stuffed in a corner, the photograph of Daddy fastened into my belongings. Mother had given me the black dress she'd worn to Daddy's funeral, and told me if I never came back home, to at least mail the dress. Now, having it seemed ridiculous; it didn't even fit me without the belt. At the corner of Eighth Avenue, a man in a decades-old smoking jacket put out a hand to help, but I remembered the words of the station clerk and held tight to the handle as the man crushed my fingers with his own. His palm was dry and cracked, and I wrested the handle from him and stepped off the curb to try and escape, but a school of passing cars held me back. The man waved me off and walked on into the Manhattan sunset, a river charred to orange that seeped through only in inches behind high skyscrapers whose faces were already dark. Past both sides of me, people streamed across the intersection, people more serious in their being than I'd ever seen — a woman in a red jacket rubbed the pocked skin of her cheek, a small girl in a felt hat with a yellow ribbon stamped her foot and cried out to her mother for a nickel, and an old man with a Dachshund puppy barked a cough full of juice. To put less distance between my life and theirs, I stepped off the curb and followed. Two blocks took me from the white street sign at 34th to the yellowed one at 32nd; I reversed myself and headed north. The September cool upset my stomach and hurt my teeth. A towheaded man with one ear gone missing blew me a kiss.

"Miss," said a man flanking my right. "Miss, are you lost?"

"Of course not. Not lost, because I do know where I am going. North. To 116th."

"Planning on walking it?" He smiled, and took in my impractical shoes, the heels of them still muddy from my walk down Queen Street to the Mt. Sterling train depot. He had a silver wedding band, and a pistol in a holster on his belt, but his ears rose when he smiled and they made me feel that I should be honest. His black wool coat smelled of new rain.

"It's only eighty-four streets," I told him.

"Good at math. Bad at accepting help," he said. He took my suitcase and carried it above his head like it was full of air. He was tall, taller than Junebug, and even finer, with copper skin and broad shoulders. He spoke without singsong, like the White people on WLEX, though when he hit the word "help," something, maybe a Georgian auntie or a South Carolinian grandpa, oozed through the bricks enclosing his accent.

"So you're walking to Harlem," he said, laying so hard on the "a" that the "r" flew off the balance. "Got a place you're staying up there?"

"I believe so."

A look crossed his face. As he slid his eyes my way, I noticed a thin line in his eyebrow where hair didn't grow. "How old are you?" he asked.

"Nineteeen," I lied, straightening my spine.

"And your people sent you up North alone?"

I wasn't alone. I had letters of reference, addresses. Fourteen dollars and forty-three cents. But his ears rose once more, and this time they told me I should lie. "I'm staying with my cousin," I told him. "She's a dress-maker."

"She should have met you at the train station, I would think," he said. In my heels, I couldn't match even half his stride, and I was almost out of breath from the pace he was keeping. "Where on 116th?" he asked.

"763 East."

"This way, then," he said, and we took a right on 42nd, which spread three times as wide as any of the city streets I'd seen up until then, with neon signs casting a daylight glow against the sunset. Where the streets bordering Penn Station had shown me a manageable slice of Manhattan, 42nd Street showed me how it was a place I'd never master. Under the electric light I was able to watch faces, but even in sharp relief all the eyes and mouths came up blank: emotion was a thing much foreshortened in the city. Even the man walking with me had suddenly donned a blank mask: he nodded at a sausage seller on the corner, but didn't smile. People — mostly other Negroes — did occasionally glance at us, taking in the man's sharp suit and close shave against my jacket with its torn hem and my hair that had lost its curl in Ohio. We passed a tailor's, a butcher's, a deli, a peep show. "Times Square, Young Sister," the man told me, and we both read the frightened little sandwich billboard standing outside the Flesh Merchant: GIRLS BOUGHT, SOLD, AND TRADED.

Two heavily lipsticked women in four-inch-high heels patrolled the corner of

Broadway, jacketless, managing the New York night without armor. No wool coats to warm their bare shoulders, no sensible shoes to help them run. The shorter one circled her arms around a lamppost as though she were steering a mast, out on a dare, maneuvering waves. We passed a newsstand, a pizzeria, an old woman sweeping a fire hydrant. A florist's. A shoe repair. A tea seller. Finally, the man stopped in front of a green pole with a globe of light atop a stair rail. Horribly, inconceivably, a stairway dropped through a hole in the sidewalk. As long as I'd lived in Kentucky, I'd never seen the opening to a mine — Grandpap had made sure of it — but now here it was, the mouth of a shaft. A metal sign stood up from the hole, with two winged green angels flanking the letters *Interborough Rapid Transit Company.*

"Here's the Nine train. Board the northbound and get off at 116th. Even there, I'm afraid you'll be walking east for some time."

"Only six streets."

"Six *blocks.* And they're avenues. You'll soon learn that the avenues are longer than the streets, and that makes all the difference in the world. Oh and" — he said, finding a five in his pocket — "take this."

"Mister, I can't."

He pushed the bill into my palm. "In a town like this," he said, "there's no room for pride. This city will eat you alive, and you're not going to be able to stop it. Just take help where you can find it, and be gracious. Get off that subway train and get yourself and that suitcase into a taxi."

I thanked him and bumped my suitcase down the steps to the subway, where I stood in line and paid fifteen cents for a token to feed the chrome turnstile. The subway was such a spread of filth — spots of old gum speckling the floor, rats crisscrossing the tracks, a woman unwittingly dragging a wad of used tissue with the stiletto heel of her shoe — that I had to close my eyes. I counted to sixteen and then back down again, and I'd done this three times when the platform started to rattle under my shoes. A head of wind grew, and a light opened itself into the tunnel, and I quickly counted 32 more to make it an even 128. I stepped closer to the edge of the platform so I could board, but the train never stopped — it just screeched quickly by all of us, blowing my hair, leaving a galaxy of dust in the air. I couldn't know why, but no one else had even expected it to stop: the man next to me had never even looked over the top of his newspaper. The train screeched past all of us, but I was the only one looking after it.

This city was so big, so full of missed possibilities and unmet connections. No easily walked trip to the Colored store, no knowing where anyone stood with anyone else. No Mother; no Caroline. Five million people, every single one of them taking their fifteen breaths per minute, walking their twenty thousand steps per day on streets that number into the two hundreds. Sweating, crying, defecating, suckling — more individual acts of love and hatred and just plain getting by than I could ever count, none of them cohering, perhaps not even between people who lived on the same city block. Another train whirred into place against the platform, spreading my jacket with its backdraft. The conductor leaned his head out of a window and ten sets of squealing doors opened to the people who rushed all around me to get on, and I got sad, thinking that in Kentucky, someone, possibly a White man even, would have stopped to help. Of course, in New York, it would be neither a matter of ill breeding nor disrespect, I could already see: it was simply that here, in this city where ten million meetings were convened in any given morning and an infinity of meals served and eaten, there would be no time for simple kindness. I was so slow with my suitcase that the doors closed on it as I was pushing it on the train. I screamed.

"Suitcase!" someone on my car yelled. The doors miraculously opened and I pulled the other half onto the car. The doors closed again, a woman with a small child in her lap sighed her frustration at the delay, and as the train started moving and threw me off balance and into the railing, I wondered whether Mr. Glaser was eating more spotted puffer at that very moment, or watching Miss L. Jones stretch her long legs along a barre in a dance studio. The eighty-five streets between me and 116th stretched out as a universe of rooms and lives and desires and bodies, and the train shot forward on this screaming tide. Across from me, a man slept with his mouth hanging open, and I turned my head, thinking it too intimate a thing to witness.

When the conductor shouted *116th!* I stood up and tried to yank the edge of my coat from beneath the woman who'd sat on it when she got on at 96th. In her confusion, or perhaps in her assumption that I was trying to pick her pocket, she yanked my coat back, and by the time she understood enough to release it, the doors had

closed once more, and I grabbed the overhead rail and waited until the conductor
called *125th!* Five fives, I remembered, and
despite the precision of it, I knew I was
unwilling to be lost there. I jumped out my
seat, then, and out the train's sliding doors
to follow the crowd — down the platform,
up the stone steps, and into the growing
crispness of evening, the relative quiet of
Harlem. Where Midtown Manhattan had
been an unending buzz, Harlem was an arrangement of well-defined noise — people
hawking castor oil, children squealing at
tossed balls, radios blasting from storefronts.
I saw my own people in all shades, from
sepia to passing; my people selling *Fire!;* my
people handing out leaflets for Pentecostal
churches; my people looking aged and
youthful and sad and flirtatious and harried
and fevered and loved. I found a woman
with large, childlike eyes beneath a red
pillbox hat. "Might you point me in the
direction of the Apollo Theater?" I asked
her.

"Aww, go on back to Detroit, bitch."

I walked a few steps and asked a boy who
sat haughtily, with perfect posture and a
smile full of judgment, on the back of an
empty mail cart. "Two blocks, that direction there," he said, pointing with a middle

finger beringed at both joints.

Two streets, then. My suitcase felt lighter. It could have carried me. The sugarsick smell of roasting cashews cleared my worries about finding a room or a bed; this street held enough energy to make me doubt that I'd ever need sleep again. By the time I finally came upon the neon sign, with red letters falling vertically from the "A" four stories off the street, I'd seen more of the earth's peoples than I'd seen in my entire sixteen years previous. Mr. Barnett had taken down his dusty atlas and shown me a map of Manhattan before I left, but now, I couldn't believe I was standing less than five miles from the Atlantic Ocean. Manhattan couldn't have been an island; it was a world.

The theater's sidewalk ticket stand was unattended, and when I entered the lobby, I found no one. I stood there in the calm quiet, scraping my feet on the thick red carpet, admiring the marble wall inserts, dizzy over my meeting with splendor. From the end of the lobby, behind the heavy double doors, came the voice of a woman counting bars of eight, and I went to find her, dragging my suitcase behind me. Leaving it for someone to steal, at that point, would have been the worst option: either this was my life, and it would require all that I'd packed, or this wasn't to be my life at all, and I'd need all that was in the suitcase to make it back to Kentucky. *One, two, three, four,* she counted: I might play piano forever, just as Daddy said I'd been born to do. *Five, six, seven, eight,* and Mr. Glaser might have been a hiccup of my teenaged imagination, and I'd be handing fifteen dollars back over to the Pennsylvania Railroad, going back to live under the rusty heels of Mt. Sterling.

As I pulled one of the heavy doors, the vacuum of the lobby's relative silence gave way to the acoustic echo of the theater, whose largeness dwarfed anything I'd imagined. Hundreds of yellow vinyl seats sat open like dandelions in bloom. Four marble colonnades held up a second floor that was just as large as the first, and from where I was standing, I could see balconies ringed around a third floor. In one of these balconies stood Mr. Glaser.

"Where the hell you been?" he asked, not kindly.

"When we pay you for a week, that means Tuesday too," said a woman in a smart black blouse and tap shoes. I matched her voice to the counting.

"I'd been waiting for Mr. Glaser at the

station —" I began, but no one was listening. My drama was no more than a passing gust of air. The woman retrieved an apple from a plate she'd balanced on the rung of an onstage ladder. She took a bite out of it before turning back to glare at me as she chewed, and a man sitting on drums examined the wax he'd picked out of his ear. Mr. Glaser disappeared from the balcony, and it was so quiet then in the theater, with everyone staring at me, that I heard his shoes as he descended the stairs. He reappeared at the back of the theater, but he didn't say hello or goodbye as he walked toward me. He walked behind the last row of seats, then right past me out the double doors.

"Well?" the woman asked. "How much longer will you keep us waiting?"

I'd been standing there gawking at them all like some county grandmother. When I realized, I dropped my suitcase and got out of my coat, which I threw over the back of a seat. It slid to the floor, but I didn't bother rehanging it. My thin flowered blouse had seemed right for meeting Mr. Glaser in the station but now it seemed wrong for my first evening of work, and the heels of my shoes, as they clacked against the three stairs to the stage, seemed wholly unnecessary. The tenor saxophonist, a boy not much older than me, with the beginnings of an unwilling mustache, gave me a look of great boredom. A male dancer bounced up and down, then scraped his taps on the floor in a tedious shuffle. Music, even onstage at the Apollo Theater, was just a job.

Only the bassist smiled at me as if we were about to do something fun or incredible. He was exactly my color, but his hair was so straight and dark and shiny as to make him look like a china doll. "There's music on the piano," he said. " 'Stardust.' " But all I could see was the reflection of my own hands in the piano's wood, ebony so polished it showed me even the wrinkles on my knuckles. I was going to play on this giant stage in this giant theater in this giant city. It seemed unreal.

When finally I turned back to the rest of the band, I found the bassist still grinning. It was the nicest thing I'd seen all day. "She's ready," he said, picking up his instrument. He spoke slowly and professorially, as though sorting through the many volumes of information in his head. "Count it off, Letty."

She cursed me all afternoon for not knowing the music, but the bassist kept smiling, and shaking his head behind Letty's back when she got outraged and sliced the air with her hand for us to stop. I'd never played with a full band, or even half of a band, and it took me some time to stop listening to the other parts enough to focus on my own, but there was something warm about sinking into everyone else's rhythm while keeping up my end of the whole. At ten 'til seven, a potbellied man came and hustled us off the stage. "I'm Porto Rico," he said when he saw me, as though I was supposed to know him. "And you must be that new blood come up to throw some spice on the plate."

I just smiled and nodded: after Letty's thrashing, I didn't have enough wits left to offer my Christian name. I gathered my music as the rest of the band packed up and off and disappeared, but when the bassist had rolled his instrument off to the edge of the stage, he came back and took my arm. "Stick around," he said, leading me down the stage steps, "and I'll show you stuff." At the back of the theater, he found my coat and handed it to me, and then he insisted on carrying my suitcase. He took me back through the lobby and up the carpeted stairs I hadn't seen, up to a third-floor studio with a hardwood floor and an old upright in the corner. I played a few chords, and found that every note missed its true pitch, but that gave the piano a wonderful, whorehouse quality, as if someone had taken a hammer to its strings during a party. " 'Stardust,' " the bassist told me, and I started playing, and then, four bars in, he asked for "Cottontail." "Make it fresh," he said, so I anticipated chords with my index finger, but then, a few bars into that, he asked for "Liza."

I strode up the bass dutifully, fast as I thought he might want to hear it, but then he asked for more right hand. "It ain't about just getting from chord to chord," he said. "You got to use that right hand too, you want to stride right." He came over and hit some flats I wouldn't have, and then stood back and asked for "A Night in Tunisia." We went through "I'll Remember April," and "Star Eyes," and then he asked for "Stardust" again. I'd played with the band for an hour already, and when I started to tire, I began playing the melodies more slowly.

"Okay," he said, taking the hint, and then he came over to the piano and practically closed the lid on my hands. "Let's go back down," he said.

This time we took yet another stair that descended to the back of the main stage, and I had to marvel at what a series of secrets the theater seemed to contain. We watched from the edge of the curtain as three white poodles, outfitted in pink clown costumes, jumped through hoops and ran in circles. Their trainer was upstage, and I could see only his hand occasionally, but the poodles were close enough that I was afraid they'd smell the chicken grease on my clothes.

"It's so funny," I whispered to the bassist.

He smiled, but he said, "They're gone next week."

"Why gone?"

"Look at those empty seats. That's why." It was the biggest crowd I'd ever seen, but half the daffodil seats still bloomed empty, and it made me suddenly mindful of what New Yorkers expected of the world. "Schiffman's bringing in more soul acts."

For a finale, the dogs climbed atop each other, the dog on top pawing the second dog's crisp uniform while the bottom dog turned around in a circle and the crowd clapped politely. Then, after they were hustled offstage by their trainer, a lady acrobat in a red-sequined leotard pulled a trampoline from the wall and dragged it to the center of the stage. She did impossible flips that made her turn in mid-air two and sometimes three times, and drew wolf whistles when she jumped up and landed in a split.

"What about her?" I asked. "She's good."

"Gone. Tomorrow, Thursday, and Friday are Gospel Week. Then she'll do four shows on Saturday, and be gone. For good."

Through all this, an older man with a porkpie hat had sat hunched at the piano, playing in such a way that I hadn't noticed him. But I didn't ask after his fate. Maybe I didn't want to know. It was all so beautiful, and yet so sad. Nothing in a city was as solid as it seemed.

"My name's August," the bassist told me, and he led me back to the lobby. We stopped at the reception desk, where he picked up a pen and a pad and scrawled out something, then lifted my suitcase again and took me through the double doors to the noises of 125th Street. I thought its business would have retreated somewhat toward evening, but it turned out that a night parade was passing by, lit occasionally by the Christmas lights on a float or the burning sparkler in a marcher's hand. A league of little girls in majorette uniforms skipped past us, waving their batons, and then a green van full of a barbershop quartet, who sang out its back window. A silent trio of marchers walked past — the man, in a war uniform; an older woman in a checkered dress with a blank sash across its top; and a woman in a flowing white robe and a scarf trailing down her back. The band around her head read ETHIOPIA, but she looked like any Negro from Cleveland. August let me watch for a few minutes, but then he seemed impatient, leaning abruptly to his right and then to his left, and he took my suitcase down the avenue and hailed a taxi.

"No. 456 Lenox Avenue," he told the driver, as I stepped in, and before he closed the door he gave me the piece of paper, on which he'd scrawled the address. "Ask for Edith."

The house at 456 Lenox turned out to be a three-story brownstone atop a mortician's; the block also held a liquor store, a wig shop, and a storefront church called Make Me a Herald. Edith turned out to be a barrel-stomached landlady who, when called downstairs by the mortician's assistant, took nineteen dollars, showed me down to my basement room, and made me promise I wouldn't have any gentleman callers. Payday, Letty had told me, would come the Monday after I played my first show. "If you haven't crawled back to the woods," she'd added. I had ten dollars and twenty-eight cents to live on for the next six days, and when I got up to my little room and unfastened my suitcase, I found that all my dresses were wrinkled. The tiny armoire in the corner smelled like camphor, and the door facing the inside of my room had been cursed with a long, muddy shoeprint on its bottom panel. I found Caroline standing in my mind, asking me what I ought to do about any of it, and I bit my lip until I tasted blood, and threw out the thought of her. Through the wall, I could smell burning vegetables. Under the noise of the traffic coming through the window, I could hear someone flushing the shared toilet down the hall. I'd packed a yard of velvet ribbon still taped to its spool, and I wondered if I might be able to sell it, since ribbon wasn't the style in New York. I was happier than I'd ever been. A brave life would be made out of such foolish acts as this.

HIM

August spread its last sunlit street fairs, its tea-sipping Tarot readers and its bean pies for a nickel, its trash-eating squirrels turned fat with extra fur. September passed, scattering the final rooftop parties of the Harlem rich, their named cocktails, their jade cuff links, their lush potted plants folded in the corners of railings. Now October has arrived, dropping a permanent cloud over New York City. Somewhere — perhaps in some portrait-modeled town north of the city — the leaves are changing, but here in Manhattan, the foliage dries to dead brown and drops to the pavement. New York, so it's said, is the corridor to a New England autumn, but the price of reaching Connecticut is too dear. And even if I were to save the fare, the train would only deposit me at a simple platform, with no one to meet and no one to telephone: I'd simply be lost in someone else's normalcy. We Harlem Negroes are bolted to this city, where every season springs one color: gray.

On the sidewalks and bus seats of the city, I've bred a city person's way of carrying things, a manner of stuffing a day's life into one little clutch purse. I've a spare pair of nylons in there, a sachet of White Rose Redi, and a leaflet from the Father Divine Peace Mission. A pair of burgundy wool mittens, because, lost in reading, I've already left five pairs on the crosstown bus. It's evidence of myself for the next person, a nice little historic trail of my days in the city, but it's maddening because nice mittens at Blumstein's are so dear. I've the book I'm reading now — *The Street* — and a bottle of hand lotion that clinks against the metal brad of my purse. *Tink, tink, tink,* it says, making me feel like an adult in the city.

Shocking, but October, with its habit of closing every window on the street, has brought me the realization that this city is more crushing, in ways more dull and gormless even, than Mt. Sterling. Making money and staying warm is all: these two simple desires unite everyone from the bus conductor to the drunk man shouting down pennies. To those ends and those ends alone, Harlemites retire to their shared homes and turn on their gas furnaces, they huddle in dry entryways to conduct petty criminal activity, or find the exact middle of a brownstone and make love. They shop in Blumstein's for wool scarves and crowd onto the north-south bus that arrives at the southwest corner of Lenox and 123rd. Certain days, as if they've telegrammed one another to agree, the women bring out closed-toe shoes and black wool coats for the cool air. Those days, the young girls frown at my lime green coat with its missing sash and its pocket full of mauve lipstick and country notions, as if I've retained my impoverished happiness on purpose, just to offend them. New Yorkers know everything there is to know about everyone in the world, or so they think, and because they already know, they don't carry a country person's wonder. The rest of the world knows there is a New York, but for New Yorkers, there is no other place: New York, as it turns out, is the most provincial place on earth.

October brings people to the Apollo in winter coats. These aren't the summer people, the girls come up from Georgia to stay with their old Aunts So-and-Such, the boys stopped over at South Street Seaport on a break from the Navy. No, not them — the October audience is full of natives, and, consequently, more demanding. This audience has ridden the subway down from 176th and Broadway in a cold rain, or over the Queensboro Bridge in a hired car with four other junior high dieticians from Jackson Heights. The singers are more queenly in October; the dancers more elastic. August, Vernon, and Jim roll joints and go up to the Apollo's roof to plan the night's repertoire: they never ask me to go. Of all the girls involved in the show, only Letty is ever consulted, but she isn't allowed to opine on the music. Whatever male mystery the three of them cook up, it pleases Mr. Schiffman — he comes on Mondays, bringing us twenties, smiling. Always smiling. On Wednesday, when the house band does not play, I sit in the Amateur Night audience and watch the audience applaud and jeer, launch careers and break hearts. In October, Porto Rico is busy. The audience hisses, and out he comes with his gun to blow a blank up into the air. As the smoke dissipates above his head, he shoves the gun back into his pocket and pulls out a long-handled broom, pushing the pitchy saxophonists and rhythmless jugglers offstage.

"Wait!" they often protest, as if their boring acts might suddenly bloom, but their false hope makes the audience even angrier.

"Get that sumbitch outta here!" they yell, and Porto Rico bears down on his broom even harder. *It's something to see before you die,* I wrote to Granddaddy. As winter bears down upon us, the Apollo will not stand for anyone who won't set her roof on fire.

Come October in New York, I'm gifted with fierce and unforgiving illness, and though its roots are not physical, it has left me so weak and distracted that Letty has to pull on my bottom lip and spoon the cream into my mouth after we order malteds at the soda shop.

"You cannot be serious," she says, catching a milky rivulet on its way down my chin. "You cannot be in love with *him.*"

"What's wrong with him?"

"Always trying to get more money out of Mr. Schiffman, that fool. He makes life hard for the rest of us. And you know, he's always making speeches about how he should get paid for every note he writes. Like he's God's gift to music. Your little Marcus Garvey in there doesn't understand how the world works."

"Letty," I say, wiping myself with a napkin where she's missed with my spoon. "You say it like he's the devil."

"No, child-friend. The devil is smarter."

Though the boy Letty first wanted me to

love, Verner, is dull as a hundred-year-old knife. Verner is our tenor sax. He's eighteen, and he's come East all the way from Kansas City, and has a cowboy's notions. After Letty tricked me into going on a date with him (*Here's your pay for the week. Take Audrey downtown for a sandwich*), Verner got the queer idea that he should hold my hand, and the even queerer idea that it would be fine for him to take his fingers and work them further up my sleeve, until he was caressing my wrist. The queerest part being that he hadn't said one word to me for the entire fifty streets south we'd traveled. He held my wrist as we walked the aisles of the sheet music store, and just after the clerk gave me my change and we exited the shop, Verner took my shoulder, turned my body into his, and kissed me. He pushed his hot, thick tongue into my mouth, and I tried to cough but couldn't get any air. He pressed me against the Colony's glass window with the force of his affections, and I had to smack him across the chest with "Love Call" to get him to stop. "That's the way!" yelled a woman passing on the sidewalk.

His eyes, when I drew back, bore the same frustration they always had, as though a voice in his head were reciting physics formulae. But that close to his face, I understood, finally, the forced mustache: beneath it was a birthmark that looked like someone had pasted sand to his lip. He'd forever be covering it with bristle and bluster.

"Well all right then," Letty said, at that night's show, when I stomped into the ladies' dressing room during the intermission and told her I hadn't come all the way to New York to be with a boy I could have met at a tobacco auction. "But I'm afraid you'll find there's much less wrong with the young ones. They haven't had a chance to turn rotten and stink."

Of Dean Jennings, Letty offered only the most neutral of appraisals. It was a week later, and Mr. Glaser had just moved through the dressing room and pushed aside three naked chorus girls on his way to demand that I play at Dean Jennings's dinner party. "Up on 132nd," he said, over the noises of women zipping up dress backs. "Nice place."

All those women — the singers with three octave ranges pushing their hair under wigs, the ninety-pound Lindyfliers who could never quite manage getting into their Ladyforms — and not one of them so much as paused mid-false-eyelash when a man walked into the dressing room. Compared to Business, Talent was just about precisely nothing — not respect, not adulation, and most of the time not even money. The house band didn't get paid every Monday at the Apollo. We got paid when Mr. Schiffman felt like sending his son, Nevil, down with his sheaf of twenties, and even then, August, the bassist, had warned me, we had to count our money in front of Robbie. If it was short, Nevil wouldn't believe us later.

"Twenty-five dollars," Mr. Glaser offered when he asked me, then, in the dressing room. "Mr. Jennings has taken a special shine to you." He disappeared without saying when I'd see that twenty-five. I had my eye on a pencil dress with zebra stripes that I'd seen hanging in the window of Blumstein's. It could wait, of course — it would be just as transformative two weeks later — but I didn't want it to disappear.

Letty commandeered her usual point in the center of the dressing room. She stood like a Nereid, with waves of sequins on her leotard and a silk shirt that fell, in layers of feathers, at her feet. "Dean's worth half a million dollars," she said, loud enough that the dozen other women in the room could hear, "and he's thirty-two years older than you are."

For most of the evening, in his three-story

brownstone on Strivers' Row, Dean Jennings hovered, ignoring his guests, watching me play from the end of his Wurlitzer. "Such a rare bird as you," he said to me when at last he thought to bring me a glass of anisette, "whose beauty flies so well alongside her talent." His housekeeper had turned the lights down when the clock struck nine, yet Mr. Jennings's pupils, in the candlelight, were like the points of needles. His voice was so raspy that I was almost sorry to hear him speak. Beads of sweat had broken out on his nose.

Despite looking like a gibbon he was confident, and Letty's half-million-dollar quote stuck with me as a solid integer I might be attracted to on principle. Dean Jennings was worth 166 new Chevrolet Bel Airs, 33,333 weeks of rent, 1,478,521 plates of fried potatoes at the corner diner. I could feel the stiffness of the Wurlitzer's disuse, but I could hear in its sound that it was the top of its line. The polished mirrors all around Mr. Jennings's parlor made the house seem bigger than it could possibly be, and watching the guests' reflections speaking to one another in those mirrors, I had the feeling that I was in the midst of something magnificent. What stuck in my heart about Mr. Jennings, though, were the dark, decaying places between his teeth, the hair alive only in patches over each ear. "My wife sails for Paris in the morning," he said, but I couldn't take my eyes off the white lines spreading like cracked glass on his tongue. "You should come play my piano while she's away."

I rang his bell Sunday at lunchtime, and, ushered in by an aproned cook, played for hours on his piano while he lay sidelong on a red leather mat in front of his fireplace. "Mr. Jennings, you're sure you'll tell me when I become a nuisance?" I asked.

"You're more than welcome in my home," he said. "And please, don't call me Mr. Jennings. You can call me Emp."

"Thank you," I said, though I made up my mind that Emp was too strange of a name to ever say aloud.

"Even after Mrs. Jennings returns, you're welcome here."

"Thank you," I said again, more quietly.

He smoked from a long brass pipe whose bottom rested atop coals, occasionally tapping his one socked foot against the other in time to my playing, and I didn't stop. I started out with a tight little Jelly Roll Morton melody, and then loosened up to open into a slow Cole Porter. With my left hand I rolled broken chords up the bass while I lay on some solid half notes with my right hand. I played some ragtime, then moved on to a composition I'd dreamed up during an Amateur Night and had yet to put to paper, though August had asked me to show it to him. Dean put out his fire and ate lunch, offered me some, listened to me refuse, napped, woke, and then slept again, but when the sun began to set, he moved from his mat to a place beside me on the piano bench. Every time he inched closer, I could smell his movements in the smoke that eased out of his clothes. He moved closer and closer, until his elbow touched mine when I hit high notes. He kissed me on the neck, and the smell of smoke on his shirt overcame me with its sweetness, and I unrolled the cover and tucked away the keys. "My coat, please," I said, and then, though I wouldn't look at him, I heard him sniffling, as though I'd announced the end of an agelong affair. To his credit, he didn't protest. He got me my coat, and had his maid show me to the door.

Letty laughed when I told her at Tuesday's rehearsal. "One wife and six girlfriends," she reported, "and I've got it from Glaser he goes through three grams of opium a day." She refused to take her opinion of Dean Jennings away from the numeric.

I laughed with her then, but I iced over and began to lean with the cold weight of my own frost. Grew uncertain that Audrey Wallace had ever existed except as a girl alone with less than nothing. Grew uncertain that New York wasn't trying to make a fool of me. I went to the little plywood writing desk that the landlady had put in my room and I got out my stationery. I wrote: "Dear Caroline, I have many stories to tell you," but I stopped there. She was with Ralph, and she didn't care about my troubles or my adventures. We couldn't reach out and touch each other forever, even if it didn't finish in fours: our season had passed, and there'd be no writing letters back and forth about boys. Through the walls of my little bedroom seeped evidence of the various permutations of love gone right and gone wrong — the tap of the bedframe hitting the radiator as a woman moaned counterpoint, the cries of a baby whose mother had gone down to the corner for news of her missing husband, the smell of the perfume my neighbor sprayed when she was ready to go dancing. Smelling her scent, I wondered whether my love, my very own love for good or for bad, would ever turn up.

Of course there had always been August,

the bassist, the four days a week we all rehearsed, hunched over in front of the window reading Mao or Dubois or the Bhagavad Gita, texts of uplift that seemed to make him sadder by the volume. August, smiling anyway, ever-smiling, nodding serenely in agreement whenever Letty got short with him. August, quiet August, speaking on average of five times a rehearsal, to tell Verner to try coming in on the downbeat, or to tell Jim that his snare seemed a hair stiff, or to tell Roland that he needed to hold Letty closer when they waltzed, lest he seem to the audience like the queer he actually was. August, coming to tell me that the house band was booked on the Rudolph Guzz Jazz Hour for Saturday afternoon; August, patting my hand and telling me it would be fine when I gasped with excitement. August, saying all this with a sweet lilt that belied his seriousness. August, quiet August, not joking with the crew who came mornings to work on the stage's settled-shut ventilation windows, not bragging with the rest of the band about weekend women coaxed up 52nd Street stairwells.

August, pulling his bass across the room to leave, passing me updated city bus maps and sticks of gum. August taking me over to the 28th Precinct house to apply for my cabaret card, slipping the cop a five-dollar bill for "processing" so I might be able to work when someone asked me to play Café Society or the Blue Note. "A quick study," August said, so he loaned me the union dues to join the Local 802. Sometimes, during a final Saturday rehearsal, I'd get sad, realizing it was the last time I'd hear him play a particular connection of notes. After we'd finished at the theater, he'd take me to after-hours clubs, places like Minton's Playhouse down in the Cecil Hotel and Tony's in Brooklyn, dark, hot places where I'd sit and sip watered-down vermouth and let the cigarette smoke sear my lungs while August went onstage and jammed with musicians like Thelonious Monk and Gary Mapp. He'd wink at me sometimes from the stage, but I took it all as a professional vibration, thought he was happy because he'd killed his solo or changed the time signature on an arrangement and gotten the rest of the band to follow. I thought he was just being a solid friend in the way that bass men are the foundation of everything. I never thought either of us was falling in love.

With his quiet came a loud scar, a line of vermilion that began at his hairline and ended at the peak of his collar. It bisected the left side of his face as though the face itself had been manufactured in two pieces, and made August look consistently to stage left as he played. Some nights he even wore a fedora whose shadow, under the stage lighting, hid his entire face. A shame, I thought, since he had beautiful skin, the same coppery auburn as mine but with a reddish flame beneath that threatened to burn through. His lashes were long as an ostrich's, and he had jet black hair that he conked, and that curled into a bubbly fizz at the roots. His eyes were as dark as a spirit's, and on the days when we had to play four or five shows, he'd shut his eyelids halfway, like an Eyptian on an ancient scroll. He made my heart race.

Still, I'd never once thought of him as *maybe him,* not until the night Roland was ill and Letty danced with a broomstick while cursing us all to hell. She was especially rude to me, once taking her broomstick and raking it up my black keys to make a point. "Gotta run to the ladies," she finally said, and we all untensed our bodies, cataloging the anger that had lodged in our arms and shoulders. We were living in the end of October, and night came rapidly: the notes in our fake books were running from discrete dots into blocks of black. When Letty left, I went to the window to try and find some final bit of sunset, some last denial of the coming winter, but all I found were street signs already set alight, the headlamps of cars drifting slowly in rush-hour traffic. I saw, caught in the high branches of a tree down the street, a red something. It might have been a cardinal.

"Dreaming of murder?" August asked. He'd come to stand behind me, so close I could smell his shaving lotion. Cloves. A hint of vanilla.

"Death'd be too good for her." I didn't turn to face him when I spoke, because I didn't need to. He'd come so close that I could feel every breath he took, hear every blink of his eyes. I heard him when he swallowed, smelled a hint of myrrh coming off him. "Anyway," I said, "I'm not thinking about Letty."

"What, then?"

"Thinking of home," I said. "You see that bird in the tree?"

He moved up to stand beside me, and looked out the window for some time before he said, "That's a bag from a shop. A little red paper bag from a shop."

"It's awfully sad that you think so."

"You're unreal," he said. "Looking out the window when there's nothing to see. It's what I keep saying to myself — you're one of those chicks with an unlimited mind. I hope New York lets you keep it."

I folded my hands on the windowsill, and August took his finger and tapped one of mine four times. Traced an imaginary line across the backs of my hands, as though drawing a string that would join them as a pair.

"I miss the sun," I said. "At home, summer stays with us all the way through November."

He relaxed his hand so it covered mine, and said, "It's a grace, your summer."

We both looked out the window, though I was actually looking at the reflection of our hands together, a hand atop mine at last. The edge of my black shawl still showed at the bottom of the window, as did two of the pearly buttons in his silk shirt.

"What's your mother's name?" I asked him.

"Auchidie."

"She must be a fine, fine mother."

We'd been whispering, of course, though Letty's bathroom trip had lasted long enough that Jim had gone upstairs on the roof to roll his marijuana. Verner, ever dull, had remained in the studio, and when August moved close to me, he began to walk about the room in small semicircles of anger, making noise that might cover our declarations. He unhooked his horn from its neck strap and set it loudly on the floor. He kicked the feet of Jim's hi-hat. "What's happening, little man?" August asked him. My face warmed as I thought of Verner's fingers up the sleeve of my coat. Verner took up his jacket and left the room.

I'd never before been that close to holding a man's hand, and I wanted August to go on standing there with me forever, wanted the dull four-counts and trivial harmonic inventions of rehearsal to cease. I wanted the world to stop rushing and growing and dying so that I could stand there and look at August's shirt in the glass while he went on saying lovely things. But he didn't stay. He went back to his bass and tuned its strings. He held it around its middle, as if he were sitting with a lover rather than so much hollow wood. When he leaned in to listen, the bass's neck brushed the scar on his face, and I got jealous. He tightened and loosened all five strings until first Letty, then Jim and Verner, returned. "What the hell is going on in here?" Letty said, to no one and everyone, meaning that we should all get back to work. Herbie Hancock was playing the theater that night, and since the day his name had gone up on the marquee, I'd been storing up anxiety in a silo fashioned of envy. Just then, all that disappeared into the dark brume of evening. Letty could snap at me for nothing, call me an idiot and a moron, threaten not to pay me, break the broomstick over my head — I wouldn't care. I'd found *maybe him,* the someone who might be my Someone. And I hadn't even had to leave the theater.

■ ■ ■ ■

Part Four:
Caroline

■ ■ ■ ■

3:10 TO YUMA

Come the fourth of June, Roy McKinley
was supposed to be taking me to the Strawberry Festival up in Lexington. It was going
to be right special, Roy told me, with a Fer-
ris wheel ride and bumper cars, and all
manner of strawberry preserves and pies
and even strawberry bread crinkly like
Christmas paper, and the town dog, Smiley
Pete, on parade with the horses what run
the Derby last year. The most special part,
for me, was going to be Roy hisself — Roy,
with them straight white teeth and a dent in
his chin like Jackie Robinson's, his hair cut
down to a shiny moss and his top two buttons undone like a singer on the front of a
record album.

Well, I reckon it weren't meant to be, that
particular day with Roy, 'cause long about
then Miss Laverna Vaughan over in Owingsville asked me to stay a spell with her boys.
Twin boys, both of them with the same

cookie dough skin turning from Mr. Vaughan's light to Miss Laverna's dark, same big
pretty eyes the color of plain coffee, same
juicy little feet with the second toe longer'n
the big one. Twin boys still fresh out of
heaven, with long puppy dog lashes. Three
weeks old and not even holding their chins
off their necks yet, but Miss Laverna'd come
down with the nerves after she had them,
so old Mr. Vaughan (so much older than
Laverna, she called him "Pop" when she
was out with her girlfriends) took her on a
little fiesta down in Tennessee. "Hoping,"
he told me, "she might feel some better."

He was picking his teeth with his thumb-
nail when he said it, and seem like he wasn't
paying me a bit of mind. He was such a fat
man that his face was in the middle of his
head 'stead of on the front of it, and ever
time he stuck his thumb in his mouth, his
second chin shifted around under his first
one. He had a look in his eyes like he was
always at a funeral, and seem like he was
thinking on how Miss Laverna might never
feel better, how she might be laying up in
her bed with her eyes closed for years upon
years while he did all the washing and cooking and nose-wiping and shoe-tying for two
loud nasty boys what'd grow up and not
remember the first thing he did for them,

be calling "Mama, Mama" when it was time to throw roses and accolades, just like anybody else. Well, Strawberry Festival was coming up but so was the winter, and Imagene was going to need a new coat and shoes. Cute as Roy McKinley might've been, I needed the money, so I stayed at the Vaughans'.

The Vaughans'd left out Sunday directly after church, and it wasn't even Tuesday lunchtime when I found myself outside listening to them baby boys screaming something awful through the window screen, with their hands all in their own shit. They ain't said nothing when they woke up, and so I stayed on outside reading the paper, but by the time I heard one of them start to cry it was shit everwhere — matted in the twins' hair, walking in handprints across their crib sheets, cased between their fat little sausage legs, packed in the roof of one of 'em's mouth. I took one boy under each arm like they was footballs and hauled them into the kitchen, unpinned their diapers on the washstand and got the water ready in the sink while they laid there just a-screaming about all the shit they done plastered. I got them all washed up right fast then pulled the plug out that kitchen sink, wrapped them twins in a towel, and laid them on the floor so they could keep screaming in peace, then I walked over to the clapboard house next door, through that high grass probably just full of cotton-mouths, and told Miss Gail Ashby in no uncertain terms to send word down to the Colored store for somebody to get a hold of Laverna and Pop.

"You can't take care a two itty-bitty babies?" Miss Ashby said. She was Laverna's friend who suggested the fiesta in the first place, and she ain't cared a whit whether I lost my mind and drowned myself in Miss Laverna's cistern.

"Ain't just little babies out here," I told her. "It's pigs I got to look after and cats I got to feed and Lord knows what all else."

"Shit," she said. Laughed a big *huh* what wasn't really a laugh at all. She leaned forward, and her front porch creaked under me. "When I was your age I had three little kids already and a mama with the chronic pleurisy to boot. Now here's just a little piece a farm, and you can't take care of it?"

"Look like Miss Laverna couldn't take care of it all by herself, and she been living out here for years. Babies need their *own* mamas, they that little."

Since Mama been dead, I ain't had the wherewithal to watch my mouth. I wait and wait for the cutting things to leave my mind, but they always leave my mouth instead, the way they was flying out at Gail Ashby right then. The righteous little daisies beside her porch was blowing in the breeze and her electric fan was circling in her front window and I was standing there just a stewing. I turnt on my heels and started marching on back over to the Vaughans', but I was still so fried I stopped halfway through the grass and turnt back around. Them cottonmouths could crawl straight off to hell. "Hey," I yelled at Miss Ashby. "If I'd of spread my legs three thousand times with thirty different men, maybe I would of come up with three little kids by the time I was eighteen, too." I shrugged. "But I ain't. So, no, I don't know nothing about two newborn babies and a piece of farm."

Well, I don't know what was said and what wasn't, but the Vaughans took the night train back. Miss Ashby told me the next morning. I'd heard the little bell on the milkman's truck, tinkling itself down the road like some kind of progress, and I went out on the porch to catch him and there Gail Ashby was too, standing over on her own porch, wearing a red sweater what stretched tight across her chest but puckered out on both sides of her belly. She'd left three bottom buttons undone to make up the difference, like they was supposed to stand to the right and left sides of her belly and say it was okay. She yelled over at me real cool — "Pop and Laverna on their way, gal" — and it was all she said. When the milkman grinned and tried to walk in her front door, she shook her head and said something low to him, so when he brought my two bottles over, he was right frosty. Took my three dimes and ain't even said thank you. Didn't make no nevermind to me, and when I held them cold bottles in the crook of my arm and licked the cream off the top of the milk, I felt specially satisfied. Seem like the cream tasted better without something on my tongue what ain't been said.

Meantime, it was the very fourth of June, and the Franklin brothers what came to collect the extra manure was talking about them twenty-one Colored boys what been burnt to death at the state home out in Arkansas. Big Myrtle was cross the way, yelling to Peggy Burke about how they done kilt Anne Fletcher out the storyline on *Guiding Light,* but ain't nobody said one word about Strawberry Festival. Come lunchtime, I ran the electric sweeper over Miss Laverna's parlor rug, then made myself a little corncake out of the meal what was left in the Vaughans' cupboard. Took some of that butter melting to cream in the icebox, dropped a pinch of paprika in it, and smeared it cross the top like strawberry frosting, even if it smelt like sin. I was just humming to myself, pursing my lips and sticking my tongue out to pretend like I was about to lick Roy McKinley's teeth, when James Bundren's little blue car came rolling down the drive in a big cloud of dust. I ran out on the front porch to meet them, and Miss Laverna jumped out the back just a smiling. Had on a happy pink housedress and a blue ten-gallon hat like you'd wear to a rodeo.

"Can't thank you enough," she said, while Pop bent his bad back over James Bundren's trunk and finished getting the suitcases. We all went back in and peeked at the boys, both of them asleep in the crib with not a drop of shit nowhere, and Laverna smiled and patted one of their little hands. It was a right pretty day out, and there was Miss Laverna featuring right then on the goodness of her babies, and I got to thinking about how the only thing what really changes a situation is time. I remembered on how bad I'd wanted to go to Hollywood all them years, and how that just went away when it didn't seem profitable, and how it ain't even mattered whether it hurt me to stop thinking about it — it was just one more thing I couldn't do. I got to thinking on how Audrey was probably up in New York making all that good money, living the life of Riley, and how there was a time when we might've run even, but now she's so far ahead of me I'll never catch up. How nothing happens for any reason — just some people are born lucky and some people ain't; how Audrey never mentioned one time how she wanted to get out of this town and now here she was the one up in New York City, how all the designs of this world are completely unthought. Righteousness don't make prosperity — if it is a God in heaven, He's just setting up there playing dollhouse. Or maybe He does fix on doing things for the rest of us, but our hopes get too heavy on His nerves. Maybe He has to tune His ear away from whoever's screaming loudest.

"You must be awful proud to be friends with her," Sylvia French told me. She been down to North Carolina for the summer with her daddy's side of the family, and now she was back, lording her gentility over all the rest of us. They stopped at a Colored motel on the way back and it'd had a big radio, and they was all flipping through, listening one minute to the Grand Old Opry and the next to Frankie Lymon and the Teenagers, when they heard the Rudolph Guzz Jazz Hour on WMAK out of Nashville. At the end of a set, Rudy scooted his mike all around the stage to talk about the band, and damn if old Audrey Martin didn't get a whole bunch of clapping from the Manhattan studio audience when she said her name. Wolf whistles even, which made Dr. and Mrs. French wonder if they had the right Audrey Martin, the one with them coke-bottle glasses. Or maybe, Dr. French said, chuckling with that thin little mouth of his'n, the fellows in New York just weren't that exacting when it came to women. Well, Rudolph Guzz asked Poindexter some questions, like what her favorite flavor Juju Bean was, and how she got started playing, and all them Frenches knew it was her. "She didn't even sound like herself," Mrs. French said. "She's journeyed up to New York and learned how to say 'picture show' just as proper as the Queen herself."

'Course, they ain't had no way to know that everthing wasn't all sunflowers up there for Poindexter. I'd get all the nitty-gritty in her letters, like how it was a big brown rat what done gnawed its way through the baseboard in her bedroom one night and kept her up listening under the bed for days after, until one day she caught sight of it in the kitchen and beat it to death with the poker. The Frenches ain't known that Audrey had to wipe the blood trail off with an old cummerbund she took home from the Apollo with her just 'cause it was the prettiest shade of eggplant and reminded her of a hill full of blackberries, and they ain't known that she left the house for work that day and watched sidewalk squares all the way to the bus stop to make sure she ended her walking on the count of four. They ain't known that to catch her left foot right on 252, she'd had to cheat one skip step, and that she been feeling some upset with the world ever since. They ain't known she wasn't wearing her coke-bottle glasses no more, that the frames just ain't looked right with her wig, that in order to be as glamorous as all them stars what came through the Apollo, she was having to feel the faces of the coins in her pocket to decide what denominations they was. They didn't know she was floating around like a dandelion seed, with her head all tilted to angles, taking on the airs of a Rockefeller so she wouldn't bump into banisters.

They ain't known, either, that one day she was walking down 132nd on her way to

Dean Jennings's house to play his piano, when she come upon a crowd in the street. Pushed herself past a ninety-year-old Filipino nun standing on tiptoes and a bald-headed White man holding a tray of roast beef and found, there in the middle of all those people, Dean's crunched-up body, its leg bone poking right through the skin over its calf muscle. Its skull crushed all the way flat in the back on account of Dean done walked right out his own third-story window flapping his arms like the wind'd catch under them; 128,205 pairs of good stockings, 657,895 long-playing record albums, they ain't known. Plus they ain't known that Audrey reckoned then that Dean was a right fool, 'cause as strong-headed as humans was, if a body was able to fly, somebody would've figured that out by 19 and 58. And then reckoned that probably, Letty Jones was that very minute thinking the same thing about country girls trying to make something out of New York City — they was fools to even try it.

Poindexter wrote me two whole pages about it, wrote me how a woman next to her'd whispered, "Dear God," and rested the bell of her open umbrella over the side of Dean's head that had exploded, so Audrey couldn't see the tomato-soft bit of cheek muscle laying on the cold sidewalk. But the Frenches ain't known that Audrey still stood there, with the smell of under-cooked beef in her nose, wondering on what it felt like when Dean hit ground, whether it was just a quick blackness come over his eyes or if he felt the folds of his brain poking out through his skull like they'd been through an egg slicer. The Frenches ain't known she stood there figuring on all that, and they ain't known she stood there re-membering on that hand he'd offered her a drink with just a few weeks previous, how he now had it pressed so unnaturally be-tween his back and the concrete that the pinky was wrapped round the thumb. No, they ain't known a bit of that. All they knew was that a lot of people in the Rudolph Guzz Jazz Hour studio seemed to love what come out from under that gal's fingers, and according to what they heard on the radio, she'd even walked round the audience sign-ing autographs while Rudy read the list of sponsors. And ain't nobody in Mt. Sterling — White nor Colored — never made the radio before.

Well, Sylvia was so excited about hearing Audrey's good luck for herself, she told ever kid in Mt. Sterling. Even old Roy McKinley done heard about it, and when he showed up on the twenty-fifth to take me to the show, I had to hear about how incredible it was that some old country gal gone to school in a farmhouse just like all the rest of us done gone to New York City and made music her job.

"Incredible, huh," I said. We was watching *3:10 to Yuma,* and when I looked over at Roy, the white of the desert was lit up all over his face, making little white dots out of his pupils and glowing in the curls on top of his head. It was one other Colored man up in the balcony with us, but he was setting right in the front row, leant over the railing like he couldn't hear. His head was right in the way of the picture, too, but the light wasn't in his hair the same way it was in Roy's, and I wondered why Roy. *"Incredible,"* I whispered to him, and then I leant over and did something with my mouth, right there in the show, what made him slouch in his seat and close his eyes like a Chinaman, clench his fist real tight against the armrest and drop his jaw open like he was floating away on a raft of balloons. When he finished, he ruint the edge of my pretty lime blouse.

"*I'm* incredible," I told him. But I ain't quite believed it myself.

FAITH

All this year since Poindexter hopped the train, she been mailing me letters. I been meaning to write her back, but ever time I read what she done got herself into up there in New York — the Saturday night cognac, the rich folks' Sunday parties, the subway cars full of fine men — my life don't even seem like it's worth the postage stamp. What can I tell her? That Grandmama's getting deaf, so deaf you have to touch her to get her to know you said something? That she whines and moans and carries on near ever night about the pain in her chest? That she's gotten thinner and thinner with all the worrying she does? How I asked her whyn't she go to the doctor, and she say we need that money to pay the iceman? That she'll go out in the backyard to break up the tomato garden and forget she's got food on the stove? That even just last night, she burnt up some food, and the house smelt so bad it stayed in my nose? How the smell of scorched turnip greens in my nightgown was so strong it woke me up in the middle of the night, and I thought, well, it was kind of a wonder? That here I am on my way to church, walking down the street, listening to the woodpecker tear up Preacher Fletcher's tree and watching the white chrysanthemums sugar up the corner of Miss Nettie's yard, and still my whole world smells like a burnt pot? How when I step up into church, I turn into my own hair and smell all those burnt-up never-eaten meals, thinking Grandmama's just one more person in that house I have to keep my eye on now? Like I said, don't none of it even seem worth the stamp. It just don't seem like nothing to write off to New York about.

Sometimes I worry she might just stop writing altogether, on account of I never send her any answer, but Ruth Simmons's mama just keeps bringing them letters with all them big proper words, and at the end of ever one, Audrey'll say I ought to come to New York, get clear out of Kentucky, see the world. Like I ain't got a little girl and a cat and an old lady and her broken-down piece a house to look after. And then yesterday, here come a new letter from Poindexter, telling me that she met a boy — *a man, really,* was the way she put it — and they'd kissed. Kissed. Kissed! And now, Poindexter says, this *man* is in love with her, just on account of some kissing. Meantime, while she's up in New York City living this fairy tale, Junebug done come to the house and seent my whole body, done felt inside it even, with his finger and his something-else, and he ain't in love with me a tall. Matter fact, he done run off with Colette Smith, on account of he done got her in a family way about the same time he was feeling the inside of me.

Ever time I think about it in the right light — this *man* in New York City — I get so mad, mad that it's stupid, store-bought Audrey whose life done turnt magical, simple-ass Poindexter who climbed up on the roof to watch the moon with me, who goofed around on the swings at school and generally ain't done a bit different in life than I had until the day she hopped that train. But here I'm the one's up in church listening to Miss Aileen plunk out them square, boring church songs, so mad at the way the world works, I'm having to cool my neck off with one of them Pinchback & Sons paper fans with Mahalia Jackson on the front.

It gets me to thinking that maybe it happened for Poindexter on account of she was truly right with God when we got baptized, so when Reverend Owington stops preaching and Deacon Greaves gets out the folding chairs, when Miss Aileen starts stretching her fingers all over the black keys for "One Lost Sheep," when I look down the pew and see that the makeup on Grandmama's face done turnt waxy and started to melt, I walk down front to rededicate myself to the Christian life.

People always do wonder what kind of mess rededicating people done got theirselves into, and when I get up and walk down the aisle, I see Wanda Hagston cut her eyes at me. Wanda's some phony who's up in church shouting her arms off come eleven thirty and then back at the bottom of a bottle of bourbon by Sunday twilight, and I ain't caring one whit what she nor nobody else thinks, and anyway ain't nobody in town who knows what I truly been up to, except maybe Ralph Cundiff over on Fourth Street, and Deacon Ragland setting up on the second row, and 'course Roy McKinley out on the County Road. Well, and maybe Oval Murden over on Seventh Street. And Brock Carlton down to the ice plant. And Junebug, wherever he done flown off to with big fat Colette. But well. Even they ain't got to know what's going on

307

in my head when I go down the aisle to set in that folding chair.

"Let's all pray for the sister," Reverend Owington says, when the music stops, and I'm shaking and crying and holding my right arm up to heaven. Ain't spoke a word the first, on account of I can't come up with the right kind of story. But I'm saying, in my head, *Please, God — take me too. Please, God, lift me up out of Mt. Sterling,* and seem like everbody in church done made up their own story about what my soul is lacking, must have, 'cause they all bowing their heads and spreading their hands out to the sky right over them, praying for me with a bunch of *well*'s and *amen*'s and shouting and speaking in tongues and *Jesuses,* like I'm dying of thirst in a desert and they're setting right there watching me broil.

For the most of it, I'm bowing my head and trying to look godly, but when I turn my head up for a minute, I see that Sylvia French ain't praying. She ain't shouting, neither. I get a good look at her getting a good look at me, with a curl to her lip like she done stepped in some shit and don't know how to scrape it off her shoe. She looks away right quick, but not before I catch on that she thinks I'm pitiful. She starts working her mouth and holding her hands up to the sky like everbody else, but that look she was giving me, it's still there, and it'll always be a part of me now, as much as the freckles on my nose. I ain't sure why she ain't over to the A.M.E. anyway. They don't do no spur-of-the-moment praying and shouting and carrying on over to the A.M.E. All the Negroes there are some upstanding, and it ain't people like me they can make into pity projects. Them Frenches been members over there for generations, and Sylvia just needs to go on back.

Come the end of service, the Women in White circle round and give me verses scribbled on scraps of bulletin paper. Psalms 20, Isaiah 41, Revelations 12 they give me, and Mother Beulah Gore leans over her four-footed cane and pats me on the back. Tells me trouble don't last always. They all walk off, looking like a flock of geese in all that white, and I try to read their writing, but the words just bounce around in my head like puppies and all I can think is that I'm setting out in the June sun like a fool, sweating out my hairdo. I know my soul still ain't right. But I remember Reverend Graves once saying that to believe is a verb, something a Christian body has to go out and *do,* so for the next two weeks I get down on my knees praying so much, I put a rip in the knee of my good stockings. I attend Sunday evening service and Wednesday night prayer meeting and even Tuesday morning's meeting of the Ladies' Missionary Circle, just a waiting for something to happen.

What happens is a bunch of regular mess like the mice laying turds in the cupboard and Imagene coming down with a fever in the middle of summer, and me not being able to go to the Tuesday night drive-in with Roy on account of I can't find nobody to sit with her. It's a new song out on the radio called "Caroline," and Tom Toy's singing *Your father is a bad, bad man,* talking about *the weight of the world is on your shoulders and I'm going to carry you away from here Caroline.* It's some more words in that song, like about how this Caroline is an orphan, and how she has hair red as fire, and I sing it and hum it and even holler it out sometimes, on account of it's like that song knows me. It's like that song is my friend, and it knows how I am supposed to be in the world. But in the end I know them words is just a coincidence, and Tom Toy ain't going to come through the radio and carry me off nowhere. I find a sworp of junebug beetles crawling on the porch post, and I notice how they're all so pretty with their gold-green backs shining in the sun, and I crush them and crush them with the heel of my shoe. Junebug guts, smeared all over the wood; all them souls, just gone.

Sylvia French comes knocking on my door one day. It's sheets of rain coming down behind her, but I just stand there looking, until she asks if she can come in.

"I don't see why not," I say, even though it's about ten thousand reasons. The biggest one right then is that the house ain't nowhere near clean, and I have to gather all my sewing off Grandmama's couch just so Sylvia can have a place to set. When I set down myself, it's in the rocking chair, on top of a dirty blanket Grandmama done took to rocking herself to sleep with. It's thick and warm under my backside, and it makes me set a little higher, so I don't mind, exactly.

"Well," Sylvia says, and she has the nerve to look around the living room at all the little projects I got going on — the sewing that I just threw in a corner on the floor, the canned tomatoes in little jars on the dinette, the Bible with little pieces of ripped-up paper put on the verses I been told to read. All of it piling up to one big mess, I know, but it ain't none of Sylvia's business.

"Whatcha need?" I ask her.

"Got a proposition for you," she says. "You are still in contact with Audrey Martin, aren't you?"

"Sure," I lie. I'm a mite surprised. I thought for sure she would of been in touch with Audrey herself, at least enough to know that I ain't in touch with her. It was a time when we all might've run together, but now Sylvia and Audrey, both of them's so far ahead of me I'll never catch up.

"Well, then. I wanted to invite her to play at a New Year's Eve ball in Lexington. Dr. Chenault's daughter is one of the debutantes this year and he said to name the price. He saw Audrey perform when he was visiting New York, and then he found out she was a local girl. You can look at this as a business opportunity for yourself. You're securing the performance, so you get a cut of whatever Dr. Chenault pays Audrey. You always were ambitious."

A few things strike me wrong, like how she keeps talking about this Dr. Chenault, like she thinks even the poor hillbillies east of Lexington ought to know who the Cotillion-throwing Negroes in the city are, and how she puts the "were" before the "ambitous," like I'm dead already. I ain't liable to cry for nobody but myself, generally, but I reckon Sylvia French got enough money, she can afford to cry for me too. Pity's a worrisome thing, and seems like she has a hard time setting with it. I want to tell her to go straight to hell, but I got to go long with her on account of I need the money. I don't even know how much it is and I still got to lick her ass.

"Will do," I tell her. "Thank you for remembering me." It ain't even the beginning of what I want to say to her. I show her to Grandmama's door, and I set on that blanket and start writing a letter to Poindexter. *How you doing?* I start. *We all of us miss you down here.* It's a lie, maybe the biggest one I've told since I got religion again. So I pray and read Proverbs and eat fish come Friday, and wait for Poindexter to get back to me with a yes or a no, but all the sudden seem like she can't pick up a pen and write no more, and the second week of all that, Reverend Graves pays me a visit. He ain't even made it to the porch when he stops and flings out his right arm.

"Sister Caroline," he says, "I believe you are wed to the things of this world." I know he's looking on all that mess in the yard — Mama's old ripped-up easy chair I can't throw away on account of I'm fixing to sew it up, and an old pair of Imagene's shoes I think I might polish over and give to the Deemers' little girl. Imagene's old shoo fly horse on its rotting springs, and the milk bottles what ain't been rinsed out and collected back yet, some of them with milk curdling up in the bottom. "Material things," Reverend Graves says, "will stifle your soul." He turns up his nose like he's going to sneeze, takes the toe of his shoe and makes a mark in the dirt right in front of an old burnt-out hotplate Roy said needs a new element.

"You need to just throw that away," was what Roy told me, when I asked him to go down to the hardware store hisself and get me an element, but I ain't featuring on people who don't save things. People who burn love notes from their own young'uns and give away the very dresses they got married in. People with no sense of what small drops in a bucket months and years are, people who don't understand how the future can't get nowhere without its memories. So when I invite Reverend Graves in for a drink of water, and he comes in the living room sniffing at all the magazines stacked along the living room wall, I have to tell him. "They got recipes I might use someday," I say. "But then I guess you wouldn't know 'bout that, since you never cook for yourself."

Well, that gets him, and all he can do is look at me right stupid, with his bottom lip hanging a little ahead of the top one, since everbody in town knows he been over to Towanda Graff's house ever evening since Laurel left her, "for dinner," is how Reverend Graves puts it when anybody asks. "Hebrews 13," he spits out, right quick, 'cause he can put everbody else's behavior in jail but he don't like it when somebody puts handcuffs on his own. "Be not forgetful to entertain strangers."

I don't bother telling Reverend Graves that him and Towanda ain't been strangers for years, 'cause I don't want to take any chances with my salvation, and anyway I reckon he's right about the things in the yard — rich man passing through the eye of a camel and all. Come Monday, I throw away some things, little things like a pair of broken nail clippers and my daddy's old transistor radio. It liked to kill me, but I figure maybe God's speaking through Reverend Graves, and I ain't going to make it all the way out to California with all them material things on my soul.

I throw out some wood what's too rotten to burn, and a bottle of fingernail polish what's dried up and cracking, and even a coat with a hem I've sewed back so many times it won't stay fixed no more. I throw away an old picture of Daddy — bamboo frame and all — but still, don't nothing happen. Audrey, up in New York City having one swank time after another, letting it loose on Friday nights and playing piano with her feet probably, and me stuck down in Mt. Sterling, waiting for her letter, pressing Imagene's nappy hair. Come Wednesday, Ruth Simmons's mama finally brings a letter from Audrey, and looking at the return address with all them high numbers in it makes me figure on how just praying and disposing ain't enough. The Holy Ghost ain't coming all the way down to Mt. Sterling just to snatch me up out of church, on account of it's something about Mt. Sterling that's maybe just strong enough to stand in His way. It's something about this town what just wants to stomp on all the Negroes what live here.

Audrey says in that letter how she's going to fix it in her schedule to come, and how she'll be happy to play at a ball but she'll be even happier to see me, and she says again how I need to come up to New York City. She tells me her phone number, and it's a big long one with a Numbering Plan code she says I need to remember to tell the operator about when I call. And then there's a part she's crossed out, about how she's so glad she left town on account of we all got to follow our daddies' dreams. And she's crossed it out with a darker color pen than the one she's used to write with, but still, I can read it. And that lets me know that I ain't important enough for her to ball it up and start over on new stationery. And *that* lets me know that I got something to prove to Audrey Martin, even if it ain't Christian to think so. My daddy had some dreams too, and them Martins ain't the only ones what can fly up out of here.

So come the first of July, when I get my piece of money from the bingo hall, I go down to Mr. Barnett's and buy me a *Herald Leader.* I check back in the ads section under "Employment," figuring somebody needs a housemaid or somesuch, figuring I'll save up a piece of money and buy me a nice dress for when Poindexter comes down for New Year's. Maybe even get myself an honest steady respectable job by the time she comes, so I can set there with all them fancy people and make out like I'm the one doing folks a charity. Ring Audrey up in New York when she gets back and tell *her* a few things. But then, while I'm thinking all that, what do I see there on page 16B, staring right at me, but an advertisement from a Mr. S. B. Fuller, who's looking for Negro girls to be cosmetics models.

It's some more tomatoes out in Grandmama's backyard need picking, and some beans that been picked what need snapping, and I have volunteered to be on the revival committee down to Second Baptist, but when I see that Mr. S. B. Fuller practically calling my name, I get down in the floor and pray one more time, throw the old busted breadbox out in the backyard, and hop the afternoon bus to Lexington. When the bus passes out of town, past the feed mill and the tobacco warehouse and Mr. Farrior's old Model T growing weeds out its hood, when the bus gets on Highway 60 and shifts into higher gear for the trip, when the lady in the next seat finally stops staring at me out the corner of her eye and gets her chicken leg back out her handbag, I tell myself I'll end up back in church anyway. Grandmama always does say people got to end up in church one last time 'fore they're put in the ground.

PARTY

S. B. Fuller didn't know where he was. That's the only thing I could figure, 'cause when I got to his office, down on Third and Limestone, I saw that the man'd drilled a brass knocker into his office door, like he was selling lipstick to Queen Elizabeth. The door was plywood covered with cheap veneer, naturally, and it'd splintered and busted through where he'd drilled it for holes, and you could see where the glue Mr. S.B.'d pushed into the cracks had dried into something yellow and bubbling and nasty, and he'd nailed his plastic nameplate over some of the glue. But there was that brass knocker setting right in the middle of the disaster, like a lady cleaning hog guts in silk stockings, trying to put a fancy lie over everthing. So I lifted it and knocked three times. I hit it soft, but I heard a little piece of wood crack anyway, and it was right peculiar but I felt more embarrassed for myself than I did for the door.

"Yes?" said the man when he came to open it. Since the ad had asked for Colored girls, I reckoned he would of been Colored too, but here he was a White man sure enough, with freckles on his nose what looked like he'd smeared makeup over them.

"Are you him, then?" I asked. "And what does the S.B. stand for?"

"It stands for Samuel. Samuel . . . Birdsell. But I ain't —" He straightened up in his checkered suit. "I'm not him."

"Well, I'm here to see Mr. S.B. Is there a better time?"

"The better time, my dear, does not exist. Mr. Fuller conducts his business in Chicago, operating from a splendid Gold Coast apartment overlooking Lake Michigan." I knew he was trying to put me in my place with the "splendid," not to mention the talk of someplace I ain't never seen. But the slow, careful way he was putting on airs, I felt like I still liked me, which made me like him. "I'm Mr. Fuller's personal representative here in Lexington," he said. "Allow me to assist you."

"Well all right then. I'm a model. Come up from Mt. Sterling. Answering your ad."

He was different from every man in the

world, I found out right then, 'cause he didn't look at my mouth when his face changed. "You've modeled before?" he asked me.

"Not truly."

"Stand up. And turn for me."

I got up, but all the sudden I ain't known where to put my hands, so I ended up twirling around with them half a foot away from either side of me, like a paper doll's. When I got back around to facing the man, I shook my hair. "It's my best feature," I told him.

"Bewitching. Can you do a model's turn?" he asked, and I made the exact same circle again, but this time I put my arms straight down against my sides, and then I stood there, looking at him looking at me. "You may sit down," he said.

"Well?"

"You're lovely." He picked up his pencil and chewed on it, took it out of his mouth, looked at the little dents he'd just made, and then back at me. "And I see you have a scar on your forearm. That must be ordinary for country girls. Quite charming, really. But I'm afraid Mr. Fuller is looking for a classic type. A beauty perhaps less stricken."

The way he said it, we both knew he was talking about my teeth, but he'd used so much fancy language, I felt like the prettiest girl in Lexington. He leant into a side drawer and brought out a big chrome case, then came to the other side of the desk where I was setting. He knelt down on one of his knees, then took my arm and started spreading makeup over it. The stuff smeared on creamy and smooth, like floor wax, and I wanted him to keep on polishing my arm like that for the rest of my days, fixing the mistake on my skin, erasing whatever'd happened with the lye and whatever other stupid things'd happened since Daddy killed Mama, and even whatever'd happened before that. That man could've erased my stupid, poor, broken life, and Imagene's along with it, and then Daddy's and Mama's and Grandmama's and Sam Wofford's, and Granddaddy Wallace's, and even all the stupid, poor living that'd gone on in Mt. Sterling before any of them was born. But the man got up. Eventually, he did get up.

"There," he said, holding my arm up where we could both look at it, "it's like you don't have nothing but an arm."

"But if you can cover that scar, why can't I be your model?"

"Shh," he said, putting a finger to his lips. "I got a better offer. How many Negro women do you suppose live in Mt. Sterling?"

Going up there on the bus, I thought I'd be staying in Lexington for months, trying on fresh lipsticks in front of a mirror ringed with naked light bulbs, while some cute little man stood back in the shadows getting his camera ready. But that man in the checkered suit gave me a chrome case full of makeup, and told me to come back to Lexington when I'd sold it all. Said he usually made people pay him five dollars before they took the merchandise, on account of he'd had people run off with it and not come back, but he had a good feeling about me. "You're not only honest but earnest," is how he put it. And so there I come, back home, on the evening bus, and that's how I ended up walking down Queen Street with this cosmetics case in the middle of a cold drizzle.

"Whatcha know good?" yells Melton Boyd, from his front porch. "Why you carrying that pretty suitcase?"

"None your beeswax," I tell him. You'd think he'd still be mad at me for knocking out his best tooth, but then he always grins at me whenever he sees me, like the empty-headed jack-o'-lantern he is.

"Packing off to Hollywood yet?" He laughs real hard after he asks it and I stick out my tongue at him — Hollywood ain't something he's supposed to know about. It's something I told his brother Tyrone while we was necking out behind his grandmama's house, which means Melton and who all else probably knows a bunch of stuff they ain't supposed to know about me. I keep my tongue out at him long enough it catches a raindrop, and I think, who cares? I'm leaving this place anyway. And when I leave out of here, it won't matter what anybody thinks they know, 'cause I'll be gone and then they won't know one thing more. All they'll have is their "she used to be's" and their "she used to do's," which is like saying they won't have a damn thing.

When the drizzle picks up to hoofbeats, I cover my head with the chrome case and run in the vestibule of Second Baptist, where Pastor's wife done agreed I might throw a Fuller party in the basement. I'm happy, on account of I'm aiming to make a piece of money, but the whole thing done like to kill my nerves something terrible. All that checking to see which mirror's in which compartment, and rearranging the lipsticks in order of deepening shade, all while Grandmama was out on the front porch setting up a howl about how awful her pains was acting up. The last Fuller party I'd thrown'd been in my very own living room, for some of Grandmama's friends what seemed like they was probably too old to even understand what cosmetics was, and I had to make sure all the makeup from that party got washed out the pink Fuller flannel. It's a tablecloth really, and it's supposed to just set under the chrome case and look pretty, but old Hesterline Martin who done lost three quarters of her mind thought she was supposed to use it to blot her lipstick.

Well, I had to wash and wash that flannel to get it in presentable order for the ladies at Second Baptist, and then I had to make sure my nice skirt and blouse was pressed, and then put on all the Fuller cosmetics I could possibly fit on my face — it's what the manual said. Grandmama was out there whimpering about going to meet her Savior, while I was swiping on lipstick and eyestick and mascara and eye shadow and rouge. I even blended the ivory foundation down onto my neck, just so it'd match my face. It clumped black on the ends of my lashes so you can't see they're really red lessun you look at the roots, and with all this eyestick on, I look like a scared rabbit, and I know the collar of my shirt'll be all messed up with foundation by the end of it all, but don't none of that matter, long as I sell something today. The man in Lexington said if I sell enough, I get to go to a seller's convention in Chicago. And there's one shindig I ain't planning on missing.

Mother Owington's already down in the basement, since she had to come open up church for me, and when I walk in, she gets up and comes to kiss me on both my made-up cheeks. "Why hello there," she says, and I think the only reason she ain't wiping her lips from all that greasy makeup is that she's a preacher's wife, so she can't hurt my feelings. She's so old she don't need makeup. Not that she ain't got wrinkles and a wattle just like any other old lady, but covering it up ain't going to improve her none. Reverend Owington ain't that straying type of preacher, so she don't need to do much to keep him, and ain't none of the rest of us she needs to impress. Seems to me like what she really needs is for something exciting to happen to her, but then as first lady of the church she's got to focus on keeping her nose clean for the rest of her life, and makeup ain't going to help one bit with that. I'm glad she's getting the free hostess's gift, on account of I always did like her, and she sat next to me and held my hand at Mama's funeral, but I wonder what she'll pick that won't be a waste on a lady like her.

"Mrs. Owington," I call her, trying to make my "t's" as sharp as the man in Lexington'd made his, "thank you for hostessing. I can promise you, you won't be sorry. Fuller Cosmetics are fine, fine stuff. And as a token of my appreciation, I would just love it if you'd select a gift of your choice. You can go ahead and look at what I got if you like." It's what the manual suggested, and it makes Mother Owington smile like it's Christmas, so I guess that manual is on to something.

While she's bent over my case, with her big grandmama-of-seventeen butt hanging out behind her, two more ladies from church walk in. Velma Ray and Wanda Hagston, both of them shaking their umbrellas out like they was twins. "How do," I say, even though I can't stand neither one of them. According to a manual, a lady salesperson cannot afford to be petty. She must put aside her differences for the sake of enterprise.

"Whyn't you have a sit down," I say then, to Wanda Hagston, on account of she's the one I like the least. And then I get the magnifying mirror out, just like the manual says do, and I show her all her enlarged pores, and all her little blackheads what look like buried ticks by the time the mirror gets

through with them. "You look like a 41," I
tell her, and when I get out the tin and open
it up, it does match almost perfectly. "Maybe
a 43?" I say, but when I sponge that on it
makes her darker, and the manual says
Negro ladies won't want that no matter how
true it is to their complexion, so I go back
to the 41 and start sponging. I sponge and
sponge, and it's hard to make her look
decent because it turns out her skin is drier
than you might think looking at all them
blackheads, and little flakes of skin keep
rolling up like carrot skin. So I end up rubbing in some of the mineral oil they put in
the side pocket of the suitcase, and that
makes Wanda's face smooth as a baby's ass.
I put a little mascara on her lashes, but I
don't go crazy with the rouge or the eye
shadow, on account of I can tell it wouldn't
look right with the mismatched makeup.
When I hand her the normal-size mirror,
she smiles like she's just seen Jesus im-
printed on her forehead, and she asks me
what else I got besides the tin of 41. So I
end up selling her eleven dollars' worth of
full face, which ain't bad considering I know
for a fact they ain't had sugar in the house
for three weeks.

Next I do up Velma Ray, who has the opposite problem from Wanda, so before I get

started I wipe her face with something called astringent. "Feels good, don't it," I tell her. "It's cleansing you." The manual says to say this, on account of really the astringent is full of enough alcohol to make your face feel like it's in hell. But people'll do anything to get clean. Say "cleansing" and they think it's something ordained by God. So I clean Velma up and sponge a little 35 on her, and since she's so yellow-skinned, I dab her on with a little blue eye shadow just for fun. When she looks in the mirror, 'course, here she comes screaming, "I look like a savage!" So I spread some brown shadow over the blue and that makes her happy, and then I lie and tell her it's the blending of the two colors that's the trick, and she ends up buying the blue and the brown plus six dollars' worth of 35.

Well, in the meantime, while I've been doing Wanda and Velma, five or six more ladies done come down to the basement looking for a good time, and I can hear them chatting each other up the wall and back down. I hear snatches of the conversation, like Miss Nettie telling Mother Owington how the salamanders are tearing up her flower bed, and old Grandmama Cundiff telling Pauline Burke how she ought to mind that she don't catch a summer cold out here in a June rain with no coat on, the 85 degrees of Fahrenheit notwithstanding. I hear people laughing, and I smell clashing perfumes, and I've got two crisp fives and seven ones in my pocket, which is a good six dollars over my wholesale, and I'm almost to where I feel like I might fall in love with the whole flock of them, when who comes and sets in my chair but Colette Smith. And she's going to be really hard to do, I can tell it. Not only because of the way her nose and her forehead shine against the rest of her dull, dull face, but on account of she's setting here holding Junebug's baby. It's a right cute baby, I got to say, with a head full of hair and Junebug's pretty Junebug eyes. But that just makes it worse. It's like Junebug setting right here watching me, asking me what the hell do I think I'm doing, being a saleslady.

"Discount's only for Second Baptist members," I tell her.

She shrugs. Says, "Do me up anyway."

I start in on her with some 23, and I got to say she does have some fine skin. Ain't a blemish nowhere, so all I'm really doing with that 23 is putting a little red over her high yellow to make her look sassy. Everbody else looked straight ahead of them when I was doing their eyes, but Colette looks right up at me, right into my eyes where things is awkward between us. And evertime that baby gets its little hand up on her shirt she takes and pushes it away, like it ain't just going to throw that hand right back up and wave it around something crazy. The way she stuffs the baby's hand back into its own lap ever time it wants her, it's just nasty.

"That a girl or a boy?" I ask, on account of it's got on green and I can't tell.

She narrows her eyes at me. "Don't make no difference, do it? Boy, it'll grow up and work down to the ice plant. Girl, it'll stick around Shake Rag and have five squalling kids by somebody who works down to the ice plant. Boy or girl, it's going to be screaming and puking on me for the next couple years no matter who its daddy's out screwing."

I take my sponge away from her face to let some air rush over her nastiness. I tell her, "I was just trying to make small talk."

"You don't need to."

I brush powder down her nose and she's still looking at me, and her eyes are so full of water the tears are about to brim, which I don't understand not one bit. Here she is setting here with the prize — Junebug's baby. She will go home and fix Junebug his

331

supper and iron his maroon ice plant uniform and tickle his baby's stomach. She'll get his good money and a roof over her high yellow head and hundred percent guaranteed loving ever night while I'm running around town following some stupid 32-page manual. She's safe, and Junebug running around on her don't water that down none. And she ain't really fat, neither. She's just soft on top, with a big blimpy bosom, and that makes her look like a cow from a distance, but really, she's got a right nice bone structure round the face, and tiny little wrists like a Barbie doll's.

"Okay, then, I'll just do your face, honey," I tell her. I still ain't sure why she's mad at me, and I can tell she ain't going to buy nothing on account of she ain't asked about the product, but she acts like she's got a right to the free makeover.

"Yeah. Do my face. You and Audrey always did think y'all knew how to boogie faster'n the rest of us. And maybe *she* does. But I bet you all the tea in China you end up stuck here just like the rest of us. Doing everbody's face."

I finish her up with a quickness, and she looks just like a clown at the end of what I do for her, and I've even put little diamond shapes on her eyelids, and when I show it to her in the mirror she drops her jaw.

"I figure that's an improvement," I say.

And then I feel like the party's over, so when Miss Nettles comes and sets down in my chair, I tell her she don't need no makeup a tall and I'm doing her a favor by telling her. Ain't nothing the manual would ever approve of, naturally, so I tell her even perfect skin needs a little mascara on the eyes to set against it. She looks over at Grandmama Cundiff and winks without smiling, and Grandmama Cundiff throws up her hands. "Darlin', we'll just buy ten dollars' worth of whatever you're selling. Figure we need to help the party, what with your mama being dead and gone."

Well, that just stops everthing. Brings it to a dead hush. Even the baby picks up that something's wrong and turns quiet, and I get so mad, thinking they all think they're better'n me because I'm out trying to make a buck off their ugly asses. But I remember what it said in the manual, about how enterprise and pettiness can't live together, and I think about that New Year's Eve ball and that convention in Chicago what ain't none of these bitches ever going to, and I smile at them all. Just like a cosmetics model would. "Thank you, Miss Smith," I tell Colette, while I shake her hand in

333

between both of mine, and then I lean over and kiss her baby, even though it's done fell to sleep. I shake Wanda Hagston's hand and say thank you. I say it again and again, six times over, and when I get to Mother Owington, I ask her whether she's picked her gift.

"Can I have a bottle of that astringent?"

I never would of figured. But I should've.

I'm wore clean out by the time I get home, so I set down on the porch bench next to Grandmama, who's sitting straight up sleep the way only dying people can do, with her hand lost through two undone buttons on her housecoat. She itches her chest in her sleep, then sets back to snoring again, and I look out on old Mr. Fleenor, wandering the stations of his yard and talking to hisself, and I wonder what he was like when he was my age, whether he ever had gals to come kiss him, and whether he ever got time to just hang between the slats of a covered bridge and fish. My cosmetics case is in my lap, and I'm stroking the chrome finish, wondering what made Mr. Fleenor into what he is now — was it too much sad or maybe too much happy.

In a couple of days I'll make another trip up to Lexington, replenish my foundation supply, and see about that Cotillion ball, what ain't even six months away. Since I'm just the middleman for the music I ain't really got to attend to the arrangements a tall, but I want to see the inside of the Strand, to see what the lighting is like and what shade eye shadow I ought to wear in front of all them debutantes, what color lipstick might show up best under whatever kind of fancy lights they got in the theater and make Sylvia French jealous. The lady running the show is one of 'em's mama, lady by the name of Sugar Raspberry. She's the first Colored lady to work at the law firm of Stites & Harbison, even if all she does is run part of the switchboard. Sylvia French took me up to Lexington to meet her one day, and I was some surprised on how refined she *ain't*. She smokes so much, she lights the end of a new cigarette with the one she just finished smoking, and when she says a word that begins with the letters "h" or "p," you got to move out of her way, her breath smells so bad. "You've spoken with Audrey on the telephone?" she asked me, and I lied yes. Grandmama ain't got no telephone. And letters is just as good, I think. Sugar Raspberry's just fascinated with the telephone on account of she pokes numbers in one all day. "Very well, then," she'd said. "I will be mailing her a contract."

I gave Mrs. Raspberry the address, but something about all of it still ain't setting right with me. I reckon it's that I still can't believe Audrey said yes, but I'm getting myself ready for the party. I went down to the fabric store and bought two patterns for dresses for me and Imagene to wear. Christians ain't supposed to be in competition with each other, I know, but it's always going to be a winner and a loser come out of a situation, and come that Cotillion ball, I don't want me and Imagene to be the losers.

Grandmama itches herself again in her sleep and moans, so I ask her, "What's wrong, Grandmama? Something bit you?"

"No, love," she says, without opening her eyes. "It's just been doing like this come lately. My chest."

I put my case on the floor and get up right in front of Grandmama. "Let me see," I say to her, and I unbutton the top three buttons of her housecoat. When it all opens up to the air, it smells like something right terrible, something you'd find under a Band-Aid after a few days if you got your nose close enough, but worse. Way worse. She's got all kinds of dry, sore skin flaking off the side of her right boob, and the skin underneath that done turnt the most peculiar color of orange. Like a grapefruit.

"Grandmama," I say. "Something's wrong."

"Ain't nothing wrong," she says, and she waves me out of her face and buttons herself all the way back up, and takes to rocking herself back and forth in her chair.

But it is something wrong, and it's a mite curious but it makes me think back to a day when everthing was still right, a day when Mama was still living and she piled both us girls in the back of Daddy's car and we went for ice cream down to the drug store. Imagene was setting next to me with her little hand wrapped around her sugar cone, and chocolate ice cream dripping all down the front of her yellow dress. It was her first time having ice cream, and I'll never forget the look on her face, like Newton discovering gravity.

"I'll call Dr. Pitts tomorrow."

"Don't need no doctor," she says, but I know right then — I'm going to lose her.

"Grandmama," I say, but she's already back to sleep. Lost to snoring, even, and as her hand shudders and falls out her housecoat, it hits me, how many things Grandmama's had sprung on her in one lifetime. And it hits me too, what she'd say if she was awake. Everbody gets them ice cream days. But everbody's going to get a few surprises 'fore it's all over with, too.

ANGELS' SHARE

Can't let cancer hit the air, the old folks say. Somebody dies, it's on account of they opened him up on the table. Once that cancer hits the air, they'll say, he was a goner. And so when we go to see Dr. Pitts, I'm straightening my back when we walk through the door, fixing my lips in a line so I'll look more like a whitegirl, getting ready to tell Pitts he ain't opening my grandmama up noway, nohow. Well, turns out, after Dr. Pitts feels all round Grandmama's boobs — over them and around them and all up under them, and then looks all up close on the sore spots with a lighted lens — turns out ain't a thing he can do for her. She don't even need to be opened up to tell it.

"Inoperable," he says, while Grandmama looks straight on ahead with that stone-hard look on her face, the one what don't tell you what she's really thinking, the same look she gave that charity lady from the

Morehead Home for Children who come around looking for Imagene when Daddy went off to the pen.

"Inoperable?" I ask him, and all of a sudden I'm ready to beg him to open Grandmama up. He's got to do something. There's got to be something he can do.

"Stage Four. Terminal," he tells me, leaning over right into my face like Grandmama ain't even there. "From here on in, you just need to keep her comfortable. I'll write you a prescription for morphine," he says, and he leans over to scribble it out.

I wonder if he's thinking my grandmama's just some old Colored lady not worth fooling with, and I blurt out, "If it's the money —" but he turns round and pats me on the hand 'fore I even get it out right.

"It was the time," he says, patting my hand again. "It was the time."

And then it seems like ain't nobody got nothing to say, on account of ain't nobody can argue Grandmama ain't waited too long to go see about things, and the quiet between the three of us grows like some kind of animal what's going to hatch and get ugly. We all feel it, I guess, because Dr. Pitts nods at us and then leaves, and I help Grandmama get out of the thin little dingy gown the nurse gave her and back into her pink blouse. I fasten all her little pearl buttons and fix her glasses back on the bridge of her nose on account of they done slipped down in her surprise. Still she don't say nothing, not "Lord help me" nor "Jesus have mercy" or even "Dammit," and it's her not saying nothing after a lifetime of talking a blue streak what makes me want to cry and cry and cry. I take a string of gray hair what's fallen down over her eye and fix it back behind her ear, and I kiss her on the cheek and leave my lips there just for a second so I can get a good smell of my grandmama.

"How much do I owe?" I ask the red-haired lady at reception, when we get out into the lobby.

She folds her lips together and looks down, so she can be sorry without having to say it. "Doctor says you'll get the bill in the mail," she says.

Part of me knows that means I ain't getting no bill, but then part of me worries I read it wrong, and Ruth Simmons's mama might be walking up the steps any day with a paper what says I owe something I can't pay. All week, the worry of it follows me around everwhere I go, and then it gets bigger and turns into something else, on account of I ain't paid for the bad thing I got

341

told. It's like skipping out on a fortune-teller before you've handed her the quarter, I think, and if I ain't paid for what Dr. Pitts said, maybe the bad thing'll get even bigger, reach out and grab somebody else I love. It gets to where I almost feel like I need that bill to make everthing okay, and so I'm walking around everwhere I go waiting for Ruth Simmons's mama to tap me on the shoulder and say, "Oh, I forgot this little thing in the bottom of my mailbag."

I'm standing in line at the Colored store Wednesday dusk, not able to remember a thing I got in my basket, just waiting for Ruth Simmons's mama to come hand me that bill, when I run into Gordon Bell, who I ain't seen in a good two years.

"How do?" he says. He shrugs an elbow at my basket. "Need a ride?" He's been looking at me all this time I've been off in outer space — that much is clear.

"Sure," I say, on account of I know I'ma end up with two bags of groceries instead of my regular one, and the next thing I know, he's loading my bags into the back of his car, and it's a big bolt of thunder what booms so loud we both jump, and the wind's blowing my hair every which way, and it's a fire engine what motors by. And when it's past, it finally registers that under all that noise, Gordon's asking me if I ever been to the distillery.

And then it turns out, Gordon Bell's got a right nice car. A 1955 DeSoto Fireflite, sea green with a beige stripe down the side. Also turns out, Gordon Bell is good people. Don't nobody got nothing much good to say about him, on account of he's real quiet and don't fool with people, but when I take my finger and slide it down the inside of his pants, just under the stitch of his belt loop where I can feel his smooth skin, he takes my finger right back out and holds my hand in the one he ain't driving with. "We ain't even kissed yet," he says. Puts ever one of his fingers between mine like we was knitting ourselves into a pattern. "And you're better'n that."

When the storm starts to hit hot, we stop on that little one-lane bridge what runs over Collum's Creek. We set there so long, listening to his radio, and I think for sure he's wanting some little piece a sugar and just don't know how to ask on account of he never talks much. But when I lean over and pretend to fiddle with his turn signal, he don't kiss me nor nothing. Just sets there tapping his foot to Ray Charles, and so I relax and settle back into my seat and watch the water roiling over rocks on its way to rise up the bank. Feels like that water's calling something out to me. Not nothing like "come in, come in," but more like "stay dry — things is finally about to change for you."

Gordon's worked at that distillery for long about six year, ever since he quit high school, and when the storm lets up and the rain turns to little pecks, he starts on back driving to show me what the distillery looks like. Turns out there's big fire, taking it all down, and we can see the smoke for miles on our way up the road. The car windows is cracked just a hair, and you can smell the bourbon on that smoke like you was pouring it over a steak. When we get to the top of Blanton Hill he gets out the car and throws his nice canvas jacket down on the wet grass so I can set on it, then he sets down next to me, on one of his coatsleeves, and I look at them smoking clouds opening up into the sky like gray seashells. "Wow," I say, but he don't answer.

It's fire engines showing up from all over everwhere, even one with NICHOLASVILLE painted on the side of it, and all their bells are clanging and all their firemen are just a yelling, but that fire's just going to keep on going and going — you can tell it just from looking. All the bourbon what's running in little rivers around the warehouse done caught fire too, and from way up on top of this hill, we can see how all them little flaming rivers connect like they was a map of Louisiana.

"What you think started it?" I ask Gordon.

"Lightning?"

"Probably. You're probably right."

Then he starts talking about all the bourbon what's burning out that warehouse. About a million gallons, he says. Enough bourbon to fill a small pond. He's telling me how part of his job is to stack the barrels on top of each other in ricks, and how even with the barrels stacked, air gets in through the wood and then the bourbon evaporates out the wood and into the air. "The angels' share," he says it's called.

"What kind of a fool misbehaving angel drinks bourbon?" I ask him, but he don't laugh. He was only a couple of years ahead of me in school but he always has been more grown up than anybody else.

"You got to keep the air wet," he says now, "keep it dark and cool." And then the way he starts talking about that warehouse, and how the company's always dreaming up ways to increase the production, you'd think he was Jim Beam hisself.

"So what you going to do now?" I ask

him, when the roof of the warehouse crashes in and sets all them firemen to shouting. So high up on that hill, I can't make out anything they're saying, but I can tell it ain't good. "Looks like you won't be going to work for a while."

"This won't kill the business. Just set it back. People got to drink. People always got to drink. There'll be some cleanup days. And if they don't need everbody for it, I reckon I might just get myself out of town." He says it calm as anything. "I got money saved up. I want to see places. Maybe even go out to Oklahoma and sit in at a drug store counter."

I rock on my butt and throw my hair back, so he can tell I'm just as fancy as he is. "Well," I say. "I don't feature on going out West to get my head beat in just so I can sip out of some White man's teacup. Me, I'm going to New York come the new year. To stay with Audrey Martin." It's a lie, naturally, but once it's out there hanging around in the air, it sounds pretty reasonable. "I got almost enough for the train ticket," I tell him. And that part ain't a lie, not exactly — I know how much the ticket costs, on account of Audrey's written it home to me near about twenty times. What's more, I've made double that off

S. B. Fuller so far.

"You'll need more than train fare, you know. Stuff costs a lot in New York. Food. Taxis. Shows."

"Well, and that's where you might come in. You want to come to a party?"

Now, I know what the Fuller Cosmetics manual says about putting differences aside for the sake of enterprise, but after that Second Baptist party and some pretty tiresome door-to-door, I reckoned I was through with women and their cattiness for a while. I took my money up to Lexington, to the man in that office, who had on the same checked suit he had on the day we met. By then, I had ninety-six dollars and a mostly empty cosmetics case, and the man told me he was awful surprised on account of it'd only been two weeks. "Honest and eager," I reminded him, and then he filled my case back up, gave me half my money back for commission, and showed me the new product line. "Sir Fuller," he said. "Makeup for the discriminating man." I knew wasn't nobody in all of Mt. Sterling what could even pronounce the word "discriminating," but when I saw them male makeup pens, I saw money. "Very modern. Very 1960," the man in the checked suit said. He made it sound like a right fine notion.

"I'ma throw a party down to the Tin Cup," I tell Gordon now. "And I want you to spread the word."

"What kind of party?"

"Sir Fuller. Male makeup."

Gordon smiles. First one I seen him crack all day. "You sure are enterprising," he says, and then I smile too, because I'm pretty sure he's the one person in town who'll get it.

"For the discriminating man," I say, winking at him.

We set up on that hill a little longer, even after the bourbon starts to get in our lungs thick like we was drowning in it, and the air gets chill. We watch them firemen still yelling and the little bourbon rivers burning, and Gordon don't crack not one word, which I like on account of in Grandmama's house there ain't never one solid ounce of peace and quiet. Then finally, when I think he done forgot I'm even setting there, Gordon says, "I know you come from a hard-working family." Ain't nobody had the nerve to mention who I come from in years, but then he gets even better, saying, "I know your father was on for a good piece a time down to the ice plant. And I know your mama used to seamstress. I remember watching her walk down the street all pressed and pretty, and I used to wish one day I'd marry a lady like her." He undoes his hand from mine and rubs me on the knob of my shoulder. "And now here you are, taking care of your sister and your grandmama and conducting sales business just like a man."

It hits me for a second that maybe Gordon Bell ain't such good people, on account of it sounds like when he does find a fine, upstanding lady like my mama, he's going to take her and strap her in behind a plow. But anyway, he can be a body at a party. "This Saturday the thirtieth," I tell him, getting up from his coat. "Two in the afternoon."

I've already asked the owner of the Tin Cup, who says it sounds like a right fine idea, so I spend Thursday and Friday rounding up some more men. For starters, I invite anybody who's ever seen me naked. Even Junebug and Ralph Cundiff I invite, on account of I reckon what the manual says about pettiness and enterprise counts for men too. Then I invite Deacon Ragland, who always calls me "young sugar" when we're screwing around.

"Young sugar," he says when I tell him

about the party, "I'ma need a little something to make me enter a house of ill repute."

I think about what Gordon said to me, about me being better'n that, and I give Deacon Ragland one little prudy kiss on the cheek. When he sees I ain't going to do more'n that, he grabs me and holds me close to his body, so close I can feel his big barrel stomach fill with air and let out again, but I just push myself away. "That kiss is just the start. I'ma need you to buy some cosmetics 'fore I lay anything else on you."

We both laugh, but only one of us is serious about the joke, and I run out his back door just dying to breathe the fresh air.

I invite Melton and Tyrone Boyd, and when Melton laughs at the idea of men wearing makeup, I tell him it's the new thing and he better jump on the wagon. "Don't let being old-fashioned get in the way of a clear complexion."

I stop at ten men, since that's really all the makeup pens I have. Come Saturday at one o'clock I get busy organizing my mirrors and gathering all the clean white cloths in Grandmama's closet. I put the cloths in a bowl of water and push them to the back of the icebox — it's key, the Sir Fuller insert says, to close the male pores before application, and anyway I figure in all this hot weather, putting a cold cloth on somebody's face is as good of a business strategy as any other. Grandmama's laying on the couch asleep, where she's been for days, and before I leave out the house I take a spoonful of morphine and put it on her tongue. She barely wakes up, so I raise her head up to make sure she don't choke on it, and then I kiss her, and I'm so glad I decided to linger that day I kissed her in the doctor's office, on account of she already don't smell like my grandmama no more with all that morphine running through her.

"Afternoon, Grandmama. Have a good sleep."

It's a right pretty day, one of them afternoons when air blows dry from the mountain, and I'm almost skipping down the street, I'm so excited about making some money. Thursday night, I went over to where Gordon Bell stays, over on Seventh Street, in that house Miss Ora Ray lived in before she died. Colette Smith was over on the porch next door visiting kinfolk, and when she saw me coming up the street she got this satisfied look on her face. But after what she told me down to Second Baptist, I ain't felt shamed about Junebug being with her no more, and ain't felt like I was standing any lower in life than she was. I figure in order to feel bad that some man left you, you got to first off feel like you ain't pretty enough and fun enough for him to've loved you. More and more, I'm figuring out how just about ever girl I know is fun enough and pretty enough, and most of the times when people get together it's all a big accident, and nothing to feel bad or good about. With Junebug and Colette, it was a specially big accident.

"What a nice surprise," Gordon said, when he opened the door, and I was right happy, on account of he said it loud enough that I knew Colette heard it. When he let me in the door I heard her baby let out a little holler, like she done got so mad she had to resettle him in her lap.

"Land sakes alive," I said, when I get in the house, 'cause Gordon done moved everthing out what was in it when Miss Ora Ray was alive. I was there a few times back then, back when Audrey's mama used to take care of Miss Ora Ray and we'd come over and listen to the lady's radio while Danaitha was giving her a bath. But now everthing's different. Gordon done took all them little dime-store paintings off the wall and put a giant clock in every room. He showed me the bedroom, and I saw how he done took it upon hisself to paint the walls orangy-red. "I think the desert's like this," he said, when I asked him why.

He showed me ever single room, even the bathroom, and I let on like I wasn't imagining Miss Ora Ray's ghost setting up in the tub, her arms stretched out to Danaitha and her mouth twisted up in something she couldn't ask, and then he took me back to the living room and I saw that he done got hisself a telephone.

"Mind if I use it?" I asked him.

"Sure."

"It's a long-distance call," I said, but he shrugged, and he scooted a chair up to the telephone stand for me before he went to set hisself down on the couch. There I was thinking no man ever been that nice to me before, and maybe there was something wrong with Gordon Bell, like he had a fatal disease, or a spaceship full of aliens hiding out in his backyard.

I picked up the receiver and dialed up the party line but I ain't even took my finger out the wheel before somebody else's voice come on. It was Mrs. Barnett, and I caught her in the middle of a sentence, talking about how Reverend Graves done sneaked some prophylactics under his order down to the store. I was aiming to hear the rest of it, or at least find out who she was telling it to, but there was Gordon Bell looking right at me and I knew it wasn't polite to listen in on the party line so I hung up. "What you know," I told him. "Everbody wants to talk tonight."

I went over to the couch to set next to him, but he scooted over until he was sitting right to the end of his own couch, like he was scared of me. He nodded his head and smiled, then looked down to his knees, and I wondered more about what might be wrong with him, like maybe he had a tail what came out at twelve o'clock midnight. "They started rebuilding the distillery yet?" I asked him.

"Yes."

I wanted to tell him it was like a radio show, and one-word answers weren't going to get him nowhere, but it seemed like he didn't really care too much about making any moves. He was just looking at his knees — seemed like he might even be the type what enjoyed looking at his knees. Seemed like he was entertained just by the sound of me breathing. Seemed like he was living a lot of his life in his head. Seemed like really, he'd make a good boyfriend for Audrey Martin.

"All right, well, can I try your phone again?"

"Be my guest," he said, and he threw out his hand to the phone.

I put my finger on the wheel and rung up a zero, and it took the wheel a few seconds to spin back around and then there was the operator on the phone, saying, "What number, please?" and I gave it to her, all them ten long numbers they got in the big cities nowadays, and by the time I got to the fifth number my voice was shaking, and I wanted to say it was on account of I ain't never actually spent money to talk to a person, but the bigger truth is that I was afraid to talk to Audrey Martin. She's a legend in this town now, for one thing, but for another she done lived in that big city and changed so much, I was afraid that when she answered that phone and heard my voice, which still ain't proper, and she heard my mind, what still ain't as big as hers on account of ain't nothing happened to me in the year she's been gone, that well of feeling she been writing all them letters from was just going to dry up. I reckoned if she talked to me again she'd see that we wasn't never meant to be friends, not really, and then it'd just be me there in Mt. Sterling with my dying grandmama and my baby sister who still wasn't even tall enough to stand on a stepstool and fry corn bread. Me with my dreams what can't never seem to come true, me with this man who was too bashful to look up from his knees.

Before I could even think everthing I needed to think about all of it, there Audrey was, telling me "Good evening," and them Frenches was right — she'd grown into a right proper way of talking.

"How do."

"Pookie?"

Ain't nobody called me that in so long, and I was right surprised on how good it felt. "Audrey."

She asked how I was, and she asked after my family, and then she said, "Tell me everything," but I really didn't have much to tell, and the stuff I would tell I wasn't going to tell in front of Gordon, so I made up some stuff about the Wild West show that came through town even though I didn't have the money to go to it and last Sunday's church service, which I did go to but ain't paid as much attention to as I made it sound like. "So you're coming down here?" I asked her, when I was finished with all that, and then finally Gordon had the good sense to get up out of the living room and pretend like he had something to do in the kitchen.

"Of course I am," she said. "I'd never break a promise to you."

"You know it's New Year's Eve?"

"Sure I do."

"Ain't that a big party time in New York City?"

She stopped for a minute. "Well, you know the Negroes in Harlem don't really go to Times Square. And big party times have never been all that important to me."

"Well, all right then. Seven o'clock sharp. I don't know if Mrs. Raspberry told you that."

"It's in the contract. I sent it back to her." She laughed. "You make a good manager."

"Well okay then. All right."

"Caroline?"

"Yes."

"You think you might come up here some day? I mean, you'll come visit, of course, but do you think you might come up here to live?"

"I don't know," I told her. "What's so special about New York, anyway?"

"Oh, Pookie. You've got to come see it. The people here are just unreal. They're not like anyone you or I have ever known. They don't care what anybody thinks — they just *do* things. There are people standing in the park playing flute. A man in the subway who dances with a doll. You just wouldn't even believe it all."

I laughed like I was interested, but it was phony and she probably knew it. "I remember when you was running to town, out of breath crying 'cause your mama done slapped you. Now look at you, in New York, trying to tell me what's real and what ain't. Well, I just don't see why I ought to drag myself up there to see some man dancing in a subway. I ain't lost a damn thing in New York."

She got all quiet, and she finally whispered "Caroline" real quiet, like maybe she was crying when she said it. It sounded like Gordon was frying bacon, and then it got to smelling like he was, and the thick aroma of it reminded me that he was probably halfway listening, and he did seem like a quiet type but who knew who he knew. And then there were those ten minutes on his phone costing more than I made in a day's worth of hog killing, and I didn't want to take advantage of him even if he did seem like some slug who wouldn't mind.

"Well, I got to go then," I said.

"I can't wait to see you."

"Same here," I told her, and we said our goodbyes.

I ain't meant to make her feel bad, necessarily. It's just that she's always seeing a rainbow and I feel like somebody's got the duty to tell her about the rain. The more I think on it, the more I do want to go back to New York with her, for a visit, anyways. I figure I'll make about fifty dollars down to the Tin Cup if I play things right, and that ought to cover all that expensive stuff Gordon was talking about. I could go back with Audrey right after she plays the Cotillion ball.

Well, when I get in the Tin Cup, wouldn't you know all of them men is there early, sucking down their beer and whiskey. Even Gordon showed up, though I think he's just drinking a Coke. "Well hello," I tell them all, and I get to working right quick. I lay the Fuller flannel out on the bar, set my mirrors out on top of it. The owner's out in the table area sweeping, whistling a birdcall ever time she bends over with the dustpan.

"Howdy," comes some woman's voice, and I turn up and she's sitting about a foot away from me and I ain't even noticed her. Except for the spread of her hips, this lady looks like a stalagmite growing out the middle of the bar stool. She's got blond hair like honey and blue eyes like a seven o'clock sky, and that kind of skin that only other

Colored people know is Black. She's smoking her cigarettes all showy-like, like she's an actress in a play and we got to watch her every puff to get the story line.

"Right nice to meet you," I tell her.

"Yeah," she says, and she goes back to her cigarette, studying it like she's never seen it before.

Gordon brings his soda over and sets down on the bar stool between me and the BlackWhite lady, but before he can even get one word out we smell something burning and he's screaming out, "God Almighty!" He hops along the counter holding his hand over a hole the BlackWhite lady done burnt in his sleeve with her cigarette. She holds her breath like she's surprised, but she smiles at him like she ain't.

"You're on fire," she says, her voice slow in all the wrong places of the Deep South. "You might just have to take that shirt off, son."

Gordon frowns at her. "Proper ladies don't smoke."

"Proper ladies?" she says, still drowning her words. "Who's a proper lady in here?" Her giggle echoes off the ceiling. "Proper ladies!" she yells. "Proper ladies! Calling all proper ladies!"

Gordon grabs her by the shoulders so

hard her boobs jog an inch to the left, and I can guess why he's mad at her — she's engaged in the wrong kind of enterprise. He puts his face right in hers. "Shut your mouth," he says, but just like all the rest of us he's looking right at her plump, soft mouth, with the skin lighter around its corners like it's filled with cream. I'm seeing a pox scar on her forehead what I might cover with a little 17, but I know Gordon's probably looking at the lovely hollow in her throat. I'm thinking how I might blend some 14 into the tired circles underneath her eyes, but I know Gordon't looking at the evening pretty of them.

"I got concealer," I tell her, and that breaks everbody's spell.

Gordon lets her go. Turns to me and says, "How do?"

But I'm serious. She ain't catty. She ain't petty. She's clearly a prostitute, which means she needs cosmetics. "Here," I tell her. "Check it out. I think ivory might be your shade. It's mine."

She palms the concealer and then comes over and sets down in front of all the other men where I done set the Fuller flannel, and as the hour goes on I get so grateful for her, because when the men get to clowning around, she makes them get serious again.

When Deacon Ragland turns up his nose at the male makeup pen and says camouflage is for the weaker sex, she tells him well then he ought to buy some of what else I got for his wife. When I put some of the pen on Tyrone's cheeks and Melton throws his hand over like a queer and starts prissing around, she asks him who the hell he thinks he is, who can walk around with pimples all over his face and still get women. Ever time they start clowning and laughing, I think ain't none of them buying a damn thing, but I end up selling sixty-three dollars' worth of makeup. I get to feeling like pretty soon, the Negroes of Mt. Sterling is going to be the best-looking Negroes what ever lived. When I finished with them ladies at Second Baptist, I thought what I'd figured out is that people ain't going to help you out 'til you get so low they can step on you while they're doing it. But here's this prostitute helping me out, and all the men-folk of the town buying stuff they really do think they need now, and when Deacon Ragland leaves with six dollars' worth of 28 and ain't called me "young sugar" once, I start to feeling like I might love people all over again.

When all the men've gone home, the lady comes and introduces herself. "My name's

Marialana. Come over tomorrow, I'll have some money. I'm in that house over on Third Street. You know the one. Second floor, first door on the left."

I do. It's a house with boards crossing all eight of its windows. Front porch with moss growing up its sides like the ground is taking it back. I knock on the door Sunday morning before church but nobody answers, so I go on in and walk up them wood stairs scratched like a hundred bobcats been dancing on them. It's water beading up on the walls longside the stairs, but I climb myself up in the name of enterprise, past the paint puckering up the banister and the roaches running long into cracks, and I knock on Marialana's door.

"Just a minute," she yells, and I listen to the drip, drip, drip somewhere in the roof, even though it ain't rained for two days, and I try not to think about my grandmama's bosom and her weak weak heart.

"How do," I say, when she opens up the door. It's a little room, but she's done it up right, even put an old Chinese rug near the door and a picture from the dime store on the wall. It's a sink over along the wall and a parakeet in the corner, dressed up in pants and a rhinestone jacket. "How do," that bird says to me. He's swinging. Hooker for a

363

mama, but he's the happiest bird I ever seen.

"Whatcha got for me?"

I open my case. "You want some 17 for your face and some 14 as concealer. I think you'd look right nice with a little purple on your eyes to make the color come out." I put the case down on her floor on account of she ain't got no dining table nor sideboy nor nothing, and I'm setting it all out on the Chinese rug when I hear somebody move behind the screen she's got set up.

"I'll be right back," she says to whoever's back there, but out pops a shirtless old man. His hair is gray and sticking up in places where it ain't been cut right.

"Pookie?" he says.

It's my daddy. Looking like something dragged up out of the sea, but still my daddy. And I don't know what else to do, so I run. I leave that makeup behind me and just run. I would run all the way to church, but he'd follow me. And he just don't deserve anything Jesus might want to give him.

■ ■ ■ ■

PART FIVE:
AUDREY

■ ■ ■ ■

BEAUTIFUL

In New York City, the music never stops.
Before rehearsal, there's the radio, Brook
Benton singing "A Million Miles from
Nowhere" and The Champs blowing "Te-
quila" through their horns, Alan Freed
whispering his excitement into the WINS
microphone, pouring Negro music over Italian people's eardrums. Then there's rehearsal, Jim spinning the hi-hat, Verner
breathing into his sax until it sounds like a
jilted woman who's sorry to be alive. After
rehearsal we work, the four of us, playing in
and around the featured acts, people like
Ella Fitzgerald or The Drifters, sometimes
three or four shows in an evening, until,
after our last show, August and I have our
nights out. We take the IRT to Town Hall or
the Village Vanguard, where we see headlin-
ers like Billy Eckstine and Ethel Waters.
After their final sets we pack off in taxis to
after-hours clubs like the Half Note on

Spring Street or Tony's in Brooklyn, where August plays until six or seven in the morning, when we taxi back uptown, happy and drunk and high, to sleep, perchance to dream up new arrangements for old standards while the rest of the city builds its hives. When I wake, long after the normal person's lunch hour, I find the dark shadows of pedestrians walking across my ceiling, and I know it's time to rise and start the music all over again.

Even last Christmas Eve, when the Apollo went completely dark at two in the afternoon, the music didn't stop, because Dr. Aubré Maynard telephoned Mr. Schiffman to request that I play a private concert. When I arrived, the housekeeper stood beside Dr. Maynard's staircase until I agreed, silently, to pass the sitting room and ascend. The sitting room, I supposed, was for proper company — the Lattimores of 137th Street and the Hornes of 132nd — proper Negroes with first-class passages to Spain and sitting rooms of their own. Dr. Maynard's housekeeper was White. She wore a uniform and had wrinkles around her eyes that suggested much mirth, a wedding at City Hall to a distant Irish relative just arrived, four children crawling through the ironing and pulling up to standing on an abused wooden table. She didn't tell me her name and I didn't ask. She never smiled at me or said, "Welcome." All she must have seen of me is that I was a Negro girl of average height, with thick glasses and hair done in a pageboy. But she no doubt recognized the poverty in the ragged hem of my coat and the envy that made me push my glasses to my nose for a better look at the jade vase from China, and so she stood at the stairs and blocked me from going anywhere except up to Dr. Maynard's upstairs parlor to play piano for him and Mrs. Maynard while I watched the ten mirrored reflections of him sitting on his sofa, occasionally nodding his head in appreciation. His brownstone held an airy second story and an ethereal third, and even the Wurlitzer's parlor with its polished floors was a realm away from my cobwebbed little shed in Edith's basement. In the corner where Janine Maynard sat, two panes of mirrors met, so that she could see the reflections of herself stacked onward to infinity. Make enough of a name for yourself in this city, and you can rise above the place, literally — escape without leaving.

"Merry Christmas," I told the housekeeper on my way out. I'd sent cards home to Mother and Grandpap, to my Aunt

Juanita and her friend Ida Mae Harris, to Caroline Wallace and Sylvia French, but I'd gotten nothing beautiful in return. Just a letter from Grandpap on lined paper, advising me that they'd all actually expected me to be arriving in the flesh.

"I'll be *here* Christmas," the housekeeper spat at me, as if it were my fault. "Stuffing a turkey's ass." She closed the door before I could tell her anything of my own problems.

Between Dr. Maynard's house and mine on Christmas Eve, the newsstand on 127th had been the only business open. There, I bought an issue of *Life* and ripped out photos of normal places — towns with lovely trees, empty ponds swimming with ducks — and taped them to the wall beside my bed. I lay down, listening in vain for Christmas carolers, remembering how the Christmas cards I'd sent home were so special they'd had tissue paper sheets over them in the store to keep them from being ruined. I looked at my magazine photos and was reminded — screaming ambulances weren't all I've ever known.

I let thoughts of Dr. Maynard's rooftop terrace surge through the grooves of my brain, and I felt the magnificence of being Audrey Martin. I didn't count the squares of sidewalk I'd taken on my way from his home to mine; it didn't matter whether I'd stopped counting at 256 or 333. I closed my eyes and saw, on the backs of my eyelids, the coal-pregnant mountains and their ceiling of sky, the women of Queen Street crucifying their laundry with wooden clothespins. All the tender things that raised me, the things that made me more than a poor girl passing by someone's sitting room. The next day, when the Apollo opened again, I couldn't sit on the notes and love them. I couldn't make "For Your Precious Love" know that I was the only person who could make the world hear it. Everyone noticed. Jim said it must be heroin, and Letty said she might as well send me to play in a saloon. Mr. Glaser said he'd put me on the first train back to Kentucky. August said they'd never. He says I'm the best piano player they've had in the four years he's been playing the theater, and they're just trying to draw blood. "Don't martyr yourself for Jack Schiffman," he says. "You save some of that special for yourself."

John Hammond caught August playing one night at Tony's and signed him to play for Columbia. It was a one-record session behind Sarah Vaughan, Mr. Hammond had told him, a chance to prove that the bass wasn't just some bastard piece of wood he

371

found on the trolley tracks, and I wondered
whether Mr. Hammond ever had much
faith in his judgments, or whether he worried that the bebop he'd heard August play
that night seemed more exotic simply because it was being played in Brooklyn.
August took a taxi down to East 52nd Street
the day the groundhog saw his shadow, and
by the time the six weeks of winter had
passed, the record was pressed. We were
hearing it for the radio. August had three
hundred extra dollars. "And this —" he
said, showing me his lyrics:

Caroline
My little orphan girl
I'm going to carry you away from here
Carry you away

"What's this?" I asked him.
"For John Hammond," he said. "You and
I are going to write something."
"Hair of fire," I told him. "Skin of honey,"
and by Memorial Day, Tony Toy was laying
his voice on a track. It was pressed into vinyl
with the red Columbia label, with *A. Martin*
written in white letters under the center
hole of every single record of its kind in the
nation, right before *A. Barnes* and *T. Toy.*
Women never get first credit, I know, and

anyway August wrote most of the song. But he lied to John Hammond and gave me first credit — he says I'm the most potent muse he's ever had, and it's only fitting.

He won't let me play it at his house, because he has superstitions. He hisses "no" when I ask. He says listening to your own song is a ridiculous kind of vanity. At my apartment I watch the record spin, watch *CAROLINE* float around the turntable, upside down and then sideways and then right side up. I hear it on the radio and sing along. For the writing credit I got paid half of what the men did. A four hundred–dollar check, I got in the mail on a Tuesday. I cashed it on a Wednesday. And felt like a bastard no more.

Yesterday, it rained so hard the grease in the streets made rainbows. Today, the sun, leagues above me, is still deciding what to do with itself for the day. When I got home, at seven in the morning, I found a letter that Edith had slipped under my door. Caroline, writing from Mt. Sterling, inviting me home to give a concert. I read and reread and then spent two hours writing and rewriting, accepting her invitation exuberantly and then nonchalantly, writing a simple yes and then telling her how she knew me before my daddy died and I knew her before her mama died, and how she knew what I wanted out of the world before I even knew there was a world. I told her nothing, and then I told her she should come here and stay. I wrote and rewrote and tossed three page-long letters in the wastebasket. Now it's nine o'clock, and I have to be at work at eleven, and the futility in those two hours will keep me from sleeping at all.

An intermittent drizzle begins to fall. Under the faltering sun, the red neon cross atop Make Me a Herald still holds its power over the block. It drowns out all other colors of light and actually colors the shadows on my ceiling. The first time I saw it, I thought I must be dreaming. Now, a man in a purple shirt walks upside down until he's cut off where he meets my wall, and then, a few minutes later, a woman with a bright yellow dress runs across the blank white space as though she's late for a coming bus. Closer to the nine o'clock hour I see a pram, and all the colors of the canopy that covers the baby within, and then a boy on a bright blue bicyle zips by, raising his hand for something just as he disappears into my wall. A man whose shadow turns up completely aquamarine floats, like a homing pigeon, into the liquor store next door. I try to sleep, but the colored shadows keep me awake with wonder.

Harlem's noises are there always, too, though the passing traffic has become so much a lullaby that I no longer understand how I slept without it. As morning tops, I hear loud voices in the park across the street, so I roll over on my stomach to look out the window and find three boys on the swings. One sits, the tight seat of his pants cradled by the swing's rubber, and the second boy actually swings, like a child, high into the air. The third boy stands in his swing, his arms thrown out in a Y so he can grip the track above his head. "That housedress!" he shouts, in a feminine voice all wrong for his young man's body. He turns in a knee and throws his head to the side, posing. "It was nasty!" he says. "James, dear, somebody needs to teach your mama how to dress."

"Alejandro," sings the second boy, in falsetto. His voice rolls in and recedes with his swinging. He hits a G, then a B flat, then holds the C for a whole bar before knocking it up to an E that's high enough to crack his voice. "My love," he sings, "my life . . . Alejandro."

I strip naked and wrap myself in a towel, then make my way down the hall to the bath

I share with the five other people who live in the basement — Mrs. Elizabeth Fogle, widowed, and her young son Johnny; Mr. Earnest Hudson and his two roommates, Reggie and Rodney Thorpe, most recently of Hunstville, Alabama, Reggie with a conspiratorial streak that made him confess that he sees Edith, on occasion, enter my room when I'm at the Apollo. Since they all wake and set off for work in the early morning, Edith has usually turned the hot water off by the time I bathe, but today she's forgotten, because when I turn the tap, I find steam rising off the downpour. Warm as it is when I sit in the tub, it's all I can do not to fall asleep. Last night at Minton's Playhouse, August came offstage and kissed me, right on the mouth, before God and everybody, and the memory keeps me awake enough to wash under my arms and between my legs. It seemed unreal, then, in the smoky air of Minton's, and even in the taxi on the way home. When August lighted a marijuana cigarette and yelled out the window, to the street we were passing, that they were looking at two famous people, I almost believed him. I let the water out and make my toweled way back down the hall, which is filled with the smell of Mrs. Fogle burning breakfast. Johnny squeals in horror at something: impossible to know whether it's something on the radio or his mother's blackened bacon. My eyes burn with the toll the night has taken.

Having dressed, I fall on the bed, on my back, and find that the shadows have lost most of their color. I find a gray dog there on the ceiling, and plastic diamonds that show up as negative space in his green leash. A cornflower-colored man walks slowly across my ceiling, half a violin case sticking out from under his arm — it's August. "Wake up," he hisses through the bars over my window. If he ever came downstairs and knocked, Edith would have me assassinated.

"Coming!" I yell. I fit my wig over my flattened hairstyle and run upstairs to meet him.

On the street, the tall church secretary unlocks the door of Make Me a Herald, looking with malice at the two men congregating outside of the liquor store. They're regulars, she and I and they and the rest of the block know, and before she enters the church, she spits in their direction, shocking none of us. A White woman emerges from the funeral parlor, holding a sheaf of papers and crying into a handkerchief. She stops in front of the colored brick to blow her nose, and she steps up close to look at the inlaid centerstone that reads THEODORE MED-FORD & SONS, MORTICIANS. The deaf girl from Edith's second floor is standing in front of the wig shop, signing to the man who moved in with her last week. They must be married — otherwise Edith wouldn't allow it — but they both seem far too young. The deaf girl throws her fingers in patterns I can't decipher, and her husband laughs. He laughs louder than a hearing person, as if notions are even more absurd when they're not connected to sound.

When I get to the bottom of Edith's front steps, I don't ask August how he is or even say hello. Instead, I make him chase me down the street, and he says it when we're running in the rain, about to miss our bus — "You're beautiful." He stops in the middle of the street to tell me, and a car swerves to miss him; its driver yells a crush of nasty words out the window, but August stays straddling the yellow divider, looking at me as if I'm Saint Agnes weeping on a rosary card. "Beautiful," he says again.

I pull the sides of my shawl together and keep running for the bus — it's Saturday, and they come only on the half hour — but the blood does stop for one second in my arteries. Weightlessness rolls under the soles of my feet. Cold, petty rain stabs the skin on my hands and face as I look back at him, but I try to smile in such a fashion that he'll keep thinking me beautiful. "Beautiful." The word is a fragile pipette, one I can't recall ever hearing aloud.

"Princess," my father called me. "Sharp," pronounced Mrs. Dickerson. "Quite a talent," said Mr. Glaser. But no one has ever measured me beautiful, and I'm afraid that the smile I give August is too big, too ridiculous, not comely at all. "You're going to get hit," I say, to break the moment, and he runs with his violin case to catch up, but the bus pulls off its spot and grunts away through the drizzle. We have twenty-eight minutes to get to our wedding appointment, a blue veins affair at Abyssinian Baptist Church.

We've had an interview with the bride's mother, Mrs. Sloan, a short, sour duck of a woman with china plate skin and a permanent crease in the middle of her eyebrows. When August suggested the Brazilian Wedding March, Mrs. Sloan gave him a stare so icy it froze his mouth for the rest of our meeting. "I'm trying to insert some Negro heritage into the ceremony," she said, "not sponsor a party for the Puerto Rican dishwashers."

Without August's voice, I had single-handedly to collect the rest of her opinions, which included a distaste for costume jewelry and virgin cocktails. At the end of the interview, she asked me to stand. "Turn around," she said, and I did, slowly so that I wouldn't stumble, and I was remembering a day when Hattie Lee Grainger gathered all us country blackberries from the ninth grade into the A.M.E. church basement and taught us how to curtsy. Frances Tate had actually fallen down trying to sink lower than anyone else, and Caroline had laughed into her own mouth until the rest of her face turned as red as her freckles. Hattie Lee demonstrated crossing one's legs at the ankle when seated, and convinced us that it was rude to sprinkle salt on a meal before tasting it. She said she'd come back the next weekend and teach us the subtlety of makeup, and all six of us ninth-grade girls showed up that Saturday but she never did, and so our charm school was much abbreviated. As I turned in Mrs. Sloan's 132nd Street parlor, I felt certain she could tell as much. Later, August would say Mrs. Sloan was either making certain I was pretty enough to play at her daughter's wedding or making certain I wasn't prettier than her daughter. We didn't meet the bride or the groom that day. After meeting Mrs. Sloan, we weren't sure we would have wanted to.

The bus moves an unbreachable half avenue and I run up Lenox waving my arms, because Mrs. Sloan doesn't seem like the kind of woman who'll stand for lateness. A small boy in the bus's back window points at me and turns around in his mother's lap to tell her, but there's so little traffic on a Saturday morning that the bus is already at 126th. We're left behind watching its exhaust rise and disperse in the mist.

"Oh, hell. We'll be late, August."

"Who cares?" he says, and with his free arm he hugs me, warming my body as we walk. "We're playing the processional. They can't start without us." He kisses me again on the lips. It's the twelfth time — I'm keeping count. The sixteenth time, I'll slip him the tongue.

"We'll have to walk," he says now, swinging his violin case at his side.

"Thirteen blocks?"

"It's nothing."

It wouldn't be if it weren't drizzling, but neither of us has an umbrella, and by the time we get to church, we're wet as cows.

"Late," says Mrs. Sloan, when we step into the vestibule, "and looking like slaves."

In the church proper, beneath its Gothic towers and crystal chandeliers, the most well regarded lawyers in Harlem frown at their wives, and their wives turn into their purses to check the freshness of their lipstick. Polite aggression hovers in the dim light. Adam Clayton Powell, the Harlem hero, is here. He's gotten people like Edith to pay their Con Edison bill in pennies until the company hired more Negroes, and every time I look up and see him sitting with his wife, Hazel Scott, I think I might applaud. "Keep the faith," he always says, but right now, in this church, the faith is in preciously scant supply. The melancholy among these churchbound rich resists him; it glances off silk hat flowers hung in resignation and leaves girls glassy-eyed in the choir loft. The ushers seat a sprinkling of final stragglers as August and I begin Pachelbel's Canon, then a large woman and her small man enter and must be seated separately, because save for a few tight spaces, this church is full even unto its balcony. As we break into the gospel Mrs. Sloan has asked for (*and by all means don't make it Pentecostal*), the groom stands in the altar with the round, open face his mother-in-law will never take seriously, and the bridesmaids wait at the rear of the church with their bouquets clutched in fright. The first and youngest one steps forward, wobbly on her pumps, and August starts his Bach fugue. The clasp of her pearls has slid around to the front of her neck. Seventeen, I'd say: in Kentucky, she'd already have two children and rotten molars. As she walks, I connect with August on the piano in a flurry of sixteenth notes, but I'm deaf to my own frequency, lost in thinking that Caroline should be here with me to see all these magnificent Negroes.

Only Caroline would think of that day in the A.M.E. basement too. And only Caroline would understand the rest of New York City as I do. She'd understand what I'm seeing when I walk down Edith's front steps and find the congregation of Make Me a Herald, holding handmade signs and shouting to passersby about the coming end of the world. She'd know what I'm really hearing when I walk by someone's open window on my way to the Apollo and hear a record skipping, damaging its own groove, playing the line "Someday you'll want me to want you" over and over again. Whoever Caroline is with at this very moment is seeing a false version of her, just as everyone around me — even August, dear August, who has spread himself over every crevice of my brain — is seeing just the New York shadow of me. I can't be sure the green he sees is the green I see; can't be sure that his orange is my orange. I can't be sure, even, that he's seeing the same wedding as me, because his face is completely unreadable. The fifth, sixth, and seventh bridesmaids break free of their escorts, I bring the congregation to their feet with the opening notes of The Wedding March, and the day becomes perfectly grotesque.

At first, the bride looks, coming up the aisle, like any bride standing atop a cake, with a floor-length veil and bouquet of Dutch roses and ribboned stephanotis that trail the ground. I can't see the detail of her face or neck, but I can make out her crimson lipstick, the diamond choker encircling her neck, the glittering solitaire half tucked into the fold of her father's arm. Her shoulders, though, are quaking. She's sniffling back tears. Her exquisite collarbone says this girl will be fine in this life: she has enough money to last it. But the beads on her train dance in the light every time she sobs, and under the bright lights, her dress shimmers over her body as though she's someone's sugared meal. She manages up the aisle to the altar, but her father has to untuck her fingers from his arm when he gives her away. From the piano, I see Mrs. Sloan roll her eyes.

"Dearly beloved," the minister begins, but

the bride never stops crying, not even when he's pronounced them man and wife. She hiccups and gobbles, and the acoustics of the church's high ceilings work too well. Mrs. Sloan never stops grimacing. When the groom lifts his bride's veil, he wipes her eyes before kissing her.

The bridesmaids rush out, in order, with their escorts, and none of them smiles. Not one of them even looks at the bride. "What do you suppose was the matter?" I ask August.

"Butler had the day off," he says, not caring. We're still under the choir loft, where he's unlatching his violin case, taking out a rag to wipe the place where he held it under his chin. He's forever packing and unpacking and repacking some instrument. He's never quite free. Mrs. Sloan's brother brings us payment, a fluttering of six twenties from inside his tux. He thanks us, but it's as if he's a robot, he shuffles away so fast.

"August!" someone screams, and a girl comes galloping out of the crowd. She's five foot nine at the very least, and she has hazel eyes and a perfect nose. Before she even says hello, she kisses August full on the mouth. "I've missed you," she says. A dimple in her chin. A lilt in her voice. She's never had an ugly day, this girl. If August thinks me beautiful, he can be thinking only in relative terms.

"Well, who is this?" she asks.

I can't help it — I scowl.

"Liz, meet Audrey. She's in the house band." Not *my girlfriend* Audrey. Not *this* is Audrey, as if my belonging to him were obvious. I've been reduced to bandmate, workhorse, a piece of his life as functional as a dinner table.

"And who is this?" I ask, and August coughs, or laughs. I know how sore I sound, and I'm perfectly aware that this is 1959 in New York City, where men and women of a certain age feel free to do whatever they wish. But my love is deeper, wider, richer than hers. I need him to know.

"I'm Elizabeth Pounds Johnson," she says, offering a hand I won't take.

"What a pleasure."

The sarcasm in my voice doesn't stop her from sitting in the seat next to August's, or from leaning forward so that her head hovers over her crossed ankles and her hair hangs over one knee. She looks at August out of the corner of one fetching eye, watches him stuff the rag in the bottom of his case to keep his violin from bumping around. She watches him pat it, in superstition, the same way I watch him pat his bass each night, and she seems neither surprised nor amused at the gesture, and I'm amazed that he's shared something so private with someone other than me. Still, I don't know they've lain in bed together, not really, until August closes one latch of his case and smiles at her as if she's communicated something just by sitting down.

"Will I see you around?" she asks.

"Hard to say."

She rolls her eyes, tosses her head back so we can see her strong heartbeat under the skin exposed by her low collar. "You will. You'll see all of me again sooner or later, August — believe it. Oh and Audrey —" she says, as she stands. "There's some hair sticking out from under your wig, dear."

I offer to carry August's violin, so he lets me carry it down 138th Street, and I try to tuck it under my arm and then cradle it like a baby when it gets uncomfortable. I almost drop it down the bus steps and he takes it back. "There is a handle, you know," he says. "And we're not in a hurry."

But I am. Running from something. I'm counting the passing bus stops, even when the bus doesn't stop at them all, trying to get to sixteen just once. Twenty-seven blocks up, we transfer to a westbound line that takes us to August's building, at Riverside and 163rd. Far from Harlem and its bejeweled princesses, but August chose this building for its marble-floored elevator, because with his bass he can rarely take the stairs. As the metal grate closes and the cage pushes us gently up to the third floor, he pinches my ass. "New York ain't agreeing with you," he says. "You need some a that squirrel meat back on your bones."

August lives just down the hall from the elevator, in 3D, a huge crate of a place with bay windows to let in sunsets and river air. Even his dining room offers a view of the Hudson, and every one of his three bedrooms is bigger than my sleeping box on 123rd. Weekend afternoons, this far up Manhattan, are almost without traffic, and in the absence of screaming wildlife, it can be quieter here than it is in Mt. Sterling. I flop faceup on his couch and count the boat motors I hear, and wonder what it must be like to be floating toward the Atlantic, casting nets in the rain and breathing in boat fuel. August's bass sits upright in a corner next to the window, as if it, too, is sniffing for river dreams.

"Stay for lunch?" he asks. "I've got chicken from last night."

"Sure. Why not?" Though I wonder who might have made dinner in his apartment, what woman's batter I'll be eating. August might be liberated enough to keep a lady dentist, but he just isn't the chicken-frying type.

Outside on the fire escape, a black cat lifts his paw one step as if to climb, but a piece of fish falls down to the landing and he charges. He licks, chews. Moves his head in feeding. "Oh, that thing," August says as he passes through the living room, pulling his tie from his collar on his way to another bedroom. "Close the blind or he'll come scratching at the glass."

But there's no need, because the cat is lost in eating, blind to human existence. A robin flies low over his head, taunting. He flies away and perches again on a step of the fire escape, flies back to the cat and away to a perch, but the cat simply watches the robin as he gets a better hold on the bones trying to slip from the back of his jaw. His ancient green eyes are lost in survival.

"Whose cat, anyway?"

"Nobody's," August yells from a bedroom. None of the three rooms are used for sleeping, since August favors his couch.

"Then why doesn't he just go away?"

"He used to live here. Whatever person lived in this apartment with him moved off and left him here."

"Poor thing! How does he stay so fat?"

"Everyone else thinks no one feeds him, so everyone feeds him. They put out milk. One time I even saw him down on the sidewalk working over a ribeye. He's the best-fed cat in five boroughs."

On the river, a motor chokes to a stop. Children's voices travel down the sidewalk outside, until they're so far away and so faint, I can hear the cat purr.

"Can I give him a chicken bone?" I yell.

"Absolutely not. I've never fed that cat a damn thing. He bothers me. Always looking in my window like I owe him something."

I consider the cat's point of view, how he's been denied by the one window he knows. "Why don't you just let him in? Make him your pet?"

"He's not cultured enough to live in here with me." He's half-serious, but here's what walks down the hallway: a scarred bear of a man in a stained T-shirt, a cigarette hanging from a bottom lip, his conk sticking up in places where his fedora crowned it at the wedding. A breath of nicotine, a soft belch. "Why don't *you* move in here with me? *You* come feed that stupid cat."

"Me? Move in with a man? My mother would die."

"How would your mother ever know?" He sits on the couch and gathers my skirt up around my waist, and the chill in the parlor brushes against my legs.

I push his hands away. "My mother knows everything."

He pulls my blouse from the waist of my skirt and slides a cold hand under my buttons. *Keep your gentlemen above the neck,* I remember from Joyce Nettles's weekly column for single ladies, but he caresses a nipple and wears me down in an instant. The chill in his sitting room raises tiny bumps on my body at the same time the heat he's causing makes my upper lip sweat. "Honey, I'm a needy man," he says, past me to the couch. Above the waist, I'll let him.

He circles his other hand around my waist so I can't pull away, and he gets on top of me. "I need you here with me all days, little mama," he whispers. And I let him some more, because I feel like he's playing me like his big, beautiful bass, and because I don't have music or numbers in my head to make me feel anything else. And then I feel something I've never felt before, and I can't help but whimper, because his cold finger feels so strange where nothing else has ever been, in this negative space I never quite knew existed. But by the time the pigeons start their afternoon warbling and the furnace kicks on, it feels as if that's just where it belongs. Thunder rumbles over the sound of the furnace and he rolls off me. "Shit," he says, and before I know it, the rain has come and he's lightly snoring. With him, I fall into shadow dreaming — orange juice puddles, wet babies drying in clay ovens, a patch of thunderclouds like a model of the sea. When the rain stops, I'm awakened by the sound of my own breathing, that and the moisture in my panties. I'm wondering if the bride ever stopped crying.

PEACE

"It's just a three-bedroom apartment," August says, sometimes. "It's not going to hurt you." He reminds me about the high rents in Harlem, and he promises he'll let the cat in to live with us, though when he says that, he's careful to add a quick *maybe.* Still, I can't believe he's talking straight: when he asks me to move in, his eyes are trained on lampposts, or sidewalks, or the spray starch commercials on the sides of buses. I can never decide why he won't look me in the eye, so I never just come out and tell him no.

And he does, of course, love me. He even loves my new wig. I'd always held a country girl's understanding of hair, a notion that a girl could either enhance her own, or, if her head became too needy, purchase a reasonable facsimile thereof. Any change in color was just silly, and addition of length was dishonesty of the worst sort. Here in New

York, wearing one's own hair is precisely not the point, though I hadn't yet realized that the costumed self might yet still be the self. A piece of luck, then, that when I went downstairs to the wig shop, the mortician's wife was there, haggling with the saleslady over a carelessly thinned fall she wanted to buy on discount for one of her deceased. It was a hot summer day, and out the storefront window I could see the liquor store's two morning regulars holding their paper bags. They stood for hours, in whatever weather, talking incessantly, always. The secretary of Make Me a Herald walked by them on her way into church, pointed down the block to the funeral home, and said, "See that? It's waiting for you."

In response, the men didn't even laugh or heckle her as she turned her key in the church's little iron door. They simply watched her, and, once the whole of her had disappeared into the storefront, first her hatted head and then her left calf and finally her right hand, they picked up their conversation from the pointless spot at which they'd left it.

The bottom row of wigs, all around the store's three walls, sat on plastic heads painted with surprised eyes and sad mouths. The top row of heads, in contrast, were faceless white Styrofoam — they could stand to be faceless because they wore the better wigs. I stood on my tiptoes and plucked a long, auburn one from its head, and I was on the bus, looking out the window at the row of shoeshine boys on St. Nicholas, before I realized that I had chosen Caroline's hair. She was seeing New York with me, then, and when I got off the bus and the watermelon seller outside the theater catcalled as if he didn't know me, I whispered to my wig, "That's what they're like here. Bold."

Jim and Verner, when I ran into them backstage, didn't notice. Letty said, simply, "Nice mop. Shiny, even. Must've cost half your paycheck." I'd changed into my costume gown already, and the ends of the wig fell to the sequined straps at my shoulders, but none of the men around melted at the sight of me. The lighting man kept lighting. The sound man kept miking. The Apollo was full of beautiful, talented women, and these were just men at work, rushing around to start the show. I walked past Bob Northern, who was cleaning his mouthpiece, but when I said hello he ignored me. He did glance at me, or perhaps he didn't — I found his eyes that hard to read. But August, when he saw me, ran his fingers through

Caroline's hair and smiled.

Through the six o'clock show he smiled, and he stopped in the middle of one of the half-time numbers just to run over and kiss all ten of my fingers, one by one. The audience rocked the floor. Letty scissor-stepped over to the piano and gave us a salute, though I know she was just trying to endear herself to the crowd: Letty hates August. "He won't be working here long," she tells me, "so don't get attached." She calls his demands for more money sheer idiocy, and she says he causes terrible trouble between her and Mr. Schiffman. She says August's broad back and thick fingers remind her of the dumb, hulking Russian she ran off and married when she was seventeen. He left her right after she grinned into a bowl of tomato soup and told him she was having his baby; she told me she'd been so pregnant she could smell water boil. She drank black cohosh and sat on the root woman's cold, chipping toilet for hours until she passed the baby, all the while vomiting into a pail because of the pain, and tapping her bare feet against the woman's gnarled wood floor, painted the most distressing shade of orange. After we all left the stage that Thursday, as August grabbed me around the neck with his free hand and kissed the top of my wig, Letty screeched that the Apollo was going to shit.

In private, that night, August begged. "Just unbutton your shirt and show me a little something," he asked, and I did, because I remember now, always, that I'm not as pretty as Elizabeth Pounds Johnson. I kept my wig on, and I unfastened my bra and showed him. But I won't let him see not one single sliver of thigh or bloomers again, not anytime soon, because of that voice in my head — *Keep your gentlemen above the neck.* August doesn't much feature on that, of course. He says every time he sees me with my blouse unbuttoned and my skirt still wrapped tight around my hips, it seems that I'm getting smaller and smaller, until I'm just about lost. I am getting skinnier, but that's because I've grown an inch taller, and the gowns on my rack at the Apollo have started to hang off my shoulders something frightful. But I'm still all here and of one piece, ready to love him.

New York City is a belching, groaning, swallowing maw. I haven't seen Mrs. Donald Green in an age. I've seen Mr. Green, heard him pounding down the stairs in the evening, then seen him on my ceiling, running across the street to the druggist's. Edith says their beautiful little girl is ill with polio, though when I told Mrs. Fogle, she said Edith was wrong — it's rubella. She seemed dismissive, though she hasn't let Johnny out to play in weeks. Through my ceiling I hear the deaf couple making love, just as loudly as they laugh. I hear their bedsprings squeaking, hear the man grunting as he pushes into her. Since he's unable to hear his own efforts, he doesn't realize the rest of us can: he sounds desperate, always, as though he's trying to climb into his wife's soul through her body. Other days I hear them fighting, the husband moaning his wordless outrage while he signs, the wife slamming cupboards, breaking glass. The day Mack Parker was found lynched down in Mississippi, I heard the Thorpe brothers crying through my wall. Wednesday nights, when there's rehearsal but no show, the blocks between St. Nicholas and Lenox fix me under the glare of their streetlamps, trap me in the silt that flows along curbs, dissect me like I'm the lowest animal. Sometimes the moon is full, and the ice around it makes a corona, as if God is blowing the moon through a smoke ring. The streets — their cold, ungiving asphalt, their eleventh-hour emptiness — these are the streets that take me home.

This morning, after work, after Minton's,

after a house party on 123rd Street raucous with marijuana and opium and pipefitters, I catch Edith in my room. I turn the key in the lock and hear my own chair slide across the floor, then open the door and there she is, not going through my things as Reggie Thorpe has imagined, but just standing there, looking at me, turning her own hands. "Letter came for you," she says. She gestures to the table, where she's lain the plain white envelope.

"You're in my home, uninvited," I tell her.

"Well, I should say not. Of course not invited. It's eight o'clock on a Monday. When respectable people keep work hours."

"You're standing in my home," I say again, and she walks out my door without closing it.

I sit down and ripped the letter open, and find a lovely paragraph from Caroline, telling me how she's selling cosmetics and making money, telling me that Sylvia French is set to marry a boy from Cincinnati, a lawyer by the name of Johnathan Troutt. *I'm looking forward to the concert,* Caroline says, and I feel myself grinning. The next paragraph is in a different color ink, and starts out, *Glad to hear all about your famous friends. You wouldn't believe it but the world turns here too,* and I'm still assuming, despite the different inks, that the letter is of one mind, but then she goes on: *It ain't that you want me to see things with you. It's that you want me to watch you. You always did. But I got people here what needs me. Imagene and Grandmama. And Gordon Bell. He's going off to the Army now, but when he gets home, I think he wants to marry me. I think at your age you got to find somebody else what sees your orange.*

I count the burls of wood on my floor, shivering when I get to fourteen. I drop off to sleep, but not happily, and when I wake, I'm even less happy, though I can't decide whether it's anger or sadness that has taken root and infected me. It's Monday, the professional musician's day off, and until August picks me up for the movie, I've nowhere to go to save myself. I walk two blocks up to 129th, where the smiling skinned rabbits, hanging upside down from their hooks in the window of Pogue's, make me weak with psychic jealousy. Two blocks back down to 127th, where five girls stand in a knot on the northeast corner. They're skipping rope to "Jesus Loves Me"; they make me weep with rage. I'm ricocheting against the universe, its accidents of passion and boredom and fright, all of them with the audacity yet to jostle me with their

400

bread bags. I break west to the less peopled end of the street, take two filthy, hot blocks under the shadow of the elevated train to 125th, where a bench sits in a tiny square of park that makes the housing project happy. I sit for over an hour in the rising heat, with the pigeons and the mice for company. Sit still enough, they forget that I'm an animal, too. It's only 75 degrees out but I'm sweating. The light coming through the clouds is unbearable.

Some boys my age pass on their way to the train and avoid looking at me, but when they're past, one of them whispers something to the other and they both laugh, too loud for politeness, unloosing their baseball caps with a synchronized toss of their heads. They're walking home from their first week of senior high school maybe, just finished lapping the gymnasium at basketball practice, or sharpening chalk as punishment. I'm not them anymore, but I'm not what they think I am, either. I'm a pianist. Quite a talent, actually. I'm just sweating on a park bench.

Three, four, five eastbound buses pass me, a mouse runs across the toe of my shoe and through the sickly vegetation, and when the eighth bus comes, the five-thirty, I get on and ride to 123rd, where August is already sitting on Edith's stoop, waiting.

"Where've you been?" he asks.

"Nowhere." It's not a lie exactly, but it floats out into the afternoon and pours a vast, unanswered sea between us. "August," I ask him, "what happened to your face?"

"You writing a newspaper article?"

"Sorry. Just making small talk, that's all."

He smiles as if he were joking. "Stitches," he says. "Right here." And he shoots an imaginary line down the left part of his face, as if I'd had anywhere else in mind.

We're walking fast to make the show, and I have to catch my breath to ask him, "But what happened?"

"String popped off my fiddle at a lesson. It's why I kept playing. Mama said I couldn't let the violin lick me."

"Well, did it?"

"What do you think?" he asks.

"You're still playing, so I guess it depends on how you look at it."

The outside of the ticket booth is washed a beautiful shade of violet, as would be the front door of a dollhouse, and the boy and girl working inside, taking money and cutting tickets, move their hands fast as falling dominoes. I add up the number of tickets they cut, stop when I get to sixteen, close my eyes for a minute and open them again.

The boy and girl both wear blue, sandwich-sized hats with white shirts creased along the sleeves, and when August hands them his money and the boy hands him two tickets, I'm filled with anticipation. I can't wait for the film to flood my mind with something unreal, if only for the afternoon. The film is *Imitation of Life.* If it's really good, I'll forgive Caroline. I'll write to her and tell her she must see it.

"So what made you keep playing?" August asks, as we hurry past the concession stand and into the darkness of the theater beyond the double doors.

"Nothing kept me playing," I say, as we stand in the aisle, searching. Despite our hurry we're late, and what's left are two seats in the middle of the second row, three separated seats in the front row. "I kept playing," I whisper, as we squeeze past half a row of annoyed people, tucking our rear ends away from their faces, "because I didn't have anything else on my mind. I'm nothing special. I just keep playing, is all."

We're lucky enough that the newsreel stops, for one precious and nerve-wracking moment, leaving the theater in pitch blackness. August takes my chin in his hand and brings his face close to mine so I'll hear him. "You are unreal, you know that?" he whispers. "You think you're nothing special, but you make that piano sound like its mama done died. All these other New York girls been out in the world so long, all they can come up with is how to get from point A to point B, but you're cosmic. You don't even pay attention to how the world is trying to tie you down. And anybody who can get along with mean-ass Letty Jones is special, with a capital S. Please," he says, taking my right hand in his left, strong hand, the one he uses to press his bass's heavy strings to its neck, "live with me. Come be with me and I'll let you interview me every day if you want."

But what I want is for him to explain Caroline's letter, and for him to tell me why the world doesn't just get tired of worshipping the sun and spin off into the universe. What Dr. Maynard's housekeeper's name is, and whether, when she bathes her four children at night, she hates them. Why condensation doesn't form on me even though the theater is cooler than the oustide, why Sonnyboy went downtown and told those White people his entire truth, how people carry on without knowing why they do. How babies can see the ugly parts of their mamas and still claim blood kin. Why some people are born talented and everyone else is born happy. I don't know that August can tell me any of this. I don't know the first thing about him. But I do know that he kissed all ten of my fingers on a Thursday, and I do know that three bedrooms, a living room, a dining room, a bath, and a fire escape is a place where a body can breathe. And that those motor-boats on the Hudson, choking on their own gas, are something like peace.

"Of course you are," August says. "It's what every country chitlin' does with their first big check."

"What's that?"

"Spend every penny of it immediately."

He flips a page of the *Amsterdam News* and reflattens the paper against the kitchen table, but he seems more amused than angry. Anyway, I don't care. I'm buying a burgundy Cartier suitcase — the one on display this week at Blumstein's — to take home with me. Instead of the thin country dresses that came with me to New York, I'm packing two black dress suits and a powder blue jacket from Macy's. I'm not, either, getting anywhere near the L&N depot — I'm flying to Standiford Field. When I remembered my journey to Manhattan, I thought about the Negro train porters in the cars, the ones not that long moved to New York themselves. I thought about those men, warming baby bottles and carrying the rotting burlap bags of all those grand-mamas from Alabama. I thought of them having constantly to manage the transport of others, and I got tired: I decided that I just don't even want to see it. Better to float in my powder blue jacket through an air-port, where no one is storing their entire catalog of hopes in an overhead compart-ment, or carrying half their life down a concrete platform in Pittsburgh.

August looks up from the paper. "A plane ticket, though," he says, as if reading my mind. "It's a little extravagant."

"It seems unnecessary to you because you're not the one taking the trip."

"It's nothing I'd ever do."

"Only because you'd never have to. Your mother lives in the next borough." Though I've never seen his mother, or even her apartment building. August has kept me studiously away from her, and the few times he's mentioned her, something in his eyes has pressed me not to ask for more informa-tion. Once we found ourselves on her block, in a taxi heading toward the East River Drive, and he asked the driver whether he couldn't move faster.

"Look, baby, if you felt like a true Har-lemite, you wouldn't be wasting all this

407

money trying to look like a fake one. Now what can I do to make that happen?"

"Nothing," I say. *Marry me,* I think. "I've got to go. I'm meeting Letty."

"Hm. All that innovation on the piano, and you couldn't come up with one reason not to meet that woman on a Sunday morning."

I don't comprehend the enmity between them, though I'm afraid, somehow, that I'm supposed to. I'm supposed to understand just how important is twenty dollars in one hand versus fifteen dollars in another, and the way love and hate, in the city, is so easily determined, because it has nothing to do with feelings and everything to do with money. My failure of understanding is a country girl's naïveté, I suppose, an innocence I must end if I'm ever to make it here.

"Bye," I tell him, and I go behind his chair and lean over to kiss him on the cheek. He grabs my arm, and there's a heat there, between us, that's apart from the bodily contact. He smiles at me, and I flush everywhere, even at the follicles on my head. "Bye," he says.

Over the months, I've come to make sense of Letty, and while I'm riding down August's elevator and then taking the bus to the shop, I think this: in New York people either pity you or envy you, but Letty does neither. She's going with Mr. Schiffman, who she actually calls "Mr. Schiffman," and it isn't a question of loving him. She says she's a kept woman, even if she's the hardest working kept woman in three states. She'd say the very same thing to Schiffman's face, I'll bet, because with Letty, what you see is what you get. She doesn't care one way or another about the unreality of being geniune. She just is.

Of course when it comes to meddling in my love life, more and more in the by and by, Letty just isn't. At the soda shop, when I tell her what happened to August's face, she laughs so hard she spits out her cream, and the other couple in the shop — a father and his young daughter — turn and stare. "You believe that?" Letty says, as a milky rivulet streams down her chin. "As long as you've been living in New York, child-friend, and you're still that green?"

"Well, since you're some sort of fortune-teller, what happened to his face?"

"I wouldn't possibly know," she says, blotting her chin with a napkin, then swigging up a third of her soda in one beat, "but he obviously messed over somebody somewhere. Most likely a woman. Or better yet, that woman's man. A fiddle string? Doesn't that sound like a bucket of piss to you?"

"I trust him, Letty. I'd trust him with my life." I've written it all to Caroline, how August waits on Edith's stoop for me every morning on his way to the Apollo, how I'd lie on a bed of nails if only I could make certain that happened every day for the rest of my life. *August's orange is my orange and his green is my green,* I wrote her, and I've almost convinced myself that it isn't a lie. Caroline didn't write back. Perhaps she's too busy. I want to believe she's happy for me.

"You go ahead, then," Letty says. "You move in with that idiot. You marry him and you get pregnant and *then* see what happens. Neither one of you will be working at the Apollo, I can tell you that."

"We're not talking about all that right now."

She sinks her straw down into her glass, but it rises again through the floaty bubbles. "Of course he's not talking about any of that right now," she says. "He's found his dumb ass some young stuff and he wants to carry it off before it grows up and gets some sense. You will see." What's left of her malt is mostly cream, and to get at it, she has to suck in her cheeks until her face is narrow

410

as a fox's. "Joe Glaser. Now *there's* someone to hitch up to. Slick. Keep hanging with him, you'll meet some fine people." August has told me all about it, how slick Mr. Glaser is, how he's double-booking the band for shows outside the theater through his Associated Booking Corporation. He pays us at a lower rate than he's booked for, then takes the difference plus his percentage of the door. August found out through Honi Coles, the theater manager, who told it as a joke, and he's raged about it to Letty and Verner and Roland, but they turn him a deaf ear. "It's a boat I ain't going to rock," is how Letty put it to us the last time August brought it up. "You know they ain't had breadlines since the Depression."

"I don't need to meet fine people," I tell Letty now. "I'm moving in with fine people."

"Child-friend, you haven't been in New York long enough to know what fine people are." She smiles and studies me like a cat, takes the straw between her second and third fingers and stabs her cream with it. Half-moons, she makes. Tiny wounds. "If you're going to listen to the trash coming out of some man's mouth, at least hear the one who can do something for you. Joe Glaser can show you the world."

She doesn't seem to understand — I've

411

already seen it.

When the other table leaves, I notice the gummy dirt on the edges of the white chairs where people have scooted on and off them over the months since they've last been cleaned, the city's soil ground into the shop's creamy tiles over the years. I stab my straw into the bottom of my malt, mining the same hard cream that Letty found, but mine is all melted into the soda I haven't felt like sipping. Soft and miserable, my lot, not at all like Letty's. Though when I sip, the compound tastes of a certain kind of holiness.

"So what day are you going down to Kansas?"

"Kentucky."

She waves her hand. "Wherever."

"Twenty-ninth of December. I'm going to buy my ticket in a few weeks."

"Excited?"

"Plenty."

"Well, good," she says, smiling. I rarely see her smile. It's nicer than anything August, in his imaginings, would grant her.

Early on a Sunday morning, the first day of snow in New York, I'm moving. Packing my three teacups and four show dresses, ripping down my magazine pictures. I meant

412

to take them to August's, to smooth down their wrinkles and let them have another life on his walls, but when I peeled back the very first piece of tape, some of the picture ripped off with it, so I just started throwing the pages one by one into the wastebasket. Gone my pretty pictures of blue adobe houses atop a mountain in New Mexico. Gone my boat-size trees in the middle of an Oregon forest. August's walls live empty, and I don't know how he'd feel, anyway, about taped-up magazine pages with serrated sides: now is as good a time as any for me to grow up, buy gilt frames, love opulence. As for the natural world, I'll be happy with the sad slice of Hudson I get if I put my face right up against his window, press my nose against the glass until it hurts. That, and a park across the street no bigger than Granddaddy's backyard.

For lack of packing space, I have to throw out all those thin little country dresses. The thinnest, a sundress I wore once to a dance in Hope, goes first. I remember loving it, fingering the pink scallops Mother had sewn on its hem while I sat in the metal folding chair watching boys pass me by; I remember watching the bottom twirl when finally I linked arms and spun with Caroline. Mother wrote me when Miss Myrtle died, and I

413

wrote Caroline, to say I was sorry. To cheer her, I told her of playing at an after-hours jam at the Blue Note, and I told her of sitting backstage at the Apollo only three feet from John Coltrane, separated by a curtain but feeling his vibrations as strongly as if I were in the bell of his horn. Still, Caroline hasn't written me back.

The delicate, crisscrossed back of the dress from Hope is held in place by buttons too small to hold the jostling of the nine o'clock train, and anyway Manhattan isn't a place for pink scallops. Not a place to remember Hope. Neither is it a place for this peony-covered dress, thin as a bedsheet, with little pills napping up all over the material where I've washed it half to death. The blue peonies never quite wash clean of city-dirt, and a hillbilly's color doesn't walk well with the sweeping crowds of Harlem, the sober browns and blacks behind which Harlem women hide their worries. My thin-strapped sandals are store-bought, but they only attract pity in a world of stiletto heels — in the basket they go. The only dress I keep is the black one that Mother wore to Daddy's funeral, and when I'm finished, the wastebasket stands so full of cheapness that I can't imagine anyone willingly digging the things out. And if they did, they'd only make themselves into a walking country girls' museum. The velvet ribbon can't go around a wig. In the wastebasket, though, it's a cinch.

When I go upstairs to tell Edith, she shakes her head so hard her curlers click together. "And you just a child. Mm, mm, mm. Ain't no limit on what menfolk will do these days."

"I am not a child."

"How old is he?"

"I am not a child."

"Where are your people, anyway?"

"I am not a child."

"And in the season of Christ, too. Running off to live in sin on the first Sunday of Advent!"

"It is not in sin."

"I bet your poor mama don't know. I sure do wish I could tell her. I get a hold of one of them letters with her address, I swear to you and to Jesus Christ, I'ma write back and tell her."

"I am not a child, and she is not my mother."

I hand Edith the five dollars I owe on the last week's rent and drag my burgundy Cartier out the front door. Even with all the Kentucky clothes gone, I had to sit on it while I buckled it closed, and now a green blouse strap hangs out the edge and trails through the snow, clearing a route down Edith's front steps. Sunlight shoots through a cloud, a string of sequins shines in the faded light, and I feel more like a little girl than I ever have, like a child with a bag full of Halloween costumes.

August is waiting in a taxi he's hailed and paid a dollar to hold, but I can't see his face for all the frost grown on the windows. I do wonder whether he's happy behind the frost, or whether he's sitting in that taxi thinking he could have done better, for his first moved-in woman, than this string bean coming with her tiny burgundy suitcase down the steps of a dilapidated apartment building. I wonder, too, why I've never met his mama. She lives in Brooklyn, only twelve stops on the IRT. I've counted.

"Any trouble?" he asks, when he gets out to hold the door open. Meaning *Were you able to pay your landlady? Or have you run out of money, as you usually have by Sunday?* On average of three days a week I get docked pay for being late to rehearsal, and August always shakes his head at me when Letty announces it. Before I got the money from Columbia, I would get paid on a Monday, need a new silk scarf on a Tuesday or a fancy downtown dinner on a Wednesday, and be going without chips for my fish by Friday.

"I'm okay," I say. Meaning *Don't worry — I'm not here to drain you.* The backseat, when I slide across, makes my skirt ride up my thigh; the taxi driver catches himself looking, quickly turns back around in his seat, and starts the meter. August hasn't seen. He gets in and closes us into our uncertain future with a loud, final *thunk* of the door, the sound of men finding young girls lost in the city.

"Riverside and 163rd," he tells the driver, and as we turn west down 123rd, past the building supers out throwing sand onto stairsteps and the children drawing their names on the sidewalk with mittened fingers, I remember about the bread and salt.

"Excuse me, sir? Could you make a stop at the grocery on 132nd?"

"Why?" August asks.

"We need bread and salt. For good luck."

"No," August tells the driver. And tells me: "We are absolutely not going there."

"Well then, drop me off. Take my suitcase home."

He stares out the windshield. In the rearview mirror, I see the driver eyeing both of us.

"I won't even be half an hour. I'll take the

bus up to your place. I've got the fare."

"No."

The driver has taken sides. He keeps steering, denying me, past the 132nd Street grocery and faster up Riverside Drive, around its twists and curves, through the rocks on either side of us in the 150's. Past the huge stone buildings and the wealthy mothers pushing their prams in the falling snow.

"This is New York, not some bayou," August says.

"I'm not from some bayou. There are no bayous in Kentucky. And everybody knows bread and salt is good luck when you move into a house."

"Old wives' tale."

"My father told me. He wasn't an old wife."

"Well, we ain't stopping this cab for some superstitious bullshit."

"It's the bullshit I grew up with. I ain't some soft-handed uptown Negro who was twelve people's Cotillion date."

Without taking his eyes from the windshield, he grabs my wrist and squeezes. "Don't be disrespectful," he says. He doesn't mean to hurt me, but his grip is pinching a piece of skin, and it stings, and water comes to my eyes.

"All right, then," I say. In just twenty blocks, the snow has picked up its pace so rapidly that buildings are mere outlines of their roofs, and our driver has slowed the taxi to a creep. We can barely make out the blue jackets hurrying into buildings, the red hats running up the street to escape the cold, the people holding their gloved hands in the air for this taxi, which they can't see is taken. The driver leans forward in his seat, wipes the windshield with the sleeve of his jacket. August coughs. I count blocks. Forty of them; four tens; good enough luck. I clench my legs together, to stave off a draft. And I suddenly know what anger tastes like when I have to bite my tongue.

LAUNDRY

"Like a hotel I slept in once," August says, hiding his head in the wire basket. He raises his shoulders to exaggerate inhaling. "Smells so damn clean." He's never had such clean clothes, he says: he's always bought them from the laundryhouse in a paper bag. They come back to him smelling of other people, of the sadness of the Chinese washerwoman and the frustrations of the roofer whose gritty pants have tumbled around in the tub with his own, of the longheadedness of the bookmaker whose shirts are never dirty to begin with, but get extra bleach nonetheless. August has never had his clothes run through a washboard, never had them whipped in the tub so they dry less stiffly. He's never had it done right like this, by a girl from the mountains.

He doesn't know the half of it, how beautiful a bedsheet can smell when you've just run out to the line and rescued it from a drizzle, how you can sink into it at night and know that the mountain's dew has become part of the threading forever. He can't know what a side of ham tastes like when it's not that long dead, or what it's like to crack open an egg wondering if there'll be a stillborn baby chick inside. I fry ham and eggs every morning — he says he's going to die from the richness of it — but really he doesn't even know what he's missing. Clothes can smell only so clean once cityair has gotten a hold of them. And the food of the city is dead, truly dead. A man's body, this food can't help.

We're both strangers to his bed. August bought it just to please his mama when he started making money, but he's spent his entire bachelorhood sleeping on the couch, above the sweet echo of street sounds. Sometimes the cat, who we've named Jelly Roll, sneaks into our room and hops into bed, running his tail along our faces. It turns out Jelly Roll is a tom, but he brings out something deep down feminine in me that I didn't know existed, and there are moments, when I'm watching him lap milk or clean his fur, that I want to drop everything and have a million babies. August loves Jelly Roll grudgingly, it seems, and only because I love him. I want to think it says something about how much August loves me. Nights when Jelly Roll wakes him, August takes him out to the living room and stays there, back on his couch. In a bed, August has no cushions in his face to push him straight into dreams, and the mattress is so very hard. My first early morning night here, he turned over and put his arm around me, burrowed his nose through my hair and against my skull, perhaps reinventing the couch. He slid his hands onto my belly, began bunching up my robe.

"Above the waist," I said, and though I said it softly enough not to mean it, he flopped back over so his back touched mine, warming us both. I was sorry, then. I'd said it more to prove something to Edith than to follow Joyce Nettles's advice.

Our bodies have told the same boring story every night this week — back to back like sideshow twins, sometimes breathing against each other, sometimes inhaling opposite each other's exhale, as one perfect pump. This afternoon, he rolls over and lays his hand on my thigh. It was a long, hard night, watching August play an after-hours studio session behind Milt Jackson: fourteen takes of one song, two glasses of cognac, and a joint. I sat, waiting, drinking, smoking . . . reading through Herbie Nichols's columns in the pile of *New York Age* magazines stacked neatly in front of Wynton Kelly's piano. I'm in and out of sleep still; the noon sun warms my closed eyes; I will myself back into dreaming. He's staring at me — I can feel his breath on my face — but I don't want to wake. Don't want to have to remind him again where his hand should be.

"Your eyelashes," I think he says, "are long as those angels' in Columbus Circle."

I open my eyes and clear my throat then, but he gets out of bed, still twisted in the sheet, leaving me naked to the cold air. He unwraps himself, then snaps the sheet in the air so that it floats down to cover my body, though I'm still left cold. He kisses me on the cheek before he showers, and I hear him turning on the living-room television, cracking eggs for himself, pouring a dish of milk for Jelly Roll. I fall back asleep, into my headache, and miss the rest of his morning. He's dressed and rolling his bass out the front door before I even open my eyes again.

On the television, President Eisenhower stands in front of the White House, saying how "deeply sympathetic" he is toward the four boys sitting in at the Woolworth counter in North Carolina. A man's been beaten and hanged upside down in a tree in Houston because of it, the initials "KKK" carved on his chest, yet Mr. Eisenhower says nothing of this. "I have a disdain for symbolic actions," he is even reported to have said, when questioned about the sit-ins. But now they are happening at lunch counters in Charlotte and Richmond and Nashville, and so Ike has to stand before the microphone, speaking of a nation's search for equality. No dirt will come this morning from the Rose Garden.

There are sit-ins in Lexington, Kentucky, Walter Cronkite is saying on the TV news, and I get a sheet of stationery and write to Caroline, asking her if she's gone to one. I don't expect that she has, and after five letters home with no return letters back, I figure she won't write back to tell me, either way. But it's always a comfort to write her, to tell her everything I see and feel. I've told her that I haven't yet let August. I tell her again that she should come live here. I tell her how Schiffman booked me and August for a private party on 131st Street last Saturday night, how, in the woman's brownstone, there bloomed an enormous, brilliant flower near the half-open window at the edge of the hall. "A corpse plant from Sumatra," the woman told me. "It blooms one day in five years. How lucky that you're here to catch it." I write to Caroline, too, of how a Nigerian prince refilled my glass of whiskey last night. I tell her how I fell asleep through the eleventh and twelfth takes of Wynton Kelly's solo. I tell her she would love Jelly Roll.

August's left eggs in the skillet, but they're cold, and my stomach is telling me no — I leave them, then, to rot. Dress myself in black slacks and a gray sweater, tie the sash tight around my new wool coat, and walk myself out of August's building and over to the Broadway bus stop. Ride the forty blocks down, and when I get up to ring the cord for my stop, startle the hunched-over nurse sitting next to me. She's still in uniform, her white hat still clipped around her hairstyle with bobby pins. She's not much older than I am, and she has the most beautiful, tired eyes. Eyes that will always look to be remembering seeing something nice, even if they've long since forgotten. It's not even two o'clock, and at 125th I'm the only passenger off the bus, the lone haunt passing through the cloud-covered chill. I find a box to post Caroline's letter, then enter the Apollo, and make my way up to rehearsal. Halfway up the stairs I slip, twisting my ankle enough to say *shit* — it's the fifth time in my life I've said it. I'm supposing that the next eleven might happen soon, here in New York.

August hadn't known, when he woke up, what his life was doing. He'd never dreamed its geometry, never felt the shape it had taken in its twenty-eight years. He'd never tallied the miles run, he said, not until he laid his hand on my thigh and saw the lashes of angels. By the time he got dressed that morning, he realized he was *responsable.* His mama wasn't walking him down the street to fiddle lessons anymore. She wasn't standing in his new apartment with her hand over her heart, frowning out his window at the streetchildren playing *in* the street (*Lord have mercy.*) She wasn't sending him down to 116th Street to buy himself a four-poster bed, or waking him up on Sunday morning to drag him downtown to some new Jamaicans' church. She wasn't telling him anything anymore — the clay of his life had become his own.

He told me that when he saw all the blank space he had dominion over, he took a taxi all the way down to Chemical Corn and withdrew a quarter of his savings, then took the 1 train down to Hell's Kitchen, where he sold off his fine Czech violin. Crossed over on the No. 36 bus to the Diamond District and bought the biggest rock he could afford. He hadn't planned any further than that, but when he got to practice that morning — later even than I did, at four twenty that afternoon — it just seemed natural to him to settle things there, in the very room where we met.

I was jazzing up "Tom Dooley," watching Verner pick some dry skin off the end of his nose, when August hurried in the door with his coat half off his shoulders and got down on one knee beside the piano bench. "Marry me?" he asked. Jim got to laughing. Letty mouthed "no" to Roland in the most horrified fashion. Verner got red around his nose like he was going to cry. When I didn't say anything, August took the velvet box out of his pocket and said, "Please?"

"Yes, yes!" I said, out of breath from the shock of it, and when he rose to kiss me, the rest of the band was struck so dumb that it took the janitor, mopping up a leak in the corner, to drop his tin bucket and clap.

I played through the evening's intro like it was a catnap dream. I saw the ladies and gentlemen of the audience but I couldn't feel their laughter, heard them clapping but couldn't see their hands. Mr. Schiffman had

427

gotten more and more serious about the acts coming to the theater — we had Sam Cooke, and Ray Charles, and we had the jazz greats like Ornette Coleman and Cecil Taylor. The shows got longer and so did the breaks we had while the feature acts were playing, and I spent more and more time sitting in one of the little bunk beds Schiffman had fixed to the wall for us backstage. The other girls actually napped in the bunks, or they sat at the metal folding table, playing cards and gossiping about their boyfriends. Vivian Harris ate dinner, salting her chicken each time she put it on her fork. I tended to read. I was reading *The Living Is Easy* when Mrs. Elizabeth Fogle came backstage.

"I saw you playing!" she said brightly. "I couldn't believe it was you. All that time you were my neighbor, and I'd never known."

"Thank you," I said, embarrassed immediately at how correspondingly little I knew about her. I couldn't even begin to guess where she worked, what she did. "How's little Johnny?" I asked.

"He's good. We're good. I'm good. I got married again." She thrust out her hand to show off her wedding band. "I'm Mrs. Earnest Hudson now. Johnny and I moved into his apartment, and Reggie and Rodney moved into mine."

I congratulated her, and she began running through what had become of everyone in Edith's building. Mr. and Mrs. Donald Green's beautiful little daughter had died, she said, and she'd caught Mr. Green's mother standing downstairs outside the mortuary, watching Mrs. Green cry. The older Mrs. Green was a haggard old woman in a fur, Elizabeth said, telling Donald, "That's the kind of thing that happens when you marry a nigger. What else did you expect." The deaf girl's husband packed off and left one day, she said, and all throughout the building you could hear the deaf girl's sobs still, all these months later. The two men who habitually stood in front of the liquor store had joined up with Make Me a Herald and been baptized, though one saw them occasionally slipping into the store for cans of beer. The church secretary had disappeared altogether, perhaps to join a kinder, gentler religion.

"And you?" she asked. "Earnest will ask, of course. Give me something to report."

I thought to show her my own diamond ring, but then I thought again, thought of her burning eggs and the occasional whippings she gave Johnny when she caught him misbehaving. Somehow, it seemed, she deserved to own the moment's happiness.

"All this," I said, motioning around me to the gowned women, the rushing stagehands. "I'm really happy."

August ran over and practically dragged me down the hall as I waved goodbye to her: he was telephoning Glaser, he said, and wanted me there.

"We want fifty percent," he said into the phone when Mr. Glaser answered. Mr. Glaser must not have recognized his voice, because he then said, "August Barnes. And my wife," he added, and Mr. Glaser must have asked *Who?* because I heard August say "Audrey." There was a long silence between them then, and August grinned at me, and then Mr. Glaser must have said they'd talk, because August said, "Looking forward to it," and hung up.

I hugged his waist all the way home that night, and when we got off the bus and upstairs to 3D, I got out paper for a letter to Mother. *I'm getting married,* I thought to write, or *You'd never guess what happened to me today.* I finally settled on a weather report, an epistle on how dirty a snow becomes in the city, a letter that would keep in touch without touching. *More good news to follow,* I left off. *Love to Mr. Barbour and*

Baby Nate. Who'd been born a boy after all, despite Mrs. Yvette down on Fifth Street, who held a string over Mother's belly and said, when it blew east, that Mother was having another girl. Mother's friend Saundra Greer said of course it was too early for Mrs. Yvette to tell such a thing, but Mother'd painted the crib pink anyway, with hearts on the headboard even. *Mr. Barbour,* she'd written in her last letter, *can't bring himself to go near it.*

Before I posted my letter, I looked again at my *Love to Mr. Barbour,* disbelieving it a little. But after my lifetime of waiting, love had finally come to me, so I licked the paste and closed the envelope: everybody deserved love, and perhaps my mother, like Mrs. Fogle, deserved finding it twice. I thought, for the first of seconds, that I'd write Caroline again, because she'd understand that eighteen felt old enough, that forever is worth smashing your mother's heart for, that love like mine and August's didn't run on a printed timetable. I remembered how we'd been in brassieres already when we saw the blood moon, and we'd run all the way to town and climbed up the roof of the Colored store so we could see the whole of it, all its craters and scars. We'd been in the middle of October, when the veil between us and the spirits was at its thinnest, and we'd thought our ancestors had sent the blood moon to tell us something. You won't die in Mt. Sterling, the blood moon said. You'll have names and lives that people will remember. I wondered, as I sealed my letter, if we'd read the moon right. I'd escaped to New York City, but so had three thousand other girls who could play the piano like a dream, and as it turned out, playing music was as much of a job as driving a tractor. Caroline, for all her big plans, was probably still in Kentucky, and it wasn't simply because there were no Colored girls on Broadway.

August was across the kitchen table, spread across a Passantino music paper, coloring the head on an eighth rest. "So when?" I asked, rolling my ink pen down the table until he stopped it with his palm. "When can we have a wedding?"

"Next fall. There'll be a week's break in the schedule. We can go on a proper honeymoon. That Colored resort in the Adirondacks, maybe. Or up to Niagara Falls."

Fall and Canada were so far off. But when we went to bed and he turned out his lamp and his hand found its way back up my nightgown, I didn't say a thing. I thought about Elizabeth Pounds Johnson, the way the dimple in her chin would stretch with the scream she'd emit if she saw the big diamond ring on my finger, and I let him inside me. "Love, love, love you," I whispered in his ear, as he shuddered in surprise.

BRUBECK

The weekend is big: we hear so on WBAI.
William O'Ree, the first Negro in the
National Hockey League, is traded to the
Boston Bruins. The Organization of Petro-
leum Exporting Countries meets for the
first time. World Airways Flight 830 crashes
three minutes after takeoff from Guam, killing eighty people. I fix myself faster and
faster to August's apartment, folding myself
into his couch to listen to him rattling the
newspaper, setting up a full-sized ironing
board from Woolworth's along the wall that
separates the kitchen from the dining room.
Counting clothes he needs for rehearsal and
performances, August goes through twelve
shirts a week, and six pairs of pants. An
hour and a half worth of Sunday ironing, he
needs, and with the board that close to the
kitchen, I won't have to wander too far from
a steaming coffee kettle or tomato soup
come to a boil. It's the warmest space in

the house, and sun from the window cheers me as I work. Afterward, I wipe the crumbs out of his silverware drawer with a soft green tea towel that's too pretty to use, really, and August listens to the Knickerbockers play a hot second half. Jelly Roll hops up on the end table, where he broke the blue-tinted flower vase that held my roses. He looks for the vase, perhaps to re-break it, but the flowers are just phantoms now. We settle into a rhythm, August and Jelly Roll and I, one no longer lived unconsummated.

Tuesday, after a crisp gray weekend, rain returns to New York. This time, it's torrential. We take a taxi to the theater, where August covers me with his umbrella while he drags his bass on the other side of him. Fidel Castro is coming to Harlem, it's been said, and a lone policeman in a blue NY PD poncho patrols a set of barricades that form a bisecting chain all around the Hotel Theresa. Letty's outside under the Apollo's awning, half in and half out of the rain. She's drinking coffee from a tiny take-out cup, and on our way in, she grabs me by the arm and holds me back. When she tosses what's left of her coffee onto the cold sidewalk, it steams. The aroma makes me click my teeth for an anxious 6/8. "Morning," I tell her, as August walks on without me.

"Nice one," Letty says. She throws me a dancer's smile so wide it can only be fake. Raindrops soak her auburn hair, turning it brown. We both stand and listen while the wheels on August's case clack over the threshold of the revolving door. *Thump, thump,* they go, up the carpeted stairs, and then the door's clicked shut. Letty fixes a wise look on her face that, from a foot away, looks like rapture. Her features, this close, are a bust's: eyes carved out of stone, nose like a slope. She's inside herself, blooming in this cold. But in an alley cat's voice she says, "Lemme see that ten-cent ring he gave you," and after rolling my finger from left to right in the day's light, she drops my hand like it was a dustrag. She narrows her gray eyes. "You may live a long time," she says, "but I can guarantee you this is the stupidest thing you'll ever do. If you do it, that is. It's not too late to back out. Move back to Edith's. I've talked to her. She'll take you back."

"Gee whiz. Thanks for being happy for me."

"Marriage is *not* about happiness, which you'll certainly discover if you marry August Barnes."

436

Letty tells me to think it over and let her know by dinner, as if the afternoon will transform August into some sort of atrocity, right before my eyes. I let her words travel around the rim of one ear and off into the falling rain. She's wrong about August, and nothing proves that more than the way, when Letty and I finally climb up to the studio, he's sitting on my bench, waiting. He gets up and scoots it out for a foot or two for me to sit down, which sets Jim to laughing again. Verner rolls his eyes. Letty just counts the slowest, calmest eight beats while August sits back down in his chair to his own instrument.

She works us like plow mules, stopping us sometimes after only one measure, having Verner adjust his reed five different times for flat notes. She works Roland so hard, making him dip her so low and lift her so high, the poor man has two perfectly round *O*'s of sweat on the cheeks of his backside by dinner break. When Roland goes to the bubbler for water, Jim laughs so hard he passes gas.

"Kentucky," Letty says to me, when we're finished and everyone else is packing off backstage to change clothes. "Come over here for a minute."

She's got on her diamond drop earrings,

and I wonder what's the occasion, whether it's Mr. Schiffman's birthday, or whether her old, broken-down, alabaster mother and father are coming again to watch the show. James Brown is playing tonight, with Brubeck, but even great artists are usually not enough to get her in the diamond drops.

"Mr. Glaser is offended."

I shrug my shoulders. "That's his problem."

"No, now it's my problem. Which makes it your problem."

"Why should it be?"

"There are things," she says, pulling up her skirt to take down her nylons, "that you clearly don't understand." She slides each sleeve off its leg, then crumples the pair and tosses it in the wastebasket, though they looked perfectly fine to me. "I think you might reconsider all this."

"All this what?"

"August. Asking for half the take. Getting married. All of it."

She's crazy. All of it is wonderful. In a couple of years, August will be famous and I'll be sharing him with the world. We'll live a whole lifetime, raising kids and making house notes and growing gray hair, and never again have nights like we're having now, rushing through Harlem in the rain, filling ourselves with late night daquiris in Greenwich Village and catching John Coltrane at the Zebra Room. Girls my age in Kentucky ruining their fingers in underwear factories and raising their armies of sad, hungry brats. This is the most romantic time in my life, and Letty's just jealous. I'm the luckiest girl in America, and she can't fell me not even one inch.

"I'm fine, Letty. Just fine. I know what I'm doing."

She narrows her eyes at me, then smiles, and becomes as serene as I've ever seen her. She walks off in her stockingless feet, and pauses at the door. She's talking into the hall, so it takes me a second to realize what she says — "it's your funeral."

Backstage downstairs, in the busy hallway, I change into one of the gowns on the ladies' rack and then gobble my dinner like a goose up for fattening, washing my catfish down with Coca-Cola to make it digest. August sprinkles clove buds under his tongue. Peculiar. Superstitious. But I'm glad he is. I take his hands in mine, knead the six soft spots between his eight knuckles, massage the length of each finger, and wish for these strong hands to make our future. All the while, he's staring at the back stairwell, which is naked of paint.

"What're you looking at, August? What are you thinking about?"

"We should find a drummer and a horn and make a record of our own. I get tired of playing other people's music."

"But we're usually playing our own."

"And there's where you're wrong. The minute you play something here, Schiffman owns it. Anything that gets recorded, he sells it. You think I'd be holding back so much if I owned that shit?" He looks out the window again as if someone were hunting him, then turns back and gives me a light peck on the forehead. "We won't find just any horn. Not a sax or a trumpet. What we need is a trombone. I bet you can't name one modern quartet with a trombone in it."

"Can't say as I can."

"Exactly. It'll make us famous. It'll make us rich. And all the money'll be ours. Mr. and Mrs. Barnes Incorporated, you know? Shit. *We* ought to be down at Birdland."

Walking onstage with this trotting around in my head, the thought that I'm actually living something far smaller than what he's thinking for us, I have to take short, shallow breaths to stop the excitement from smashing me flat. Backstage, while the six of us stand there getting our heads ready, while the crowd chants *A-pol-lo!* into the blacked lights, I grab August and kiss him. I put my cheek to his and transmit whatever chemicals make up forever. Only the purple floor lights, the ones Schiffman wired into the floor to keep the performers from tripping, shine.

Letty floats by our kiss, then Roland and Jim, then Verner. They're just spirits in the corner of my perception, tiny rises in body temperature I feel when they pass closest. When I break loose from August and look into his eyes, the lights are tiny purple ovals in his black pupils. Everything runs in slow motion: *A-pol-lo! A-pol-lo!* all the way up to the balcony, and the smell of grease in the lights, and the rush of cool air from the box fans in the catwalk. These people in the audience, I know, are the same people I pass in the streets, the same ones getting on the bus at seven in the morning cussing the conductor for running early, and the ones getting on the bus again at four, cussing him for running late. The same ladies who threaten their children with belts for moving an inch on the sidewalk, the same boys who take pisses in alleys when they think no one is looking. Right now, they all sound like angels. Even my skin feels electric, like somebody's rubbed witch hazel all over it.

"We've come so far," August says, "but

there is farther to go. We'll save two, three thousand dollars, and we'll split. With the money from Columbia, it shouldn't take us more than a year. We're going to be out of this world. Cosmic."

I scratch my shoulders where the sequins bite them, and August takes my hand and leads me out past the curtain. "Ladies and jagomints!" yells Vivian Harris. Everyone laughs. Vivian has the spotlight, and the rest of the stage is black, but as soon as we get to the edge of things, someone turns a spot on me and August. "Well, would you look at these two lovebirds here," Vivian says, and the surprise of the light and her voice makes us drop hands and blink. "Tonight is the very last night for bassist August Barnes and his intended, pianist Audrey Martin. Let's hear it for the happy couple!"

The crowd sits poised to scream, and that's what they do, and it takes me going on a couple of minutes to realize that sweet, kind Vivian Harris has just fired me onstage. She's announced *my* last night. But then, there's nothing to do but sit down and play — it isn't in either August's or my natures to do anything else. Letty and Roland dance their steps as though nothing untoward is happening. Verner keeps blowing and Jim keeps beating, and it hurts me to realize that neither of them is surprised. When the Famous Flames step onstage, and James Brown comes out in his cape singing *Please Please Please,* we all hustle back behind the curtain, but no one speaks a single word to me, not even when I go to sit on the same bench where Verner is sipping gin from a tumbler.

Through the ladies' dressing-room door, we can both hear August and Letty skreaking at each other, Letty's unintelligible words high as a monkey's, August's voice booming in its lower register. *I wanna be your lover man,* James Brown sings, sliding his mike to the floor as he drops to his knees. The Famous Flames bring their horns louder, thus containing the viciousness backstage. The other women in the dressing room seem to be dropping their own opinions into the argument, and every once in a while laughter erupts in the dressing room, or a chorus of *umm-hmms,* but Verner hears nothing, it seems — he sips his gin like a fish, with his Adam's apple bobbing up and down and his eyes wide with trying not to look at me. I think to myself how dumb I've been, how young and unhip to New York, but then how grown-up too, since something in me is already miles above the petty shit Letty's just dropped on us. I'm blind with nerves about the two thousand dollars we haven't saved, but after all, a true Harlemite cannot give anyone the satisfaction of seeing her upset. I get up from the bench and walk — concentrating so as to hold my head high and not swing my arms like a gorilla — to hunch against the back door of the dressing room.

"She can't even play a bar without humming it," Letty is screaming.

"High yellow whore," August shouts, and something thumps against the wall.

Letty comes running out of the dressing room with her arms pinned to her sides and her hair in a topknot. As she strides away, August bursts through the door and grabs me by the arm, a hair rougher than Letty did in the afternoon. He drags me to the stage, where he takes his bass by the neck like it's an unfaithful lover and drags it across the floor. The endpin scrapes the hardwood and leaves a groove that will last until the floor is refinished, but the chattering audience, immersed in intermission, notices nothing.

"Where're we going?" I ask him, as we break curtain.

"To our future."

We hustle ourselves down the stairs at the back of the theater and into the lobby.

Brubeck and Paul Desmond have taken the stage, and they're playing something fast, something rocking, something that won't slow down for me to hold it. I try, but I can't make out a time signature. In two years' worth of nights, I've thought I was redefining music itself every time I played a run, and here it turns out I can't even hear outside the four. Desmond kicks in on his sax just as August rolls his bass through the door, *thump, thump,* and I hold back to count beats. There must be a signature. All music has a signature. It simply must be. "What will we do without seven hundred dollars?" I ask August, to stall him at the door.

"Manage." He holds the door open for me to walk through, but I'm standing there, in the lobby, trying to count. Whatever it is, it doesn't finish in fours. It sounds like the surface of the sun as heard from outer space, bigger than I can understand. "Come on," August says, shaking his hand in impatience. "We're through here."

"I trust you," I tell him, and walk through the door. Down the avenue, at the Hotel Theresa, a crowd of Cubans stands behind police barricades, waving Cuban flags, and the swell of them bursts onto 125th Street such that a car has to swerve to avoid hitting a little dark-eyed girl in pigtails. Fidel Castro's in there now. Word has it he's talking to Malcolm X. So much resistance. So many blueprints. August hails a cab and we zip up to 163rd, up the marble-floored elevator to August's apartment, where he takes off his shoes, flops on his couch with his arm resting atop its back, and says, simply, "Shit."

A letter's been slipped under the door. August stepped over it on his way in the house, because it's lying with the *Times* and the Walgreens circular, but when I pick it up I see that it was mailed to me at apartment 3G, and the tenant must have recognized the name and brought it over. *Mr. Stanton Wallace,* reads the return address, *211 Queen Street, Mt. Sterling, Kentucky.* I have no idea how Sonnyboy has found me, no idea what he could want. But it doesn't seem appropriate to open anything before August's had his cigarette, so I wait, wondering if I'll ever again have my name announced to an audience of angels.

■ ■ ■ ■

PART SIX:
AUDREY

■ ■ ■ ■

ICE

I'd meant to be landing in Standiford Field
on December 28 with a songwriting credit
to my name, a new leather suitcase hanging
from my hand, and a diamond big as a
filbert on my finger. Once I arrived, I'd
spend three days letting my grandfather
beat me at checkers. I'd cast new, wide-eyed
wonder at the stories he'd repeat without
remembering why. I'd speak loudly to his
deafness. I'd studiously avoid Mr. Barbour
and build, somehow, a bridge between me
and Mother: after all these years, my life
would wash out more clearly for her now
that I, too, had found a husband. On New
Year's Eve, I'd ride with Sylvia up to Lexington in Dr. French's new Simca and, with
the three other musicians Mrs. Raspberry
had recruited, play for twenty two-stepping
debutantes; I'd be fêted by the same Negroes who wouldn't even have told me hello
on the street when I was a girl in Mt.

Sterling.

But it wasn't like that, not at all. "You know you shouldn't even ask," August said, when I reminded him I was traveling.

"But it's my money."

He gave me a peculiar look. Not a worried or angry look, but a look that said he wasn't going to argue — he was just going to tell me. "It's our money," he said, "and you're not going to use it on a plane ticket."

I still felt it was an argument, and mine to win. I shuffled around all afternoon, unpacked my clothes in front of him and then repacked them in the privacy of our bedroom closet, stroked Jelly Roll's fur in the wrong direction on purpose. Over dinner, I told him I would go on the train. "It's not a big deal," I said.

"I've already booked us a gig for New Year's. Either you can spend all that money going to Kentucky and not even break even by the time you get back, or you could stay right here in New York with me — your *husband* — and bring four hundred dollars home from the Roseland Ballroom."

You're not my husband yet, I wanted to remind him, but it wouldn't be in keeping with the spirit of things. Instead, I excused myself from dinner and lay on the floor in our bedroom and cried until I was nauseous.

I hadn't cried so hard since my daddy died. The floor was cold enough that the physical pain drowned out some of the hurt in my heart, but still, I kept thinking how love caused a person to make the bitterest sacrifices. I'd get married and have a sweet bouquet, but when their stems were bound with twine, the flowers would be crushed.

I'd meant to call Caroline as soon as August decided, but I didn't know what, exactly, to tell her. I could tell her that my fiancé's father had died, since that had been true for many years. I could tell her that the tickets for the flight were sold out, since she wouldn't possibly know how air travel happened. I could tell her nothing at all. That whole night in bed, while August snored and Jelly Roll padded up and down the hall, excuses darted through my mind and then sat a minute before leaving. I saw the faces of the innocent sixteen-year-old girls who were looking to have a good time and see a local girl made good, the faces of their mothers and fathers, who would suppose I thought myself too important for them all, not knowing that what was keeping me in New York was the same lack of money I'd always known. The next morning, after August left for Sunday dinner with his mother, I went to the post office and mailed

Caroline forty of the vinyl 45's we'd been saving in the corner of his living room. *CAROLINE,* in white block letters. — *A. Martin* — *A. Barnes* — *T. Toy* underneath. Every debutante and their mother would have one. I shoved them into my Cartier and dragged them to the post office, where it cost me a fortune to post them in the mail. I imagined Ruth Simmons's mother lugging the heavy package up Miss Myrtle's porch in her mail bag, imagined Caroline reading my note. "I'm sorry for the short notice," I'd written to her, "but I cannot visit on the 31st. Words cannot begin to express my regret." In fact, there were too many words, far too many to print in one letter. "Please send this gift to the members of the Cotillion on my behalf."

The disappointment felt like it might ruin me.

Come New Year's Eve, I did play the Roseland with August, then went with him to an afterparty in Queens, where we kissed at the stroke of midnight, oblivious to everyone else in the room, their paper 1961 glasses and their whiskey-soaked drink umbrellas. The next Monday, August put most of the four hundred dollars into our joint bank account, and laughed as he gave me fifty dollars' worth of what he called "mad money." I was going to use part of it to take him on a date. I'd meant to spend my nineteenth birthday sipping grasshoppers from my fiancé's straw, leaning my head against his cologned shoulder while we watched Thelonious Monk play Town Hall. Every day in December, I'd walked past the posters pasted to construction barriers, orange edging with sky blue letters, the *T* of *Town* and the *H* of *Hall* slightly enlarged, Thelonious himself immortalized in black silhouette at his piano, as though he would never again rise to eat or kiss his wife or use the toilet. I'd pass under the scaffolding and note the date — January 25, 1961 — and the address — 113 West 43rd. I'd even collected change for the bus ride downtown and back, as I was so often without small change in New York City. For once, before our relationship became something else altogether, I'd wanted to treat August.

Too late now: we're married. It's what I did with my nineteenth birthday. We'd just bused ourselves into Hickory, North Carolina, and August took me to the downtown courthouse and we signed the papers. I had no white dress, no bouquet of daisies. August had no best man, and no gold band from me because I hadn't had the money. Strange, considering August and I played almost twenty New York weddings together, but we had no one to play at ours. Melodies settled in our ears as we walked up the courthouse steps, but neither of us could be certain we were imagining the same song as the other, let alone the same arrangement. We would have been too embarrassed, standing before the judge and the court clerks, to hum.

August had, at least, French-kissed me for a full minute while the judge who'd called him "boy" tried to hand us our papers. I couldn't tell whether it was defiance or love. "What were you thinking," I'd ask him later, "all that time you were kissing me?"

He'd only joke. "Daydreaming about lunch. Every fiber of fish and every pecan in the pie."

For a honeymoon, we've taken the bus up to Kentucky to tell Mother.

"You're what?" she yells, as though her hearing is shot. "Married?" Mr. Barnett, on his way out to the country to pick up a side of beef, has dropped us off at the edge of Mr. Barbour's yard, where we walked up the stone steps to find Mother sitting in one of his green metal glide chairs. Dead of the coldest January on record and a full week before Groundhog's Day, but the sun has come out between snows and offered a day

454

of warmth that will save the minds of the people of Mt. Sterling. Sunday, for once this year, might live up to its name: at ten in the morning, sunlight glances off the iced-in branches and gives the trees a fiery new life. Lucky for Baby Nate, who's two years old and weary enough of the house that he's trying, nail by nail, to tear down what his father built. When he hears Mother upset, Nate makes his wobbly run to her chair, where he balances himself against an arm and tugs at the bottom of her rose sweater. She swats his hand away without even looking at him. "How can you be married?" she asks me. "You're only nineteen. You just turned nineteen yesterday!" Mother turns to August, speaking to him for the first time. "And how old are you?"

He rocks forward, and I can see the outline of his knuckles in his pockets as he clenches his fist. "I'm thirty. Ma'am. Just turned. My and Audrey's birthdays are the same week. Isn't that something?"

"My good God," she says, then yells through the open window at her back. "Jonas! Get out here!"

"I'm sleep, 'Naitha," he whines. "What you need?"

"Just get yourself on out here!"

Even Baby Nate is silent as the four of us

listen to each stair creak with Mr. Barbour's sleepy weight.

"What — oh — hey! Audrey's back! Who is the young fellow? Ain't chaperones usually ladies?"

"Well, that'd be her husband," Mother says. She scoops Nate into her lap and cries into his hair as she rocks him.

"Oh, hey now," Mr. Barbour says. "You know your mama's been dry as a bone, going on a year now. We don't want to upset her, make her nerves come back." He puts a hand on Mother's shoulder. He shuts his eyes tight and opens them again. So recently has he been asleep, he's likely wishing he were still standing in his dreams. "It'll be all right," he says to Mother. "We'll get to the bottom of all this." But the seconds pass, and he doesn't find any other words. He seems unable to take his eyes off Mother's shoulder. Water begins to drip from the tree at the edge of the porch, making pocks in the snow.

"This what people do in New York City?" Mother asks. "Men marry babies?"

"I'm not a baby. And I'm — we're not in New York anymore."

I can't remember ever seeing my mother cry when she wasn't also drinking, and without a cushion of alcohol to keep them fierce, her eyes seem gelatinous in their misery, like a beaten horse's. "Where you been living?" she asks. "Why ain't you let us know where you was? I oughta kick my own ass for ever letting you trot up there in the first place."

"No, Mother. It's been wonderful. I'm having a wonderful life."

"Wonderful is married at nineteen? Your daddy was alive, he'd kill us all. I guess you're pregnant."

"Not yet," I say, "but it isn't for lack of trying." I can't help but grin at August, whose face has gone ashen. Mother starts sobbing. Mr. Barbour just keeps staring down at her shoulder. Over and over he rubs her back through her sweater, as though he's looking to unweave its knit. "Our gig at the Apollo got . . . well, no matter — we're on the road. This week Charlotte, then Greensboro, then Winston-Salem. Next month, we'll play the islands. I'll be living on a beach, Mother!"

"That so? Your daddy went off to live at the beach. Next thing you know, he's dead." Mother puts a hand over her mouth, inadvertently bumping Nate's forehead with her Bakelite bracelet. It couldn't have hurt, but my brother begins to wail, and Mr. Barbour lifts him from Mother's lap and carries him

457

back into the house. Poor Baby Nate, who hasn't yet learned to count. I myself have this gift of numbers: no matter how far things deteriorate, August and I have to be back on the bus to Charlotte in twenty-six hours and eighteen minutes.

"Audrey. Get the keys to Jonas's car and get out here. We're going into town."

Mr. Barbour's kitchen stands darker than it should, given the sun's sudden winter appearance, and I find myself wondering if anything at all good ever penetrates his windows. Baby Nate screams louder, even, as Mr. Barbour bounces him on his knee, and Mr. Barbour himself looks more afraid than he did on the porch, but he's not at all surprised when I ask for the car. "Take care of your mama" is all he says. He hands over his ring of four keys.

Mother's learned to drive in the months I've been away, and I can't help but be proud of the way she shifts into her different gears and paddles her foot from clutch to foot-feed without missing even one beat of crying. A dead rabbit lies splayed on its side in the shoulder of the road, and I'm reminded that to be in the country is to be surrounded by death, always.

"I'm sorry, Mother," I say.

"Don't be. My mama never loved me

458

right. She had too much grief for love to live with it. I got kicked out the nest while I was still hatching, and all I knew was to do the same thing to you. Matter fact, I figured if I loved you the way you ought to be loved, it'd just make me mad for what I ain't had when I was coming up. I never got enough of nothing, not till I met your daddy, and then he went off and died. I thought your daddy was the onliest thing what ever loved me. But do you know you're just about the onliest thing I ever loved?"

Ahead of us, a branch of ice falls from a tree and is crushed beneath Mr. Barbour's wheels. Finally, after all these years, the building that houses the bakery is being rebuilt. It has a new roof now, and a large windowless shoproom where icicles hang. Mother rolls down the window to clear the condensation that's gathered on the windshield, and with the breeze coming in, I should feel chillled. I don't.

"Maybe I was flapping around the house like a bird with one wing, but I want you to know —"

"I do."

"You don't. You know what you *think* mamas are supposed to do. You know the ways you *wanted* to believe I loved you. But I'm telling you, you don't know the half of it. And I want you to know that that boy, that man — what's his name?"

"August."

"He ain't the be all end all. He ain't the only one what ever loved you. Me and your daddy, and your granddaddy too — peculiar as he is about showing it — you are our whole life, girl. Always have been. When you was borned, you ain't never seen three people so happy." Mother keeps her eyes trained on the road, but she takes one hand from the wheel to hold mine. She smiles. "We think you're the bee's knees." She coughs, then lets her smile go. "Leastwise we did. Until you went and got married 'fore you could even get a chance to smell yourself."

We're in town now, riding down Queen Street, with all the people on their way home from church waving to Mother as if she is, by herself, a parade. Pauline Burke yells howdy to our open windows; her psoriasis has worn so far in the harsh winter, her face looks like something hanging from a deli window, but the warmth of her smile breaks the ravaging of her cheeks. Junebug, still tall and fine, but with a rangier walk and a certain increase of want in the way he holds his shoulders, doesn't really wave at us. He's more honest than anyone else: he waves at the car.

"Go on in here now," Mother says, pulling the 210 alongside the Tin Cup, "and get your ma some Early Times." She pushes a five-dollar bill into my hand, propelling me out of the car with the passion in her fingertips. *Take care of your mama,* Mr. Barbour said, but once I'm standing outside in the bright sun and graying slush, I can't be certain what that entails. Junebug catches up to where I'm standing on the sidewalk and passes me, but his head stays swiveled in my direction. He's dressed in a regular workshirt and suspenders; he hasn't been to church. I think maybe, like Mother and Mr. Barbour, he has his reasons. He touches the brim of his cap in respect, and someone standing across the street might mistake him for having a newfound appreciation of me, but I'm standing close enough to see his eyes. He's staring at the cerulean fins atop the trunk of Mr. Barbour's car.

"Nice to see you too, Junebug."

"You really do look like a citygirl," he says, halting his stride. "Hear tell you had a record on the radio, but I ain't never got to hear it for myself."

"It wasn't my record," I say. "I just wrote the song. I bet you have heard it."

He doesn't ask which song, because he

461

doesn't care. He wiggles his cap right and then back left on his head. "Think you'll ever come back to Kentucky?"

I shrug, and he snaps his head back around to shuffle on down the street. Through the white cinder-block walls of the Tin Cup comes laughter, the shouted end of a joke, more laughter. I breathe deeply of the winter around me, then step in the bar's front door.

"Them Cats is doing all right this year. No thanks to Coach Rupp —"

"Aww naw, you pour lye down the drain it's gonna eat them pipes right up —"

"Gotta grease up the sow 'fore you reach up her nethers for that piglet —"

"Then she took my boots and threw 'em out in the snow while I was sleep —"

The little radio atop the ice chest carries on with its Nat King Cole chorus, and at last the men of the bar fall silent. They build me a wall of stares. The Tin Cup is always so stuffed with men, I thought they could smell it when a new woman walked through the door, but they're just now noticing me.

"That the little Martin girl?"

"The one what went off to New York?"

"I believe it is."

"Heard tell she was on the radio."

"Well, little bit, you done growed right

462

up," says the Tin Cup's owner, who's standing behind the bar, crushing ice in a grinder. He's let his conk grow out, and even under the crown of his natural, his polished gold-cuffed links and black leather vest whisper a proprietary slickness, a sophistication that will own Queen Street even if it will never transcend it.

"Thank you," I tell him. "But it's probably just my new coat."

Still the men stare, some of them at my shoes, others at my hair, still others at shapes they visualize beneath my wool coat. The WLEX announcer breaks the music with news: *Eight days after launching the seven-ton* Sputnik V, *the Soviets have used the orbiting satellite as a launch platform for the interplanetary probe* Venera I, *which is aimed at the planet Venus. The United States launched* Pioneer V *toward Venus in March, but the signal was lost a month later.*

"What you need?" the owner asks. "You're a little short in the tooth yet to be liquored up on a Sunday, smart girl like you. And I ain't seen your mama here in a good long while."

"I'd just like some —" I begin. I've arrived at a minute I've come to a thousand times before, in a hundred different lifetimes, and this time the hard, blue crystals that have tied me down are snapping loose. *Take care of your mama,* Mr. Barbour said.

"Peanuts. I came for peanuts."

"Peanuts? Well, all right, if that's what you want."

"This some kind of New York thing?" somebody yells from the bar, and all the other men laugh.

I try to hand the owner Mother's five dollars and he shakes his head. "Your mama's gonna be all right," he says, as he pours half a bag of shelled peanuts into a paper sack. I breathe deeply of the Tin Cup, of my mountain people and their gorgeous, ruinous ways, of something that's no longer my mother's.

When I slide back into the car, I watch Mother watch me. The bun she's so carefully coiled this morning has slid down to a loosening bump on the back of her neck, and she doesn't seem like my mother at all — she's just a sad, nervous widow too old to have a two-year-old baby and too young to have a daughter who's gone and gotten married without so much as a how do or a go-to-hell. Mother leans into me and puts her hand out for the sack. "What's in here?" she asks, peering in. "Peanuts? Peanuts!"

But she's smiling, and then she starts to laugh.

Ice on the road has turned to slush and then to water, and trees on the way out of town stand naked, relieved of their icy sleeves. Spray hisses under Mr. Barbour's tires and dirties the sides of his car, and I imagine him outside later, washing it with his bucket of soapy water, drying it with his chamois. I hope it'll stay warm for him. He loves my mother. To teach her to drive, he's had to sit in his own passenger seat and look over at her and see a woman more bold than afraid, a woman defaulting on the sadness she owes her past. I've finished eighteen, and I'm on my way to twenty. Five fours, a nice rounded-off number. Between Mother and me now is an end, a beginning. She turns on Mr. Barbour's radio, and I sink back into the vinyl seat. I can't know the time exactly, but in less than twenty-five hours I'll go from being some of my mother's daughter to being all of August's wife. And for that, for my hurry, I'm already sorry.

FAMOUS ONES

When Grandpap sees me coming up his sidewalk with August, he stands up from his new porch swing and shakes his head. Not so much at us, I gather, as at himself — after sixty-eight years in the world, he can no longer always be certain of what he sees. Age has carried his body a far piece in the year I've been away, or perhaps it's just that I never noticed the pinching of his mouth and the blossoming of hair in his ears when I had daily watch of them. He says my name with tears in his blueing eyes. I'm his lone pigeon returned to roost, and he holds his embrace of me for such a length of time that I'm able to count a score of shy heartbeats traveling up his chest. I'll leave it to August to tell him we're only visiting.

"Granddaddy, this is my husband."

He shakes August's hand as gently and easily as if I've offered him a sandwich. "Right pleased to meet you," he says, but he hikes up his pantlegs and sits back down without offering August a place in the swing. He doesn't invite us into the house, though the sun is just starting to dip behind the mountain and our arms are chilled underneath our coats. "How old is this feller?" Grandpap asks me, without taking his eyes off August's.

"Thirty," August answers.

"I asked my granddaughter."

"Thirty," I say. "Says so on his birth certificate."

"Thirty. That means he ain't in high school. Which means he must do something for a living." Grandpap keeps August locked in his sights. "Now I *am* talking to you," he says, and sets himself to rocking.

"I'm a bassist. Sir."

"A musician?"

"Yes, sir. I make a comfortable enough living out of it, sir."

"Well, that's good. Ain't too many of 'em what does."

Grandpap manages to lower his bushy eyebrows and make himself look satisfied, but it comes out that he isn't. Over a dinner of breakfast — hotcakes he's smothered in butter, and sausage with hot pepperseeds he's ground tiny as dustflakes — Grandpap rakes questions over August. How long has he played for money? *Eight years.* Who has he played with? *Jaki Byard and Elvin Jones.* Anybody we would of heard of? *McCoy Tyner?* Naw. *Pharoah Sanders?* Maybe. Where all has he played? *Café Society. Connie's Inn. The Five Spot.* You get booed off the stage? That how you met my Audrey? *It was a regular gig we had together. Sir.* Had? What happened?

I've got seventeen hours left to find Caroline, and answering all Grandpap's doubts will take a lifetime. "Granddaddy," I say. "Let the man eat his supper."

"Your daddy's dead, so I'm the man has a right to know."

"They threw out my contract. Sir."

"Well, then. People don't generally throw things out midstream lessun the things is causing them trouble." Grandpap sets his fork and knife down on either side of his plate so that they stand like soldiers waiting for orders. August looks glumly at his island of hotcakes. He bites into a piece of sausage, and spice waters his eyes.

"They threw out his contract," I say, "because he was living on his feet."

Grandpap's eyebrows ruch upward again and he retakes his silver, pushing his knife through the tines of his fork to saw out a piece of sausage. "Man oughta make sure he can feed his wife before he goes standing on his feet," he says, but he doesn't sound like he means it. He chews and swallows, making a couple of minutes during which neither August nor I dare breathe. "So," he asks, "if you can play bass, that means you might can fiddle, too."

"Yes, sir."

"Well, it just so happens I got one in the backroom."

"Granddaddy," I say, but he's already up and tapping himself to the back of the house.

"Hey, Lolita," August whispers. "What's old Grandpa really going back there for? His jar of arsenic?" He rolls his eyes, and I giggle. Grandpap returns with a blank expression that confirms he's heard nothing.

"Well, all right, son," he says, handing over his fiddle. He thrusts his splintered bow forward, grazing August's forehead with its frog, but he won't acknowledge having hit him. He won't apologize, either, for interrupting the man's dinner. August takes up his bow and sews together a child not quite ragtime and not quite bluegrass, a movement so undeniably precious and rare as to make me and Grandpap feel that this is the afternoon for which we've lived eighty-four collective years. He heads into 5/2 time, shuts himself into the pentatonic scale, resolves back into bluegrass, and Grandpap dips his head with the shame of having to wipe away a tear. If August knows then that our ears are melting, his face reveals nothing: he's simply saving the day with his hands. He plants the fiddle deeper in the crook of his neck and frowns, transects Grandpap's fiddle with the camber at every possible angle; and the thing he hatches takes me and Grandpap back past the telegram from South Korea, back past the time either of us ever saw the word COLORED atop a water fountain, past that day in childhood when we first discovered our fingers wouldn't reach the sky no matter how high we stretched. August plays, and my grandfather and I are reborn.

"Best damn fiddler I ever heard," Grandpap says, when he's finished. The curtains are still parted, and I can see the moonlight as a faint smear across the tops of the trees; snow will be back in Mt. Sterling by morning. Grandpap invites us to stay the night, the weekend. "But don't y'all dare think a living here," he says, as August hands him back his fiddle and bow. "Ain't a body south of the Mason-Dixon line knows how to treat a black man got that kind a talent. Y'all need to move on over to Paris. France. That's where all the famous ones goes."

For the night, we do stay. In our sharp, black, New York clothes, we spoon up and sleep together in fits on Granddaddy's narrow sofa, August's pants against my nylons, the soft part of my nose sunk into his starched collar. I remember how, if you're a young person, it's a virtue to be out on a Friday night in Mt. Sterling, and I wonder at how old I've grown already, that the thought of doing so repulses me. I wake at midnight. And at three in the morning. And again at four thirty, having dreamed that I fell asleep and had a dream. I'm exhausted the next morning, but it feels wise: I have only five and three-quarter hours to find Caroline, and from Mr. Barbour's house, it would have taken me all morning to catch a ride.

I'm not at all certain what meeting her will make me have to say, whether I owe her apology for not coming on New Year's Eve or excuse for coming so soon thereafter, or the neutrality of being — like her — not so special after all. Just a girl who tried. By the middle of January in this new decade, neither August nor I were able to find gigs anywhere. Joe Glaser, it seems, was powerful enough to have both my and August's cabaret cards revoked. What's worse, we didn't find out until we went looking for gigs. Where we'd been friends, we'd become poison. At Clark Monroe's Uptown House, the stage manager shook his head and said his hands were tied. At Dan Wall's Chili Shack, the owner just chuckled to himself and walked away, as though he were already looking at two ghosts. John Hammond hadn't been touched, it seemed, and August played a session on the eleventh, but we both knew it wouldn't be enough money. Through a friend, we got on with the Theater Owners' Booking Association. Everyone knows it as T.O.B.A., though August calls it Tough On Black Asses, because the Southern audiences want blood, sweat, and tears at every show. They're interested in showmanship, not musicianship, and in 70-degree winter weather, it's too hot, in any case, to play art. It feels odious to lay on a note for two measures; it feels like we ought constantly to be playing Dixieland. August, in reaction, wants to solo constantly. He's forgotten that the bassman is the foundation. It's like someone's thrown us a medicine ball. In the long run, it might be that holding the ball isn't the hard part, but catching it has been something awful.

When I see her, I won't tell Caroline

about that. I'll tell her, instead, the story of us in New York, of nights spent jostling beautiful, sensitive crowds, and subway platforms full of girls with their own spending money. I'll tell her how I'd forgotten about my mother's black dress because each night, the costume girl wheeled out a whole rack of show gowns. I'll tell her she should have come; she should have been there. I'll tell her about the Negro girl on Riverside Drive who etched the faces of famous people in pink chalk.

August is drooling a spot on the flowered couch pillow, and when I roll to standing on the cold wood floor, he rouses and turns over so his face is in the couch. Still, he sleeps. Grandpap's bedroom door is filled with his heavy snoring, and it's easy, if I miss the louder floorboards, to steal his winter boots from inside the door. At the back of the house, in the old keeping room, I take three pairs of wool socks from his drying rack to snug the boots against my feet. If I take August with me to see Caroline, August with his crisp black shirt and his quotations from Mao's *Little Red Book,* it will be like speaking Portuguese. It won't do to wake him, then, and when I leave through Grandpap's front door, I hold the spring so it won't creak, letting its coils slink along my fingers.

At seven on a winter's morning, the frontier beyond Grandpap's porch stands empty of life, without humans or animals or visible foliage. The sun has sunk itself and not returned, and the heavy winds have rolled overland in the night and refrozen the earth. From every chimney on Queen Street, smoke recycles itself into the gray sky, and the singed air stings my nose and leaves a sooty film on my tongue. It means mothers are cooking breakfasts, and fathers are warming their feet at fires; older sisters are pressing their hair and warming babies' bottles. It doesn't mean that anyone on Queen Street cares that I'm here, or is waiting for me to be anywhere save the inside of their radios or the hard places they reserve in their hearts for folks run off and grown strange. Off the porch, then, I stumble, down the sidewalk and into the frozen mud of the street. Grandpap's boots rub hard enough to blister, but the layers of sock protect my feet. Enough time passes that the early morning wind stops and gives way to silence, and though its song stays in my mind, I know it's just an echo deep in my soul. When an engine finally breaks the quiet, I trudge the exact middle of the road, daring the car to run me down, which I myself can't believe. Any monster could be driving, waiting for a young, stupid, frozen girl to misjudge her place in the scheme of things.

Mrs. Wofford comes into view behind the wheel of her station wagon — pink and wrinkled, with cruel eyes and blazing orange hair. She leans across her seat and rolls down her window in jerks. "Where you headed?" she asks, in the loud voice of the slightly deaf, and I can't believe how much two years have ravaged her. Her roots, at the hairline, show half an inch of gray. "Where you headed?" she asks again, when she sees I'm just gawking at her, and I lift my hand in something not even dismissal.

"Are you listening to me, gal?" she yells, as I start to walk. Another motor crawls along in the distance and then comes to pass her. A tired-looking couple in a dented sedan, the letters D–O–D–G–E pressed against the muzzle of its grille. Mrs. Wofford inches along the street beside me. "Well, it's right cold out here, and you with not even no hat. You're liable to get frostbite on them ears, you don't get inside right quick."

She rolls up her window as she says it, and drives off with no further advice, spoiling the virgin air with exhaust as she rocks through the ruts. I watch until her car disappears, then I take up walking again in the direction of the White grocery and the carousel. I'm traveling. Just like everyone else on the planet.

Atop No. 211 stands a man hammering a shingle onto the roof. It's remarkable, but my thoughts are only of escaping the cold, and I think nothing of him until he shouts out: "Audrey? That you?"

"Yes."

It's wholly unremarkable, as if I've been waiting for him to call out to me for years.

He tucks his hammer into his waistband, pulls a handkerchief out of his back pocket, and wipes the sweat from his eyelashes. He's wearing a wool cap with flaps down over his ears, and he's pulled it down over his eyebrows, and I wouldn't know him at all if it weren't for the way he's standing, that sturdy, sure way he used to stand and smoke when he got home from the ice plant. I've known, since I received his letter in New York City, that this was a possibility, but when he says, "Nice to see you," all I can manage is one more quiet yes.

I think Pookie's some lost without you, he'd written. *I'd tell her to go up there and live with you in New York, but she won't talk to me. Won't let me see Imagene.* He'd written me about prison, told me his number was

*everything. Just everything. When you got
your hair cut, what you got called whenever a
body needed to say something to you. My
number was 3852. I wrote it at the top of this
letter on account of I forgot I had a name, so I
threw the page in the fire and started over.*
He'd told me something he told me he'd
never told anyone else, about Mauris's feet.
*It wasn't that I didn't want to tell them where
they were. It's just that they was mine and
mine alone. She'd danced with me and not
them, and she'd rubbed her pretty feet up my
legs in the nights when it was cold. I was in
love with her feet just like I was in love with
her. Wasn't none of nobody's business where
they was.* No apology had come from his
words, and no explanation. It was just
information: an outrage of ink.

He's painted the four corner columns of
No. 211 fire engine red, but the rest of the
house is still its same yellow, neglected and
peeling during the six years Sonnyboy has
been in Eddyville, so it seems as though the
house is bleeding. In the yard, magificently,
strut two peacocks. The male thinks me
enemy or maybe mate, because he spreads
his full complement of feathers, with their
hundreds of eyes looking to be seen. He
obscures his mate with his display, then
struts forward twice and gives the sea of

eyes what small breeze penetrates through the cold.

"Where'd you get them?" I ask him.

"From them beatniks up the mountain."

"You raising them for the eggs?"

"Their eggs are the nastiest things you ever tasted. And they ain't easy, either. I'm out hand-feeding them before the sun even comes up. Dead snails. Worst smell you ever dreamed up. No, I'm raising them for their companionship."

The male's eyes are black peas in his sea blue head, and he's so fiercely beautiful that I need to apologize just for looking at him. In New York, I've seen the genius of tile mosaics laid into the street, the shimmer of a thousand silk blouses. But this bird's body, the blinding turquoise bleeding down to its purple nethers, is a summit of possibility a million times more brilliant than anything a hand could create. I might fold him into his meat and tuck him into my suitcase, see what August says when the bird pops out in North Carolina with his feathered eyes in the air. See whether Jelly Roll tries to eat him. Elaine Prince, living up by herself on the mountain, complained to the law when a couple of the hippies' peafowl got loose; they flew over her fence and ate a row of her corn, and she shot one dead.

Now, looking at all those eyes, windows to hundreds of truths, I know she'll go to some special corner of hell for doing it.

"Well. I found a cat, up in New York. All animals are beautiful, aren't they?"

"People are too, when you look through them," he says, and I wonder why he doesn't just climb down from the ladder, so he can stop yelling. "When'd you get home?"

"Yesterday."

"You seen Pookie yet? I know she'd be right happy to see you."

"I'm looking for her now."

"Folks say you've been gone a good long while."

"Just a couple of years."

"Well, you know a lot can happen in two years. People change."

"You think Caroline's changed?"

"She won't talk to me, so I can't know it. But you know, it might be that Pookie's the one what's grown up. And I know being in the pen doesn't compare to anything you've done, young lady, but let me tell you, sometimes, you think you've gone somewhere and been to something and you've changed so much down in your soul, but it turns out it's the folks what stay home and learn to live in their own skins who's made out in the growing-up department. And in all the five years I was in prison, I never grew up so much as I did in ten days of solitary."

"Well," I say.

"And you know Pookie always was a smart one. All smart folks go through some evoluting, I guess. If they didn't, they'd get awfully bored."

"Well."

"Well. You have a nice day. Right nice to see you." He nods, then goes back to his roofing: 3852, I think, was lucky for him. It finished in fours.

Where Queen meets Fifth, I find Miss Myrtle's house. Her storm door is skinned, in places, of its paint, and the spring that makes the screen door snap back to has fallen off its hook. I knock three times before Imagene answers. "What" is all she says.

"Why aren't you in school?"

"They ran out of coal this week, so Caroline said it's too cold to go. She don't want me catching the pneumonia."

Two years have grown Imagene taller, melted off her baby's belly, but she's still a child. A flock of freckles has come in on the bridge of her nose, and her missing front teeth have grown in crooked: she looks so much like Pookie that it seems a redundancy when I ask whether she's home.

"Nopey dope."

"Know where she might be?"

"Hey — ain't you supposed to be in New York City?"

And then I remember this about her — even when Imagene was an infant, Daddy used to comment on how loud she'd holler in church. "I'm home visiting," I tell her.

"Bring me anything back?"

"Sorry, Imagene. Maybe next time."

"Is it true it's mens up there'd just as soon kill you as look at you?"

"You know where Caroline is?"

" 'Cause that's what Grandmama used to say. Said your mama was a damn fool to let you go off like that."

"You know where Pookie —"

"Said you'd probably come back filled out on dope."

I zero in on a small, pale freckle on Imagene's cheek, then lean over and kiss her there. She's doomed in so many ways, but blessed with boldness. It's the way of girls nowadays. "Bye, Imagene," I say. "I'll see you later."

"All right," she says, and ducks behind the storm door, to the magic of an empty house on a school day. "You might find her at the Tin Cup."

The sun, reduced to a white circle behind clouds, hovers to my right. Nine o'clock or so, meaning I need to find Caroline soon. Over the buckling, frozen mud I run, then, and past the salt thrown in front of houses with spare money. Down the alley and into the cinder-block building. When I walk in the bar, the row of stares again blinds me, and I'm grateful to be in such a hurry as not to let them stop me.

"You seen Caroline Wallace?" I ask the owner.

"Lemme get you a Coke-Cola," he says. He pulls a bottle from the refrigerator and uncaps it on an opener lodged beneath the bar. "Caroline's right behind you," he says, handing me the cold bottle. The stares are still quiet, and I'm afraid to turn around, to let them see how afraid I am to see my best friend.

"I am," she says. "Over here." She's bent over the pool table, taking aim — longer than I remember her, with fingers strong and thin like a woman's and her hair twisted into a durable but elegant chignon. Her acne has disappeared altogether, and her face is as clear and beautiful as the moon-shaped back of a china plate. She's grown into her teeth. Gone off and left me in turns.

When she puts the nine ball in the corner

pocket, the stares, doubting the import of girls, nod their heads and turn back to their whiskeys. *Aw shit,* says the man playing with Pookie, as he chalks his cue and looks over his possible shots. Ice clinks in glasses. The stares talk and laugh. Peanuts are stirred in bowls.

"Got to dress them horses, you want 'em to make it through a winter like this —"

"Well, the wind died at sunset, so he got stuck out there on that sailboat, the fool —"

"And then she found the boil on my butt —"

"Caroline," I say. "I'm home."

She crosses her arms and smiles at me. "You ain't a bit more home'n the man in the moon," she says. "You'll always be a citygirl. Now, forever, and always. What the hell is that on your finger?"

"I got married."

She sets herself into a fit of insincere laughter, then uncrosses her arms and slaps the pool table, and I have the same sick feeling I had when I told Mother and Grandpap. "Who the Sam Hill hell married you?" she asks. "That guitar player?"

"He's a bassist."

"Figures."

I try to haul myself out of her acidity, the

scalding sourness of a girl who once held hands in fresh-cut grass with me, who climbed up on the roof with me just to look at a big red moon. I try to stop the lump in my throat, try to think of the pretty bus ride back to Hickory and beach days to come. But I've loved Caroline more than anyone since Daddy, and now I don't think she's ever loved me at all. I need a hole to breathe through. I drink from my Coke, but the carbonation's already gone a little flat. "How's Gordon?"

"Well, I wouldn't know. He came back from Fort Lejeune talking 'bout 'the man' this and 'the man' that, and right about the time I got up enough nerve to ask him what man he was talking about, he went straight on up to Louisville. Sure ain't took me."

"Sorry."

"I ain't."

But I can see how two years have made her eyes sadder at their corners. Her man goes back to the table and files his shot, bouncing the ball off the side. "Shit," he says again. "Your turn." He hands her the stick. I follow her around the table.

"Who're you?" I ask him.

"Who am I?" he says, imitating the pitch of my voice, not in a kindly way. He chews on his toothpick, twirling it angrily between his lips. "Who am I?" he asks Caroline, who doesn't even look at him. "I'm Al Capone," he says. He walks over and nudges her in the ribs with his elbow.

"Stop," she snaps. She takes a shot, sinks the six. "This here's Benton. He come down with Cousin Harrel from Chicago last week, 'cause things is a little hot for him up there. He's going back come spring and I'm going up there with him."

"So you two just met?"

"You ain't the only one can leave town."

"Never said I was."

"Who in God's creation you think you are, anyway? And why are you here hunting me down? What is it you're trying to find? Poor little country girl ain't know her ass from a hole in the ground? Some orphan with red hair?" She starts singing, " 'I'm going to carry you away from here . . . Carry you away,' " and then her eyes start to glisten with the moisture, and she says, "your own life is so boring, you ain't got nothing better to do'n write a song about somebody else's?"

"It wasn't about you."

She gets close to me, so close I can smell the licorice and worry on her breath. "You. Of all people. Even you. Got to make yourself feel better trying to feel sorry for somebody else."

"I didn't even write it."

"How do you think I felt?" she says. She's trying to whisper, but she's so mad, it feels like a scream to me. She's so angry that when she speaks she bends a little at the waist, and though her arms stay pinned rigidly to her sides, she makes her hands into righteous fists. "Do you ever think about anybody but your damn self?"

"I'm sorry — I really didn't — I never thought —"

"That's the thing. You never think. Never have."

"If you don't believe me, at least accept my apology."

"For what? So you can feel good enough about it to write more songs about me?"

"Never mind," I say, backing up. "Whyn't you spend the rest of your life trying to pretend you ain't special to nobody. I don't care anymore."

"Ha!" she laughs, a short blast like the sound of a trumpet, and she's right — I'll care forever. "Ain't none of us country girls never going to mean a bit of nothing to nobody. We wasn't raised to. Sooner or later," she yells, "you're going to figure things out."

I drop my Coke right at her feet, and as it

shatters my body moves, and I don't know whether I'm trying to hug her or slap her, but when I reach for the pool cue she moves it, leaving me to stumble forward against the table. Capone laughs.

"Little bit done flew off the handle," says one of the stares.

"Ladies. Ladies," says the owner. He runs over and starts picking up shards of glass. On the floor all around him, soda bubbles wink in the dingy light.

I wheel around again, run past the stares and push out the door into the bright light, clean winter. Down Queen Street and back to Grandpap's house. One: Put his boots back. Two: Pack things I'm likely to forget. Toothbrush. Hair grease. Three: Pack things I'm likely to remember. Sunday skirt. Eyeglasses. Four: Four. Four loses itself in the lack all around me, the emptiness of people who refuse to love. But then I remember: Get a jar of Grandpap's pickled tomatoes for the ride back, because Negroes are not allowed in the bus depots. In a day I'll be in Hickory, boarding the band bus to Winston-Salem, to the ballrooms that feed us and the crowds who rattle the floor with their love. I'll be back in a nice feathered bed beside my husband. Back in North Carolina, trying for something I've never known. In my new life, which Caroline cannot touch.

LIGHTNING

Days on a beach are days of small deaths:
the quiet balls itself into a punch, and the
chill air sharpens mornings that march
toward nothing. Jelly Roll naps for the most
part, resting up for a long night of pretending to hunt. Boredom builds barriers of
dread across the mind's peace, and the rolling carpet of water carries itself off to no
visible end. The Outer Banks is not for those
who haven't yet squared reality with infinity. I excuse myself. I couldn't have known.

For August, who has always lived in the
city, Ocracoke is an escape, a cleansing.
When we first arrived, he sat each morning
burying his toes, wondering like a child at
the orange sea glass and the crab skeletons
strangled in seaweed. Nights, he made me
go out with him to watch the lonely beacon
of the lighthouse, to listen to the boats
bringing their whistles of mourning from
the mainland. But after two weeks here,

even he's beginning to see past the magic, straight through to the endless non-ending. Outside of the dances, he no longer plays his bass. He won't even let it out of its case, and complains that the humidity is wrecking its varnish. We make love sometimes at dawn; mornings, I cry. Thinking about how I've embarrassed poor Caroline, I tell him, and he makes the most awful face before leaving me in bed alone. He reads the *News-Record* and fights with me over what it tells him, calls me country and a clod, says my entire reading life has been wasted on fantasy, wonders aloud how he ended up marrying so far beneath himself. Then, as though being in the same room with me will reduce his IQ, he goes to stand on the back porch of our boardinghouse. As though staring at squirrels should be more engaging than speaking to his wife. He hums to himself, looks for loose feathers to give to Jelly Roll, peels bark off a tree trunk. From the window I watch, appraise: his work is beginning to reveal itself up one of the lower branches. If we stay here long enough, he might undress the whole tree.

I believe our landlady notices, but she'd die before she said anything to her *dear, bad August,* for whom she has the incurable sweets. She giggles at everything he says —

even if he pronounced the grass green, she'd laugh. Her name is Janet Silvers, and she looks to be twice my age, and I cannot say for sure that she's never married, but the photographs on her mantel are of people long dead, people of bonnets and monocles and unpressed hair. Besides her house and two others, she owns a restaurant in town, a fish fry. She's always working, then — boiling beans in the morning, or sweeping gutters between the lunch rush and the dinner crowd, or mopping the dining hall after she closes. All of which gives her little time to blink her long lashes and swish her fat ass at August, but when she gets home she does that anyway, with the energy of an athlete. Some nights she plays the piano, and August and I spread out on the sofa and listen out of politeness. The missed flats, the chords sounded out note by note, her keyless voice: she struggles with every measure, stopping midphrase with her fingers glued to the wrong keys, her mouth hanging open in slow confusion, and I think that only someone who hated the piano could insult it so.

When she's at work I play her piano naked, while the gnarled, knotted wooden stooltop imprints itself on my ass. If it's a warm day, I'll open her parlor windows — neighbors be damned — and let the wind wake my skin: August will hear me and get out of bed, unable to resist the invitation. It'll be before the morning paper from Wilmington, before editorials on foreign policy and news of the nation's banks have raised August his few rungs above me. He'll roll the piano's top down to my fingers, take me back to his bed: mouth me, mold me, love me. After, in that odd space between love strong enough to put tears in my eyes and the separating business of the morning, we listen to the birds. Seabirds, forest birds, Northern birds on their winter holidays, more birds than either of us has ever heard in a lifetime. Even in the night, they party on, these birds, and in the morning, they still rise before dawn.

August's mother calls him daily, some-times twice in one day — she never called when he was in New York, but she's assailed by loneliness now that her bird has left the nest. "Wow," he'll say, after he hangs up Janet's receiver, because his mother has asked if she might mail him some socks, or deposit money into his Chemical Corn ac-count. Once I heard him tell her, "I'm a married man now. My wife is responsible for that sort of thing." She hung up on him then, I suppose, because he shouted, "Hello? Hello?" into the mouthpiece before he replaced the receiver. "If my brother had lived," he told me, "my mother would have somewhere else to spread her neuroses." He won't say whether she's yet congratulated him on our marriage.

The Black folk here resist our attempts to get to know them. The greengrocer has never asked me my name, and the fishermen avert their eyes and vary their paths when they see August frolicking in the sand. Only one person breaks our day: Sanders. He comes calling to share what he calls brunch: vodka with a finger of cranberry juice. He walks through Janet's house — around her parlor, into her bedroom, into ours. We hear him stop, turn back her star quilt, rummage through her chest of medallions. He brings his glass back drained, and has me pour him another from his own bottle. "That's my fruit for today," he'll say, guffawing, but he is well preserved, given his diet. Skin smooth as an apple's. A thick mustache without even one gray hair in it.

He and August sit at the kitchen table, looking through the pages of Janet's *Life.* A surprise: Janet doesn't seem jolly enough to enjoy *Life,* but she keeps a subscription.

"Where'd they take that picture?" Sanders asks, full of excitement.

"Caption says Hiawassee. Georgia."

"I've been there!" Sanders says. "I've done that!"

"Where haven't you been, man?" rejoins August, but it's charity — when Sanders brags of his travels, he makes going downstate sound like sailing the Spice Islands.

"One place I ain't been," Sanders says. "That's up in Janet Silvers."

Sanders laughs hard at his own joke, then leaves. Women to chase, tin cans to collect, tales to sell to other stoops. "Y'all need to get out of here and live a little," he says on his way down the front steps, but when he leaves, we lunch; we screw. August finishes the middle pages of the paper. Night falls, and Janet comes home early from the restaurant and makes a point of sniffing the air. "You've had a guest?" she asks me. "A smoker?"

"No, ma'am."

She hands me a letter, addressed from Miss Caroline Wallace, 832 Queen Street, Mt. Sterling, Kentucky. "Don't you lie to me, Missy," she says.

"I wouldn't dare."

Before she can object, August does. "My guest," he says.

"Oh," Janet says softly, and giggles.

It's the third letter Caroline's sent to North Carolina. Mother said she came out to the county one day, dressed in a man's jeans with a long look on her face, asking for my address. I'll throw this one in the trash, where I've thrown the others, and August will ask why I don't want to hear from someone I spend mornings crying over. I'll tell myself I don't believe she could be saying anything that would be productive for either of us. I'll tell him nothing.

The next morning, after Janet leaves, I sit naked and play until my fingers are sweaty. I play through an imitation of Janet, move on to Rachmaninoff, then Joplin. Then, some miracle — I improvise the end to a song August started writing before we were married — but still he doesn't stir. A storm is beating in the Banks, and the piano's bass competes with thunder. When I stop, wind blows down the sand, scattering its noise into the millions of grains. "Dumpling," I say, when at last I stop and go in to him. "Are you sick?" He's buried his face in Janet's good goose pillow, sandwiching his head. "Dumpling," I ask again. "You okay?"

"Lightning," he says, in a voice melted with crying. "Out here, it's so loud."

I sit on the bed and rub his trembling shoulders, then lean over to push my breasts into his naked back. I warm his body with mine, and this, this minute empty of music or talking or contracts or sex or envy or pity, this minute is a birth, two souls' definition. This minute, I know, will leave the Outer Banks and live with us forever. I kiss the back of his neck, move his hands from his ears. A grown man afraid of thunder. The most incredible thing I've seen yet.

We cry together until the rain tapers to drizzle, until we fall asleep. We push into opposing arms and legs, breathe sour air into each other's faces. We have only so many hours to be ourselves before Thursday night begins that weekend, before we turn into August and Audrey Barnes, one half of whatever-T.O.B.A.-has-named-our-band-this-week; before we have to deliver happiness we haven't quite found for ourselves. We tangle hard in the sheets, and we don't wake again until we hear Janet's key in the front door.

"Yoo hoo!" she calls, a child forever puzzled. "Y'all home?"

To be awakened by her voice is to be mauled by savage animals: August's heart beats wildly against mine.

"We're here," I yell, "but we won't take dinner tonight. We've got twenty minutes to make the ferry."

"August," she yells, though she's come close enough to the door that I can hear her stockings rub together as she walks. "Would *you* like dinner? I've got sweet potato pie . . . hot rolls . . ."

"No, but thank you just the same."

The storm has left the air colder, and we have to link arms and huddle together to feel at all human. "I don't think Miss Janet likes you," August says, laughing.

"Now you're married," I tell him, "you'd better get used to women not liking your wife."

Hatteras

A gruesome Thursday. Cold. Rain breaking up the ground out in Janet's backyard, coming down like weights. I've been down so deep that it's like waking from two separate sleeps. One an unmooring of the mind: dreams of music from the night before, of White girls' dresses fanning out over hooped slips and the Black waiter taking the cut-crystal bowl to the kitchen to mix more punch; what I'd have said, in a different world, to the White ferryman who spat at my feet on my way down his plank. The other sleep a drugged cocoon of lost functioning, from which I have to rehinge my slack jaw upon waking, and wonder if the clouds in my eyes aren't permanent. We've played fifty shows in a month, and I've never seen a crowd so hungry as the one I saw last night. Julius, our drummer, was as wet at the end of the night as if he'd gone swimming, and I sweated so much that I think the stink will never come out of Mother's dress. Mark's solo still echoes, his sax at the tail end of it so like a human scream that I'm still hunched over in panic. And in the real distance of the morning: the telephone.

It's rung five or six times by now — it has to have, to wake me up — and I run to the living room, where the little black machine sits in its anointed place atop a doily on Janet's end table.

"Hello?" I ask.

"Hello," the woman says. Then comes her silence, her deep breathing. "Are you Audrey Martin, then?"

"Audrey Barnes. Yes, ma'am."

"Well, I'm August's mother."

"The other Mrs. Barnes, then," I say. I'm smiling, but when she says yes, I can hear that she's not.

I've daydreamed her call a hundred times, her welcoming me to her family (abridged as it is), her sharing stories of August's youth and instructions on how to feed him. I've rehearsed my end of things, my thanking her for the wonderful man she's raised, my wishes for Sunday tea in her parlor, my general graciousness. I can't let her have any doubts, can't give her mind one centimeter of space that registers as regret. But when she says, "Made me chase you down, did you?" I know it's already too late for us.

"It's not what we intended. When we got down here, things happened so fast —"

"Well, such a short time as you've been married, it'll be just as easy to have it annulled."

"Annulled?"

"Revoked. As though it never happened."

"I know what it means, but —"

"Yes, that's it — you can have it annulled. Then, if my son still wants to, you come back to New York and do it properly. I keep telling him. And he needs to come back home anyway. I don't know how you were raised. But I raised my son to be a musician, not a migrant laborer."

If her son still wants to. She keeps telling him. Things he's never told me. I didn't know he even spoke to her.

"And your people are from where?" she asks.

"Mt. Sterling. Kentucky."

"Whosy wheresit?"

"Kentucky."

"Louisville?"

"No, ma'am. Eastern Kentucky."

"Well, I've never heard of any Colored people from Kentucky," she says, as though I'm either lying or White. "I guess he thinks that makes you exotic."

500

When August gets home, cloaked like a Spanish bandit in his gray poncho, I don't have the courage to tell him his mother called. "You went out in this weather?" is all I can think to say.

"Things wash up on the beach in a rain. There wasn't any thunder this morning, so I wanted to see for myself."

"And what did you find?"

Jelly Roll's been gone three days. August has spoken of it in only the most oblique of terms. This morning, his pant legs are soaked. His feet are bare. His thick eyelashes are still beaded with rain. "Nothing," he says. "Didn't find a thing."

And why look for the truth? The crowds come to us as happy as they know how to be, and Sam Reevin, the T.O.B.A. manager, always smiles as he counts the take. We're making enough of a cut, August promises, that we'll be able to go to New York and start our own quartet by Thanksgiving.

All this time we're playing on the islands, our minds are boiling over with it — Harlem. We walk down Main Street in Hatteras and can't help but hallucinate 125th, and we wonder where are the gassed crowds, the street preachers calling the end times, the septuagenarian Modelles and Hatties hobbling to remnant sales. We miss the happy ribboned schoolgirls entering the Colored library, the packed trolley about to jump its groove. When we play corny little veterans' halls, when we watch bowlegged old men two-step with women a foot taller than themselves, we wonder where is The Sweeper when you need him. All the smiles are forced down here. All the debutantes wear polyester. Someone has cut the electricity of hip somewhere in Philadelphia; down here, we get no juice.

In any Southern town, Thursday nights are the Negroes'. Thursday crowds come with gas; Thursday crowds almost save us. Women — flour white, cornmeal yellow, red-boned, pitch-ochre — in dresses of dandelion, pineapple, goldenrod, and grape; at eight o'clock they swirl and dip together in clusters. They toss their freshly pressed hair and isolate their hips into celestially fleshed arcs, all for the men lined along the wall, wearing their own different tensions of curly hair, standing in their own many shades of brown skin so striking against the white shirts they wear like a dancing uniform. By eight thirty, the wall has moved to the center, pulled into orbit by the magnetic force of the women's bodies. Here is the thin-lipped, long-nosed woman who takes in White people's wash over in Buxton, dancing with her eyes to the chin of the round-shouldered hog farmer from Avon. There, the miner who hauls his three littlest children to the Hatteras Colored School in a little red wagon, dancing shyly with his sick wife's sister, who is a spinster at twenty-eight. Women with connecting eyebrows or men with sinus-ridden breath pair off with second cousins once removed.

And always, on Thursdays, there's a fight. Nine times out of ten it's the usual permutation of one man pecking down another, quiet fighting with clean punches and wrestling that would make Gorgeous George jealous. Then comes that tenth fight, two girls making a firecracker, one lilac blouse closing her eyes before she winds up to slap her boyfriend's other girlfriend, another Butterick pattern grabbing her classmate's hair and winding it meter by meter around her hand. The girls scream. They spit. They scratch. They shout *bitch slut whore.* They pretend to fight over men rather than admit their anger over another girl's lighter skin, or the store-bought cut of her dress. But even against the ragged dance of violence stands this power: the beauty of those segregated into assembly by the rules of the world's common ugliness. Sometimes, when I watch the Thursday dancers,

I can almost understand whitefolk: these people are so beautiful, it wouldn't do not to oppress them.

Fridays and Saturdays are sloppy seconds. The White people, always, need a fair amount of liquor before they'll dance, so the first hour, we play a set repertoire. We fool around in our heads, devising mnemonics for our grocery lists and ordering the elements of the periodic table. We don't reach very far into our souls, because the White people won't even hear us until around nine, when a couple might move to the center of the dance floor and brush a quiet circle around each other. Eventually more will come, and they'll fan out into a chimera of misplaced legs and jerking shoulders, but they'll never quite seem to hear us; they'll never stop talking to one another over the punch bowl, never get over their individual bodies to move to something as large as an entire Motherland. Julius plays the difference, marking Fridays and Saturdays by barely using his left hand. He looks to one particular burl in the floor and loses himself in thoughts of his only child back in Louisiana, a baby born dying, with wrinkled skin for eyelids and a six-year-old head already bald in patches. Julius has shown us his son's photograph: the child, despite the hat hiding his baldness, could be his own grandfather. We had to smile to keep from sucking in our breath. Thursdays, when Julius extends his reach and the beat carries his body and he's dripping sweat by eight thirty, I do believe Julius is able to forget. But Fridays, he sits and stews, waiting for the liquor to mottle the White people's skin into different colors. Waiting for one of the men to get drunk and jump upon a table to twist like a stuck screw. Waiting for liquor to give one of the women, her hair stuck to her face, the inspiration to sass a barkeep.

Mark, our sax, is the hottest thing I've heard come Thursday. He sands down his reed and keeps his horn an octave higher than it wants to go, so that it sounds like a menopausal woman calling cows. "Where'd you get that *sound*?" August asked him, the first night we played.

Mark grinned. He's fifteen, with rabbit teeth too big yet for his mouth, and a huge roof of hair. "I'm thinking," he said, "about that girl's *ass* over there. See how round? Every time she moves, I play that ass. It's like a —" he said, tapping his foot to start a rhythm, and he picked up his horn and blew us some free gold. August says I don't even know how amazed I should be. I'm just nineteen, he says, and haven't seen it enough times to know, but Mark Parker is going to be a star. Maybe, I say, because Friday and Saturday, he stares into the bell of his sax and plays anybody's idea of a tea party. A sad aphoniac he is on Fridays and Saturdays. Only half of himself.

There comes, though, one crazy Saturday that leaves us thinking we've been wrong about the whole scheme, because the most willowy of polka dot dresses, with the shiniest blond bouffant hairdo, throws a beer bottle and kills a man. The dancers become the show, and we play two more measures before we even catch ourselves, before Mark throws up a hand and we stop to fall into the moment's inertia. "Penny!" yells the girl standing next to her, and I think I shall never forget that name. "My God, Penny!" the girl yells again, though Bouffant has already begun to shudder. She has, at such close range, broken open the side of his face. She bunches up the big red polka dots in her hand while the dead boy lies at her feet, bleeding into the gloss of the hardwood floor.

A boy wrestles Bouffant to the ground, pins her arms to her sides with his legs, and starts punching her as she turns her head left and right trying to protect her face.

She's able to wriggle under his crotch just enough that he misses her mouth. Her hair comes undone and long blond snakes of it slide all through the dead boy's blood, and you'd think Bouffant would scream but she doesn't. She just keeps dodging punches, grunting as she moves, and hers is the only sound besides the five quick footsteps in the hall.

Instinctively, Mark begins packing his horn and August his bass, even before the police swing through the heavy doors of the dance hall: we know the official record will not tolerate the accusing words of any Black person. The only one-set night of our season, then, and though we won't easily forget what we've seen — the paper-thin skin of the boy's temple, puckering out into blood, the other boy's knuckles, going white as he finally made contact with Bouffant's face and then punched her and punched her again.

"I bet that kid deserved it anyway," Mark says, on the ferry back to Hatteras. He's feverish. Unable to stand still. He's staying with some of his daddy's people over in Ocracoke, but this night, out early from working, he'll be able to go find the long-legged girl he's been with all winter, throw a rock at her window, and sneak her out of her mama and daddy's house and down to the beach.

August shakes his head. "The sorrows of gin," he says.

Julius is at the rail of the ferry, looking as lost as I've ever seen him. Instead of beating his drums he's back home to his rear room in the little yellow boardinghouse Mr. Glaser found for him over on Fourth Street, back to his dent on the cheap, hard mattress, where he'll sit with his legs under his chin and wonder whether his sick child is hurting, this clear night of stars. Julius sends all his money beyond expenses back to Louisiana for the child's medicine. He can never afford to telephone, so he'll have to imagine the waves he hears out his window are the child's deep and easy breaths. When I go stand beside him, he offers a nod to the sea. The ferryman drives fast, kicking spray against our hands; the engine drowns the mighty noise of the Atlantic. The ferry crowd, at nine thirty, is so different from the drunken lots of partiers we ride home with at midnight. These are men come home from fishing, women and children returning from visits to relatives.

When we get home, Janet is killing her piano. At nine thirty she's already in her white nightgown, absurd in its formality, with a lace drawstring that she's tied in a bow at the bosom. An expensive choking of lace around its collar, as if it's wishing to have tea with the Queen. She's wrapped one front section of hair around a foam roller: she'll wear her bangs tomorrow in one uncombed blister. Her cold cream is a film of grease on her cheeks. "Good night," she tells August as we walk through the door, and she scampers away so that he can't examine her bedtime incarnation.

"That bitch," I tell August, "will take five dollars of my hard-earned money this month."

"Shhh," he says, patting my hands. "Shhhh."

KEY LIME

Saturday night, it rains an apocalypse. The crowds stay home, mostly, and we play an almost empty hall out in Nags Head, one wild drunk table of five, getting ever louder, ever drunker; one solid couple dancing every single song, having a night out in the rain, perhaps, because they'd promised each other. The couple leaves at nine but the table stays until closing, so we keep playing. But five people's energy isn't enough of a meal, and with nothing for us to feed on, we play a wholly uninspired set. Like the music you'd hear at a grocery. The ferry is docked because of the storm, so we take a taxi all the way down 158 back to Janet's house, and when we get there, we find that Caroline has turned up. She's curled up on Janet Silvers's couch, dressed in the most beautiful purple and pink spackled dress, its bodice as clean and uncreased as if the wind has picked her up and blown her the six hundred miles. A curtain of deep auburn hair has fallen over her face, so that all we can see are her made-up lips. Vermilion, they are. Maybe scarlet.

"Poor thing," Janet whispers. "I told her you were out playing a show. She said you've never written back to give her your travel schedule."

"That's because I never invited her here in the first place."

But Janet's not listening. "Poor thing," she says again, and pulls Caroline's hair gently back so we can all look on her pale face. Deeply asleep like that, she doesn't mind her teeth while she snores through her open mouth. She looks like the Easter Bunny. It's perfectly gruesome. "Poor child," Janet whispers again, as if it's my fault, the dark circles under Caroline's eyes, the hair now splayed in different directions over Janet's throw pillow.

Come Sunday, they're both at the breakfast table by the time August and I wake, Caroline in one of Janet's dresses, halving her canteloupe slices; Janet bustling around the kitchen, slamming cabinet doors, sniffing pantry shelves, looking for something. "I'm skipping church," she says brightly, "to make lunch for this poor angel."

Skipping church is probably a real detriment to her chances at marriage, since Pear Adams, Sr., a widowed deacon twice her age, has been (she's confided to August) *making inquiries.* It's upper choir Sunday, but poor Deacon Adams will have to do without her angel's voice this week. August smirks as he pours my glass of orange juice, as though he's read my mind. "Chrissakes," I whisper to him. "My money puts food on that woman's table."

"Miss Janet says y'all are moving on next week," Caroline says. "Guess I was lucky to find you."

August, missing somehow that this situation isn't a polite one, walks over to shake her hand. "Nice to meet you."

"Well, you too! We were all wondering what kind of boy Audrey went off and married. You know, them people back in Mt. Sterling always did think I must've been something special, just 'cause I was walking down the street with Audrey Martin. I'm supposing that's true for you, too?"

I'm leaning a hip on Janet's icebox, keeping an eye on Caroline, who looks, sunk in the middle of Janet's dress, like a child playing house. "One tablespoon vanilla, a half teaspoon nutmeg," Janet whispers to herself, as she bends over and peers into the exact middle of her cookbook, whose essential pages are marked with cuts of ribbon.

"Why are you here?" I ask Caroline.

She looks in my eyes as though she's expecting to meet someone she's never known. "Everbody deserves a vacation," she says.

"You couldn't run down to Lake Barkley?"

"Whatever," she says, chewing.

"Well," Janet says, as though our conversation is causing her physical pain.

"May I help with the food?" I ask her.

"You know nothing about food. Get out of here."

The Outer Banks' best treasures wash up after a rain, so August goes out beachcombing for horseshoe crabs and moon jellies. Caroline and I watch from the edge of Janet's back porch as he disappears down the shore, letting the brown foam of the tide wet the cuffs of his pants. He skips deep footprints into the sand, but as soon as he's left a trail of six or seven, the tide comes to erase his evidence.

"Think he'll find anything?" I ask Caroline. She's leaned forward with her palms turned in against Janet's porch, swinging her legs in the empty space beneath.

"I don't know, but he sure is getting black out there in all that sun."

"Really, what are you doing here?"

"Years, you been bothering me to visit. Now I'm here, where's your sense of hospitality? You don't," she says, sliding off the porch, setting a line of determination into the side of her mouth, "know how to treat people."

"I'm sorry, Caroline. All I ever wanted to tell you was that I'm sorry."

She waves a hand at me, says, "To hell with that." She kicks off her shoes and runs down the shore after August, running until she disappears, about a mile away, and then all I have are her poor orphaned shoes, lying atop the sand. I feel silly looking after them, so I drift back inside, where Janet has come out of the kitchen to let pots boil. She's up on a ladder now, cleaning the three triangular windows that form a semicircle in her lintel. She puts all her upper arm strength into wiping, and comes away with a year's worth of hardened crust.

"Can I help with that, at least?"

"I've told you once — get out."

She's blocking the door with her ladder, so I have to swing it right into her — not hard enough to upset anything, but she does flinch in anticipation of falling. On her porch, sunlight shears a sheet of pain across my eyes and I slam her door back closed, with enough force that it makes the loose four in her house number rattle. I'm down her front steps, then, and into the strangest fog: the post-rain sun glows orange through the haze that has erased rooftops and porches. Even the next house over is invisible, but birds still call. Always, down here, the birds call — they're twenty-four-hour maniacs. A length of wind comes, smelling of Pookie's hair pomade, and I think I'm going mad as a plover, but then who's to say this one square inch of wind hasn't blown right through her on its way up the beach? Who's to say it doesn't pick up the scent of her, the new sadness in the hollow of her neck, and bring it here to reproach me? We've been friends for more than a decade now: I might have welcomed her. I might simply have laughed at her joke about August, and made everything all right between us. But there's a new, hard thing. An impossibility between us that I hadn't seen until we were standing beside the pool table together, with soda bubbling all around our feet. The thought brings tears to my eyes, and I have to get myself off Janet's sidewalk.

With the general store closed, the butcher's and the bait store locked up, the crowds of this town have nowhere to spend their money on a Sunday but the corner green-grocer's. Behind his back, they call him a heathen for changing money on a Sunday, and yet he does enough business that he doesn't have to come out again until Wednesday. I've seen them lined down our street, the men and children sent out by the mothers on their day of rest, and among them I know I'll be safe, with no one asking me whether I don't belong to anyone, not one of these strangers caring a whit whether I've been loved. I breathe more fog, searching for another pocket of Caroline, but she isn't there. In the corner of the shop, I handle the lemons up from Florida, drop them in their bucket — three beats in an uneven tempo — and wonder how I might put them to use.

When I get back to the house, Caroline and August are back from their walk and sitting in Janet's living room, Caroline beaming, August looking terribly unhappy. "I need to refresh myself," she says, and skips off to the bathroom. August has three shells in his lap — he's picked the most unusal ones — one spotted like a dalmation, one fragile and uneven with a striated underbelly, one bluish and shaped like a miniature conch. "Ain't no money in shells," Sanders told him once. "Peoples is laughing at you all up and down the beach." Coming from a man whose entire livelihood is junk, this seemed absurd. Now, August rolls his eyes toward the bathroom. "Folks really speak that way where you come from?"

I giggle. "It's a miracle I wear shoes."

"She's so loud. And was pulling up her bra straps while I was talking to the Baptist Reverend. And she passed gas. More than once. It smelled like the sewer. And then she told me you always did want to marry into money."

"What?"

"She said you wrote her a letter and told her you snagged a rich one."

"It's a lie. I can't even imagine why she'd tell you that, but it's a lie."

Caroline runs from the bathroom with a yelp and I follow her into my and August's room, where she falls back on the bedspread and starts fingering the grooves in the chenille. "This is right fun," she says. "Is this what you've been up to?"

"We work all night," I say.

"Shoot. You don't know what work is. And try raising a young'un all by your lonesome on top of it."

"I'm sorry about Miss Myrtle."

"Well, I'll be damned if it didn't take you long enough to say so."

"By my reckoning, Imagene just turned eleven. If you've run off on her account, you're having an awfully delayed reaction."

"She's still a child. And she still needs protecting. And my daddy's back in town, and it's a mountain of work just keeping her away from him. Come Mama's birthday, here he was putting flowers on her grave when we come up the hill. I had to beat him off like a crow."

Such an image it is, Sonnyboy with his prison-grayed hair, hobbling up the hill to pay his respects, only to be beaten back by his own kin. And so confusing to remember Mauris's funeral, all the spiritual energy spent on her soul's ascendance, only to have those left behind become consumed with her body's physical location.

"Let's get back to why you're here."

"Just came to see you. Ain't it okay to visit a body?"

That evening, Janet returns home and starts heating up the dinner she's made. She has a big floppy bow across the top of her dress — always she is thus decorated in her war of femininity, with big floppy bow or lace drawstring, as though her entire wardrobe is aimed at gating off whatever sexual suggestion exists beneath her neck — and though the bow points up happily, her mouth now does not. She sets a soufflé on her long cherry table, then follows up with a basket of bread and a dish of candied beets, pork chops, some sweet corn casserole, and creamed spinach. "Have a seat, y'all," she says. The table seems awkward and false, the four of us with such different agendas. But after several lost starts having to do with the sinking of the Yancey Street pier, Janet sends us on a rhythm with the week's best town gossip, including her own annotated history of the White preacher's wife and her accidentally Cherokee baby. "She might've known he'd come out too dark to pass," Janet says. "Salt and pepper don't mix back into salt."

Caroline hums while she chews, gnaws the last flashes of meat off her pork chop and sucks the marrow out of its bone. She starts in licking her index finger and Janet squirms. August pats his own hand. When Caroline puts her elbows on the table, Janet puts her own elbow in the air and makes a big show of brushing it off. When she tells a joke about St. Paul at the pearly gates, Janet points out how inappropriate on a Sunday. When she speaks of the weather back in Mt. Sterling, Janet says she can only imagine the bugs and the heat. And of course Janet meets everything I say, even my compliments on her sweet tea, with a pursing of her already sour mouth. She's like a show dog with a bark for every occasion, her red bow hiding the parts of her that might move.

"How long have you two been married?" she asks us, trying to forget about Caroline.

"Since the end of January," Caroline answers for us. "Her mama like to die over it."

"How'd you meet?" she asks.

"At work." August chews hatefully. "At the Apollo."

"Ahh," Janet says. "Love at first sight."

"I wouldn't say that," says August, and without chewing, I swallow a hunk of sweet bread. "If I'd seen her walking down the street, I might not have looked twice. Hell, it took me about a week just to understand what she was saying." With one of Janet's crisp white napkins, he dabs his chin, missing altogether the shiny veneer of pork chop grease slicking his lips, and it makes me think of all the ways he's never been careful.

"You can't be serious," I say.

"I cain't," he says, making his "*a*" long, and Janet laughs.

"Different backgrounds, naturally," says Janet.

"Different planets," August says. He

smiles at me, the same smug smile a boy might give to his dog after he's tricked it into licking its private parts. "I find it amazing I ever met such a person."

He's said this to me before — once, on a city bus, as he rubbed the place between my third and fourth fingers, smoothing out a kink of muscles worn to fury by the night's long performance. Once, he said it to me as we sat down to a meal at Velvet's. He'd looked toward the door one last time, because we'd been waiting for Mr. and Mrs. John Tilghman, old friends of his to whom I'd later be introduced as "the backbone of the band." Not seeing them then, he'd looked around Velvet's great high-ceilinged dining room, at all those Negroes, not one table of them worth less than a quarter of a million dollars, and then back at me, at the thin shoulders of my old silk blouse. "I find it amazing I ever met such a person," he'd said, and his words had warmed me on such a cold, snowy night.

Now, his words cut me open. They're the words of a classically trained violinist married, out of unplanned need, to a girl who grew up playing church songs by ear. The words of a boy from the better end of 138th Street run smack into a girl from the cowpath. Janet's left her kitchen window open, but so long after the heat of her cooking, it's cause for a draft. August's words sound like the words of someone who's run upon a rare breed of goat, or a new old world monkey. A sip of sweet tea doesn't send my bread down: it won't go anywhere. The lump my feelings are making in my throat is pushing it right back up.

"She thinks she's so smart, but she's so tiresome she got to go and write *my* life into a song. She's lucky she met you," Caroline says. "You know, her mama's a drunk."

"What's this about?" Janet asks, her pupils as wide and black as a shark's.

"Audrey's mama. Everbody in town knows it. Did you know it, August? Ain't you met that lady? You know, Poindexter's sitting here trying to act right cute, but she's really just like me — she's just from a fancier part of the street. Don't mean she ain't got a outhouse. It means her outhouse was decorated."

Silence, then, and I look to my plate, wishing the corn would roll into a demonically possessed pattern on its own accord, or the bread would jump up and dance — anything to turn off the horrible echo of what Caroline's just said. She gets up and shoves her white napkin into her plate, right into the candied beets. The stain will never wash out;

no matter how many times Janet hangs it in the sun to bleach it will still be there, bleeding. "You might think you're the only one what can embarrass a body, but you got another think coming," she says, and she walks out Janet's foyer and slams the door even harder than I did this morning, so hard the ceramic angel falls from the wall and breaks.

"Why, she didn't even taken her dessert," Janet says, more quietly than I've ever heard her say anything.

August and I watch the little hand on Janet's clock make its revolutions. Four minutes pass, and a fifth reaches its middle before Janet leaves the table and we hear her in the parlor, blowing her nose. She's left her high heels in the foyer, it seems, and in her stockinged feet she brings the biggest pieces of her angel to the kitchen, sets them on the counter, and proceeds to serve her final course. It's stunning — a key lime pie whose icy surface is broken with perfectly squeezed florets of cream. A slice of lime twisted across the middle of each piece, and I don't know when she's had time to go to the greengrocer's. A perfect dessert, but like everything else in life, never meant for everyone at the table.

WRECKING BALL

I'm on Janet's couch, dreaming about the telephone, when it rings. "I want to speak to my son," she says.

"I'm sorry, Mrs. Barnes, but he's out for the morning."

"Out where? Where could he have got to at seven in the morning?"

"Fishing."

It's true: August has gone native on us, with a straw sunhat, a long rod, and a reel that looks like the barrel of a gun, a Fred Arbogast Jitterbug on the end for bait. He's out every day before the sun, even when we've gone to bed at two. You'd think I'd sleep through his leaving by now, but I don't. It hurts enough to wake me every time.

"Fishing?"

"Yes, ma'am. He catches quite a bit, actually."

"All my son's going to catch out there is a

cold." She herself clears some phlegm in her throat. "I should think you'd be able to keep him in, mornings."

"Well, he is a grown man."

On her end of the line I hear the faintest music, a rising and falling of delicate chimes like the movement of a music box. He hurts me, this son of hers, so much. I don't have the netting to hold it all in, and the sad, sticky gum of it comes spilling out of me at the craziest times: he drinks a bottle of Bolt's Seltzer and I want to press his forehead to mine and kiss him; he writes a figure in his bankbook and I want to take him to the hard bed we're renting, lay him down on Janet's bleached sheets, watch him beg. He buttons his overcoat and I want to drown in him.

"Please tell him I've called."

Without saying goodbye she rings off, and I'm left with the knotted, lonely loop of my morning. The phone slips out of my hand to its cradle, rattling emptiness.

Janet's charging me extra for Caroline's board, even though Caroline has slept here only one night of the four she's been in town. Days, I don't see her nor hear tell of her. Only the one night I've seen her, curled up on the couch just like the first night we found her. Same dress, even, kept just as clean. Something in her face has filled out in four days, and with her hair French-braided back and the Fuller 14 on her cheeks, she looks just like a doll.

Next week, we leave for South Carolina. We've paid fifty dollars for promotional cards and posters in Greenville, Anderson, and Abbeville, but that's only three cities, and beyond them we don't know how long we'll stay. Eventually, Sam Reevin says, we'll hit Georgia, Alabama, Florida. We have no way of knowing what we're in for, no idea what new and outrageous indignities await us in the Deep South. Reevin's told us to stay in the Colored part of town, but even there, Jim Crow has found us. We could be killed for kissing in front of the White-owned soda shop, Sanders has warned us, for White people are offended by the notion of Negro love. We can't even think of flagging down a White taxi passing through, no matter how torrential the rains. We've found Jim Crow's rebellious stepchild, too: the Negro woman who works at the Colored window of Egan's Fish & Chips regularly gives away food when she takes a notion. I'd meant to ask Caroline if she'll travel with us to South Carolina, maybe sell her cosmetics on the road, but I haven't even seen her to ask her where she's been.

Janet has gone in late again to the restaurant, leaving hungry fishermen stranded without breakfast. Monday, a lady tenant came to complain that Janet hadn't pruned the bushes. Tuesday, a man came by the house to pay her because she hadn't gone to collect his rent. That same day, she mopped the restaurant without gloves at closing, and came home smelling of Lestoil. Wednesday, a White man came to the house to look at her piano.

"Fifty dollars," he said.

"Fifty? That's just about what Daddy paid for it! And that was back in 1927!" The man rocked confidently on his heels, and she looked down at the floor. "Take the damn thing," she said, in a bear's voice. "Come get it this afternoon if you like."

With the piano gone, her house is a jail. She leaves meals on the kitchen table, but doesn't call us in to eat. She's stopped sectioning August's grapefruit in the morning, and she strips our beds to nothing and leaves the fresh linens hanging on the line for me to collect. The day the piano left us, she telephoned a store in Hatteras and bought a television. Had it delivered that evening, before a neighborhood thrall to its spectacle. Now, she watches *Gunsmoke* in the parlor while we sit in our room and listen through the door. She gets up and takes a skein of knitting back to the sofa for *I Love Lucy,* and we leave the door open two cautious inches to watch her watching. She finishes twenty loops of a blue winter scarf and throws it back under the sofa, puts her feet up on the table to rub her tired heels. At the end of the show, when Ricardo kisses Lucy on the cheek, she gives a little cry, and slowly, we turn the knob to close the door.

Everywhere in America, people are gathering for television parties in front of new consoles full to their thirteen inches with shining celebrities, but to 547 North Walnut, Hatteras, North Carolina, no one is invited. Instead, for entertainment, the street watches the crane swing the lead wrecking ball into the old Slone's grocery. It takes an entire day's shift to destroy half a wall; most times, when the ball hits, it doesn't even break brick. Janet watches her television alone and falls asleep long after the wrecking ball does, her mouth open, the static roaring.

Finally, August escapes to shoot dice with Sanders — something he'd promised, when he first came here with his city-shined shoes and Harlemite notions, never to do — but without invitations of my own, I'm shut in here on Walnut Street without even a piano to play. Alone with Janet, I listen through the walls and peep through the crack in my door and read her as one would digest an issue of *True Confessions:* as a jeremiad, a caution, and a counsel. I could study her life backwards in frames. Learn how never to end up alone, by doing the exact opposite of what she has. In the company of the television, she begins to eat heavier meals: biscuits with milk gravy at nine o'clock, two chunks of rhubarb cobbler at ten. She's a dying star, expanding.

Mathilde, a tall, precariously thin girl on our street, has one roller skate, perhaps found in the garbage at the edge of someone's yard, or received as part of a once-new pair for Christmas, or taken from an unthoughtful bundle her mother's White people sent home with her. The girl launches herself with her shoed foot and glides down the street on the one quartet of rusty wheels, so gracefully that we who are watching don't even wonder after its mate. She skates down the sidewalk in front of the grocery's undoing, the wrecking ball beating a counterpoint to her moves.

By the time Auchidie calls again, I've watched Mathilde lose her footing and stumble four times. "Don't think you'll keep my son from me," Auchidie says, when I tell her he's out fishing again. "Don't you dare." And I don't blame her for not believing me, since it's two o'clock in the afternoon. But he's out shooting dice, which is nothing I can say.

"He loves you dearly," I tell her instead. "Why would I want him not to?"

"The way girls like you are," she says, and hangs up on me again.

The rest of the day I spend on Janet's front porch, rocking in her favorite chair in my good sweater, waiting for August to walk up her sidewalk, letting the slight chill slide up my wrists, testing the air for my best friend's hair pomade, reading and rereading the same three lines of *Tell My Horse* while the plover calls to its mate and the Atlantic washes up the broken rock of distant continents. The sheer power of the wrecking ball as it pounds into the ceiling of Slone's distracts me, and the skating Mathilde lures me in with the *tum-thaa* of her exertions, and the crazy old tomato seller with her caged lovebird makes me watch as she cleans her ear with her fingernail. I wait for August or Caroline until the sun is low and orange, but it's Janet who comes home early, rouged like a Raggedy Ann doll, her hair out of its bun and curled so that the bottom hangs in a hunk on her shoulders. Not an auburn-haired China doll dressed in purple; not Caroline. I'm tamped down by sadness until seven, when August finally returns, just in time to bathe before our show in Swanquarter. "Do you still love me?" I ask him, once he's dressed.

"What a question." He picks out his conk and pats it back down, and it's redundant, I suppose, to tell him he must answer yes or no. I close the toilet lid for a seat.

"Why does your mother hate me?"

"She doesn't," he says, turning sharply sideways to look at himself in the mirror.

"You know she does."

He loses some of the wire in his shoulders. Guilty. I sit on the toilet lid and quietly watch him preen. He brushes the lint off his jacket and knots his tie. "Let's go, then," he says, and flips off the bathroom light.

Out in the parlor, a four-piece White band stands in the frame of Janet's television, boys with slicked-back hair crooning like a gospel choir, the teenaged audience stretching behind them, from one top corner of the television to the other. "Good evening," Janet says, without looking at us.

"Night," says August, and we clink out the door together, too embarrassed by her misery to even get our coats from the closet. She's more emptying than anything a human soul should have to endure. In the street, August looks to either side of himself, taking in 180 degrees of night. It's North Carolina warm, 70 degrees on an April evening, so warm neither of us even need our jackets anyway, and August's profile breaks the clouds gone silver over a full moon. In the distance we hear laughing from neighboring porches, a guitar coming from somewhere on the beach. August scratches his ear as if divining, knowing the Colored taxi doesn't run at night.

We end up hitching a ride from a White man with Tennessee plates. August loads his bass onto the truck bed and hoists himself up before pulling me in, and I hitch my dress up and squat on my stockinged knees so as not to pick up too much of the bed's dirt. An ax lying in the truck with us, and a dull-toothed saw. We ride through the Negro part of town, then past the warehouse further out, then to the open air of the beach, and I get sorry for bringing up his mother, or his loving me. When we jump off the dock, August offers the driver a quarter, but the man waves it away. "Thank you, sir," August says instead, clipping the *sir* the way any obedient Southern Negro would. One month we've spent down here. Kennedy invading Cuba, Eichmann on trial in Israel, but in North Carolina, Blackness outdefines everything else.

The ferry line grows and shortens and branches and finally, the boat growls into the inlet and the boatman rolls down the ramp. The people in automobiles drive to the center, leaving a right and a left alley for pedestrians. The gears of the boat shift into play and I stare at August, who's staring at the ocean. You can see it in people's eyes sometimes, a sadness, like they know they're going to die, and it will probably hurt, and no one will be able to stop it. I see that sadness in August's eyes just now, and I say, "I'll always be here for you," but the spray of the wake overpowers my voice so I have to yell it — "I'll always be here for you."

August recoils from this, physically, rolling his eyes and moving his left leg one step down the deck. He stands this way, a leg-length apart, for the whole ferry ride, staying apart from me even when I try to go close on my tiptoes and whisper it in his ear again, even when I take his hand and slip it under the back of my sweater. It's a cold, limp fish, his hand, a hand that won't hear me and cannot feel me, a hand that has felt my need and found it unbecoming. I let him go, kiss him on the cheek, take his chin in my hand and turn our lips together, but his don't move. "Please," I say, "don't be mean." The ferryman throws his rope to the man on dock, and August pats me on the back once, twice, three times, as if I were his daughter or sister or puppy.

At the Pavilion in Swanquarter, the girl in the ticket booth has a thin, nervous efficiency about her, long bangs pressed out over intelligent hazel eyes, and when a man in the crowd, upon seeing August's bass, asks us to let him in with us for free, she shakes her head no.

He's a tad stout, with a nice enough jacket and a bowler hat, and something in his eagerness reminds me of my father, dressed like a doctor for Lyric night. "We know him," I lie. "From way back."

"Whatever," she says, waving him in. "It's y'all's bread."

August shakes his head at me, and the man hurries in the door without so much as a nod of thanks.

Through the open doors we can see that the Pavilion, inside, is full to capacity already, women in small circles bumping into one another's backs when they laugh, men trying to flock against a wall already lined end to end with bodies, kids out for relief on the warmest day of the spring so far. We can see through the front doors that it's the biggest crowd we've had on these little islands, and Sam Reevin must have premonited as much, because he's here, in person, sitting on a chair under the Spanish moss that grows along the Pavilion's front porch. He grins at us, tips his hat. Something in his eyes, the way they don't hold a gaze, makes me want to ask August where we'll find our own trombonist. "Full house already," he says, "seems like the word's spreading fast. She can't let anybody else in until somebody in there leaves. You'd better get in there and set it off."

We're hot into our groove fifteen minutes into the first set. To the Pavilion have come Negroes from as far away as Kitty Hawk and Pamlico, and the hardwood floor is so crowded that an easy time is impossible: only the best dancers and the prettiest women will get respect enough for a wide berth on the dance floor. August solos and I calculate the trajectory of his notes, so that I match them every time he finishes a measure. He lets me do it twice, and then, the third time I try, he plays an accidental. He presses hard into the neck of his bass and plucks loud, dissonant notes. I try to play Monk to his Mingus then, but it doesn't sound quite right, so I let him be.

Little tall Mathilde, who can't be more than thirteen, is swaying with herself against the curtained wall. She's drinking all the liquored-up punch from the table near the stage, and smiling at Mark and clapping the downbeat and having herself a time. Even with the bodies crushed into each other she's an easy spot because of her height and the loud pink lipstick that's too old for her, and in a pretense of adulthood she moves stiffly, as though someone has fused her spine. At some point I miss, she's asked to dance or maybe even asks a man herself, because when Julius takes his long drum break, I look up again and find her dancing with a bald man whose gold tooth winks under the Pavilion's strobe lights. She keeps an arm's length between them, and when he tries to whirl her around she doesn't understand what he's trying to communicate, and they both end up hurt, rubbing their wrists and laughing. I look to August and wink, but he hasn't seen her, doesn't wink back. It takes him a minute to smile at me.

Even so, even with that beat of silence, he did smile. He didn't even know why, but he smiled, and when I think about that, I feel righter than I have for a long time. I'm just about to start believing in being saved again when the first screams come from the other end of the Pavilion. The half of the floor closest to us empties in a motion fluid as an ink bottle's as people begin running for the front entrance. I hear a series of gunshots like firecrackers going off, and people crush toward the front doors; they scream. A woman not five feet tall, in a black mini-dress and heels, gets tripped up in legs. She's under everyone's feet but no one cares, and her screams are the loudest, until she screams no more. A woman close to the door — maybe she has asthma or just weak-ness or maybe bad luck — is on the floor, coughing, and a man kicks her out of his way so he can get closer to the door. From somewhere, finally, someone brings the lights up on the empty dance floor.

"Mathilde," I say, but August shakes his head. I think of the girl's mother, tall and thin and tight-lipped like Mathilde herself, and I wonder whether she even knows her daughter is here. August grabs his bass by its neck and pulls me, with his other hand, along the length of the wall toward the rear of the building. Dust from the wall makes a screen on my arm and I lose August, snatch for his hand, find it again. "Damn," he whispers, and he squeezes my hand until it hurts. We slide backstage this way, and come to a door with a window, the moon shining through it to make a four-paned projection on the opposite wall. The door's marked DELIVERIES ONLY but some force of goodness has left it unlocked, and we exit into the vacuum of cool air and it's as though I'm breathing for the first time, but then suddenly a dog is upon us, a big slobbering German shepherd whose ears are as high as my waist, and as quickly as anything August has pushed me out in front of him.

The dog sizes me up and doesn't even bark before he runs away, but August keeps his palm on my back anyway, pushing me, making me his human shield. "Wow," is all I can say, when he finally realizes and withdraws his arm. We both laugh uncomfortably, but something has changed between us. "You're not in love with me," I tell him.

"In love is when your heart beats faster every time you see somebody. In love is once in a lifetime, maybe not even that. Do you feel that way, Audrey? Do you?"

The full moon illuminates the detail of the cars in the parking lot, washed and polished just for the night. Two or three, maybe, that won't be driven home. I want to run back into the gunshots, drown myself in the ocean, do anything but stand and hear August say this. I could respond to his question, but he wouldn't like my answer. "What about Mathilde?" I ask him.

"What about her?"

"We can go back in and see."

"I'm keeping my Black ass right here in this parking lot."

After all the dust of the backstage area, tears feel good. I close my eyes and walk away as he calls my name. When I get to the front door, I see Reevin walking the parking lot with a money box under his arm, smoking a cigarette. The Colored ambulance has arrived, but already among those watching under the corrugated tin roof there hangs a sense of futility. People have stopped shooting and screaming, and a group of men are leaned in the door. The one doctor in the back of the ambulance sets his mouth into a straight line: he's here to collect the dead rather than save the living. Two of the leaning-in men pull a body out the door, and then the paralyzed, asthmatic woman, having been mistaken for dead, screams out as they throw her onto a gurney. A man shudders in an agony of injured nerves as he's put on another gurney and rushed into the ambulance with her, but from the looks of him — the white matter of his brain showing, one eye gone missing — simply dying would have been a blessing.

"Audrey!" someone yells. "Hey, girl! We were looking all over for your show!" It's Caroline, Caroline in that same purple and pink dress, sitting on the hood of a silver Studebaker. Closer to the car, I see that there's a man sitting behind the steering wheel, engrossed in his cigarette. She hops off the hood, runs over, and hugs me. "I knew all this time I should have come to see you. Your life is a gas, it really is. This here's Jimmy," she says, taking me over to the window, where I give the man a small wave.

He stares at me. "You the pianist?" he asks.

"Yeah."

He nods.

She takes me away from the car so that we're standing in Jimmy's headlight, and she whispers, "I know that bitch is charging you 'cause she told me she would. I don't know why she don't like you, but take this." She hands me a twenty-dollar bill. "You go on to South Carolina. I'm staying here."

"Here? In Swanquarter?"

"Durham. Jimmy's taking me to Durham. He's a banker there. They got Colored banks, girl!"

A hearse arrives and is filled with four bodies; the undertaker leans out of the car and vomits into the gravel. An older woman in a pink nightgown and house slippers shrieks when a young man in a blue suit is taken out of the building. "Warren! Warren!" she wails, running to where he's been unceremoniously thrown to the gravel. "Warren, my Warren, you sleep tight, and Mama's gonna make you some Cream of Wheat come morning." My world has stopped, but Caroline's is still moving. She's talking, talking about the brand-new pair of shoes Jimmy bought her, and the hamburger she breaded up and fried for him, the little mechanical rabbit at the dog track he took her to, the Colored resort where they're staying and the maid who comes and sweeps their patio every morning. My world has stopped, but she doesn't feel it. Her orange isn't my orange. No one's is.

"You all right?" Caroline asks. "You don't look too good."

But I look right through her dress, right through its illumination in front of Jimmy's headlight. Right through Caroline, through the Studebaker, and even through the water of the ocean beyond. I can see my future. "I'll be fine," I tell her.

■ ■ ■ ■

Part Seven:
Caroline

■ ■ ■ ■

DITCH

When Baby Nate got up on two years old,
Mr. Barbour rented one of them big bull-
dozers from the county and dug him out a
pond. Didn't nobody know what he was doing at first, ruining his own earth like that,
and when the men down to the Tin Cup
asked him why he was tearing up his yard,
he lied. "Looking for bones," he said. "Hear
tell it's some Cherokee buried out there."
Well, he got lucky, since spring brought
rains harder than Mt. Sterling'd seen in near
about a hundred year, and while the rest of
us was putting old feed troughs down in
our cellars to catch the water, Mr. Barbour's
pond was getting deeper and deeper. Ever
time lightning struck, here went Mr. Barbour, tutting out to the side of his house
like a rooster, looking down the rise with
his hands crossed over his belly. He got all
wet, naturally, outside watching it rain like
that, but he wasn't caring a tall, and bit by

bit folks figured out he wasn't looking for no Indian bones to float up.

He started to call that old ditch his lake, and people had to remind him, all gentle-like of course, that it was just a pond. He built hisself a wood deck out to the side of it, but when the rains stopped come May, that pond dried up something powerful, and you could see almost to where he done stuck the posts in the mud. He bought a little paddleboat, but the pond wasn't deep enough for him to get anywhere but right out in the middle. No matter, 'cause come June the sky brought us more misery, rain so strong it kilt all the corn. Mr. Barbour's pond rose up again even higher, and he went to Burtis's and bought hisself some live catfish to let loose in there. Pretty soon them four fish done beget forty, and then the forty begat four hundred, but still he wouldn't let nobody near his pond. Not until the Fourth, that is, when we saw him out there fishing with Audrey. Of all people. We ain't even seen her come into town on the bus.

We drove by a time or two in Cousin Harrel's car just to catch a look at her, sitting down there on that deck fishing with her hateful stepdaddy, dressed all wrong for fishing, in city clothes and black stockings, dangling her high heels over Mr. Barbour's lake what'd grown a green scum and sprouted a passel of dragonflies. Look like she ain't even cared none whether she lost that shoe, and it made me nervous ever time I saw it, 'cause them shoes was stiletto-heeled and shiny black with straps round the ankles, and you could tell by the way they was shaped they cost plenty of money. Imagene saw it too. "Look at that ijit," I said. "She gone lose that shoe."

"Y'all think she cares one whit about some lost shoe?" Imagene said. She been less and less on actual conversation since we walked out the county hospital with Grandmama's patient's belongings bag, so whenever she did say something, I didn't oppose her none. "She's a princess," Imagene said, "all the way from New York City. She probably got fifty pairs of shoes by now."

We girls ain't been fishing since before Daddy kilt Mama, but we knew enough to know that Mr. Barbour's pond wasn't fit for fishing no more nohow. In the early mornings, it looked like any other pond fed into and out of a river, with fog rising off it just like God Hisself done dug it, in His original version of earth. But by the heat of noon, that pond would be standing solid green, like it was out of a fairy tale and some wicked witch was going to rise out of it and start saying spells. The four hundred fish probably done died down to ten, was what Cousin Harrel said. Ain't no way they could get any air under all that algae. Yet and still, there they sat, Audrey and Mr. Barbour, staring at their poles hanging into the water, not saying a thing, so deep in concentration they ain't took note of us slowing down to drive past them twice. Part of me had a notion to go over and talk to her, tell her about how Jimmy told me, on the way to Durham, that he was married. Ask her what happened to that guitar player and why she was back up home. But then another part of me hated her. When you've wanted to be somebody else so bad for so long, it hurts real bad when you finally figure out it ain't never going to happen. And that part of me what hated her got to thinking, well, here she is, with her mama's old black dress on, just like any other girl done got left by her man. She's a little like that pond — in the end, she just couldn't handle the lack of air. Turns out God made her need the same things as anybody else.

Cousin Harrel's friend Maywood come down with him this year, and he stayed until the blossoms started to fall from the trees.

"It's just like a carpet!" he said, first time he seen them falling in the yard. "A beautiful carpet!" He was a cityboy, I reckon, and ain't never seen none before, because he took all twenty-three years of hisself and laid down in the grass. Even rolled around some. "Get up from there," I told him, " 'fore you get all eat up with the chiggers." The blossoms was still sticking to his hair, and he went inside and took near about an hour picking them out, looking in the mirror at all those white petals stuck to his head like a swim cap. It was right cute, tell you the truth, and you could kinda see how Maywood might've been if them gangsters up North weren't all the time chasing him.

I reckon Audrey saw some other side of him too, at some point I ain't knowed about, 'cause the very next day her and Maywood was walking hand-in-hand down the sidewalk in front of Mr. Barnett's store. His hair was all clean of blossoms, and he had on a shirt the color of a shark's hide, shiny silk that rippled and turnt dark where the sun wasn't hitting it. Audrey had on another one a them thick city dresses what was almost too hot to wear in the summer, and them spiky heels what was starting to wear down from all the country walking she was doing. I stayed about ten feet behind them and followed them in Mr. Barnett's store, and then I went in back and stood near the ice cream cooler so I could watch them in secret.

"I think I'ma stay down here with you," I heard him tell her. He said it real loud and pinched the inside of her thigh, and she turnt right around and kissed him, her head turning against his like a gear, tongue probably all down his mouth. Naturally, all us girls was doing things behind closed doors, but Audrey was the first I ever seen acting like she was some White girl in the movies. "Sweetness," he said, when she let him come up for air. "I'ma stay right here."

"Whyn't you take me to Chicago? Ain't nothing but peckerwoods down here."

"Yeah, well. It's just a bunch of *city* peckerwoods up there. Dressed-up peckerwoods with new cars. I could take 'em or leave 'em."

But by the time the rain turnt the blossoms to foam out in the yard, Maywood done gone back up to Chicago without either one of us. I cut off all my hair again and snipped my good purple dress to ribbons. Cousin Harrel said to count my blessings.

Then one day — and I remember it clear as anything 'cause I was outside with a can when she did it, watering Grandmama's poor peonies to death 'fore they could even come up right — Imagene wrote something on the mirror what like to shock me to death. I remember walking to the bathroom and finding it, written in angry red Fuller Flair lipstick across the sink mirror: AUDREY AND RALPH.

"Audrey and Ralph what?" I yelled at her, when I went back out in the living room. I went to stand over her where she was sitting on Grandmama's couch and I shook her shoulder. I talked to her softer — "Audrey and Ralph what?" But she wouldn't answer me. Wasn't till the next week, when I saw Audrey walk right down High Street and into his house without knocking, that I knew what Imagene been talking about. Audrey done moved out of Mr. Barbour's house and in with Ralph Cundiff.

Well, before it was all said and done, she got Ralph into a bunch of mess I never would of gotten him into. It's a lot of people who are satisfied to think that if ain't nobody in Mt. Sterling never done it, then it ain't worth doing nohow, but not Audrey, and I guess she got Ralph to thinking that way too. Tyrone told it to me when we was cruising around in his car, how Audrey took him over to Louisville to play at Johnny

Flanagan's club. Johnny's real name was Marion Dent, Ralph told him, but couldn't nobody ever tell he was Irish with a name like that, so he put JOHNNY FLANAGAN out on the sign above the bar to get people to come in. And they did — them people came out to Irish Hill in herds, from all over Louisville, and Johnny Flanagan's got to be a big enough place that it was like a Louisville event.

Well, old Marion Dent hated hisself some Negroes, maybe on account of he felt like he been treated like a nigger so many times hisself, so it upset him something terrible when the rich smart asses from 'round U. of L. started ringing him up on the telephone to ask when such-and-such a strange nigger might play Johnny Flanagan's. People done stopped wanting to dance, he saw, and now they just wanted to sit and smoke and listen — 1961 was breathing some new kind of strange air into the country. And what's worse, them smart-asses wanted weird shit, music with no beat, music what didn't make sense lessun you done read a bunch a books about it. Marion Dent hated strangeness, and Coloreds, and books. But he loved money just a little bit more'n he hated all those things, was the way Ralph told it to Tyrone, and he certainly loved money more'n any idea he had about what music ought to be, so he decided maybe he ought to appeal to the new clientele and get hisself some onstage niggers. He got hold of Mr. Glaser somehow, and it turnt out Glaser done figured out every single move Audrey'd made. You think she might've been too proud to go but she needed the bread, so when he called, she grabbed Ralph and they hightailed it on over to Baxter Avenue.

Her and Ralph got to Johnny Flanagan's early on a Saturday night, some sore about the fact that a policeman at the corner of Bishop and Payne had asked where two niggers like them might be going that time a night. Downright mad about the fact that the trolley bus conductor downtown had tried to drive off while Ralph was still getting hisself down the steps. But they was all ready to go, on the promise of fifty dollars for the weekend, almost all theirs with nobody in the middle but Glaser.

"House rules," Marion Dent said, soon as they got through the glass door. Ralph'd stuck his hand out to shake, but Marion Dent ignored him. "No eating out front in the restaurant," Dent said, "and no using the patrons' restrooms. There's one for the cooks, in the back of the kitchen. When you finish your set, you will kindly leave the premises immediately. What you do in the neighborhood afterwards is your business, but I highly recommend you head on home, as the police officers in Irish Hill do like to keep the neighborhood clean. And absolutely," he said to Ralph, "no conversation with the White ladies in my establishment."

"What planet is this?" asked Ralph, after Dent done walked away. I guess Audrey done been down in the Deep South so long she'd gotten comfortable with the idea of taking money from people what hated her, but Ralph been up with Gordon Bell to Indianapolis Temple 74 to hear Malcolm X give a speech, and like he told Tyrone, up here it's a new day for Negroes. He said he'd just gone up on the bus with his woman to hear her play and keep her safe on the streets at night, but after Marion Dent's list of house rules, he half expected Baxter Avenue to swallow him up whole.

One by one the rest of the band got there — Joe Jarman with his tenor sax, Milt Greenlea with his drumsticks, and man by the name of Percy Heath on bass. Percy Heath was a skinny, light-skinned cat, with a goatee and a little bit a hair sliding off the top of a head long as a squash, but when he took his bass out of its case and started tuning up, Ralph said Audrey got to making eyes at him, and he had to cough to remind her he was sitting right there watching.

Joe Jarman done put his sax case on the floor for a rest, but when Marion Dent came over and ticked off all them house rules, Jarman picked his case back up. "Brother," he said, tapping Greenlea on the shoulder. "I know you need the bread, but this I cannot do."

Greenlea just shrugged. He done told them all how since he didn't care none for public transportation, he had a fistful of parking tickets from the city of Chicago, all waiting to be paid.

"Well, there you have it," Ralph told Marion Dent, and the band all turnt to watch Ralph talk, like it made perfect sense for a stranger to be sassing Dent on their behalf. "If we don't see two hunderd extra dollars right this second, we're all walking right out the door into civlized society."

"Who's this nigger here?" asked Marion Dent, and at that moment, Ralph told Tyrone, even he didn't know. He'd surprised the hell out of hisself. He wasn't even shaking, he felt so right about what he done said.

"No niggers here at all," he told Dent. "I just see men. What even *are* niggers?"

The band had to laugh, and Dent's eyes

got all wide like a scared bunny's, and Ralph said he looked around at all the tables behind him, at the men and women talking and smoking and what-all. He turnt back to Ralph and winced like somebody done punched him in the kidney. "One fifty extra," he said, and Jarman put his tenor case back down.

"Just for that," Ralph said, "it's two fifty extra or nothing." Jarman picked his case back up, and even Greenlea nodded in agreement. "Don't none of us need the money that bad," Ralph said, even though he knew that was a lie for all of them. Ralph hisself done got behind on his rent, trying to help his mama get her teeth fixed.

"Two hunderd extra then," Dent said, as Jarman hitched his case to the crook of his arm. "But break one a my rules, and you're out." He walked away, hunching a little. Funky house rules or no, he'd be out one and a half times what he should've.

Heath took his bass to the stage, with Jarman and Greenlea following him, and all the White people got to clapping. Then Audrey went out and sat at the piano — she always went out last, since she was the Black Woman Surprise — and the crowd went wild. The men hooted a little, and a lady in the front row whistled with her fingers in the sides of her mouth. Then Marion Dent went to the stage with some beat-up old White man following him, and crooked his finger at Audrey to get up off the bench.

She just sat there pretending she ain't understood, even if she had.

"Get up," Dent said, all gruff. "I thought you were the singer. You ain't playing here."

"It's free jazz, bubba. We don't have a singer."

"Just get up, nigger."

"I'm not getting up anywhere, lessun you want to pay my man even more money."

Dent stuffed his hands down at his sides and said into the mike, "And on piano, Louisville native Langston Basso."

"Who?" somebody in the crowd said, real loud, and everbody laughed.

"Let the lady play!" somebody else yelled.

Dent stared at Audrey like she was a rat he done caught trailing through his dinner, but still she didn't move, so Dent pushed Basso in the back so hard the man almost fell over the piano bench. Basso sat down, or anyways he sat on the edge of the bench, since Audrey still ain't moved an inch, and Ralph said it to some people, it might've looked like they was about to play a duet, but to him, looked like Basso was about to be Audrey's page turner.

"And on piano," Dent said again, "Langston Basso!"

Basso got up and bowed, then sat back down, but nobody clapped. Some of the rich-looking folks started to boo. Ralph was standing on the edge of the stage, and Dent got right up in his face then.

"Mister, what is your problem?" Ralph asked him. "Do you want this band to play or don't you?"

"That your wife?" Dent asked.

"Yes, she is," Ralph lied.

"Look. I really don't give a damn. I don't care, she's your grandmammy. I won't have no niggers at my piano."

Ralph told Tyrone the man's eyes was so narrow you could of slid pieces of paper through 'em. The take was up to four hundred, and Ralph'd never been good at math, but now that there was money involved he done took ten minutes to do some calculating and figured out Audrey's share, fair and square, at a hunderd. A hunderd was still more'n he seen sometimes in a month, and so he started to feel like such a man that he forgot his woman.

"Double the four hunderd," Ralph whispered, so Audrey wouldn't hear, "and she leaves. Anything less than double, and ever one of us leaves."

"You just get her up from there," Dent said. "Right now." He took eight hunderd-dollar bills out his pocket and dropped them right in front of Ralph's shoes. Even the hecklers got confused then, and they got all hushed. Right on up until Ralph nodded at Audrey to get up, and then, when she did, they started in again to booing. Audrey made a big show about it, scooting the bench back and walking all the way round the stage. Ralph said about three quarters of the audience just gathered themselves up and went on home.

Well, old Dent lost money that night, 'cause the crowd that was left didn't even spend three hunderd dollars, not even on drinks. But Ralph lost more'n that, 'cause Audrey hitched on home. Ralph got hisself to Mt. Sterling early that morning and said he found a scared little girl down on High Street where before he'd had a woman, and a fence that done growed up between their two spaces of love.

She was a person like nobody he'd ever known before, is what he told Tyrone, and all them years he'd been thinking she was an impossible dream. And so when he put his hand on her hip in bed and she flinched, it like to make his stomach drop clear out of his body. "I'm sorry, baby," he said, taking them two hunderd-dollar bills out his wallet and snapping them to attention, "but you do realize you could put a down payment on a car, just off this one night?"

Audrey didn't say nothing.

If he'd put his arms round the back of her and kissed her neck just then, he might've saved everthing, but instead he said, "Well, you could."

"You go on then," Audrey said into the pillow, so Ralph couldn't even make out what she was saying. "You take that two hundred dollars and buy your*self* a car. Like it's the most important thing in the world."

DADDY

Next time Audrey even got near a piano was at her granddaddy's funeral. We was all there, the whole town, seem like. Wasn't on account of the deceased, 'cause old Grandpap Martin just been sitting around in that old musty closed-up house for the last three years of his life, not ever coming past the porch to say how do nor go-to-hell, his Christmas tree still standing with popcorn and tinsel come July. We wasn't at the funeral, neither, on account of the tragedy of his son, since that done happened seven years prior and people done largely forgot about Lindell. We wasn't even there on account of us all wanting to see that bulldagger Ida Mae Harris what Juanita done took up with, 'cause it warn't never a secret noways that they was sweet on each other. No, I'd say if anything drew that crowd to fill up Queen Street Second Baptist, it was us all wanting to see the tragedy of Audrey Martin herself.

She ain't let us down, neither, playing and crying and snotting and humming to make us think we was watching something supernatural. She made the high notes on that piano sing, and when she hit the low notes, seem like they done some of her crying for her. With lightning killing the sky outside, making it look like the earth done died at one o'clock in the afternoon, and Reverend Owington going on about how the wrath of Jehovah extends from the lone sinner to his entire family, the whole service was like God speaking to us directly. Even so, I wasn't listening right much. Just thinking about Grandmama's funeral, and how all the other ladies her age was tipping around that casket thinking they was too fancy to die. Grandmama, laying there in the casket with them cat-eyed glasses with the rhinestones what she loved so much, and me wondering what'd happen in fifty years when they was out of style and she was still sitting in some easy chair in heaven, pushing them back up her nose. At Grandpap Martin's funeral wasn't nobody whispering, or writing notes back and forth on the funeral program, or even chewing gum — we was all scared to even so much as look anywhere but at that body in the casket. It was like Grandpap was presiding over us all in his death the way he never could control anybody in life. Just then, looking at him all laid out like that, his eyes closed against ever knowing anything else, I remembered when he yelled at me for cutting my hair, that time me and Ralph been trying to sell him some coal, and I felt ashamed that I done cut it all off again, over some man.

Seem like Audrey was a little shamed about Grandpap looking down from heaven and seeing her with Ralph, 'cause right before everthing started, when Ralph came to the piano and tried to talk to her, she just sat there stiff as a board and wouldn't so much as look at him. "Baby —" he started to say, but the way she closed her eyes into whatever she was playing said it all, how she was disgusted at herself for ever even looking at some county mope like him in the first place. The nerve. I wanted to kiss him on his baby soft ears and tell him it was all right 'cause she always been something different anyways. He was my first love and I'd never be shamed of him, I wanted to tell him, but seem like that would of been the entirely wrong thing to do right then at a funeral. Audrey's mama and Mr. Barbour was there, with Baby Nate, and she did let them hug her some, even held Baby

Nate in her lap up on the piano bench and let him plunk a few notes in the time when folks was getting seated. She got up and passed Nate on back to her mama when it was time for her to start playing. Ralph was one of the folks had to hand the boy back through the pews, but Audrey ain't seen it.

My daddy was there. I still ain't talked to him but I'd seen him in town, putting his money in the bank right at eight in the morning when wasn't nobody there but the bankers, getting his shoes shined in the square like he couldn't do it hisself at home. He stayed out the Tin Cup, I guess out of respect for the owner, but he did go down to Mr. Barnett's regular, to play some numbers, and didn't none of Barnett's customers so much as bat an eye at him. He was back, and it wasn't what I'd expected. Women loved him. Look like they just *wanted* theyselves a wife-killer, wanted him to do them in too, maybe, make them invisible to everbody else what was hurting them everday in ten million other ways. They wanted him to kill them back to their true selves, maybe, 'cause in the one year he been back, he done had a chain of 'em, one kind after another, from Versailles to Shakey Farmers, until he got to be responsible for the melancholies of half the women in eastern Kentucky. They loved him and they fed him, and the paunch he come home from the pen with got to be the size of a Teddy bear's, and that made him even more irresistible, seem like. He'd got gray in the five years he been locked up, and you might think it'd make him look older and sadder but really it just made him look distinguished, and in his church clothes, he looked like any other man in Mt. Sterling baling tobacco and feeding his family, and maybe that's what made folks just plumb forget, forget that Mama ain't done nothing, that he done kilt her just like you'd butcher a hog. Down to the Tin Cup, the story even got to be that it was Mama who done this or that, that Mama was getting ready to run off with some man, that Mama done took Daddy's money and lost it playing the numbers.

Well, there he was at Grandpap Martin's funeral, looking all respectable, and he went up to Audrey and give her a big hug afterward, and I didn't make nothing of it at the time, but then, but then, but *then.* One night at the county fair, the strangest thing. Imagene run over saying she seen Audrey with Daddy at the cotton candy stand, and damn if she ain't had one a them big stuffed turtles, the kind your man wins you when he shoots three balloons in a row. "He ain't never won me no turtle," Imagene said, and she poked out her little lip the way she done when she was a little bitty baby, and I had to tell her he ain't never won me no turtle at the fair neither, and with me, he done had an eight-year head start. But there, with Daddy and a prize, was skinny little Audrey Martin, Audrey Martin who you'd never catch no more without her black city clothes, Audrey Martin who sat closed up in that house playing piano just like her granddaddy and her daddy before her, Audrey Martin who done got so afraid of the world by then that she wasn't even living in it. Not a week after Grandpap's funeral, she moved out his house and into No. 211, and you'd see the two of them out in the mornings 'fore Daddy went to work down to the ice plant. Talking to each other on the front porch, Audrey leaning over the rail just like Mama used to do, watching the flowers she done planted. Sometimes her mama would even let her babysit Little Nate over at No. 211, and the three of them'd be walking down the street holding on to each other's hands: after all his chain of women, Daddy done clipped it off at the end with Audrey.

And then I was the only one I had to share the outrage with, 'cause Imagene been too little to remember what happened to Mama, and Grandmama done passed. In a way, I'd always thought it was some all right Grandmama passed, 'cause she couldn't never get used to what was going on in the world, the girls with their afros and halter tops riding through town on their way up to Lexington, and them White boys with sandals come down from UK, all keen on the Colored girls sometimes, talking 'bout how amazed they was that it was plenty of Black peoples in Appalachia. Grandmama'd stand on the porch, crying tears big as money, 'cause she done outlived her daughter and then outlived herself. She'd walk back in and rub that little pit in the wall where I threw the poker at Daddy and say, "Just left a little mark, that's all." Well, it's a bunch of little marks what kill us all in the end. And when I see Audrey walking down the street between Little Nate and Daddy, I'm awful glad Grandmama ain't lived to see that. I still remember how she begged God right before she died, and I hated her house then, 'cause all that was really left in it was me. Her ashcans was so clean and so nice I didn't want to throw nothing in 'em.

And I remembered back when I'd of had Audrey to come over and share this all with, all my grief and all my wanting, and you know I'd never tell Audrey this now, but it was a time I loved her something terrible. She would of come over to the house and thrown my grandmama's false teeth in one of them ashcans and got us both to laughing something awful about it, and just thinking about her doing some such thing, I knew I'd loved her better than I'd loved my own self. But she grew off and left me. I'd always be poor old Caroline Wallace, what stayed in Mt. Sterling and watched all the men go off and leave her, and Audrey'd be the smart one who kept finding Love, even if Love was some old piece a thing what done been to the pen and got old and gray and fat around the middle. August is her tragedy, but it's me who ain't never been loved, not even by my own daddy. There's something in her heart what's still alive, something my heart ain't never had in the first place.

I saw her in Mr. Barnett's this morning. I cut her off in the cleaner aisle, but she just pushed into my arm and walked around me, so I called her a bitch. She probably thinks it's on account of her being with Daddy, but it ain't. She don't know me no more, and I don't know her. And even though it's been a long time happening, she's such a force she done broke my heart without even meaning to. Seventy times seventy the Bible says you must forgive, and we even got baptized together, but I can't forgive her even once. That girl was a diamond, here in the middle of all this coal.

PART EIGHT: AUDREY

Summer

Of all my days in Harlem, there is one that has lodged itself like a poor, trapped bird in my memory, throwing itself constantly at the borders of my mind, trying to get out and make itself happy, and that's the day August hauled me out of my little room on 116th Street — away from my landlady still shaking her curlers — in the name of taking me to a better life. Even then, I knew better, knew better even as I hauled that poor dented lime green suitcase down the steps by myself, even when I sat down in the taxi and August didn't so much as hold my hand. I'd ripped down all my *Life* photos but one: a shot of a man and a woman dancing across a beautiful hardwood floor, the woman's stockings glowing, through some trick of lighting, as if her legs were candles. I left that for the next young, dreaming girl to live in Edith's room: August and I had never danced. We never would.

Down Beat called once, in 1963. August was on tour in the Netherlands, the reporter said, and the magazine wanted to do a pictorial. His mother had told the reporter that Elizabeth Johnson Barnes was August's first wife, but Elizabeth Johnson Barnes had pointed the reporter in my direction. "How did she know where I lived?" I asked him, but there was one piece of information he was without. He asked me what it was like, being with August during the early years of his career, but I couldn't tell him. "I no longer know that form of music," I told him instead. "You may find this incredible, but a whole language can disappear." He just breathed into his mouthpiece — thrown, no doubt, by my answer — and as a train rumbled past in the distance, so long it was beginning to sound like a river, I tried to come up with something conciliatory, something that sounded like an answer, even if it was untrue. "You can love the music without loving the men who go with it," I told him. "A lot of people are good at a lot of things, but not many of them are good at love." I told him goodbye, and asked him please not to call me again.

What else could I say? "We never danced," I might have told him. But then, I'd never danced with a man — not ever. My clunky youth had been full of boys who saw only the thickness of my glasses, boys who heard only the words that owned more syllables than their own. Now, I've danced, and danced again and again and again. I didn't know, the first two songs, that he was Stanton Wallace. His body had become powered so slowly with regret that you didn't even notice his height until you stood next to him. I only knew, at that Blackberry Festival dance in Hope, that he was someone who had traveled away like me and come back the better for it, someone who felt stronger, when he held me, than anyone else in two counties. He was everything I needed and didn't need. To someone less melancholy, he'd have been a marvel.

Because Mauris exists only in his memory, she's a saint, and I can't compete with her. I haven't raised two of his babies, and I can't weave yarn together to make beautiful patchwork shawls for them come the fall. I can't even sit quietly in pink lipstick. And I can never again be a young wife, full of hope. What I do now is play at the A.M.E. church for ten dollars on Sundays and teach the little girls who come to my house straight from school on Tuesdays and Wednesdays, that and try to stay out of Grandpap's house and away from Daddy's ghost. At home, Stanton teaches me things, like how to survive getting to know yourself, and how he stayed in solitary for three days and came out knowing he'd never need anyone else. Solitary is pitch-dark, he told me, like being lain in a grave with the continued burden of breathing. The room is cleaned once a month when the warden takes pity on the guards who must walk by and smell it, and the corner toilet smells so awful already that you hold your bladder so as not to make it worse. First, in the darkness, you see people you love, then people you know, then the ancestors. Food comes in through a slot at the bottom of the door and you see the animals it was before it was on the stove. You see the guards you can't see, and the warden you'll never see, and his ancestors, and his poor great-great-great-grandmother who died of consumption in the middle of a Dutch forest. Then, Stanton says, you see yourself. You see yourself ugly first, and then you see yourself beautiful. But you understand that both selves are all the reality there is.

An answer I wasn't even looking for, but one I've always needed. We're born alone and we die alone, Stanton says, and everything between is an illusion. I think he's right. All this time I thought I was supposed to be out finding something special in this world, but these days that have come, these days when I welcome little Olive Gaye into Grandpap's parlor and ask her to please not swing her legs while she plays "Alouette," I wonder if maybe Auchidie and Caroline were right: Special is not how we were raised. I remember how Pookie and I climbed the roof the night of the enormous moon of 1955, how we held hands and supposed we'd never again see such a big, red moon, how we wondered whether it wasn't the end of the world and we were the only two people who knew.

Now, I know it was just a blood moon, a trick of atmosphere and humidity, a simple message to sailors and farmers that it's going to rain come the morrow. Every adult the world over, from the mango seller in India to the milliner in Poughkeepsie, has seen one. Even little Olive Gaye, sitting there swinging her legs, thinking none of the other girls in her grade have pink and purple polka dot bows brought specially down by their daddies from Cincinnati, oblivious to the fact that her very own seventh birthday party was really an affair thrown for the entertainment of others, even Olive Gaye will see a blood moon. Maybe on a roof.

Still, my daddy's in that house, trying to tell me something. He doesn't rattle windows, or make signs on walls, or walk the floor in the night to make the hairs on my neck stand on end. Instead, he whispers me this story, every time:

Your granddaddy spent the whole nine months before you were born hunched in suspense, folding and unfolding the things he'd bought for his first grandson. There was even a pair of breeches he bought from a store in Lexington, a store he'd heard of from the White people he delivered to, a store he'd got lost on Limestone trying to find. "Y'all buck up now," he said to me, the day you were born, "the next one'll be a boy." But when I bent over that crib and studied the fine hair on your ears and the mottled red on the soles of your feet, I knew there could never be another child. There isn't another child in all the world.

ACKNOWLEDGMENTS

At some point, early in the first draft of this novel, the late fifties became my life. It was not a place that was initially comfortable for me, and I want to thank everyone who gave me the creative space I needed to see the remarkable complexity that was there under the sepia-toned, unexamined surface, all the folks who helped make these characters and this world come into being.

I am grateful to Jesse Lee Kercheval for her guidance during my year at the University of Wisconsin's Institute for Creative Writing, where I wrote the short story that later grew into this novel. I'd like to thank Crystal Wilkinson, Lindsay Shadwell, John Branscum, and Honorée Fanonne Jeffers, who published pieces of this novel in *Mythium Journal, WomenArts Quarterly, Red Holler,* and *poemmemoirstory,* respectively.

Tamara Fish, Andrew Lewellen, and Dalton McGee all read early drafts of this book and deserve a thank-you for their insightful comments. I am eternally grateful to my marvelous agent, Gail Hochman, who had faith in me for many years, and I'd like to thank Melanie Tortoroli at W. W. Norton for all her assistance. My brilliant editor, Maria Guarnaschelli, has my undying love for all the patience and tenderness she gave this book. Maria offered me so many gifts, not least of which was the many one-sentence questions that generated a hundred pages of revision, and her ability to see the castle in all of my sand. If there is a mystical dimension to the religion of editing, Maria Guarnaschelli is its spiritual leader.

Thank you to God for all the amazing. Thank you to my mother, Angela Townsend, for being my first, best teacher, and for blessing me with the gift of literacy. Thank you to my father, Wendell Townsend, for offering me the story of resistance that became the backbone of this novel. Thank you to both my parents, and all the other baby boomers who patiently answered my questions about the past. Thank you to David Gides for believing I would do this even before I quite believed I would do it, and for showing our children so much love while I was chained to coffeeshop tables. Finally, a huge thank-you to my children, who slept while I dreamed, who, with their breathtaking sweetness, give me more joy than I ever imagined possible, and who dazzle me on a daily basis into seeing what lies beyond the visible.

ABOUT THE AUTHOR

Jacinda Townsend is a Hurston-Wright Award finalist and former Carol Houck Smith Fiction Fellow at the University of Wisconsin. A graduate of Harvard University, Duke Law School, and the Iowa Writers' Workshop, she was also a Fulbright Fellow to Côte d'Ivoire. Her writing has appeared in *African Voices, Carve* magazine, *The Maryland Review, Obsidian II, Passages North, Phoebe, Xavier Review,* and other journals. She teaches creative writing at Indiana University, and lives in Bloomington, Indiana.